SHARON BARNES

Shanghai Sunset

The Great Adventures of Breeze Lee (Book 1)

First published by S&D Publishing 2025

Author's reassurance to the readers: NO artificial intelligence (AI) was used in the development/writing/editing/proofing/formatting/publication of this novel. Edits were completed by several individuals. We have tried to make this book the best it can be. I do apologize if there are any typos or grammatical errors, we are human after all and no one is perfect.

This book does contain scenes of violence, flashbacks of the violence, has profanity, and sexual content. It also addresses very real topics such as domestic violence, alcoholism, depression, and teen pregnancy. If any of these topics or content bother you as a reader, then please do not read this book.

First edition

ISBN: 979-8-9918869-3-2

Illustration by Chris Ross
Editing by Bonnie Lill

This book was professionally typeset on Reedsy.
Find out more at reedsy.com

To all the individuals out there that are victims of domestic violence, don't give up. You are beautiful and you deserve happiness and love. I hope this book will encourage at least one person to leave a bad situation.

This is a work of fiction and fantasy, however this novel does touch on very real topics such as domestic violence, alcoholism, depression, and teen pregnancy.
- Sharon Barnes

Friendship improves happiness, and abates misery, by doubling our joys, and dividing our grief

Marcus Tullius Cicero

Contents

Acknowledgments

To my family- Daniel, Bryant, Justice, and Hermione, thank you so much for encouraging me, standing by me on this journey, and loving me. Zeva, thank you for bringing such joy into my life and helping Mimi to embrace her creative side more and more everyday. Brixton, we will hopefully get to run around soon playing witches and dragons and yelling crazy phrases as we throw hats in the air just like me and your sister do. Eric thank you for your friendship, wonderful book cover designs, and an amazing website. When I took the leap of faith on this publishing venture you were right there cheering me on. April, Jody, and Nancy thank you all for being my sounding boards, beta readers, and friends. Finally, thank you to all of my friends that are a part of Writers Round Table your advice, suggestions, patience, support, and for sitting through the countless hours of revisions of my manuscripts, thank you so much. You are an amazing group of people and I am so happy to be a part of your group.

BREEZE LEE

Breeze had blood pouring down the left side of her head, but she didn't care. Her opponent would tap out or pass out; this win had her name all over it. The referee motioned that the fight was over. Breeze refused to loosen her hold on her opponent's neck, she had to know for sure that the fight was over, and that is when she felt the tap on her shoulder from the ref. She released her opponent, jumped up, and ran around the ring.

Her dad, Jon Lee, her Uncle Han, and one of her dearest friends, Kidd Knight, rushed her. Her dad picked her up and spun her around.

"Awesome spinning back fist. That rattled her. I'm proud of you," Jon said.

Breeze's opponent had just eased up off the mat. The ref was making sure she could stand unassisted before he announced Breeze the winner. The dazed look on Lady Ice's face made Breeze smile. Lady Ice had walked into the ring three minutes earlier with a cocky attitude. Breeze felt honor in the fact that she had just deflated Lady Ice's ego balloon a notch or two. Jon, Han, and Kidd moved off to the side of the ring when the ref and Lady Ice walked over to the center of the ring. The two women stood on either side of the ref; he held both of their wrists and then lifted Breeze's arm. The MC spoke loudly into the microphone, "Winner by Knock Out from a rear naked choke, BREEZE LEE!"

The crowd started cheering and yelling. The energy in the room filled Breeze's soul. Breeze exited the ring. Jon and Han looked at her head and doctored it.

Kidd waited until they were done treating her wounds, and then he wrapped her in a bear hug and squeezed. "Thailand will be yours for sure."

"Yes, it will. It will be mine and Jazz's for the taking. I am starving."

"No joke. My stomach feels like it is about to eat my backbone," Kidd said.

Han laughed, "Jon we better feed these two quickly before Kidd turns into Jazz and rips off Breeze's arm and eats it."

"Oh, Lord, Kidd hasn't even met Jazz yet, and he is beginning to sound like him," Jon teased and patted him on the back.

Breeze shot Kidd a warning look. She knew that he wanted to flip her dad off just because he could but she knew the outcome would be a grueling workout with both her dad and Han. Kidd smiled at Breeze.

Kidd walked close to Breeze. "Do you think Jazz is surviving his tournament with Jana?" He winked at Breeze.

She pushed him over. "Of course, he's surviving. Jana loves Jazz. He has two fights left before his tournament is over. Once the tournament is over, they will be going to Joe's Crab Shack or an all you can eat seafood buffet." Breeze flashed him a grin. "Wish we had an all you could eat buffet here, for Dad. He would sleep for a year if that was the case."

"Where is your boy this weekend?" Kidd asked.

"I don't know. Probably on an errand for his Daddy." Breeze shrugged.

They talked as they walked the two blocks. Han and her dad were slightly behind them. When they entered the hotel, Jon swore because there stood Matt and Mickey. Han wrapped his arm around Breeze's shoulders.

"Gentlemen, what brings you here? If you even think of sneaking out or scheming tonight before we fly out, I can assure you we will be in the gym from now until three in the morning when we have to leave to go to the airport," Han told them with a cocky tone.

All of Breeze's friends started talking at once.

"Never," Kidd said.

"Just here to celebrate her wins," Matt said.

"I'm hungry, I knew Jon would feed us," Mickey teased.

Jon and Han were too busy staring down her friends to have seen the slight nod that Breeze gave Kidd.

"You boys will come up to my room while Breeze goes to her room to shower. Han will go to her room just to be on the safe side," Jon stated.

"Yes sir," Mickey, Matt, and Kidd all said.

Breeze texted all three of her friends after she was in her room.

Breeze: Are the cars locked and loaded? We race for two hours once Han and dad are asleep. We will be back before any of the Japanese Warriors can alert Han.

Kidd: Steak and shrimp?

Breeze: Of course.

Matt and Mickey didn't respond right away because they were with Jon and they didn't want to put him on edge any more than they already had by showing up unannounced.

3

Matt went to the bathroom and quickly responded to Breeze.

Matt: It's all good. We got ya, girl.

Breeze: Purr…fect!

Breeze sent Jazz a quick text.

Breeze: I won. THAILAND one step closer. Matt and Mickey were waiting at hotel & Dad was cussing. Racing later. Love you. Best of Luck on your final two fights.

Jazz: Wish I was there. We could really celebrate with all of us together.

Breeze: Dad and Han would call in all the brethren.

Jazz: Wouldn't be the first time.

Breeze: I know, right. I have to hurry. Han in the living room waiting. Later.

Jazz: Love ya, babe.

Breeze walked over to Jon's room about twenty minutes later with her luggage in hand. Han went to his room and grabbed his suitcase and carry on bag. Everyone put their luggage in the trunk, they loaded up into the SUV and went to a local steakhouse. Jon and Han started to relax during the meal because they were talking about the fights. Han and Jon both praised Breeze on her speed and technique.

"Can I go to Thailand to see Breeze compete?" Kidd asked in a pleading tone.

"Son, we will see what we can do," Jon said.

Han looked at Jon. "Can we handle Jazz, Breeze, and Kidd together in Thailand, especially if Jazz and Breeze win that tournament?"

"Of course." Jon smiled wide,"Jana will be there, too."

Mickey made the sign of the cross at the mention of Jana's name. "May the force be with you all on that trip. I sure hope Jazz has survived this weekend. Life would be dull without

4

him."

Matt stared at him. "You're an idiot. You do know that pain is coming your way for that little gesture, right? Not to mention that little comment."

"She loves me," Mickey said.

Matt, Kidd, and Breeze were all laughing. Han and Jon exchanged looks and smiled at Mickey.

"Mickey, Jana loves us all; however, she won't even break a sweat while you are dry heaving on the mat from the workout she will put you through," Breeze said.

Mickey shuddered at the thought then gave a slight shrug. Jon and Han rubbed their hands together and nodded at him. While they were eating, Mickey and Kidd got up to go get everyone refills. Mickey waited until they were close to the soda station before he slipped Kidd a vial.

"Three drops are the max right now. We don't need them drooling on themselves until later when we are back at the hotel. When you get in the SUV, give it to Breeze, but make sure it is unseen."

"Are you sure they won't taste it or know something is off?"

"I am not stupid. Yes, I am sure. It has even worked on Jana, and she was none the wiser."

Kidd's mouth dropped open, and he playfully acted like he was bowing to Mickey.

"Thank you. Thank you. However, I can't take all the credit... Jazz and Breeze did help me. Breeze was even the test dummy a couple times to ensure there was no after taste, funny taste, or side effects."

"You should have given Jazz a full dropper so he would sleep for a year," Kidd said but was smiling so Mickey knew he was teasing.

"Don't let Breeze hear you say that... you might be left drooling on yourself along with Han."

Kidd shook his head and acted like he was zipping his lips and throwing away the key. They walked back to the table with all the glasses and passed them back to the appropriate owners. When they finished dinner, they went back to their rooms. Jon made sure that Han stayed in Breeze's room while Kidd, Matt, and Mickey stayed in his room. They were less likely to get in trouble when they were not alone with Breeze. Thirty minutes later, Mickey texted Breeze to let her know that Jon had passed out. Breeze responded quickly to let them know that Han was also down for the count. They all walked out and went to the SUV that was waiting at the curb. Breeze nodded to the driver and handed him an envelope of cash. They were racing tonight, not fighting. Breeze couldn't risk fighting and having more bruises or, worse, broken bones. That would be too hard to explain. Ten minutes later they pulled up to the circuit's gates.

"Password?"

Breezed leaned forward. "**Shanghai Sunset**."

The bouncer motioned them through. They all got out, went to the registration table, paid their entry fees, and received their wristbands.

Two Korean warriors walked up to the group of friends. "Breeze." They both greeted her and bowed.

She bowed in return. "Hey, Zion and Yu. What's up, brothers?"

Zion walked up to Breeze and wrapped his arm around her waist. "Hey, girl, what are you doing?"

"Celebrating. What about you?"

"Taking a day off, so please don't make us have to track,"

Zion said. He quickly looked around. "Where's Jazz?"

"I wouldn't dream of it," Breeze said. "Oh, you know, at a tournament with Jana."

"Whew!" Zion acted like he was wiping sweat off his brow and slinging it to the ground. He reached over and pulled her flush up against him. "Please, behave."

She tilted her head up slightly to meet his eyes. "Always."

"Ahh, hell!"

He released her. He popped her butt hard and turned to join Yu. Zion and Yu walked off to go to another section to race. Breeze spotted three of her other friends, Sasha, Max, and Brian. Breeze walked by Sasha and gave her a little finger wave. Matt didn't miss the gesture.

"Girl, I know you do not want to be in the gym with Jon and Han after the kick ass tournaments you were just in for four days," Matt said and shook his head. "And, I know, I don't want to be in the gym with them after you piss them off."

"Relax, darling. That gesture, if you must know, was for them." Breeze gestured toward the retreating figures of Yu and Zion. "Sasha will be issuing challenges to Yu and Zion to keep them on their toes," Breeze said.

"Oh, I can't wait to see those races," Matt said.

Sasha walked over to her bike and threw her hand up to issue a challenge to Zion. Max issued a challenge to Yu. It was on like Donkey Kong. Brian stood back and watched, then he decided to issue a challenge to Mickey.

"Oh, I know he didn't," Mickey said and made three snaps in the air.

"Yeah, he did," Breeze taunted back.

They all started racing. Breeze watched as Zion and Sasha raced. Zion won, but barely. Yu lost to Max, just by a hair, but it was enough to lose. Mickey lost by a bike length. He was ticked. He turned around and issued a challenge to Sasha.

Breeze looked at him and said, "Mickey, how much money do you have to lose tonight?"

"I got enough. I'm getting my pride back. Shut up," Mickey said.

Zion walked over and just smiled. "Good luck with that, brother. Good luck with that." He walked over to Breeze and wrapped his arms around her. "Girl. Did you issue that challenge?"

"I was not the one who threw my hands up. That would be Sasha."

"Yeah, I know how you and Sasha work. I got my eye on you, girl."

"I'm sure you do," Breeze said.

Kidd came running over to where Breeze and Zion were standing. Kidd had some serious attitude. "She's with us tonight. You need to take your hands off her. She's mine for the night."

Breeze looked at Kidd and said, "I am not a doll that gets passed around."

Zion looked at Breeze and mentally touched her mind. *"Do you wanna play?"*

"Always." Breeze said. She turned to walk off to her next challenge. Kidd started to follow her, but Zion threw a challenge at Kidd.

"OK, so that's how it's going to be?" Kidd asked.

"Yeah, that's how it's going to be," Zion said.

Breeze was laughing hysterically. Zion was fired up. Kidd had never seen Zion fired up, ever. He might have thought he had, but he hadn't. There was a shift in Zion's posture when

8

he issued the challenge. It was his warrior stance. Kidd was a fighter, not a warrior.

"Oh, boy, Kidd, I wouldn't put slips up if I were you," Breeze said.

"That's the bike Jana had built for me. I am not racing for slips, no way. Cash only, brother, cash only."

Zion smiled, "That's okay, I'm happy to take your cash any day of the week."

Zion and Kidd made their way over to wait their turn to race. They watched Sasha and Mickey race. Mickey lost to Sasha. Mickey paid Sasha and walked back over to where Matt and Breeze stood. He wanted to see Kidd race Zion. Zion smoked Kidd. Kidd flipped Zion off as he walked back to where Mickey and Matt stood.

"Breeze, where's Breeze?" Kidd asked frantically.

Mickey whipped around. "Shit, it was a distraction. Hell, no, we aren't fighting Yu, Han, Zion, and Jon at the same time because Breeze wanted to take off."

About that time Breeze tapped Mickey on the shoulder. "What are you stressing about? I told you we had two hours. I was racing."

"You need to tell somebody," Mickey said.

Breeze threw her hands up in an I give up kind of gesture and rolled her eyes at him. Zion walked over and gently pulled Breeze to him and kissed her lips. Breeze winked at him, and they put so much passion behind that kiss. Breeze loved messing with Kidd, and Zion was happy to assist any way he could.

Kidd started stammering and stuttering, "Uhh no, I don't think so. I'm going to tell Jana." Breeze turned and looked at Kidd. Everybody in their circle looked at Kidd. "Oh, hell,

Breeze, I'm sorry. I didn't mean that. I'd never tell Jana. I'm so sorry, Breeze."

Breeze threw up her hand to issue a challenge and pointed to Kidd.

Zion took Breeze's hand and said, "You got this."

"I know I do."

Kidd did not stand a chance when that challenge was issued. Breeze not only smoked him, she'd left him in the dust coughing and sputtering. Now everybody was issuing challenges to Kidd because they thought he couldn't race. Kidd quickly won his money back and reassured the circuit that he was there for a reason. He just wasn't at Breeze's caliber, apparently. All of Breeze's friends were making the most of the two hours that they had at the circuit.

Zion walked up to Breeze at the end of her race with Kidd. "I like you fired up, Breeze."

"Thank you. I like you fired up, too."

Zion sighed. "Has Uncle called you?"

"No. However, if I am supposed to be on an assignment, then I'm sure he will be in touch," Breeze said.

"We will meet you at the airport. It will be Uncle, me, Yu, and a couple other warriors. It will be for a two-day assignment. We will be back Sunday evening to ensure you can go to school on Monday."

"Okay. Well, I'm going to enjoy this evening while I can still walk and don't have to have stitches along the way. I've only got thirty minutes left before I have to leave to go back to the hotel."

Breeze hoped that Zion hadn't seen the sadness in her eyes; however, his expression told her that he had noticed something. He didn't ask any questions, and that was good.

She wasn't looking forward to going home to her mom's house or seeing Taylor. Her relationship with Taylor hadn't felt right for a while now, and she had been thinking about ending it. She was starting to feel like a caged animal with him and his controlling nature.

Every time she was with her dad and Jana, she felt a sense of freedom with them. However, she never felt that way at her mom's house. Her dad and Jana accepted her fully for who she was and all her glorious glitches, whereas her mom chose to believe that Breeze was normal and a girly girl. She had been a fool to think that Zion hadn't noticed the sadness she felt. His posture showed he was on alert. *Always the warrior,* she thought.

She knew if the opportunity arose while they were on the assignment, he would talk to her, and she would be honest with him. The streets were fun and flirty with no rules. However, once they stepped back into their normal everyday lives, they were warriors, through and through. They followed all of the rules to the letter. They could not date unless Uncle granted them permission. Breeze saw concern on Zion's face. She refused to let her relationship with Taylor ruin this evening. At the end of the two hours, Breeze and all her friends told everyone bye and loaded back into the SUV to go back to the hotel. Once they were back at the hotel, they split up and went to the appropriate rooms. Ten minutes after Breeze arrived at Jon's room, Han came over. They loaded up and went straight to the airport. Matt and Mickey had made sure that they were on the same flight home with them. Jon just shook his head.

While they were unloading the SUV to go to check in and return the rental, Jon told Breeze that Uncle had called. They would take her stuff and she could get it before she went back to Memphis. Zion, Uncle, Yu, and two other warriors were waiting when they walked off the plane. Breeze texted Jazz to let him know that duties call, and he had agreed to wait at her dad's house until she returned from the assignment, then they would go back to Memphis together. Neither Breeze nor Zion had acted like they had seen each other a few hours earlier.

Zion made sure to ask how the tournament had gone while they were standing there waiting. Breeze quickly told everyone about the tournament. Uncle was proud; he knew that Breeze and Jazz were both training extra hard for Thailand. They were also entering as many tournaments as possible. Zion and Breeze were leaving in one car, Yu and Tony went in one car, and Uncle and Chris were going in another car. The car ride to the location gave Zion plenty of time to ask some questions about the sadness he saw. He also knew from Uncle that both Jana and Kidd had some serious concerns about her relationship with Taylor.

"Breeze, if you ever need to talk, you can always call," Zion said.

"Thank you. I appreciate it."

"As a friend or as a warrior."

"I know. I just want to focus on this assignment right now. However, if I need to talk, I will call you."

BREEZE'S TRAININGS

Breeze was drenched in sweat from the grueling workout with her sensei. It had been such an intense work out that her muscles were screaming. She didn't care; it meant Thailand and the title were steps closer. Her private lessons with her sensei were almost as intense as her trainings with her dad and/or her Uncle Han. The last time that her muscles screamed like this was when she and Jazz were training with Han during the summer before their freshman year of high school while they were in Japan before their warrior tests. They had trained at such an intense level that summer that they tested three months earlier than scheduled.

The time before that was when they represented her dad in an international tournament, had lost badly, and were in the gym the remainder of the trip with both her dad and Han. The flight home from that competition, both she and Jazz had sat too long, and when they got off the plane they looked like robots that had not been oiled or maintained. She laughed at that thought. Mickey still reminded them of that competition often. Breeze knew that the hour session with her sensei was coming to an end; she could feel it.

Her sensei bowed, and Breeze bowed lower as a means of respect.

"You are on fire, Breeze. I think you will take Thailand by storm," Sensei Travis said.

"I hope so," Breeze said, then walked to the locker room.

Breeze entered the locker room, closed the door, and gently put her hand to her stomach. How was she going to tell her family and her friends. She hadn't even confided in Jazz, her best friend. How would he take the news? Would he stand in her corner or tap out? She was trying to stay busy and keep her mind on other things, but that was getting harder and harder now. She showered quickly, got dressed, and let her sensei know that she was leaving.

Breeze walked out of the dojo, got in her car, and cranked up the radio. She was listening to Johnny Cash's song called "Jackson." She started laughing. She was bored, and it was never a good idea for her to get bored. She thought about the challenge where she snuck into all her friends' houses while they were sleeping and stole all their clothes. She had left them a ball cap and a note, nothing more. The scavenger hunt was all over Jackson, and they had to find their clothes without being caught. Mickey was the first to find an article of clothing and it was a white sock. Breeze started laughing harder. The memory of Mickey with his cap covering his bare essentials and one white sock on, was priceless.

She spotted Jazz's car driving down the road toward his house. She called him, and he answered on the first ring.

"Let's race," she said.

"You got it."

"To Matt's?"

"Yep."

They disconnected and took off. He was going with her to Jackson for the weekend. They both knew all the back roads

14

from Memphis to Jackson and where all the speed traps were along the way. Breeze smiled to herself because her plans for the evening were coming together beautifully.

UNDETECTED

A thought occurred to her, and she grinned. It had been a while since she had been on an adventure; she was overdue for one. Getting out of town undetected was something she typically did with Jazz or Kidd, but today she had different plans. She called Matt, and he answered on the second ring.

"Hey Breeze. What's up? Are you on your way to Jackson?"

"Yes, Jazz and I are on our way there now. Call Henry privately, please, two for Cuba, there and back three hours later. That will be plenty of time for a car slip or two and enough time to piss off Jazz and Mickey."

"The names you want given to Henry?"

"Cleopatra and Donatello."

Matt laughed and hung up.

Next, she called Jazz again. "Hello Darling."

"What's up?"

"You up for a challenge?"

"With you, always."

"Against me. It will be you and Mickey versus me and Matt."

"Hell Yeah. I am ready for a win in my pocket." He paused for a second. "My sensei wants me to train Sunday morning because he is out of town Monday and Tuesday. I know we had planned for a full weekend together, but I have to leave early on Sunday."

"Sucks for you," Breeze teased. "You could tell your sensei that Jon Lee will be working you on Sunday."

"Har-har. I would like to be able to stand and walk on Sunday. I will work out with my sensei, thank you much. Are you going to keep yapping or are you going to tell me the challenge?"

"I am sure dad would love to hear that. I will tell you about the challenge when we get to Matt's house."

Breeze turned down a back road and saw Jazz turn in right behind her. She knew Jazz would be frustrated because he was behind her, which meant he was losing. They all loved to win, even if it was against each other. She thought of the Willie Nelson song, 'On the Road Again,' and started singing. On the way to Jackson, Jazz was getting jittery with excitement. He loved Breeze's challenges. She mentioned Matt and Mickey, it was probably an in-state challenge, nothing out of country for sure… hold on, this was Breeze. It could be off planet for all he knew. He laughed at the thought of them being in spacesuits and racing in flying cars. His cell rang, and he answered it.

"I like it." Breeze said.

"Damn, I wasn't blocked."

"Slacker. That would be as cool as racing on dragons."

"Hell, yours would probably eat Mickey."

"Nah, life would be boring without him," she said.

"Did you ring just to bust my balls about not having my thoughts completely blocked?"

She took a deep breath. "I forgot to tell you; I broke up with Taylor last night. I gave him everything back, including the engagement ring."

"Forgot? How the hell do you forget something like that?"

"Not worth a second thought."

"You're right, he's not."

Breeze turned off down a backroad and Jazz followed. He left the car running when he got out. They would be on the road soon; they weren't far from Matt's house. When Breeze got out of her car, Jazz charged her, picked her up, and spun her around.

"Was that why you were distracted at school today?"

"Yes and no. Mainly I was bored."

"Ahh hell, does this challenge require me to be swimming naked with sharks?"

Breeze roared with laughter. She hadn't thought of that, but she liked it. Jazz noticed a slight bruise on her cheek, and he gently touched it.

"Is that from your workout or him?"

"Him, but it's over now."

Jazz leaned over and gently kissed the bruise. He placed his hand on the opposite side of her face; she turned her head and kissed his palm. She touched his mind. They both felt freer when they spoke mentally, since they were both telepaths.

"Thank you for always being there, Jazz. I love you."

"I will always be there for you and with you. Now, if you don't mind, I have a challenge to win."

They ended the mental connection and got back in their cars. Breeze spun out with Jazz right on her bumper. They were racing, and Jazz had every intention of finishing in the lead; however, Breeze had other intentions. Breeze had a lot on her mind. She needed her friends and the distractions right now. She was worried, and she could not let it show, not now, anyway. She would deal with all that later. She wasn't sure how she would deal with it all, but she would, to the best of her ability. She unconsciously touched her stomach and sighed. She got her thoughts back on the road so she wouldn't lose this race to Jazz. They raced to Matt's taking every back road they possibly could. Breeze spun into the drive with Jazz right on her tail. Matt and Mickey were waiting when they pulled up. Matt held out his hand and Mickey slapped a ten in it. As soon as the cars were stopped, Mickey ran to her car.

"Breeze, spill it. Are there women and money in this challenge?"

"Mickey, Mickey, Mickey. How about you try to not be left behind…again." Breeze smiled at him.

Mickey flipped her the bird and grinned.

"Ok, here is the challenge. We will have a seven-hour window and let's keep it undetected, ok? I really don't want to be grounded for a month or worse in the gym with Dad and/or Han."

"Han? Is he here?" Mickey squeaked out.

"No, but you know he will be happy to fly in from Japan just to watch us sweat in the gym," Breeze said.

"Undetected, undetected is good," Mickey said and made the sign of the cross.

Matt pushed Mickey. "Breeze, please continue before I slap this fool."

Breeze shook her head with a smile. "The first part of the challenge is that we will race from the old quarry to Dyersburg and back. We must bring back one souvenir from a little mom and pop shop that is at least ten miles out from here. The second part of the challenge is to run by Dad's house and snap a pic of one of Jana's new art pieces. The third part of the challenge is that we race from here to Erin and back. One person from the team must get out at the train caboose and have their picture taken on the other team member's phone with a time stamp for verification. First team to return in the seven-hour window, wins."

"What's the prize?" Mickey asked.

"Dinner at Mr. Wu's, paid for by the losers."

Mickey began jumping up and down. "Man, I love that place."

"Can it be in any order?" Jazz asked. He was forming a plan in his mind. Breeze shook her head, and Jazz swore.

"Gentlemen, let's start our engines."

Matt threw open the garage door. He selected his Challenger. Jazz decided to stay with his Mustang. Mickey locked up the garage. Breeze took the driver seat of Matt's car and Jazz stayed behind the wheel of his car. Mickey was riding shotgun with Jazz. The two cars lined up, side by side. Mickey turned on Aretha Franklin's "Respect." On the second R-E-S-P-E-C-T they took off to the quarry. Breeze and Jazz stayed neck and neck until Jazz had to shift behind her because a car was coming. Breeze looked in her rearview mirror, she was laughing. Matt looked back and saw Jazz was right on her bumper. Mickey was pounding his fists on the dash and yelling for Breeze to get out of the way. He really wanted to win this challenge. Matt laughed.

"Lord have mercy, I would hate for him not to get Mr. Wu's."

"He would kill us, you know that, right?" Breeze teased.

"No joke."

Jazz hit a side road to come into the quarry from the right. Breeze went up and took the next sideroad. The outcome was the same. Breeze was in the lead. She spun into the old quarry drive and Jazz flew up beside her. She was laughing when Jazz got beside her. She turned a hard right and flew down the road leading out of the quarry. Matt grabbed hold of the bar above the door and swore.

"What time does this challenge end again?"

"11 p.m.," Breeze said.

"Ok, well then, I might find my stomach and heart around 3 a.m."

"Nah. You will have a cigar and an 8-ball whiskey in your hand around that time."

"Oh, yeah, I forgot."

Breeze saw Jazz pull into a store lot. She blew past him. She knew that was where he would stop; she would stop at a place on the way back from Dyersburg. They made it to Dyersburg, Breeze made the turn to head back to Jackson, she made a call and flashed Matt a smile. She had called a new little coffee shop, placed the order for their coffee and a keychain with their logo on it, and paid. It would be ready by the time they got there. Breeze whipped into the lot, Matt jumped out, ran in and out, and got back in the car. They were back on the road in no time. Matt took a sip of his coffee.

"This is good. I think this is my new favorite coffee shop. So, we are finishing this challenge?"

"Yes, sir. It is the next challenge that we won't finish."

"You are so bad, and I absolutely love it."

"It will start at two in the morning and end at ten in the morning." Breeze said with a smile.

Matt could only imagine what Breeze had in store for Jazz and Mickey. He knew that Breeze would need to keep those two busy to ensure he and her got on the plane.

"They will have a scavenger hunt with clues at each location."

"OMG. Did you get bored?"

Breeze nodded and flashed Matt a sly grin.

"Holy shit." Matt said.

"Keep on, and you can stay and play with the others," Breeze teased.

Matt threw his hands up in surrender.

"I thought you would see it my way," Breeze said.

Breeze beat Jazz to her dad's house. Matt ran in, told Jana he needed to see her newest pieces of art.

"Challenge?" Jana asked.

"Yep."

"Oh, Lord, does Jazz still have clothes?"

Matt simply shrugged. Jana shook her head.

"What those two won't do is not worth mentioning."

Jana had just shown Matt the new pieces when they heard Jazz's car. Matt snapped a pic and ran out.

"Thanks, Jana."

"Anytime," Jana called out as he ran to the door

Mickey tried to trip Matt as he ran past but failed. Matt was barely in the car when Breeze pulled out. He slammed his door as she was hitting the main road. He didn't say a word. There was no point. Breeze turned off and got on the interstate only to be greeted by road construction and the interstate being down to one lane. Bumper to bumper traffic. She got off at the first possible exit. Breeze swore because she just saw Jazz's car go by and was seeing his taillights as she was getting off the exit. There were cars in front of her or she would gun it and find a way to get past him. She was not losing this one.

"Siri, call Sasha."

"Hey girl," Sasha said.

"Hey."

"What's up?"

"You up for some hide-n-seek for a scavenger hunt, Breeze style?"

"Hell, yeah. What are the perimeters? How many are playing?"

"It would be from Jackson to Memphis. Two in the morning to ten in the morning will be the time frame for the scavenger hunt. There will be four to six players. Objects are to be left, a pic of each object and the location found would be for verification. Each stop would be a new clue to the next location."

"Sweet."

"Matt will be texting you the list of objects from my phone. If you think of anything else, just add it to the list. Do you mind calling Brian and Max to help you set it up? They both know the rules and have played before. I will text you the names of the players involved in case you decide to set up clues with the person's name, or you can just label one through six and we will draw numbers to see what clue belongs to which person."

"Hell yeah, I will call them. We will use the numbers instead of names."

"Since you are setting it up, if you want to change anything, that is totally up to you. The location and time frame are the only things that can't change."

"Oh Sookie, Sookie, I get to play."

Breeze busted out laughing. "Ahhh, hell, I think Jazz is rubbing off on you."

"Never. It is all you, girl."

23

"Thanks. See you at the finish line." Breeze ended the call. "Call Zion." The phone rang twice; Zion answered it, and Breeze heard a woman in the background.

"Sorry to interrupt."

"You're not."

"You up for a scavenger hunt – Breeze style?"

"As long as I am not tracking you, then I am game."

"Zion, do I need to issue a challenge?"

"No, we are good. I'm still trying to recover from the last one. Hell, I think half of the brethren are still recovering."

"Only half? Damn, I am slipping."

Matt yelled, "DUDE, SERIOUSLY. My stomach and heart are still in Jackson. Shut it."

Zion laughed. "Yes, I am game."

"Good. Call Yu. Meet at Matt's at one thirty in the morning."

"Do you ever sleep?"

"Where is the fun in that?"

Breeze ended the call. Matt turned his head and looked at Breeze. She was grinning like a kid with her hand in the cookie jar and her other hand in the candy jar.

"They are so screwed."

"Distraction for us and yes, yes they are."

"I love you, girl, but I am glad I will be with you."

Breeze pulled into the little parking area at the Betsy Ligon Park just as Mickey was jumping in Jazz's car. They spun out. Breeze swore. "Hurry." Matt and Breeze ran to the caboose, snapped the pic, and ran back to the car. Minutes were like hours in a car race. She hated to lose. They all did, but still…

Jazz was sitting on the hood of his car and Mickey was leaning out the passenger side window when Breeze and

Matt pulled up.

"Well damn, looks like dinner is on me. It's a record six hours and forty minutes. Nice."

"Dinner? I want lunch." Mickey said.

"We will see. It really depends on how tired you are after the next challenge."

Jazz stared at Breeze. "What next challenge?"

"No worries. You won this one. Mr. Wu's is on me."

"Breeze."

"Yes, darling."

"Oh, hell, Mickey, we are swimming with sharks naked."

Breeze laughed. "I keep forgetting that one."

"Fools. Shut it. I mean damn. This is Breeze; she can come up with crazy shit herself without you giving her ideas. I kind of like keeping all of my body parts in one piece, especially my manhood, and not as shark food." Matt said with irritation.

Breeze was laughing so hard she was gasping for air. It took her a good five minutes to calm herself enough to speak. "Zion and Yu will be here at one thirty. The challenge will begin at two in the morning and ends at ten in the morning. Sasha, Brian, and Max are setting up the scavenger hunt as we speak."

Mickey was bouncing in his seat. "Teams?"

Breeze shook her head. "Nope, individuals only."

Mickey could not contain his excitement. He jumped out of the car and ran around to Breeze. "Prize?"

"Everyone will list what they want as a prize before the scavenger hunt begins."

Matt just shook his head. "I need a bigger garage."

Jazz laughed. "Is that your wish for a prize?"

"No, but now that you mention it, good idea."

Breeze flashed a grin at Jazz and walked inside the house. Jazz took off after her.

"I love it when you get bored." Jazz said and spun her around.

"Thanks."

He leaned down and kissed her lips. He saw a brief sadness cross her eyes when the kiss ended.

"What? What is wrong?"

"Nothing."

"Breeze, I know you."

She pulled out her phone and showed him the texts from Taylor.

> **Taylor**: You are mine. You whore. Did you run off with that asshole Jazz? I mean it, you are mine.
> **Breeze**: No, I'm not. It's over. Now good-bye.
> **Taylor:** It's over when I say it's over.

Breeze had not responded to the last text. Jazz begged her to not let Taylor ruin their day, their weekend, or their time together. Breeze reassured Jazz that the only thing that was happening this weekend was her smoking him on the next challenge. She walked into the kitchen and made herself a snack. At one in the morning Sasha texted Breeze to let her know that Max had just finished with the last two locations. Breeze grinned and gave Matt a brief nod. Jazz was playing against Mickey on the PlayStation 5, so they did not see the exchange between Matt and Breeze. Yu and Zion walked into the house at one twenty in the morning.

"Glad to see that fine ass of yours is still in town." Zion said.

Breeze got up, walked slowly over to Zion, and stroked his

cheek. "I have a challenge to win, but if you would rather chase my fine ass from here to Korea to Romania and back, I can arrange it."

Zion quickly flipped Breeze over his shoulder and popped her butt. "Oh, I know you can. I like this better."

He kept Breeze over his shoulder. Breeze wiggled and tried to get down, but Zion acted like it was nothing to have her draped over his shoulder. Breeze reached over and grabbed a cushion off the couch and hit Zion with it. He turned them both slightly, and she threw the cushion at Mickey and hit him on the side of the head. Everyone was laughing until the text came through from Sasha. Zion set Breeze down so they could each read their phones.

[SCAVENGER HUNT—Breeze Style]

- **Individual Challenge** (NO teams)
- **Begins** at 2 a.m.
- **Ends** at 10 a.m.
- **Locations:** Jackson to Memphis and everywhere in between.
- Complete list delivered **10 seconds** after the final instructions are sent

Rules:
📷Pics of objects **and** location **only**
🔍Clues at each location for the next location
📍First location the tree outside of Jon's Dojo
📝All clues are numbered 1-6
—Only read your number!
—Every clue is different, yet the same.

27

The clock felt like it stopped as they waited for the list to come through. When the list came through, they all scrolled to the end and saw that there was a total of one hundred seventeen items on it. The final object to be received from Sasha was the Ace of Spades.

Breeze laughed. "I think Sasha had fun with this. I need to recruit her more often."

Every man in the room turned to look at Breeze and shook their heads. If that was the case, then they would never find her.

"We think we are good," Yu announced.

"Ahhh, I feel a challenge or two in you guys' future. I might get soft or out of practice with getting around you fools."

"Mickey, the timer, please." Jazz said before Breeze could issue another challenge and they were all tracking her instead of playing this amazing scavenger hunt. Matt numbered pieces of paper 1-6 and placed them in a jar for everyone to draw their number. Matt wrote the number down as each person drew from the jar, their name, and their requested prize if they won.

Breeze drew first.

3. Breeze – A bracelet from Romania

6. Jazz – A tat

4. Matt – Indian Motorcycle

2. Zion – Mustang 1965 completely rebuilt for streets

5. Yu – Charger (black & red)

1. Mickey – A steak dinner for 2 at Longhorn Steakhouse with $100 spending money for him and his date

Zion looked at the list. "Breeze, a bracelet, really?"

"From Romania... duh."

"I see that, but a bracelet," Zion said in complete disbelief.

Breeze walked over to the list and added the note, * last place must go to Romania, find the most unique bracelet, and bring it back*. She looked at Zion, "Now, is that better?"

"No, not really."

"Five minutes," Mickey yelled.

Everyone grabbed their keys and went outside. Once the timer went off, there would be a mad dash to their vehicles. Mickey, Yu, and Zion chose motorcycles while the other three chose cars. When the timer went off it was a scramble. Breeze and Matt had privately agreed to do the first and second locations so as to not throw up any red flags. Breeze was the first to the tree at her dad's dojo, and it still took her three minutes to find the object. She snapped the required pics, read the next clue, and took off. Zion was right on her heels. Breeze made it to the Koi pond, found the second object quickly, snapped that pic, read the next clue, and took off.

Everyone's list had the same number of items on the list and the same items listed; however, the order of the objects and locations were different for all of them. Each location had six objects hidden with the next clue for the individual by their numbers; if they forgot their number then they were screwed. Breeze's next clue led her to a different location than Zion's did. They were everywhere and focused on the task at hand so when Breeze and Matt went different ways, everyone thought they were following clues. Breeze and Matt made it to the airstrip undetected.

"Cleopatra. Donatello. Welcome." The pilot greeted them. The plane was down the runway and in the air before the others had found their fourth item on the list.

"GIRL. That was an AWESOME CHALLENGE, kind of sad not to finish it," Matt said.

"Really?"

"I said kind of."

"There is always next time," Breeze said.

Matt laughed. "Yes, there is."

Breeze went to the restroom and changed into her street clothes. When she returned, she sat back in her seat and drank a coke. Matt had an 8-ball of whiskey and was savoring it.

"Good thing Mickey isn't here, Jazz would have to beat him off with a stick." Matt said and toasted her.

Breeze just shook her head.

SELF-ABSORBED

Taylor paced his room. He could not believe Breeze had thrown all his stuff on the ground and just left it for him to pick up last night. *Who does she think she is, anyway?* He had not slept well at all. Guilt and a broken heart caused him to toss and turn. He looked at the box on his bed. The engagement ring was in its original box on top of all the stuff in the box. He had never cared enough before Breeze to give jewelry to a woman, let alone an engagement ring. He shouldn't have lost his temper with her again. He kicked the dresser and grabbed his phone. He looked up the local florist and ordered a dozen red, orange, and pink roses. He ordered two dozen yellow and white roses to be delivered to her mom's house. The card read: Breeze, I love you. I promise you are my world. Love, Taylor.

He paid with his credit card, hung up, called a florist in Jackson, and placed the same order to be delivered to her dad's house. Both orders would be delivered Saturday morning around ten. They would get past this and work things out; he was sure of it. He decided he was going to the Blues Club tonight. Maybe she would be there. He was hopeful, then that hope turned to anger. If she was there, she would probably be with one of her goon "friends" like Jazz or Kidd. "WHORE," he yelled, and the glass he had been holding shattered against his closet door. "She makes me crazy." He pushed the intercom on the wall.

"Yes, sir."

"Send someone up to my room to clean up glass."

"Yes, sir."

A couple of minutes later there was a knock at his door. He opened the door and saw Claire, the head of housekeeping, standing there. She curtsied and walked in with a broom, dustpan, and cleaning supplies. Taylor pointed to the closet door. She made quick of her work and left the room quietly. Claire had a new woman on the cleaning staff, but she didn't want her first day on the job to be one where she might be seduced or running from the house screaming. The younger Mr. Smith had come home drunk last night and was in an absolute foul mood. The new girl did not need his fury; that was why she had gone herself. Claire had worked for the Smith family for a long time, and she knew how to fair their storms.

She heard the locks click on Taylor's door and the heavy metal music start. She shook her head. It was going to be a long day. She hoped and prayed that Taylor's father was not in a bad mood, too, when he arrived for the evening. She quickly made her way down to the staff area and got everyone's attention.

Claire clapped her hands. "Listen up. Everything is spot on today, no mistakes. Kitchen staff, these will be the meals for the day; for lunch grilled cheese and homemade chicken stew for dinner lasagna and garlic bread. Exactly the way that Taylor likes it."

All the staff nodded and quietly went to complete their

duties for the day. Taylor was pleased at lunch to have the homemade chicken stew and the grilled cheese extra gooey the way he liked it. He even complimented the chef and kitchen staff. Claire cleaned the dishes after he had seconds and brought him vanilla ice cream with hot fudge drizzled over top of it, with a cup of coffee to go with his dessert.

"Thank you, Claire. You are so good to me."

She bowed and stepped back into the shadows. She smelled the slightest hint of liquor on him. His mood and liquor were never a good combination, especially this early in the day. She had seen the box on Taylor's bed when she had been up there, but she knew better than to ask questions. Obviously, Breeze had broken things off with him. She was surprised that Breeze had stayed as long as she had. Breeze was always so respectful and kind to all the staff, but she could stand up to Taylor, too. She didn't put up with his moods. She would give them back to him on a silver platter.

Taylor slid his chair back. "It was good. I'm going out. I will be back for dinner, then I will be going out again."

"Yes, sir. I will let the kitchen staff know."

He ran upstairs, freshened up, grabbed his keys and wallet. He was hoping to see Breeze after she got home from school. He had to talk to her. He needed her. He had a feeling she was going to Jackson this weekend. He was hoping she wouldn't go straight there after school. He decided that he would go to the shopping center close to her school and hang out until two forty-five that afternoon. At least that way he could get in front of or behind her when he saw her car pulling out. He thought about picking up flowers and delivering them to the school, but he didn't know for sure how she would respond to that. Taylor texted Breeze.

Taylor: *I'm sorry. Can we talk?*

Ten minutes passed with no response. He remembered the school had spotty service. He drove to the shopping center. He decided he needed a few things and went shopping. He bought himself a few new shirts and the cologne that Breeze liked on him so much. He shopped until two-thirty that afternoon, paid and made sure he was in his car by two forty so he could see her car when she passed. He waited, looked at the clock; it showed 2:49. He waited some more.

He saw Jazz's red mustang go by and figured Breeze would be by soon. By three she had not come by yet, and he was getting mad. "Why does she always make me wait?" He looked at his phone; still no text from her. He hit his hands on the steering wheel, then he remembered that she would be at the dojo today. She had gone the other way. He quickly pulled out and went to the shopping center near the dojo.

He shopped there for about thirty minutes, then he sat in his car and waited. He had been there a little over an hour when he saw her. She was driving by; he could see that she was smiling and laughing. He had not slept the night before, was in agony, and she was smiling. "BITCH." He pulled out three cars behind her. His phone beeped, and he quickly looked at it. It was Breeze.

Breeze: *There is nothing to say. You can keep your apologies, it is over.*

He threw his phone across the passenger seat. She was going to talk to him, one way or another. She took off and he sped up. He saw her turn off down the road to go to her house.

34

He stopped at the light and swore. Once he finally was able to turn down her road, she was already getting back in her car and driving off. She drove past him and flipped him off. Shock and fury flooded him. He went up the road and turned around. He saw Jazz's car and then he saw Breeze's car; they looked to be racing.

"Damn it." He hit his steering wheel again. He called a couple buddies. "Hey, are there any races tonight?"

"Not locally. There are some in Atlanta, New Orleans, Las Vegas, and Dallas."

Now he was really mad. He sped up to try to get them in his sights again, but they were gone. He drove back by the dojo where she took private lessons, but her car wasn't there. Hopefully, she would call once she received the flowers tomorrow. He did not want to go home right now; he would just get mad all over again. He was going out tonight to get his mind off Breeze. He would go home around five or six for dinner, then he would be hitting the clubs. He called a few friends, invited them over to eat, called Claire to let her know that there would be guests for dinner, and he began planning his evening.

Taylor arrived home at four forty-five, ran upstairs, and changed. He was wearing name brand blue jeans, a nice t-shirt, and expensive shoes. He made sure to wear Breeze's favorite cologne. He put on the silver rope chain that Breeze had given him and walked downstairs. His friends arrived at five thirty. They ate, cut up, and were out the door by seven thirty to hit the clubs. Taylor grabbed a light jacket off the coat rack by the door. It wasn't cold, but the air had a light chill to it. The glories of Tennessee especially in the fall and spring: it could be hot as hades during the day then cool or cold in the evenings and night. Taylor decided on the Blues Club as the place to start. The four men were gorgeous, most people assumed they were models, but none were. Money and power seemed to roll off them, and it was an elixir to most of the women in the clubs. As soon as they walked into the place, women were offering to buy them drinks or inviting them to join their tables. The four men had made sure to drive their own vehicles in case they ended up leaving with someone. That rule had been in place since they first started driving.

Taylor spotted a tall redhead near the bar, and he made his way over to her. Once he got closer to the woman, he realized that it wasn't Breeze, but the woman was pretty, so he continued over to her. She looked familiar, maybe he had seen her here before. It didn't matter, just another face of many.

"Hi," Taylor said with a flirty smile.

"Hello," Sasha said.

"May I buy you a drink?"

"Not tonight, cowboy. I am here with a date."

"Come on, it's just a drink."

"Aren't you Breeze's boy?" Sasha asked.

Taylor's eyes narrowed. "No, I'm not, but even if I was it is just a drink."

"You mean she finally dumped your sorry ass? Good for her. Now, excuse me." Sasha turned and tried to move past Taylor when he grabbed her arm.

Sasha pulled hard with her arm and kneed him in the crotch at the same time. A big guy started walking over. He stood six feet three inches and weighed in at two hundred eighty pounds and was solid muscle.

He touched Sasha's arm. "You ok?"

"Peachy. Breeze's ex-boyfriend thought he would put his hands on me, but I fixed that thought. We're good. Ready?"

Brian nodded. He allowed Sasha to get in front of him. He kept his eye on Taylor as Sasha made her way out. He stepped closer to Taylor. "Sasha is off limits just like Breeze is."

Taylor grabbed Brian's shirt. "Breeze is mine."

"Funny way of showing it, putting moves on other women."

Taylor shoved Brian. Brian simply laughed. The bartender was watching Taylor. Brian waved. "See ya, Lucas."

"Later, Brian."

Brian looked at Taylor and gave a slight nod. "Later," Brian said and laughed all the way out to the car.

Brian thought it was funny that Taylor honestly thought he was bad enough to start something with him. His muscles weren't just for looks. Now if Taylor's three buddies decided to jump in and assist Taylor and it became four on one, that might be a different story, but Brian wouldn't let it get that far. Sasha smiled when Brian got in the car.

"He is a loser. I can't believe Breeze fell for him."

"I'm surprised Jazz let that shit fly," Brian said.

LET THE GAMES BEGIN

Sasha and Brian continued to drive to landmarks to hide items and clues. Sasha was pumped about this challenge. She had a feeling it was a cover up for something else but who knew; this was Breeze. She thought about calling Breeze to give her the heads up about Taylor being at the Blues Club, but then that would tell her a location. The items that were placed ranged from plastic rings, plastic frogs, plastic animals, sunglasses, colored stones, pencils, erasers, balls, etc. Most were purchased from the novelty aisles at Walmart, Dollar Store, and the Dollar Tree. The items were for pinatas, birthday party packs, or party favor type items. Sasha's favorites were the emoji balls and the pirate rubber duckies.

Max called Sasha a couple of minutes after she finished her last location. He had just finished and was planning to meet them at a local café, after she texted Breeze. Sasha would be at the final location around nine in the morning just in case someone finished early, which she seriously doubted would happen. She sent Breeze the confirmation text at one in the morning.

Sasha: The task is complete. The scavenger hunt

is ready when you are.

Breeze: Perfect, text the full instructions at 1:50 a.m. then immediately send the list.

Sasha: Absolutely. Can't wait to see the winner.

Breeze: It's me… you know that.

Sasha: More than likely.

Breeze: Once the winner proves their win, announce to all of us. A total of 6 players; Matt, Mickey, Jazz, Zion, Yu, and myself.

Sasha: I am surprised Zion is not sitting on you.

Breeze: LOL. Why is that?

Sasha: Oh, I don't know… your last adventure. See ya around 10 a.m.

Breeze: Hee-Hee… you were a perfect decoy. Yes, you will. I will have your delivery in hand too.

Sasha: Yes, I was. Sweet. Thanks.

The texts were sent just as Breeze instructed. Sasha, Max, and Brian watched from a distance as everyone raced to the first location. They saw Breeze get the second clue and then took off. Brian texted Max to see if he had changed Breeze's third location. He had not.

Max texted Sasha.

Max: You a decoy "Red"?

Sasha: Nope

Max: Sure?

Sasha: Positive. See you at the café in 10 mins.

Once they were seated at the café, they discussed where Breeze could be going. They gave up because that discussion could go on forever and the possible locations were endless, though they doubted that she was on her way to Japan. The thought of Breeze going to Japan had them all laughing. It was amazing that Han hadn't moved to Tennessee to try to help keep her in the country. They talked about some of the times that Sasha had helped Breeze get around Han, Jana, and Jon. They ordered and ate while they talked. Sasha knew that Zion had been called in a lot to try to find Breeze, and it amazed Sasha that they had not found Breeze more than what they had. She had skills, that was for sure. Brian told Max of the development that they had learned about Breeze's single status.

"It is about time. Taylor is a jerk. Every time I have ever seen him it is like he thinks he is God's gift to women. Yeah, he has money, but big deal," Max said.

"For Breeze, you know it wasn't about the money. I am not sure what it was, but it wasn't the money," Sasha said.

Back in Jackson at two thirty in the morning, Jana was awakened to a roaring in her head. She eased up out of bed and went to the kitchen. She grabbed a bowl, tea leaves, and a glass of water. She sat at the table and began scrying. "Show me." She saw Breeze and Matt sitting and laughing; there was a roar of engines. "Show me Jazz." Breeze's image faded and she saw Jazz and excitement. He was running and laughing. She saw Zion and Yu running. They were looking for something. Jazz spotted something and pulled out his phone and took a pic. Zion was on his heels. "Show me Breeze." The image was still of her and Matt. She noticed that Matt was holding a glass with dark liquid in it. "Whiskey." She looked closer. "It's not a car. Plane?"

She watched them for a few minutes and then switched back

to Jazz. She saw a flash as Mickey raced by Jazz. "Memphis? Interesting." Jazz and Mickey were looking for something. Jana noticed a glimpse of something and watched closely. Mickey lifted an object and took a picture and then a second picture; one picture was of the object and the second was of the location. The object looked like a rubber duckie dressed as a pirate, and the location was the Piggly Wiggly. Jana started laughing. She remembered earlier when Matt said it was a challenge.

"Oh, my lord, Breeze got bored. Thank goodness they all still have their clothes on." She switched back to watching Breeze and Matt for a couple of minutes. The sounds were different. Matt was relaxed but excited at the same time. Breeze was on cloud nine. Jana picked up the word undetected from Breeze. The plane was descending, and Jana watched as Breeze became focused and grabbed a duffle bag. Matt sat the empty glass down. He allowed Breeze to exit first. When they got off the plane, there were two street cars waiting. "Racing, where?" Jana watched a little longer.

Breeze danced to the car she was driving. "Three hours then back here so we can get back to Tennessee before the challenge ends. We have some slips to win right now. Welcome to Cuba." Breeze threw her arms open wide and turned in a circle, opened the driver door to her car and stood there for a moment talking to Matt.

Matt laughed. "Don't forget my cigar."

"Cigars. You must share."

"Oh, yeah. I forgot."

"How pissy do you think Mickey will be?"

"He gets Mr. Wu's."

"Left behind, again."

41

"Oh, man. I am staying here. He will be one soggy cookie."

Breeze winked and got in the car. Jana sat back. "Unde-tected." Jazz, Zion, Yu, and Mickey are on a challenge while Breeze and Matt are in Cuba racing. Interesting. Jana started laughing. Cuba was part of the challenge but directed at the trackers and the other master schemer. Jon came up behind Jana and rubbed her shoulders. He leaned over and kissed her neck.

"You are laughing so I will take it that we don't need to track."

"Nope." Jana explained what she had seen.

Jon started laughing. "Mrs. Lee, how have we survived?"

"Quite nicely, I would say. Thank goodness all of their abilities have not been discovered yet or we might never find them." Jana said.

Jon lifted Jana up, turned her to face him, and kissed her. "I think my heart has stopped. There is enough craziness without their other abilities being revealed."

Jana laughed. "We would both have to show them that we could out do them, regardless of whatever ability they might discover."

Jon laughed harder. "As long as I can find our house, it's all good."

Jana and Jon went back to bed. Jana would not tell Breeze she knew about Cuba unless the need arose. Breeze and Matt raced for two and half hours then went back to the plane. They won cash and several slips. Matt arranged for the cars to be loaded and shipped to the states. Customs would delay delivery for several weeks. They left and went to a little shop and bought seven cigars. There was one for all the guys, her dad, and two for Matt. The flight from Cuba to Tennessee was not that long at all.

Breeze decided they still had time so they could play the game a little bit once they were back in Memphis. Breeze changed back into the clothes that she had been wearing before she boarded the plane; she didn't want it to be obvious that she had skipped town or anything like that. Breeze had set up the scavenger hunt for others to play several times. She was thinking about all of the places that she would have hidden things. Sasha had played and assisted with the set-up previously, and even though the game was never the same, there were some locations that were in all of the games. There was no way around it. Memphis was their home, and they knew the area. She refused to use her ability of telepathy to cheat. There was no fun in that. She thought about places around Jackson and Memphis.

"The Blues Club, the arena, Grizzlies Stadium, The Factory, etc. will be just a few of our next several stops. I am going to think a little bit more about Jackson. I am sure I can come up with possible other places."

Matt laughed. "When you get bored again, please make sure you call me."

"Now Matt...where is the fun in that?" Breeze said in a sappy sweet southern dialect.

"Oh, hell."

"Can I have Zion's cigar?" Matt handed her one. "Don't give the others their cigars until Zion finds his." Breeze rubbed her hands together. "Or a new item added to the list...nah, too easy for Jazz to figure out he was left behind...again."

Matt looked at Breeze. "Again? Like recently?"

Breeze nodded and held up four fingers. Matt was still laughing when the plane landed. Breeze got in her car and drove straight to the Memphis locations. Jazz was pulling up when Breeze was running in; she found her item and clue. She snapped the pics and took off. Zion was jumping off his bike as she was getting in her car. Jazz was running out. Zion briefly thought about not seeing Breeze since the first two locations, but he gave that little thought since it was a scavenger hunt. He hadn't seen Matt at all and Mickey only a couple of times. Hell, he hadn't seen Yu much either. Sasha, Max, and Brian knew Breeze well and had set this up beautifully.

Breeze and Matt knew there was no way to make up for the hours they had been gone, but they could do their best to find as many as possible. They would not cheat as it wasn't in them. Breeze looked at her watch: eight thirty in the morning. One and a half hours remained. She looked at the full list and thought hard, then she read the texts again with the rules.

"And everywhere in between." Breeze spun out and hit the small towns between Jackson and Memphis. She found a good number of the items there. She had her final clue and raced to the location. Zion came out of a side road and was quickly catching up. He was on her tail, so she gunned it and laughed.

"Siri call Sasha."

"Zion is on my tail. I will whip in, hand you your package, and a little something for Zion. Give it to him and his ace of spades. Please and thank you."

"Sure thing."

Breeze hit a back road, turned, saw Sasha, eased up to her and handed Sasha her package, as well as a postcard with a note on it and a keychain for Zion. Breeze looked in her rearview mirror, saw the front end of Zion's bike and took off.

Zion pulled up to Sasha. She handed him his Ace of Spades. She verified the items and the locations with the pictures and sent the text.

> **Sasha:** *WINNER – ZION. Everyone text me your number of items and I will compile the list for second through six places.*

The texts came in quickly to Sasha. She giggled at the numbers and shook her head. She compiled the list and sent the text.

> **Sasha:**
> *Winner – Zion*
> *2nd – Jazz*
> *3rd – Yu*
> *4th – Mickey*
> *5th – Breeze*
> *6th – Matt*

Zion looked at Sasha. "Breeze is fifth. Are you sure? She was in front of me."

Sasha smiled, walked over to Zion, and handed him the items from Breeze. Zion took the postcard and keychain. He turned the postcard over and read the note. Zion thanked Sasha and got on his bike. Ten minutes later Zion pulled into the all-night diner, walked in, and slid into the booth across from Breeze.

"Well, hey there sweet thang." Breeze said in a thick southern drawl just as the waitress walked up.

"What will it be?"

"Coffee, please," Zion said.

"We are ready to order as well," Breeze said and smiled at the waitress. "I would like blueberry pancakes with bacon and scrambled eggs extra cheesy with salsa on the side."

"I will have the same. Thanks." Zion said. The waitress walked off. Zion sat back and looked at Breeze. "So."

"So, what?" Breeze asked.

The waitress refilled Breeze's coffee and sat Zion's cup on the table. "Your food will be out soon."

"Thank you," Breeze said and looked back at Zion. "Congrats."

"Thanks."

Breeze took Zion's hand and turned it over. She placed a key in his palm and gently closed his fingers around it. "Pale blue. It is locked and loaded."

"I will drive it proudly."

"I know you will." Breeze picked up her coffee and sipped. Zion continued to stare at her and smiled.

"You are so damn beautiful...even when you are scheming." Zion said.

"Scheming? I'm not scheming. I'm eating or about to be."

"Hmmm. Spill it."

Breeze laughed. The server walked over and placed the plates on the table. "Enjoy."

"We will have four more joining us soon. All of them will want coffee once they arrive. Can we slide the table over to connect with our table?"

"Sure." The waitress started to set down her tray so she could move the table, but Zion slid out of the booth and moved the square table to align with their table and sat back down. He saw the envelope by his plate and opened it. He pulled out the cigar, smelled it, and looked up at Breeze. She smiled at him. He slid his plate across the table, got up, and slid in beside her. She grabbed his coffee and put it by his plate. They both looked up at the sound of engines and motorcycles.

"Breeze, I am going to sit on that fine ass of yours."

"You didn't have to track."

All the guys walked in talking with excitement. Breeze nodded to the waitress. She set the cups down, filled them, and left an insulated coffee pot on the table. She was about to lay down menus when the guys all said. "We will have what she is having." This caused the waitress to laugh. "Coming right up."

Jazz sat in the booth across from Breeze, Mickey sat beside him, Matt sat at the table on the same side as Breeze, and Yu sat across from Matt. "So, what was everyone's numbers?" Mickey asked with excitement.

Jazz stated that he had one hundred twelve, Yu said one hundred eleven, Mickey sulked and said one hundred nine, Breeze said seventy-five (this made Mickey smile) and then Matt said fifty.

Mickey had just taken a sip of his coffee and sputtered, and then said "Fifty? Were you sleeping? I mean, damn."

Breeze gave a slight nod to Matt. Matt pulled out envelopes for Yu, Mickey, and Jazz, and handed them to each of them.

"Yeah, Mickey, something like that," Matt said with a deep hint of sarcasm.

Jazz looked at Breeze, then Matt, and ripped open his envelope. He held the cigar. "Cuba," Jazz said.

Breeze nodded. Mickey was still psyched about the challenges, so he just inhaled the smell of his cigar. "I will enjoy this dearly after I enjoy my dinner at Mr. Wu's. Thank you

Breeze and Matt."

Zion looked at Breeze. "Mr. Wu's?"

"Yeah, those two won an earlier challenge because I got stuck in bumper-to-bumper traffic… I was smoking those fools until that happened."

"Dream on," Jazz teased.

"I can issue another challenge that would involve you naked and dancing through the parking lot."

The waitress almost dropped her tray when she heard Breeze's comment. Matt caught the tray before anyone could wear their breakfast. "Thank you," she said, and blushed.

"I promise he will keep his clothes on until we are at least outside." Breeze said.

The waitress smiled. "Hell, he could lose his clothes in here - they all could, I wouldn't mind. However, I think my dad, the cook and owner, might have an issue with five men running naked in his restaurant."

"Oh, all right… we will wait," Breeze teased. Jazz shot her a look.

"What, darling?" Breeze asked Jazz as the waitress walked off.

"No worries, Jazz, I got her," Zion said and placed his hand on her thigh.

Yu busted out laughing. "This was fun."

"Yes, it was," Breeze agreed.

Matt laughed. "Undetected as requested."

They sat, talked, ate, and cut up for over an hour. Jazz was getting irritated by the constant buzzing of Breeze's phone, but Breeze was just ignoring it.

Jazz touched her hand. "Forward them to me."

"Nah, I'm good."

Zion looked at Breeze, then Jazz, and sat up straighter. "Breeze, what is it?"

"My ex, it's nothing that I can't handle."

"Your ex? You mean Taylor? You broke up?" Zion asked and Breeze nodded.

"Good. I don't like that fool," Mickey said.

"Most people don't," Breeze said and drank her coffee.

Zion patted her thigh and mentally touched her mind. *"You ok?"*

"I'm perfect."

"Obviously, you broke up with him. Is he threatening you? Do I need to intervene, or do I need to call Uncle?"

"No, but thank you. I'm fine. Taylor will find someone else soon, I am sure of it."

Zion ended the connection He could tell that Breeze didn't want to talk about it or talk about Taylor. Uncle had already been watching Taylor because Jana and Jon had concerns. Zion looked at Breeze and noticed a shadow of a bruise on her cheek. He reconnected with her mentally.

"Did Taylor put that bruise on your cheek?"

"Zion, I am good."

"That is not what I asked."

Breeze sighed. "Yes, but it has been dealt with. I don't want him or anything about him to ruin my mood, my weekend, or anything else in my life. It is done, so please relax. I really am fine."

"Are you sure?"

"Yes. It is over for good this time."

Zion rubbed the keychain in his pocket that Breeze had recently given him and relaxed. He would call Uncle once he was on his bike; he would do it mentally. Zion and Yu laughed when Mickey got up and danced out to his bike.

"Mr. Wu's, Mr. Wu's, yeah baby, Mr. Wu's." Mickey sang as he danced out.

"Breeze, I blame you. You created that hot mess," Matt said as he pointed up and down at Mickey.

Breeze simply smiled, dropped the tip on the table, and went to the register to pay the check. Jazz stayed with her and wrapped his arm around her waist. The waitress looked a little bummed to see Jazz's arm around Breeze. "Nicole," Jazz said softly to gain her attention. She looked up at him. He slipped her a piece of paper. Nicole quickly looked at Breeze, and Breeze gave her a reassuring smile.

"We are best friends and always will be," Breeze said and paid.

"When is your next off day?" Jazz asked Nicole.

"Friday."

"Beautiful, just like you. Meet you here at four on Friday so we can go to dinner and a movie?" Jazz asked. Nicole glowed with excitement and nodded.

"The tip is on the table. Thank you," Breeze said.

Jazz touched Nicole's hand. "I will see you Friday. I'm Jazz by the way."

Nicole was smiling when they left.

Breeze bumped his hip. "Have fun."

Breeze got in her car and pulled out first. She sighed, once no one could see her. "What am I going to do? Zion is off limits, Jazz is my best friend, I refuse to ruin that relationship or friendship, and Kidd is my brother." She took a deep breath, turned up her radio, sang, and jammed all the way to Matt's house. She cleared her head and focused only on the music.

Zion was third behind Breeze. He briefly let Uncle know the situation and Breeze's single status. Uncle simply nodded.

Zion could tell Uncle was not happy, but he was letting it slide because Breeze said she had handled it. Breeze was a capable warrior and fighter, but emotionally she seemed off right now. Zion didn't like the bruise. Jazz had seen it, he was sure of it. "Ahh, respecting Breeze. I can see that, but allowing it, I don't think so." Zion said to himself.

Jazz tapped Zion. *"Relax, brother. I never allowed it. Breeze demanded I not get involved because she handled it, but I still went toe to toe with that asshole a time or two. The last time was when I walked in the Blues Club and he was all over another woman. Breeze deserves better, we all know that. I am glad she ended it with that fool."*

"I don't like it."

"I know. Neither do I. She wears make up more often as a means of cover."

"He will not touch her again, or Taylor and I will be toe to toe." Zion reassured Jazz.

Jazz nodded and ended the connection. Zion had the confirmation that he needed. It wasn't the first time that Taylor had struck her. Zion cleared his thoughts out of respect for Breeze. He would think about it later. They all went to Matt's and crashed for a few hours. Zion was up around four in the afternoon, next was Breeze. Zion made coffee and was sitting on the back porch when Breeze walked out. She gently touched his shoulder, smiled, and sat in a chair beside him. They sat in silence for a few minutes, just enjoying the view and their coffee.

"I am inviting Sasha, Max, and Brian to dinner at Mr. Wu's tonight. I think they earned it."

"I'd say so."

"Will you and Yu join us?"

"Of course. Thank you for inviting us. I would like to test drive my prize."

"Well…" She stood and held out her hand to Zion. "…let's go." Just as Zion was getting up, Breeze's phone rang. "Hey mom. What's up?" Breeze frowned. "Really? Please give them away or throw them away." Breeze chewed on her lip as her mom made her protests on the other end of the call. "Mom, stop. I do not want them, and I don't want to see them when I get home. Don't you have that bridal shower today? I bet Dorothy and her daughter would love them. Remove the card, rip it in half and throw it in the trash. Tell Dorothy and her daughter they are a gift from me, don't tell them anything else." Breeze began to smile and laughed. "Ok, mom, I love you, too. Bye."

Breeze had just hung up when Jana called. "Hey, Jana." Breeze let out a disgusted sound at whatever Jana had said. "Throw them away." Breeze nodded and laughed. "The same arrived at mom's house. It truly is a shame that he has no clue that I'm not a flower kind of girl. We broke up and that is his ploy to try to win me back. It's not working. Thanks, Jana. Talk later. Bye."

Zion had taken their cups to the kitchen, refilled them, and returned while she was on the phone. "Everything ok?"

"Yeah." Breeze took a deep breath and let it out. "Taylor sent flowers to Mom's house and Dad's house for me. It was an insane amount of flowers, dozens of roses in all colors."

Zion shook his head. "Does that happen often?"

Zion knew the signs of domestic violence and the hairs on the back of his neck were standing on end. He prayed that the bruise on her cheek was not a frequent occurrence, but the signs were more obvious than he liked to admit. Jazz's confirmation earlier and the flowers as an apology really made him want to go pay that asshole a visit. Zion did not let his thoughts show, but he was seriously pissed that a man would think it was ok to put his hands on Breeze. He would report back to Uncle when he had the chance. Breeze simply shook her head, held up her phone, typed out a message, and showed Zion before she clicked send.

> **Breeze:** *Received the flowers, still nothing to say, we are done. Go find someone else.*
> **Taylor:** *Breeze, I love you. I'm so sorry.*
> **Breeze:** *Heard it before. Control is not love.*

Breeze handed her phone to Zion so he could read the texts, put it on vibrate, and put it in her back pocket. She looked at Zion. "How about that test drive?"

Zion grinned, showed her the key, and they walked down off the back porch around to the garage. Breeze unlocked and opened the garage, and Zion spotted the car. He ran his hand over the car as he walked around it. His head shot up and met her eyes. "You built this?"

"Yes. Dad, Jazz, and I built it."

"It's wonderful."

"Wait until you drive her."

Zion opened the driver side door and motioned for Breeze to get in. He slid in beside her, and he fired it up. It purred. Jazz was standing on the front porch when they pulled out. Breeze waved and Jazz nodded. He walked out to the garage and locked it up. That evening Breeze rode with Zion to Mr. Wu's.

As they entered the restaurant Zion tapped Jazz. *"She seems off. Are you sure she is ok?"*

"I sense it too, but I am not picking up anything besides that. I think she is ok. I know Taylor is burning up her phone. She texted her mom and Jana and told them if they need her to call my phone."

"Keep me posted. I leave on assignment tomorrow."

"Of course, brother."

They ended their connection and enjoyed their meal. Zion had a lot to think about, but it would be after he enjoyed the evening with his friends. Mickey ate to the point that everyone thought he would throw up. Thankfully, he didn't. Sasha, Max, and Brian were still excited about the challenge and were dropping hints that they would love to have another one soon. Breeze laughed. "Playing or hiding?"

"Hell, both are fun." Brian said.

"Careful brother, some of her challenges involve us losing articles of clothing along the way," Jazz said.

"Sign me up," Sasha said and grinned at the men.

Max, Brian, and Mickey all spewed their drinks.

Zion busted out laughing. "Can you at least wait until I am back from assignment so that I can be a part of that or be a witness?"

"Breeze, would you look at that, Zion wants to see Jazz naked," Sasha teased.

Zion threw his napkin at Sasha. "Not bloody likely, but I would like to win that damn challenge."

"Dude, you do realize that on one challenge, we started off naked and the challenge was to find our damn clothes, right?" Jazz said.

Matt just nodded and agreed. Yu was laughing so hard he had tears streaming down his face because of Zion's expression.

"Where the hell were we?" Zion asked.

"Assignments," Breeze said and shrugged.

"Seriously?"

"We would not play about something like that," Mickey said.

When dinner was over, everyone went their separate ways. Zion and Yu went home to get rest before their assignment. Matt and Mickey had dates. Brian, Max, and Sasha went clubbing while Breeze and Jazz went to collect the items from the scavenger hunt. Jazz was thankful that Breeze had ridden to the restaurant with Zion because it meant she didn't have her car. When they left to go get the items, she would have to ride with him. Jazz was determined that they would talk to ensure that everything was alright.

Breeze's phone was off. It was nice not to hear it buzzing like crazy. Breeze got in the car and turned up the music. They danced and sang halfway to Memphis until Jazz turned off the radio and took her hand in his.

"Breeze. Please, what is it?"

"Nothing, besides I want him to move on and leave me alone."

"Yeah, me, too. You seem off."

"Really? Cause I got around you, again." She pulled out an envelope and handed it to Jazz.

Jazz swore. Jazz knew defeat and he hated it as much as the next man. "Cuba doesn't count. Matt was with you."

"I know." Breeze said.

Jazz groaned and opened the envelope. He gaped at Breeze. "Holy cow. Seriously?"

"Yep."

"Oh, hell. I am calling Yu and Zion."

"Good luck with that."

Breeze turned the music back on and danced like crazy. They collected everything and returned to Matt's to sleep. Jazz had to leave by ten in the morning, so he could make it back to Memphis for his workout. After Jazz left, Breeze called Kidd.

"Let's race."

"Yeah babe." Kidd said.

Breeze stayed in Jackson until eight Sunday night, and then she drove back to Memphis.

JAZZ'S WORST NIGHTMARE

It had been a month since Breeze broke up with Taylor. Taylor was not giving up. Jazz was becoming more and more frustrated with Taylor. Jazz had spotted him sitting and lurking several places throughout town waiting on Breeze. The texts were constant and ranged from groveling to absolute foul and vulgar. Jazz could tell it was bothering Breeze, but she would insist that she was fine. Breeze left school early today for a doctor's appointment: she would call him when she got home so they could hang out.

Jazz had just arrived home from the dojo. He placed his keys on the entry way table, and when his cell rang, he answered it without looking at the number because he assumed it was Breeze. "Hello."

"Jazz, it's bad." It was Jana, not Breeze.

Jazz grabbed his keys and went rigidly straight. "Jana? What's bad? What's wrong?"

Jazz could hear that Jana was in a vehicle and had been crying.

"Jazz, he tried to kill her. She is enroute to the hospital; they are not sure that she will make it. Please hurry."

Jazz was running to his car. "Where?"

"County General."

"I am on my way."

"Jazz, we are on our way. If you see her and we aren't there before they take her to surgery, please tell her we love her."

Jazz choked back a sob. "I will, Jana. See you soon."

He called his mom to let her know what Jana had said. He broke down; he was crying. Everything over the past month flooded him. Thank goodness it was County General Hospital in Memphis because he was not sure he could have kept his wits about him if he had to drive to Jackson, not with Breeze's life on the line. Jazz made it in record time. He tapped Breeze mentally; her thoughts were scattered, and there was a darkness there that he didn't like. Her aura was dark and gray, not full of all her normal vibrant colors. He felt her wish that the darkness would just take her. His heart felt like it was being ripped out of his chest.

"Breeze, please hold on. Fight, Breeze, fight. I love you."

"Jazz? Pain, so much pain. I see darkness."

Silence fell between them. It was unnerving. He pulled into the parking lot as the ambulance was unloading her. He was in a full run, still mentally talking to her and encouraging her to hold on. He told her that Jana and Jon loved her. He told her over and over again how special she was and how much he loved her and needed her in his life. She would mentally mumble his name and then go back under again. Breeze's mom and stepdad were at the ER door when they unloaded Breeze from the ambulance. Mary and Stan were both crying, and Stan had blood on his hands, shirt, knees of his pants, and shoes. Jazz felt sick knowing that was all Breeze's blood. Stan must have been the one that had found her and tried to stop some of the bleeding. Stan saw Jazz first.

"Oh, thank God, Jazz." Stan hugged him tight.

"What happened?" Jazz asked.

"When I came home, I saw blood, lots of blood. She had drug herself into the living room and knocked the phone over and called 911. I picked up the phone when I heard dispatch trying to get a response. I told them to hurry, and I began working on her until the EMTs arrived. I just know that Breeze told the dispatcher to hurry, that her ex-boyfriend had stabbed her. They said she was in and out of consciousness and couldn't get much more from her. She did give them her name, date of birth, and Jana's cell phone number."

The EMTs were running with Breeze's gurney now. "Female, Caucasian, seventeen years old, allergic to IV dye. Multiple stab wounds, has been beaten repeatedly and has abdominal bleeding."

The doctor was now beside the gurney with a nurse. "We need to get her to the OR stat. Call radiology. Tell them we need a portable CT Scan in OR ASAP."

The nurse ran to the phone and made the calls while the EMTs and the doctor continued to run down the hallway. Mary, Stan, and Jazz ran with the gurney as far as they could go until medical staff told them they couldn't go any further.

Jazz knew that Jana had called Matt, Mickey, and Kidd, but he knew he had to call Uncle or a fellow brethren. He decided to call Zion. He dialed the phone, and Zion answered on the second ring.

"Hey, Jazz. What's up?"

"It's Breeze." Jazz swallowed. "It's bad, she might not make it."

"What? She is not on assignment."

"No. Taylor tried to kill her."

Zion took a deep breath and let it out. "Where?"

"County General. She is on her way to surgery now. Jana and Jon are on their way."

"Thanks, brother. I will call Uncle and Yu. Keep me posted, please."

Jazz agreed and ended the call. He paced the corridor. *"Fight, Breeze, Fight."*

Fifteen minutes later, Jana, Jon, Matt, and Mickey walked in. Jana hugged Jazz in a bone crushing hug. "Han is on his way."

"Good." Jazz took a deep breath then spoke again. "Jana, she can't die, she can't."

The tears were streaming down both of their faces. Jon was talking to Stan and the nurses. He walked over to everyone and relayed all the news they had currently. It was worse than he had thought. Jon sat down hard in a chair and placed his face in his hands.

"Jana, where is Kidd?" Jazz asked with concern.

Jana choked back a sob. "His father won't allow him to come see her. He threatened him if he even tries to come see her. Kidd is an absolute wreck."

Jon stood, walked over to Jana, and wrapped his arms around her.

"Both of our children are in absolute hell right now," Jana said to Jon as he held her.

"I know, love, and right now so are we. I will not lose my daughter because of that asshole," Jon said.

Jazz was in shock about Kidd's dad. Breeze had told him briefly about Kidd's crappy home life. It was still hard to believe that Kidd's father would deny him seeing a friend who was fighting for her life. The room was so silent that you could hear the fluorescent lights humming and the clock ticking. The minutes turned to hours, and those hours turned to even excruciatingly longer hours. It was gut wrenching not knowing anything. Jazz wanted to be with Breeze, he was anxious, and he felt like a wild cat in a cage.

A young doctor walked in. "Are you the parents of Breeze Lee?"

Jon, Jana, Mary, and Stan all stood. "Yes."

"I am Dr. Thomas Witkowski, one of the surgeons that worked on your daughter. Breeze is in recovery up on the ICU floor. She will not wake up for a few days. We have had to put her in a medically induced coma to allow her body some time to rest and begin healing. We lost her twice on the operating table. Her injuries are extensive. She is lucky to have made it this far.

"The next twenty-four to forty-eight hours are critical. If we get through the forty-eight hours, then we will start bringing her out of the coma. I have let ICU staff know that two people can go in at a time, and one person may stay with her overnight. Everyone except the person staying overnight has five minutes to visit her. Two people are allowed a maximum of ten minutes." Dr. Witkowski took a breath and looked at all the people in the room. He saw the worry and the fear in their faces. He hated what he was about to tell them, but he had no choice; he had to prepare them. "I am not going to lie to you. I will be surprised if she pulls through this. The only two things that are on her side right now are that she is young and that she is physically fit."

Mary was hysterical again. Stan was trying to console her, but there wasn't much he could say.

"Follow me. We will go up to the ICU floor. There is a waiting room up there that the rest of the family can wait in while two people go in to see her."

"Jana, I will stay nightly, if that is ok." Jazz said.

"Mary?" Jana asked.

Mary jerked a nod through her sobs.

"Thank you," Jazz said.

The ride up to the ICU floor was harder than the hours upon hours upon hours in the waiting room. Matt placed his hand on Jazz's shoulder. Jazz met his eyes and nodded. Mary and Stan went in first. The doctor warned everyone that seeing Breeze would be hard. Boy that was an understatement. While Mary and Stan were back seeing Breeze, Jazz informed everyone that he had called Zion. He would step out in a few minutes to update him. Jana nodded. Now the brethren knew.

An officer walked in and spoke to Jon and Jana. "Mr. Taylor Smith has been arrested and charged with battery, assault, breaking and entering, and attempted murder."

"Has bail been set yet?

"Not yet."

"Please keep us posted."

"I will. I am sorry for what has happened to your daughter." Jon shook the officer's hand and thanked him. Every person in that room knew that Taylor's father was filthy rich and was involved in questionable business. They all doubted Taylor would spend much time behind bars. Jazz stepped out to make calls to Zion, his parents, and his Sensei.

Zion answered on the first ring. "Tell me."

"They lost her twice on the operating table but brought her back. She is in ICU in a medically induced coma. The next forty-eight hours are the most critical. The doctor said he would be surprised if she makes it; her age and being physically fit are in her favor for survival." Jazz knew to give it straight and not sugar coat the situation. "Taylor has been arrested, but no one thinks he will spend much time in jail."

"I need to call Uncle. Can anyone see her?"

"Yes, two at a time. One person at night. I will be staying nightly."

"Good. Thank you for calling. I must call Uncle now. He is flying in from Korea."

"Han is on his way from Japan, he should be here soon."

The call ended, and Jazz called his parents. His parents would be by to visit as soon as his dad got home from work. His mom said it was ok for him to stay during the evenings and nights; however, he had to go to school daily. He had known they wouldn't mind. They loved Breeze almost as much as he did. He told his mom what clothes he would like for tomorrow. There was no way that he was leaving today. Thank goodness it was Friday. Next Jazz called his sensei and planned for private lessons during the day on weekends while everyone else was at the hospital, and his sensei told him that they would make up the missed weekly sessions once Breeze was out of the hospital. After the private sessions were over, then he would go home and pack for the next week. He would do his homework in the evenings while he sat with Breeze.

Mary, Stan, Jon, and Jana had been back with Breeze while Jazz had made all of his calls. He came back in as Matt and Mickey went back. Jazz looked at Jon, he was pale, and his eyes showed worry, stress, and anxiety all rolled up in one. Jon's eyes said more than any doctor ever could. The door opened and Han walked in. Jon, Jana, and Jazz all stood and bowed. Grams, Kim, and Jim walked in behind him.

Grams hugged Jana. "How is my granddaughter?"

"Fighting to live." Jana said with pure conviction. Grams sat down and wrung her hands. Jazz walked over and sat with her. He took one of her hands in his and held it. Han walked over to Jazz and placed his massive hand on Jazz's shoulder. Jazz looked up and met his eyes. Han saw the fear and worry. Han tapped his mind.

"Jazz, she will fight. She will live."

"She is fighting. I didn't pick up on any of this."

"None of us did."

"She broke up with him over a month ago. I don't get why this happened now."

"Is there ever a reason for domestic violence?"

"Well, no, but still, why now?"

Jazz was in absolute agony and hell. Everyone was, but Jazz was punishing himself for things he could not have prevented. Matt and Mickey walked back in; both were looking worse for wear. Grams patted Jazz's leg, stood, and went over to Matt and Mickey. She hugged them both. Han waited then went with Grams to see Breeze. Jazz was relieved that there were only two more people left to see Breeze before he could finally go back to be with her. He placed his face in his hands and leaned forward. His head felt like it would explode. He heard the door swing open, but he didn't bother to see who it was at that moment. He felt a hand on his shoulder, and he looked up to see Uncle. He started to stand and bow, but Uncle stopped him. Uncle sat beside him and wrapped his arm around him.

"How are you, Young One?"

"Not well. This is killing me," Jazz said honestly.

Uncle nodded and hugged Jazz tightly against his side. Nothing else was said. They sat there in silence until Han returned. Han walked in and immediately bowed to Uncle. Uncle lowered his head in acknowledgment. Han walked over to Jana and Jon and spoke in a brief whisper. Grams was rattled. Uncle released Jazz and went to Grams.

He hugged her and spoke in whispered Japanese where only she could hear him. "Old friend, shh now, she is strong, and she will survive."

"Wait until you see her, old friend. I am not so sure. It is worse than any nightmare."

Uncle kissed the top of her head and hugged her tighter. He now realized how bad it was. Grams was always a positive person even when things seemed like there was no light at the end of the tunnel. The grief hit him hard. Breeze was the daughter he never had, and he refused to let her die like this. Kim and Jim stepped out to go see Breeze. Jazz would let Uncle go back alone and then he would go back. Jazz was so anxious, and there was this pressure in his chest. Han walked back over to him and asked him to join him outside. Han looked rattled in a way that Jazz had never seen. Jazz got up, but it was like he was in a trance. He was numb as he followed Han out. The tears were streaming down his face, and he didn't even bother to wipe his cheeks. He didn't care. All he cared about was the person lying in a bed fighting for her life.

"Jazz."

Jazz held up his hand. "Han, I can't lose her."

"You need to prepare yourself; it is bad. Worse than seeing her cursed or ambushed and unable to do anything. Young One, I know you love her more than a friend and agreed to not push that issue with her because she is your best friend. Jazz, I need you to use every ounce of your love for her and

65

encourage her to fight harder. She needs your strength and your love. There is a darkness to her aura that I don't like."

"I know, Han. I saw it when I was talking to her mentally on my way here. She was trying to embrace the darkness because of the pain."

Han grabbed Jazz in a bone crushing hug. "I love you Jazz. You are as much my nephew as she is my niece; I can't lose either of you. If she dies, I know you would not be the person that you are now. I need you both to fight for her to live." Jazz nodded and hugged Han back. They both were crying. "Go. Uncle will be coming out soon."

Jazz walked back in just as Uncle was coming out. He bowed to Uncle and made his way to see his best friend. He took a deep breath to steady himself and walked into his worst nightmare. The machines were beeping and dripping. Jazz's chest felt so tight that he couldn't breathe. He forced his feet to move even though they felt like concrete blocks were on them. He spoke to her mentally and physically. He reminded her of their last adventure and the scavenger hunt. He reminded her that Sasha, Brian, Max, Zion, and Yu needed another adventure or two. He talked about the first time they went to Japan together.

All of the beeping and the sucking and pumping of the ventilator were nerve racking, but seeing her face so swollen, cuts, gashes, and bruises everywhere rocked him to his core. She fought Taylor. He knew she did. He had the element of surprise, otherwise there would be no way that he would have been able to do this much damage. She was used to fighting in the arena and the underground, there were few who had ever beaten her, and none ever came close to causing this much damage. He knew his time was almost up. He held her hand and stroked her hair.

"I love you, Breeze." Jazz said through the tears.

He mentally heard her call his name.

"Yes, Breeze, I am here. I will be staying the night with you, but right now I have to step out so other people who love you can come see you."

"Jazz."

"Yes Breeze. It is me."

"Pain. So much pain."

"Shh, I know. I will heal you as soon as I can."

"Pain."

"I love you, Breeze."

"I love you."

Breeze fell back into complete unconsciousness. Jazz kissed her lips gently and quietly left the room. As he was stepping into the hall, he saw Zion. He quickly went to him.

"She mentally spoke to me briefly. Brace yourself, brother." Jazz said.

"Uncle is having guards stationed everywhere outside and inside the hospital. He is not taking chances that Mr. Smith will not try to finish what his son started."

"I am glad he thought of it, because my only thought has been Breeze."

"That is why he is Uncle. He thinks of everything." Zion said.

Jazz patted Zion's shoulder and walked back down the hall. He did not go back in the waiting room; he walked down the corridor to the elevator and rode down to the main floor and walked out the front doors. Uncle, Han, Jon, and Jana were standing there. Jazz bowed deep and walked over.

"What is the plan?" Jazz asked.

"Nothing at the moment, Young One," Han said.

"We can't, because then it would be seen by the authorities as retaliation and the first people they would look at would be this family," Uncle said.

"So, we do nothing? That son of a bitch can't get away with this." Jazz was furious.

"We did not say that. We said, nothing at the moment," Uncle said.

Jazz understood that this was far from over. He bowed and walked back to go in the hospital but stopped short when he heard his mom call out his name. He turned to see her and his dad speaking to Jana, Han, Jon, and Uncle. She ran to Jazz and hugged him tight.

"It's beyond bad, mom."

"I did not see this," Cindy said.

"No one did, and we didn't sense it," Jazz insisted.

"She must have blocked it even when she was fighting to live," Cindy said and hugged him tighter.

That night after everyone left and Jazz was left alone with Breeze, he mentally and physically talked to her about anything he could think of until exhaustion pulled him under, and he fell asleep in the little fold out chair that was a bed of sorts. He awoke with a start; machines were beeping and screeching like crazy, and he could hear nurses talking quickly and feet running. *Oh God, she is crashing.*

"Don't you leave me Breeze. You fight. I need you. I love you so much. You fight."

Silence. Complete silence. He was on his feet and staring at Breeze and her lifeless body as the nurses ran in. The nurses immediately began working on her. Jazz watched as they put the paddles on her chest. They yelled clear, and her body rose off the table. They did it twice, and the machines started beeping like normal. Once they had her back, one of the nurses gently guided Jazz to the door.

"We will let you back in once we are sure she is stable." She patted Jazz's arm and walked back into the room.

She pulled the curtain so no one could see in, and Jazz slid down the wall in disbelief. He gathered what little strength he had, went down to the main floor, and called Jon. Within minutes of the call, Jon, Jana, Han, Grams, Mary, and Stan arrived. Everyone was pale and shaken. No one could go in to be with Breeze because the team of nurses and doctors were still working with her. They all went up to the ICU waiting room until they could go back to be with her.

The silence in the room spoke volumes about the anguish and grief everyone was feeling. The reality that Breeze might never leave this hospital was too much to handle. Jana sat down hard and leaned forward with her face in her hands. She rocked slightly. Jon had his hand on her back and was rubbing it in a slow, soothing way. Han was sitting with Grams. Mary was crying, and Stan looked in a complete daze. Jazz would pace and sit, pace, and sit. After fifteen grueling minutes, the doctor came out and spoke with them. They could finally start going back to see her. Han recommended that they each take two hour shifts to sit with Breeze for the rest of the day. No one wanted to leave, not now, but they also knew they needed sleep. Han was going to take the first shift after everyone went back and saw her before they left.

Jazz tapped Zion. *"Brother."*

"What's wrong?" Zion asked.

"She crashed, but she is back. We are starting two-hour shift rotations of staying with her. One at a time from now until she is

69

stable enough to be brought out of the coma."

"Damn it. I am leaving today on assignment and will be gone for several days or I would take a shift, so would Yu. Hell, all of the brethren would."

"I know. Han called the Japanese brethren. A few are flying in and others are getting with Uncle in Korea once he is back there."

"Is Taka flying in? Keep me posted. I will let Uncle know."

"No, Taka is not one of the warriors flying in. He is on assignment out of country. I have already informed Uncle. I accidentally called out to him when the machines went crazy. He was immediately linked with me. He saw everything that I saw." *Jazz had just finished his sentence when he felt the mental nudge of Uncle alerting him to stay open for communication.*

Zion understood the hell that Jazz was feeling. Uncle had pulled Yu and himself to the side to see if they had sensed anything in the last month. He also called in several other warriors that had worked with both Jazz and Breeze to see if they had sensed anything. None of the warriors had and that concerned Uncle. Uncle had men everywhere. Mr. Smith was furious that his son had been arrested. He did not care that Breeze was in the hospital or that she was fighting for her life. Zion refused to relay that information to Jazz. Uncle had forbidden all warriors from doing anything until he gave the order. That was probably the hardest order Zion had ever taken in his life. He had plans for Taylor, but now all he could do was sit and wait.

"I will stop by either before I leave for my assignment or when I return. Tell Breeze, when I get back, I am ready for another challenge. Let's see if we can get her fired up so she will fight to live. She loves challenges and adventures so let's use that to our advantage. Have Mickey bring some beats that will make her want

to dance."

"I had the same thought, brother. Let's do this Breeze style, shall we?" Jazz said.

"You know it."

Jazz walked over to the door. "I am getting coffee. Would anyone else like some?"

Everyone there wanted coffee.

Uncle mentally called out to all his warriors. "Warriors, all assignments have been canceled for at least one week. The priority is protecting Breeze, Jazz, the Lee family, and the hospital. I will not risk leaving to go to Korea. Anything Jana or Han needs you will follow there orders as if they are mine. I need everyone to meet me at my house in twenty minutes. Jazz you are to stay where you are. I have alerted Jana and Han that Zion and Yu will be taking up rotations as well."

Jazz was relieved that Uncle had decided to stay and that Zion and Yu would be there as well. He wished Kidd was here. She needed everyone that she was close to. Jazz got everyone their favorite beverage. Thank goodness there was a twenty-four-hour coffee shop in the hospital. The conversation with Zion had sparked a fire in Jazz, and he was going to use it to the best of his ability to help Breeze through this horrific event. Han noticed a difference in Jazz when he walked back in with the coffee.

"Young One?" Han asked.

"What?"

"What are you up to?"

"Nothing, oh, Obi-wan." Jazz said.

Han looked at Jazz and saw a hint of a challenge in his eyes. He knew Jazz would not leave Breeze to go on an adventure, not now. So, what was he up to? Then it clicked, and Han roared with laughter; Jana looked at Han in shock and then at Jazz. She saw it too. Mary and Stan had received their coffee and left before Han burst out laughing, which was a good thing. because they would have thought he had lost his mind. Jon had just walked back in the waiting room when he saw the scene in front of him.

"Damn," Jon said and laughed with Han.

"Whatever works, and she is out of the blasted place," Jana said.

Jazz rubbed his hands together. "Really?"

"Hey, now, that is still my daughter." Jon said.

Jazz threw his arms up in surrender and a truce before they decided to sit on him. Han took the first two-hour shift. Jon took Grams back to the hotel so she could sleep. Everyone was staying at a hotel, including Mary and Stan. Their house was a crime scene, and they could not enter it or have it professionally cleaned until the police told them it was ok. Jana and Jazz stayed in the waiting room. Neither of them were going to sleep, not any time soon. Jazz walked over to his backpack and pulled out some cards. They had nothing but time. Jon returned and sat down and played with them. They had been playing for about thirty minutes when Zion and Yu walked in. They did not miss a beat, they walked over and joined in the cards. Han walked out at the end of the two hours. Jon took the next shift, but before he went in, he allowed the others to go in to see her while he got more coffee. Jazz waited until Jon returned with his coffee before he walked into the room to see Breeze. Zion grinned as Jazz passed him with the cup of coffee.

"Work your magic, brother." Zion said.

Jazz nodded and walked in the room with more confidence

than he truly felt. He took a deep breath, removed the lid of his coffee, and spoke. "Yo, Breeze, I have your favorite beverage here, and it is all mine." He sipped loudly. He saw her right hand twitch. "You smell that? Oh my goodness, this is better than Starbucks." He slurped again. "Yum. If you want some of this liquid gold you better come get it."

Breeze's hand moved and so did her foot. Jazz continued to taunt and slurp. He even walked over to the bed, took a big drink by her ear, and leaned over and kissed her so she could feel it on her lips. She moved her hand again and she moaned mentally where Jazz could hear her.

"That's right, it is all mine."

He mentally heard her. *"Jazz. Coffee. Mine! Need it, Jazz."*

"You want coffee, Breeze, then you fight to get out of this hospital. You fight and come back to me. Zion will be sitting with you for a couple hours. Do you think you can get around him?"

"Jazz. Coffee. Zion? Hmm."

"Yes Breeze I am here with my coffee. Yes, Zion will be here later. I love you. Your dad is coming in for a little bit. I love you and will see you soon."

He took another huge sip and slurped and kissed her one more time before he left the room. His spirits were better. Jon was standing outside the window in front of her room watching Jazz. He was firing her up, and there was movement with her hands and foot. *Good, Jon thought.* Jazz stayed in for his five minutes then walked out with a smug smile on his face.

"She is all yours," Jazz said to Jon and walked back to the waiting room.

Jon just shook his head. It was a good thing those two did not date, because he wasn't sure that Jana, Han, Uncle, or himself would survive that craziness.

Days had passed and the doctor was pleased with Breeze's progress. Today was the day they were going to try to bring her out of the coma; they had left her in the coma for a couple extra days just to give her more time to heal. Everyone was there. You could have heard a pin drop in the waiting room while the doctor and nurses worked with her to slowly bring her around. This waiting was almost as bad as the day she was admitted to the hospital. Mickey was holding flowers and balloons for Breeze. Kidd was sending her something every day. It was his way of supporting her when he couldn't physically be there.

Finally, the doctor came out. "She is stable. If she continues to breathe on her own for the next twelve hours, then we will move her down to one of the other floors." Mickey actually whooped.

Breeze held her own, and they moved her down to the fourth floor. Jazz mentally let Uncle, Zion, and Yu know of her status and her room number. Uncle was pleased. He let Jazz know that he would be in Korea for a while, but if anything happened or changed, he was to let him know immediately.

Zion arrived that evening with flowers and birthday balloons in his hands. He was surprised to see Breeze propped up. Her color was better. "Hey, girl."

"Zion?" Breeze said with a raspy voice and through the fog of pain medications.

"The one and only."

She smiled and fell back to sleep.

"That is the norm right now." Jazz said.

Zion sat the flowers on the table and walked over to the

bed. He took her hand and gently kissed the top of her head. He leaned over to her ear and whispered in Korean to her. He spoke so softly to her that Jazz could not hear what he said. It was private, only for her to hear anyway. Zion stood up, gently squeezed her hand and said, "Happy Birthday, Breeze. Once you are out of here, we will celebrate Breeze style."

"I know her birthday is in a couple of days, but I will on assignment at that time."

"Thanks. She will appreciate it."

Zion spoke briefly to Jazz and left.

Jon, Jana, Stan, and Mary arrived not long after Zion had left. Jazz decided that he needed to step out. The four of them took chairs and sat in Breeze's room. Stan looked at Jon and Jana. "Mary and I have been talking. We think it would be wise if once Breeze gets out of the hospital that she moves in with you guys. Please do not misunderstand, we love having her at our house, but we know that you can protect her better than we ever could."

"We have been having the same conversation, and we agree fully." Jon said.

Mary had dark circles under her eyes. "Her safety is key. I can't believe that this has happened to her. I am so glad that she could fight, because if she hadn't had the training that she did, she probably would not be here right now."

Never in a million years would Jon or Jana think they would hear the words, 'glad she can fight,' come out of Mary's mouth, but she was right. Once Breeze woke up, they all let her know their decision. She nodded and was happy to be moving in with her Dad. She loved her mom, but her dad and Jana accepted her and her glitches where her mom did not. She had a gut feeling that Taylor would try again and probably while she was still weak. Apparently, her family had the same thoughts.

Breeze looked around the room. She could have sworn that Zion had been there. She thought she had talked to him. Once everyone left, Jazz came back in, and Breeze asked him if Zion had been there. He pointed to the flowers. "Card?" Breeze asked. Jazz got up, retrieved the card, and came back to the bed. He read her the card. She smiled and held her hand out. Jazz gave her the card. "Kidd?" Jazz pointed to the newest arrival. "He needs to save his money," Breeze insisted.

"This is his way Breeze. It helps him feel close to you since he can't be here."

"Oh, ok."

Jazz knew the latest round of pain meds had kicked in, and she would be out soon. Two days later all the immediate family came to the hospital. Jana had cleared it with the doctor for a small cake and ice cream to be brought in. Jana had picked up a small cake for the family and a couple gifts for her to open. This was not the eighteenth birthday that any of them had ever dreamed of her having, but they would have a big celebration once she was home. Jana brought in a large cake and small cups of ice cream for all the nurses and doctors on that floor. Breeze thanked everyone, ate a small piece of cake, and opened her presents. They all could tell her heart wasn't in it, but she was trying.

Three grueling weeks, along with seven surgeries, and more tests than she cared to count, was how long Breeze had to stay in the hospital. She was ready to climb the walls when the doctor came in and announced that she would be going home the next day. She did a little happy dance, and then there was a sadness that had washed over her. She pushed it to the side.

Everyday Jazz offered to let her drink, but she refused. He was frustrated by her refusal, but he respected her decision. In time he would get her to drink. Breeze wasn't sure she would ever be whole again. She was broken down to her soul. If she drank from Jazz, she was afraid he would know and see everything. She loved him too much to let that happen.

HOMECOMING

Jana gave Kidd, Matt, and Mickey instructions and money to go to the store and get all of Breeze's favorite foods while they were in Memphis bringing her home. Kidd was so excited he bounced when Jana told him Breeze would be home tomorrow. Han had stayed in the United States while Breeze was in the hospital, but he was leaving the day after Breeze came home to go back to Japan. Han stayed with the guys so he could help get everything set up. He had some of his brethren ship some of Breeze's favorite Japanese candies, sodas, and snacks so they would be at the house when she returned. The brethren were thrilled to be able to do that for Han and for Breeze. She was family.

Kidd made sure that they went by Hobby Lobby and Michael's before they went grocery shopping. He bought Breeze sketchpads, pens, pencils, acrylic paints, and several packs of canvases. Mickey had gone to the little Oriental shop that Breeze loved so much and bought her a Korean doll, and then he went to a Latin shop and bought some upbeat music cds. He would spin some cds for her later, but right now the Latin beats would have to do. The house was perfect when she arrived. The back of Jana's Escalade was packed with balloons and flowers. They helped Breeze in the house, and Kidd almost bowled her over when he finally saw her, but he stopped the second he saw her. She was covered in bruises. The memories of his mom flooded him. He gently walked up to Breeze and hugged her. "I love you, Sis."

Jana choked back a sob. It was the first time that Kidd had openly called her that. Jon took Jana's hand.

"I love you too, Little Bro."

Grams, Han, Kim, Jim, Matt, Mickey, and Kidd all stayed for dinner. Jana made a wonderful beef stir fry with homemade spring rolls and yokimondo. Dinner was divine. Jana saw a sadness in Breeze's eyes, but then she could tell that Breeze was trying to focus and not let the sadness show. Breeze had come in the kitchen to take one of her pain pills, and Jana hugged her. She stepped back and put her hands on Breeze's shoulders.

"Breeze, this was not your fault, and none of us blame you."

Breeze said thanks and hugged Jana. Jana didn't like the overwhelming sadness that Breeze was exhibiting. She was not the same happy-go-lucky, ready to take the world by storm, scheming on a dime person that her family and friends loved. This was not Breeze. Jana understood tragedy changed people, and she was determined to help Breeze mentally, physically, and emotionally. She would have her daughter back, no matter what. She would take the schemin' Breeze any day of the week over this Breeze.

THE DEPTHS OF HELL AND BACK

Breeze knew that she should be thankful to be alive, but she felt like she had climbed into the depths of hell and was pulled out only to repeat the process night after grueling night. She woke up in a cold sweat yet again. She looked at the clock and it read three in the morning. *Great, the witching hour and I have to deal with my demons, she thought.* She groaned in the darkness, she crawled out of the bed, and went to the bathroom. Her emotions were all over the place, and she blamed it on pure exhaustion, but she knew it was more than that. The hole that was in her heart was so large that you could put the Grand Canyon in it, not to mention she felt like a failure in more than one way.

How would Jazz react if he truly knew what a fraud she was and a failure as a person? Would he still accept her and love her? Zion's face popped in her mind. She wondered what all her fellow brethren thought of her. The hole in her heart felt like it had doubled in size, which she knew was not at all possible. She locked herself in the bathroom, turned the water on, sat on the cool tile floor and began sobbing. This was not the life she ever envisioned for herself. She was a fighter and she was beaten down by someone who is not a mixed martial artist. She had been beaten down in the ring numerous times, but that was to be expected; to be beaten down by someone else was unacceptable, she was and is a warrior twice over.

She missed her sense of freedom, she missed the streets, and she missed being in school and seeing her friends. She had homebound and virtual classes for two weeks while she was in the hospital. She would have had it all three weeks; however, for the first week she could not hold her head up due to all the medication that they had her on for pain. The accident occurred three weeks before the end of her junior year of high school. She celebrated her eighteenth birthday in the hospital; lucky her. Her plans to be in several stateside and international tournaments had all changed in an instant. The doctor told her that it would be anywhere from six weeks to three months before she would be able to fight, train, or workout. She needed a sense of normalcy. Doing martial arts, training, and working out gave her a sense of being, and it helped with her sanity. That was her normal, and most of all, it was her life. The waiting game was torture for her.

The days seemed to pass by turtle slow. She wanted to race, dance, and fight. She had been home from the hospital for almost two weeks and was bored out of her mind. She was taking an online college course, but it was only a couple hours a day, and she was ahead on all the assignments and projects. Thankfully, this piece of her life had not been taken from her. Breeze was at her desk thinking; the frustration and negativity of the situation were wearing on her. She snapped the pencil she was holding and threw it. She stood and paced. She honestly felt like a caged animal.

She needed some human interaction besides her family. She needed to get herself and her life back. Since she was home and not going anywhere unless with Jana or her dad, she would sit in her room for hours and sketch or paint, but her thoughts kept going back to that day. Her drawings had a darkness to them, and she hated them. There was paper everywhere on the floor where she had wadded up pages. One of the drawings that she had done put her mind back to when she was in the hospital. She sat on her bed and cried when she was alone. She wished the darkness had claimed her because it would be better than the recurring thoughts of that day or the what ifs. Her nights were worse than her days. She would wake up drenched in sweat with her covers thrown all over the place. After several days of that, she decided to take one of the prescription sleeping pills. It helped her relax and fall into a deep sleep until she heard screams, deafening screams.

She jumped up ready to fight then she realized that the screams were her own. She closed her eyes and tried to slow her breathing, but she could still see all the blood, the knife, and his cold, menacing stare. Would this nightmare ever end? She grabbed her pillow and cried herself to sleep. She tried to make herself dream about fast cars, dojos, and the title fight in Thailand, but no matter how hard she tried, the screams kept pulling her back and his face kept reappearing. The dark circles under her eyes were becoming harder and harder to hide. She was in count down mode. She would mark her calendar every night before bed. She wanted an adventure, hell, she needed one.

Han called every day to check on her as did Uncle. Jazz would call every day physically and mentally. He had three weeks of kick ass trainings to make up for. God, how she wished to be training right now. She wished to be doing anything besides just sitting and waiting for the next attack. There was no doubt in her mind that Taylor would try to attack her again. She needed to get out or talk to someone or scheme or issue a challenge, something, anything. She looked at the clock. She dialed the international number and waited. After the fifth ring she was ready to hang up when Taka answered.

"Hey, Taka."

"Hey, girl. How are you?"

"Doing good. Do you have time to talk?"

"I wish I could. I was just walking out the door for an assignment. Can I call you later?"

"Sure. Later." They said their good-byes.

Breeze sighed. She decided to call a fellow brethren, so she called Zion.

The phone was answered on the second ring. "Hello."

"Hey. Are you busy?" Breeze asked.

"No. What's up?"

"Can you come get me and take me to a café?"

"Sure. When?"

"Now or whenever."

"I will be there in fifteen."

"Thanks. Feel like driving one of the rebuilds?"

"Two wheels or four?"

"Does it matter?"

"No, but it would still be nice to know."

She laughed. "Two."

"Hell, Yeah."

"What if I had said four?"

"Oh, you know, probably the same."

She laughed again. "See ya in fifteen."

Breeze went down and let Jana know that Zion was on his way. Jana nodded. Breeze made sure she knew that they were taking her Indian motorcycle.

"You are letting Zion drive it? Holy cow, it is official, the world is coming to an end."

Breeze gently pushed Jana. "He will take great care of it."

"Hmmm." Jana laughed. "So, has Jazz driven it yet?"

"Oh, hell no."

"Girl, I would not want to be you when Jazz finds out."

"Are you telling him?"

"I am not stupid," Jana said.

Breeze went back upstairs to change. This was not a date, but Breeze wanted to feel sexy and not like chopped liver. She knew Zion would call Uncle to let him know that she called, and that was ok. She knew Uncle would be alright with any of the brethren if she called, but right now she needed a friend and fellow brethren, so that really narrowed the field. She put on jeans, boots that laced up to the knee that went over her jeans, a cute t-shirt, and a simple jacket. She wasn't dressed for the streets or anything, but she felt more like herself. She heard his car pull up. She ran in to brush her teeth and walked downstairs.

Zion was wearing black jeans, combat boots, and a t-shirt. He was holding his black leather motorcycle jacket and his helmet. He smiled the second he saw her. "Ready?"

"Yeah. You?"

"Yes. I am ready to see what I'm driving."

"Oh, oh… I see it is all about the wheels and not about me."

"Well…" Zion teased.

Breeze walked by him and pushed him back. "Fine, you can stay here." They were walking through the kitchen to the backdoor out to the garage. Jana was at the sink when they came through. She turned to face them. Zion bowed to Jana and she bowed in return. "Bye, Jana. Not sure when we will be home, but it won't be too late." Breeze said.

"Ok. Behave and try to stay in Tennessee tonight."

"Ahhh man, I was planning on going to Vegas."

"Well, at least you have one of the best trackers with you."

"How has that worked out for you guys?" Breeze asked sarcastically.

Jana laughed. Zion did not say a word. He knew better. He really did not want to track her tonight. Breeze walked into the garage and flipped the switch. Zion gasped. It had been years since he had been in the garage, and their collection of cars and motorcycles was vast, but that was not why he gasped. There was a 1959 Indian Enfield Chief parked over by Jana's motorcycle. It was black and in mint condition.

"No drooling on the merchandise, especially since that is the ride of the evening," Breeze said with a smile.

"Are you kidding me?"

Breeze simply shook her head and handed him the key. He handed her his helmet so he could admire the bike. She gave him a moment to take it in and appreciate it while she got her helmet down off the hook on the wall. After the second circle around the bike, Zion got on and fired it up. Breeze handed him his helmet, placed hers on and got on behind him. He eased the bike back and pulled out. When they got on the road Breeze encouraged him to open it up. He did not need too much encouragement. He was in heaven. They pulled into the café lot and Breeze slid off. She took a picture of him on the bike before he got off. She shook her head and motioned for him to go around the block a couple of times.

He shook his head and got off the bike. They placed their helmets on the bike and went in.

"Why not?"

"A couple times around the block is not going to satisfy me. That would just be a freaking tease."

Breeze laughed. "I thought you would like it."

"If you ever bring that to the streets and put it up for slips. I will be glad to take it off your hands."

"I do not have stupid on my forehead."

"Just saying."

"Keep dreaming."

Breeze and Zion ordered sandwiches, chips, scones, and coffee. They laughed and talked for a couple of hours. Zion never once mentioned Taylor or the accident and neither did she. They had a second cup of coffee, then Breeze encouraged Zion to take her for a ride. Again, it did not take a lot of encouraging. They rode to Erin and back. After that they rode down by the old cabin, then to her house. Zion had her home by ten. He parked the bike and walked in to say his goodbyes. Jon and Jana were watching a fight.

"Want to join us?" Jon asked.

"Sure."

Breeze smiled and grabbed a bean bag chair. Zion looked at her.

"Uhhh, this is mine. If you want one, then go get one." Breeze said with attitude.

"I was going to let you have the chair and ottoman, but I think I will take it for myself now."

Jon laughed. "Zion I am so glad that you and the other brethren can put up with all that sass."

"It is hard at times, but we try our best."

"Yeah, I know the feeling." Jon said.

"Hello. I am sitting right here," Breeze said.

"We know, princess," Zion teased.

"Oh. Oh. I know he didn't," Breeze said.

"He did," Jon and Jana said in unison.

Breeze nodded, grabbed her bean bag, and hit Zion with it. Zion tried to block it, but the bean bag was too big. He tried to stand, and she knocked him back.

"Princess my ass," Breeze said.

"Well…" Zion started to say when Breeze gave him a I dare you look.

Jana was laughing. "I am getting popcorn, would you guys like some, and Coke?"

"Yes, please," Zion and Breeze both said.

The front door swung open. "Honey, I'm home," Mickey said as he walked in. He was followed by Matt, then Kidd. Kidd looked at Zion and shook his finger at him. This caused Zion to bust out laughing. He knew he was referring to the last time they were at the streets, and Kidd could not say what he wanted to say because they were in front of Jon and Jana. This caused Zion to laugh harder.

Matt walked over to Breeze and slung his arm over her shoulder and whispered where only she could hear. "So, does Jazz know?" Breeze had no idea what he was talking about and gave him a questioning look. Matt said one word; "Indian." Breeze started laughing. "I thought not. It's your funeral." He dropped his arm, shook his head, and walked into the kitchen.

Breeze was still laughing. When she would try to stop, she would get the giggles. No matter how hard she tried she could not stop. Zion touched her mind and she showed him the conversation.

"Are you telling me that I got to drive that sweet ride and Jazz hasn't?" Breeze nodded. *"Life is now complete. I have one upped Jazz."*

Breeze would giggle, then hiccup. Jana walked in and just looked at her. "Zion, I am going to give you both bowls of popcorn, so Miss Thing doesn't knock it over with the fits she has going on."

The guys ran in with their bowls and their Cokes. Mickey looked at Breeze and shhh'd. her. Breeze's hysterical giggle/hiccups just got worse.

Zion touched her mind. *"We could let Kidd know about the last challenge."* Breeze gasped and shook her finger at Zion. *"I thought that might sober you up."*

"Thanks."

"Any time. There is always the next time at the streets."

"You are so bad."

"Put up that bike, and I will take any challenge thrown at me."

Breeze ran her hands together and smiled at him. *"Not bloody likely. It is MINE."*

Zion smiled, handed Breeze her popcorn, and leaned back in the chair. Everyone got settled and watched the main fight. Jazz called while they were watching the fight. They spoke briefly, but while they were talking, Matt was making gestures and saying "Vroom, Vroom." Zion laughed and held up the #1 and pointed to himself. Breeze told Jazz goodbye and grabbed the closest decorative pillows, threw one at Matt and hit Zion with the other one.

"What did I miss? What just happened?" Mickey asked.

"Jazz got left behind," Jana said.

Mickey looked at Breeze, Matt, and Zion. "Well, it's about

damn time," Mickey said and went back to eating his popcorn. The fight ended, and Zion left around midnight. Jana offered him one of the spare bedrooms, but he insisted that he needed to go. Zion approached Breeze before he left. They were alone in the foyer.

"Thank you for calling me. I had fun, and that is one sweet ride."

"Thank you for answering the call. You're right it is, and it is MINE."

"Anytime. I will see you later," Zion said as he leaned over and ran his finger down her jawline.

"Yes, you will," Breeze said with a grin.

Zion looked at her; there was a hint of scheming in her tone. He wrapped his arm around her waist. "Do not make me track you."

"Who, me????" Breeze batted her eyes up at Zion.

He laughed and walked out the door. He was now on alert and it felt great. He saw a little bit of the old Breeze. He tapped Jana and Jon. *"Be on alert. Breeze just hinted to scheming."*

"OMG. Right now, I would take it in a heartbeat." Jana said.

"Me, too. It would mean I have my baby girl back."

Zion agreed and ended the connection. Next, he tapped Uncle. "Be ready, we may be tracking soon."

"It's about time. Good work."

"Excuse me?"

"You helped Breeze get a sense of herself back, which she desperately needed. Jazz hasn't even been able to do that. I do believe if she schemes, the challenge will be issued at you or Yu."

"I get the feeling it will be towards Han and then us."

Uncle busted out laughing. "I will let Han know. You informed Jana, correct?"

"Yes, sir."

"Beautiful. Absolutely beautiful."

"I never thought we would be begging for her to scheme," Zion said.

"I know. Thank you," Uncle said and ended the connection."

Breeze took a sleeping pill and went up to her room. She was glad that she had called Zion. She decided that she was not going to get lost in self-pity. She was a fighter and the hell with Taylor and his dad. She was broken, yes, but she was still Breeze Mercedes Lee. She was going to fight or scheme or whatever it took to get her true self back, come hell or high water, she would get herself back. She rubbed her hands together. "Who?" she said to herself. "Han and Zion. Maybe. No, they will expect that. I know." Breeze laid down to sleep and for the first time in what felt like forever she did not dream of the accident. She dreamed of fast cars and motorcycles. While she was sleeping, she felt Uncle, Han, and Zion's mental nudges to make sure she was not scheming. She woke up the next morning feeling well rested.

She got up and started doing some light stretching and toning exercises. She was sore, but it felt good to be doing some type of physical activity. She drew the outline of a dragon on a cliff and motorcycle down below. It was the first drawing she had done in a while that felt light and promising. Jana came up while she was drawing.

"That is beautiful."

"Thanks."

Jana hugged Breeze and walked out of the room. She tapped Uncle. *"Thank you for allowing Zion to answer that call. I see our Breeze shining through."*

"All of my warriors know that if Breeze or Jazz call, they are to

answer and to alert me." Uncle said.

"You know what I mean."

"I do." Uncle sighed. "I am surprised that Taka has not flown in."

"All the Japanese warriors are aware as well as the Korean warriors. Han has kept him on assignment. The last thing we need, are those three back together." Jana said.

"Good point. If Han runs out of assignments, I have plenty I can send him on." Uncle teased.

Jana laughed. "I will let Han know."

Uncle ended their connection and called Grams. It had been a long time since one of their meetings, and it was time.

Breeze finished the drawing and now she was ready to transfer it to a canvas. She went down and asked Jana if they could go to Hobby Lobby or Michael's. Kidd had been in the kitchen and came running out. "Yes, can we?"

"Yes, children, give me ten minutes."

Kidd looked at his watch and tapped the glass on it. "Clock is ticking. Chop, Chop."

Jana stood there with a hand on her hip and shook her finger at her children. This just made Kidd tap his watch again. Jana turned and her long hair shone in the light. It had a blue sheen to it, but the auburn highlights made it seem like there were flames dancing through it. Kidd elbowed Breeze. Breeze just flashed him a smile. Jana was back in the living room before the ten minutes were up. Kidd had grabbed her VW keys instead of the Escalade keys.

"Son, do you really think the bug is going to be big enough with you and Breeze shopping at Hobby Lobby and Michaels?"

"Hmmm, good point. We can put Breeze on the roof, and

then we will have room."

Breeze took off and beat them both out to the garage. She was in the front seat of the bug when Kidd and Jana walked out.

"Sucks for you, you are in the back. If anyone gets strapped to the top it will be you, dear brother," Breeze said.

Jana laughed and got in once Kidd was in the back. Breeze turned up the radio and they jammed all the way to Hobby Lobby. Breeze picked out two large canvases and a pack of canvases, she decided on the standard, 8x10 sized ones for right now as well as some tubes of acrylic paints. Kidd was working on a couple statues so he got some supplies at Hobby Lobby. He was hoping that Michaels would have more of what he needed; if not, he would have to go to Lowe's or Home Depot.

"Have you checked out back in the shop?" Jana asked.

Kidd just looked at Jana. He had no clue what she was talking about. "The shop? Do you mean the garage?"

"No. The shop. Our working shop. Where we have spare parts, scraps, wood, leather, etc."

Kidd shook his head. He really didn't know what she was talking about. Jana had assumed that Matt or Mickey had taken him out there or Jon had when they were working on a car.

"I will show you when we get home. We will go to Michaels and look, if you don't find what you are looking for, then you will probably find it in the shop," Jana said.

Kidd turned around. He didn't see Breeze. He looked at Jana with fear in his eyes.

"She is here. No worries."

Breeze came around the corner with some material in her

hand.

Kidd rushed her. "You scared me."

"I am in an art store. Do you really expect me to stay in one place?"

"Jana says there is a shop at your house."

"Yeah. I assumed you knew that."

"OMG. You do know what ASSUME means, right?" Kidd said with annoyance.

Jana was laughing and continued to laugh all the way through check out and to the car. Kidd made life as fun as Breeze did. The trip to Michael's was brief. When they got home, Kidd stood and tapped his foot.

"Help carry everything in, then Breeze can show you the shop. Lord, both my children need to learn patience," Jana said and shook her head.

Kidd did as Jana asked. Breeze was happy to show Kidd the shop.

Once they were out at the shop, Breeze whispered. "You up for old times?"

"Absolutely."

"Good."

Breeze said nothing else. She unlocked the shop and watched as Kidd went into artist and mechanic overload. "You can use any of this stuff that you need. I will leave you alone so you can continue to drool. Be ready when I call."

Kidd nodded and continued to look around the shop. He thought of a couple lights that he would like to make, and the car parts that he wanted to use for that were in here. He set the items to the side and then walked over to a shelf labeled scrap and found exactly what he needed for the sculpture. He began working. Breeze came out an hour and a half later and told him that lunch was ready.

"After lunch, we are going for a ride," Breeze said.

"Daylight?"

She nodded and walked back into the house. She knew the alerts were up with the brethren, Han, and Uncle, but her Dad and Jana did not suspect Kidd of scheming with her. That thought made her smile. If they only knew! I mean, come on, he was her brother. Did they honestly think she didn't teach him how to scheme? Breeze and Kidd would get where they were going and send the challenge out. Kidd came in with rust and grime on him, so he washed up, and then took his seat at the table. Jana had made gumbo and rum pudding. It was delicious, as always. Breeze announced that they were going to Matt's and would be back around ten. Jana nodded. Jon told them to behave and went out to the garage. An hour later Matt and Mickey arrived.

"Hey, Jana. Is Breeze in the garage?" Matt asked.

Jana whipped around and looked at him. "They are supposed to be with you. Damn it." She sent out the mental alert. *"Uncle and Han, alert the trackers. They have an hour lead."*

"Breeze and Jazz?"

"No. Breeze and Kidd."

"Zion and Yu are on their way."

Breeze was sitting in her seat on the plane when she felt the excitement. "Do not think of anything, Little Bro. Matt and Mickey set off the alarms before I could issue the challenge."

He nodded and went back to his book. She felt Han, Zion, Yu, and Uncle try to tap her. Then she felt Matt, Mickey, Jana, and her Dad. Next would be Jazz. She knew it, even though Jana had not called him yet. She began to count from 10 to 1, when she got to 5, she felt the mental nudge of Jazz. She was completely blocked. Now it was time to play.

"GOOD EVENING fellow brethren, family, and friends. This challenge will end at 9:30p.m. CST, for those of you that are out of country. Ta-ta for now."

Jon walked in the kitchen and wiped off his hands. "Really?"

"Yeah, and she has involved our son."

Mickey began whistling and Matt looked at the floor.

"So, it is not the first time for his involvement. I should have known. I swear you all are going to be in the gym with me," Jana said.

Zion and Yu walked in, spoke briefly with Jana and took off. Zion had sensed it last night and earlier today, but no red flags. Zion caught their scent and focused on it, then it shifted. "Interference."

Yu looked at him and understood. They were in the air or on water. He would take the water route and Zion would take the air. Jana and Jon were working from the house. Matt and Mickey were reaching out to circuit contacts. It was silent.

"She has had five weeks to think and plan," Jana said, and Jon threw his hands up. The trackers had actually gotten close a couple of times. Close but no cigars. At 9:59p.m. Breeze and Kidd walked into the house. Breeze was grinning. Zion and Yu were standing in the living room with Jon, Jana, Matt, and Mickey.

"Better luck next time," Breeze said and danced off.

Zion wrapped his arm around Kidd's shoulders. "I got your number."

"Really? What is it?" Kidd laughed and danced off.

Jana looked at all the men in the room and spoke to them mentally. *"Do not let your guard down. It is official, high alert."* They all nodded and went about their business for the night. Uncle just shook his head when his trackers filled him in.

Breeze went up to her room, sat on her bed, and looked around. She had a blast with Kidd, but now that she was home and in her room the wave of loneliness and depression washed over her. She would be going back to school in August. She was thankful to be living with her dad, but she missed her home in Memphis, plus she missed seeing and hanging out with Jazz. Their senior year was now going to be apart. It was just another thing that was destroyed by Taylor. Her anger bubbled up and she threw her shoe at the closet door. She thought about her friends in Memphis and then thought about her friends that were here. She knew a lot of people that went to school here. She would be attending the same school as Kidd. Breeze busted out laughing. "YES." She knew she could have fun with that.

Zion's face popped into her mind and she laughed even harder. She was excited. She had a long way to go, but she had things to look forward to, and school was one of them. The next day, Kidd decided that he would stay at Matt's for the next few days because Jana was now watching them like a hawk. He would turn and catch her staring at him, which just caused him to laugh. Breeze walked by after dinner that night and reached behind her back and finger waved to him. Breeze stayed low key for a week after her and Kidd's adventure. Once the week was up she thought it would be enough time for the trackers to start relaxing their guards so she planned her adventure. She snuck out, made it to New Orleans, she turned down Bourbon Street and ran right into Yu and Matt.

"Ugh." She threw her hands up in the air. "I am off. Don't worry, it won't happen again." Yu let Uncle know that they had her and told him that he saw pure determination in her eyes. Uncle thanked his warrior and called Jana, Han, and Zion.

Two days later, at two a.m.; Breeze slipped out of the house, down the tree, turned to run toward the shadows when Zion stepped out.

Breeze growled her frustration. "Oh, hell no."

Zion simply smiled. He had tracked her for years and rarely had they even come close to catching her.

"Zion, just know, this will NOT be the norm."

"Well, sweetheart, why don't you take that fine ass of yours back up that tree and get some sleep."

"Or you could go to the streets with me."

Zion shook his head and pointed up to her room. She was mad. She would figure out how they had found her the last couple times, and she would get around them again. She was taking this as a full-on challenge. She climbed back up the tree, and when she got in her room she waved to Zion and closed the window. She mentally reached out to Jazz. *"Busted again. I am off. Can you help me figure out how they are catching me?"*

"Absolutely."

Breeze and Jazz worked on getting around all the trackers for two long grueling weeks. Jazz had even gone out one night as a means of distraction for Breeze, and they both were caught. They knew their thoughts were blocked, they weren't acting any different, etc. They were both ticked. Han was thrilled that the trackers were finally coming out on top, but he knew his niece and her best friend, and this was just the beginning. Breeze relaxed and didn't think of anything.

Finally, one night Breeze made it out undetected. She had just entered the circuit and was about to remove her disguise when she spotted Taylor. Thank goodness he had not recognized her, and he was too busy with other women. Breeze turned and went to a different section of the races.

She reached out to Zion and Yu. *"Where are you?" She knew her tone was frantic, but she didn't care.*

"We are in Atlanta for the evening, racing. Why? What is wrong?" Zion said.

"I am here, too. HE IS HERE."

"What section are you at?"

"Motor cross. He was at cars a minute ago."

"Stay there. We are on our way."

"Ok." She sounded like a terrified child to her own ears. She absolutely hated being this afraid.

A few minutes later she saw Zion and waved. He saw an average looking blonde wave at him. He walked over to her and wrapped his arm around her.

"Shall we race?" Zion asked.

"Yeah."

They both knew that if they left at that moment, Taylor might take notice and it might send up red flags. Zion had every intention of getting them out of there as soon as possible. Breeze leaned into his hold and whispered, "Three o'clock."

He nodded, leaned over, and kissed her cheek. "No worries. He will not touch you. Go win some cash. Yu and I have him in our sights. One of us will race while you race and the other will be on look out. Do not come out of your disguise for

98

anything."

"You are not working tonight. That is not fair to you."

"I am a warrior, Breeze, and he will not touch you."

Breeze raced for slips on the first race and lost badly. She was distracted. Thankfully, the car she lost was one of the cars she was still trying to work out the kinks on and not one of her main rides. She learned a long time ago if she was in disguise not to bring one of her main rides. It was too obvious that it was her if she did. When in disguise, she also always covered up her dragon tattoo. Again, it was too obvious that it was her if she didn't. She was mad that she lost, but then again it was another layer to her disguise. Zion won his race, but barely. His focus was not on racing. He accepted the cash and walked back to Breeze. She greeted him with a kiss. Breeze heard a familiar voice behind them, and she was thankful that her disguise was so good that Kidd and Matt didn't even recognize her. She knew it would be, so that is why she selected it. It wasn't the first time that she had worn it, but it would be the last because the trackers now knew it.

"Glad to see your interests vary." Kidd teased.

Zion ended the kiss slowly and looked up at Kidd. "My interests are as varied as yours."

Kidd walked off laughing. Matt was lining up to race when Zion and Breeze noticed that Taylor was now following Matt and Kidd. Zion alerted Matt mentally that Taylor was following them, to keep their guards up one hundred percent. Matt thanked him and was relieved that Breeze was not here tonight. There was no doubt that Taylor was looking for Breeze. Taylor was not a racer; he only came to the streets to meet women and to keep an eye on Breeze.

Breeze sighed. "Can you take me home?"

Zion stroked her cheek. "Sure."

"Thanks. If you just get me to the plane, I can take it from there."

"No way am I leaving you alone. Not now."

She nodded. She was glad that he was going with her all the way home. Her fear and anxiety were through the roof, at the moment. Zion let Yu know that he was leaving with Breeze and encouraged him to stay. Yu would keep Taylor in his sights and report back to Uncle. Zion understood that the constant threat of Taylor and looking over her shoulder all of the time was a good reason she was not healing mentally.

"Where is Jazz?"

"He is in tournaments all summer. We were both supposed to be, but then my plans changed abruptly." She looked away from Zion and turned her head to the side. "I wish Taylor would move on with his life. He has other women that he sees and goes out with, so I don't understand why he still has his sights on me." She shook herself mentally. "Zion, I am sorry that your evening was ruined because of me."

Zion gently pulled her arm to stop her walking and turned her to face him. "What if it was me and I needed help? Would you help me or would you focus on staying here?"

"I would help, of course. You don't even have to ask."

"Then why would you think that I would not do the same for you? You are a warrior as I am, but more than that, you are my friend. I am always there for my friends and fellow brethren."

"Thanks."

Zion and Breeze started walking again, and then he saw the bike. He drove, and Breeze road on the back. They made it to the plane about fifteen minutes later. Once they were on the plane, Breeze changed and then laid her head on Zion's shoulder and went to sleep for the forty-five-minute flight back to Tennessee.

When they landed, Breeze sat up and took a long, deep breath. "Zion, I don't want to go home. The walls are confining and feel as if they are closing in on me. I can't go to Memphis to see my mom or Jazz because Taylor lives there and is always lurking around. I can't go out alone for fear Taylor will catch me while I am out. It sucks. I just want my life back. Can we just go somewhere and hang out?"

Zion offered a movie or bowling. Breeze mentioned the new black light putt-putt golf place and Zion agreed. It was open until two in the morning, which was perfect; after they finished golf they would go get breakfast at Waffle House, then Breeze would go home. Zion sent Uncle a text while Breeze was sleeping on the plane. Uncle was relieved that she had called Zion and Yu, and they responded so quickly. Breeze had not asked Uncle to intervene yet, but if she didn't call soon, then he was going to have to pay her a visit to discuss Taylor and the situation at hand. Right now, he was keeping her and Jazz safe from a distance.

JUNE 20th - KIDD'S DAY

Kidd was thrilled to be staying at Jon and Jana's house. Tomorrow was his birthday, and they always made it fun for him, not to mention Breeze always made it extra special. He had a feeling that Han would be flying in for his birthday, but he believed that it was more than that. He had a sneaky suspicion that Han was hoping to ensure that Breeze stayed in Jackson. That thought made Kidd smile. He knew Breeze would take that as a challenge. Breeze had been caught by Yu, Matt, and Zion, and she was mad. She kept mumbling that she was off and that she would figure it out.

Zion stopped by the house not long after Kidd arrived and spoke briefly to Breeze. He touched her elbow gently and led her to the dining room so they could speak privately.

"Has there been any word from Taylor?"

"Yes, but I forward everything to Jazz."

"Forward them to me please."

Breeze looked at Zion and searched his face. He was in warrior mode. She could tell that he was ready to fight at any moment. "What is it?"

"Taylor and his father have ordered a hit on you and Jazz." Zion always gave information direct and to the point. Why sugar coat it? There was no need; she was a warrior.

Fear shot through Breeze. "How much?"

Zion had never seen that much fear cross Breeze's face in all the years he had known her. Then there was the sadness that touched and radiated to her eyes.

Zion placed his hand on her cheek. "You are safe. Uncle ran interference."

"How much?"

Zion sighed. "$250,000 for you and $150,000 for Jazz."

She bowed and walked off. Zion watched her leave the room. The look that crossed her face when she turned to leave ripped at Zion's heart and gut. If he didn't know better, he would have sworn it was a look of grief, but no one had died. He knew she was trying to get the old Breeze back, but he saw the sadness, no matter how hard she tried to hide it. She straightened her shoulders, turned back just as she got to the stairs, and faced Zion's direction.

"Please tell Uncle I'm not running. If he needs me for bait, then I'm up for it."

Zion walked closer to her. He was speechless for a moment, then he regained his composure. "He won't risk it, Breeze."

"Tell him. Zion, please. I'm tired of looking over my shoulder, tired of not being able to go out alone for fear that he will be lurking around, and most of all I am tired of being broken." A tear streaked down her cheek and she flicked it away. Breeze bowed low. "Thank you for telling me."

She stood, turned, and ran up to her room. The tears were streaming, and she refused to break completely down in front of Zion or any other brethren. She refused to be seen as weak to them. She had worked too long and too hard for her warrior status for Taylor to strip her of her honor as a warrior. She hated this. She was sick of the tears and the fear.

103

She sat at her desk and just collapsed into gut wrenching dry heaving sobs. She was bawling, and she couldn't stop it. She held her stomach, rocked, and cried. The more she tried to stop the tears, the more they came. She was in absolute hell. She hated Taylor and everything he stood for, and she hated him for everything that he had taken from her.

Zion was extremely concerned about Breeze's comments. His biggest concern was Breeze saying she was tired of being broken. Her injuries seemed to be healing as expected. Was she referring to the scar across the side of her neck? He didn't think so. He needed to talk to Jana. Once he left, he would call Uncle and relay what Breeze had said. Zion found Jana in the kitchen.

"Jana," he said and bowed when she turned to face him.

She returned the bow. When he stood and she saw his face, she became rigidly still. "Zion, what is it?"

"Hits have been ordered on both Breeze and Jazz. Uncle sent me to warn her and you guys as well." He took a breath and thought of his words carefully. "I am concerned about Breeze. She seemed to be in better spirits after we went out on the motorcycle but now her sadness seems to be worse. I have been with her on many assignments. We have been ambushed, assaulted, attacked, beaten, and bloody, she has always bounced back or come back with a vengeance. She is not bouncing back this time."

"I believe she thinks that she is weak because she was beaten and caught off guard."

"Breeze weak? She is one of the strongest, most loyal, and determined warriors that I know."

Jana nodded at Zion's words.

"I know it is not typical for guys to go up to her room, but

104

may I speak with her?"

"Absolutely."

"Thank you." He bowed and quietly went up to Breeze's room.

He heard the sobs as soon as he neared the door. *What the hell? This is not Breeze. I have never seen her like this.* He quietly walked up behind her where she was sitting in her bean bag chair looking out the window and gently touched her shoulder. She jumped up and spun around like she had been shot. Zion jumped back just a little so if she swung she wouldn't connect with his jaw. She stared at Zion like a deer in headlights. He didn't think, he just reacted. He took her arm, pulled her into his arms, and held her against his chest. He stroked her hair with one hand and rubbed her back with his other hand. She cried even harder.

I don't deserve his kindness, but it feels so good.

"Breeze, I want you to know that you are not weak at all. You are one of the strongest warriors that I know. Will you please talk to us?"

She cried harder at his words. "Thank you, but I can't. There is nothing that I can say." Breeze choked out the words between sobs. He held her for about ten minutes until she realized that he was in her room.

She pushed back from him. "OMG. You can't be up here. You will get us both killed."

He laughed. "Relax. Jana gave me permission."

Her mouth dropped open. She started giggling and touched his mind. *"Do you think that permission would be granted if she knew about the streets."*

Zion actually blushed, then smiled. She was still crying a little. He continued to hold her for about ten more minutes until her tears finally stopped. They both turned their head to the sound of someone running into the room. Kidd gasped and pointed at Zion.

"Permission granted by Jana," Zion said smugly to Kidd.

Kidd looked over his shoulder to make sure Jana wasn't coming, turned back to Breeze and Zion, shook his finger at Zion, and clucked his tongue at him. He could not find the exact words he wanted to say but, they understood his intent.

Breeze leaned over to Zion and whispered, "Do you really want to mess with him?"

Zion gave a slight nod then he heard a stair squeak and stepped back. A moment later Han was behind Kidd in the doorway. Kidd had no clue until he was lifted in the air and began cussing like a sailor.

"BOY."

"Uncle Han." Kidd said with some serious attitude.

Han lowered Kidd to the floor and bowed to Zion. Zion returned the honor.

"Breeze, are you behaving?" Han asked.

"Unfortunately, Obi-wan." Breeze said and rolled her eyes.

"Beautiful." Han said.

Zion started laughing at the exchange between the three. Han could make most grown men quake with fear, but not Breeze and her friends. Han looked at Zion. Kidd got the giggles and danced off. Han watched him go down the stairs and then looked back at his niece.

"Breeze, do I need to take you and Kidd to the gym?" Han asked.

Breeze flashed him a smile, danced past him, and ran down the stairs. Kidd was at the bottom of the stairs waiting for her.

"You ok?"

"Of course."

"You are such a horrible liar," Kidd said.

"Just the normal crap, plus Taylor. I am ready for him to move on and leave me be. I'm ok; besides, it is your day and your upcoming birthday. It is not about me." She took a breath and focused. "Ya know, at least your cake will not have flowers on it."

Kidd gave her such a baffled look it was not even funny. "What are you talking about? Your cake didn't have flowers on it."

"Not on the cake from Jana, but the one my mom had for me. Yeah, it did. It was covered in flowers."

"You hate flowers," Kidd said in shock. "Does your mom NOT know this?"

"She still thinks and hopes that one day I will be a girly girl."

Kidd's mouth fell open and he just stared at her, then he pointed at her and shook his head.

" I know," Breeze said to his unspoken comment.

Once Kidd had regained his composure they went in the kitchen to assist Jana with making dinner and setting the table.

Han and Zion stayed upstairs. Han lowered his voice. "Jana said there is a hit ordered on Breeze and Jazz. She has alerted all of us. I have also alerted all of the Japanese brethren."

Zion nodded. "Good. Uncle is keeping feelers out. He also has eyes all over them." He looked at Han and decided to say what he needed to say. "Han, she is not healing emotionally. I know victims of domestic violence typically take longer to heal, but this is Breeze. There is a sadness to her eyes. I know she tries to hide it, but it is still there."

Han touched his shoulder. "I know brother. It is killing all of us to see her like this."

"Uncle said to tell you, if you need us, we are completely at your disposal."

"Thank you."

"It's not my place, but I am asking. Do you think Taka would be able to help her?"

"We have discussed that. We are not sure having Jazz, Breeze, and Taka in the same state would be a good idea."

Zion thought about it. "Yeah, probably not the best idea. There might be a whole lot more trouble with those three together again."

"Now, add Kidd in with those three."

"On second thought…NO."

Han roared with laughter. Zion shook his head, and they walked down together. Kidd and Breeze were in the living room playing on the Wii. Zion said his good-byes and left. Jana made lasagna for dinner. Matt, Mickey, Jana's sister Kim, Kim's husband Jim, and Grams all came over for dinner. Han sat beside Kidd at dinner, and Breeze decided that she would sit on the left of Kidd. Jana sat across from them with Jon beside her. Breeze was unfazed. She looked at Kidd and grinned. He started laughing. He had to excuse himself from the table so he could leave the room to compose himself, but also to read the small piece of paper that Breeze had slipped him as he sat down. **Go to the bathroom 10 minutes after dinner, look below.** Kidd folded the paper and put it in his pocket and walked back into the dining room to eat.

"Kidd, you get one present tonight. The rest are for tomorrow. Would you like to pick it out now and open it or wait until after dinner?"

Kidd jumped up, almost knocking Han over as he hurried to the table with the presents on it. He went to grab one and it started vibrating as he picked it up, he dropped it back on the table and threw his hands up. Jana had the camera ready to snap the picture as Kidd reached for the present. His expression of surprise and uncertainty was priceless. Jon was laughing as he was holding his phone.

Han picked up the package and handed it back to Kidd and shook it at him. "Well?" Han asked.

Kidd snatched it and ripped the wrapping open. It was a new cell phone. Kidd gasped. "Thank you."

Breeze had bought him a go phone a while back, and he was completely fine with that. This one was a brand new, top of the line, iPhone.

"You are on our family plan. It has unlimited talk, text, and data," Jana said.

Kidd ran around the table and hugged Jana and Jon. "Thank you. I love it."

Han smiled at Jana and nodded. Everyone sat back down and ate. Kidd had seconds on dessert. After dinner, Breeze and Kim helped clean up the kitchen. Kim and Jim left after that because Jim had to work early the next morning. Grams was staying the night. Kim would be back in the morning for breakfast and the birthday celebration. At exactly ten minutes after dinner, Kidd went into the bathroom. He gently opened the cabinet, he quietly searched the cabinet, and behind the extra rolls of toilet paper he found an envelope with his name on it. He opened it and was completely confused.

Welcome to the Scavenger Hunt
   Clue#1

Tall with leaves near a building where we store our vrooms

Kidd put the clue back in the envelope and walked out. Everyone was standing outside the bathroom door waiting on him when he walked out.

"What?" Kidd asked.

"What did your clue say?" Mickey asked with excitement.

Kidd was shocked. He thought it was something between him and Breeze. Kidd told them the clue, and everyone scattered to run outside. Kidd looked at Breeze.

"They couldn't play until you found the first clue. Now it is on. You better hurry," Breeze said, and Kidd turned to run out when Mickey ran in waving his first clue.

"Move your ass. I am not losing to Han." Mickey said and ran back out.

Uncle, Zion, Yu, and several other warriors arrived while everyone was out back. Uncle laughed when he saw everyone except Breeze and Grams running around.

Breeze walked over to Uncle. "Would you like to play?"

"No young one, but my warriors can play."

"Excellent," Breeze said and rubbed her hands together. Breeze told all the warriors the first clue and they took off.

Zion looked at Breeze. "Decoys Red?"

"Never."

Zion and Yu laughed but ran to catch up with everyone else. Mickey was all over the place.

"It looks like an Easter Egg Hunt for adults," Uncle said. Grams was laughing.

"Yes, pretty much, but with a twist of Breeze."

Han ran toward them, bowed, and ran off to his car. Mickey

ran to his motorcycle followed by Jana, Kidd, Matt, and Jon. The warriors were quick. They left two minutes after the others.

Breeze grabbed her keys, "Shall we?" She said to Grams and Uncle as she walked toward her car.

They both nodded. Breeze drove them to Matt's house. Uncle was laughing when he saw the chaos of people running around. There was obviously some kind of stand-off between Han and Mickey. Mickey was holding two pieces of paper and waving one at Han yelling "Andale! Andale!" and would pull the paper back out of Han's reach.

"Mr. Wu's went to his head, Breeze," Matt yelled.

Kidd spun around. "Is Mr. Wu's the prize?"

Breeze shook her head. Kidd turned just in time to see Han snatch the paper and pin Mickey as he read the clue. He jumped off of Mickey and took off. Breeze motioned to Uncle and Grams to get back in the car. She took off and they went toward the interstate.

"Where are we going?" Uncle asked.

"Waverly."

"Breeze, when did you have time to set this up?"

"Are you kidding? I have nothing but time right now."

"My granddaughter is so much like Jana. It is never a good idea to let them become bored," Grams said.

"We will beat them there," Breeze said.

Uncle shook his head at her. "Breeze, that is an hour twenty minutes from here."

"Not with me driving."

Grams started laughing. "Lordy, she is so much like Jana, Han, and Kim. Breeze, where is Jazz?"

"He is at an international tournament. It is a week long

tournament."

Grams saw the sadness briefly touch Breeze's eyes and noticed that it was quickly gone. Breeze did not drive as fast as she normally would since Grams and Uncle were with her, but she still made the drive in a little less than an hour. Breeze pulled into the Walmart parking lot, parked where they could see cars pulling in, and could see the front doors. Ten minutes later Han and Zion were racing into the Walmart parking lot.

"They have to buy three random items. Everyone's list is different." Breeze explained. "They have to pay at register three to receive their next clue by saying, 'Breeze sent me to get a purple people eater.'

Uncle looked at Breeze and she flashed him a grin. They watched as all the others pulled in seconds after Han and Zion. Kidd tripped Mickey. When Mickey went down so did Matt, Yu, and another warrior. They were all visually upset and once they untangled themselves they were running after Kidd.

"All's fair in love, war, and Breeze's scavenger hunts."

"I can see that," Uncle said just as Jana pushed Kidd out of the way and ran past him.

Jon jumped sideways as Mickey pushed his way out of the pile. Han was the first out of Walmart. He had his bag and clue in hand. Zion ran out, and he was ripping his envelope open as he ran. Zion whooped loudly and ran for his motorcycle. Breeze laughed. She threw the car in drive and drove to the carnival that was in town. She got out of the car, grabbed a stack of envelopes from the glove box and waited. Uncle and Grams stood beside her. They heard the cars and motorcycles pulling in quickly. Breeze handed each person an envelope as they ran past. They all went to various games and began playing. Competition and winning seemed to be the theme of the evening.

Uncle thought about how much planning had gone into this scavenger hunt and looked at Breeze. "So what is the grand prize?" he asked.

"Fun... of course," Breeze said.

Kidd played the milk bottle game, won a giant monkey, and ran over to Breeze. He grabbed her hand and started pulling her toward the game. She pulled back lightly and handed Grams and Uncle each an envelope.

"Have fun, we will be here awhile. Meet back here at ten o'clock." Breeze turned and started walking off with Kidd.

Kidd leaned over and hugged her. "Thanks for this. It is a blast."

"Glad you like it. Enjoy your night, but I am about to smoke you at the milk bottle game."

"Dream on," Kidd said.

Breeze paid for them both, then the challenge was on. They played until Breeze won a giant Raggedy Anne doll. After that they went to the water balloon race game. Everyone joined them at this game, took a seat, and started playing. Jon won twice, Uncle won once, and Han won once. Jana threw her hands up.

"I'm off. Absolutely off. I'm going to the Gravity Pull." Jana said and started to get up.

Mickey jumped and looked at Jana. "Race ya." He took off running.

Jana just looked at her watch, then at Jon and Han. They gave Mickey a ten second lead then they took off after him. Han caught up to Mickey, ran beside him, and grinned as Jana ran past.

"Better luck next time." Han jeered at Mickey.

Zion on the other hand was not letting Breeze or Kidd out of his sights. He had a feeling this was a decoy for another challenge. Breeze walked up to Zion with a candy apple in hand and patted him on the back.

"Relax brother. This is too much fun."

Zion just looked at her and gave her a skeptical look. He was not letting his guards down now. Everyone met in the parking lot at ten o'clock. Breeze handed Uncle her keys. Matt snuck up behind Kidd and blindfolded him. Jana took his keys and threw them to Breeze. Mickey pushed over a motorcycle that had been parked behind a building so no one could see it. Breeze handed Jon an envelope. He walked over to Kidd, handed it to him, and spun him around three times. Mickey, Han, Zion, Yu, and all the warriors stood where they were blocking Kidd's view of the bike. Jana removed the blindfold and Kidd ripped open the envelope. He looked at the key. He knew it was a bike key and not a car key. He looked around scanning the lot, the only motorcycles he saw were those that belonged to Mickey, Zion, and Yu. He turned and they parted so he could see the bike. It was a new Yamaha Y2F-R6. Kidd walked to the bike and ran his hand from front fender to rear taillight and back. He looked at Breeze. She nodded.

"Happy Birthday from all of us," she said.

"Are you going to get on it or am I driving that sweet ride home?" Han asked.

Kidd just gaped at Han, then quickly jumped on the bike. Matt and Mickey whooped when he fired it up. Jana handed him a new helmet. He put it on, flipped the visor up, "Race ya home," and took off. Everyone ran to their appropriate ride. Breeze laughed. Even Uncle and Grams were in the spirit. Uncle and Grams spun out in front of Mickey and Han. Zion pulled out behind Breeze. She looked in her rearview mirror and laughed. He could eat her dust all the way back to Jackson.

Kidd was kicked back on the bike when everyone started pulling in. He was grinning. "It's an AWESOME ride. Thank you."

Breeze walked by Kidd and ruffled his hair. "You know in thirty minutes it will officially be your birthday," she said.

Han rubbed his hands together. Kidd just laughed.

"Breakfast will be at nine in the morning. Get some rest," Jana said.

"Yes, you will need it. We have a full day planned," Jon said.

Uncle told his warriors to go home, but to return no later than eight thirty in the morning. Zion tapped Breeze. *"So you can behave?"*

"Who said?"

Zion whipped around to look at Breeze; she busted out laughing and walked in the house. Uncle shook his head and left with his warriors. Before Uncle left, Zion asked if he could be on guard duty for the night. Uncle agreed. Last year or the year before they had got around Han on Kidd's birthday, but they hoped that would not happen this year. Zion set up post outside in the trees close to Breeze's window. An hour later Breeze called his cell. "Get some sleep. I am not leaving."

"I don't believe you."

"I am unlocking the front door. You can come up and chill in the chair in my room."

"Uhhh, no. I want to live."

"Call Jana. She will welcome it," she laughed. "Plus we could mess with Kidd in the morning."

Zion hung up. He thought about leaving but knew better. *Shit, If I am going to die I better do it honorably.* He called Jana. They spoke briefly, and Jana greeted him at the door a couple of minutes later.

"I have let Jon, Han, and Uncle know of my approval. Go before she uses this time to get out."

Zion was quick. He ran up the stairs soundlessly. He texted Breeze that he was coming in. He received an ok as the response. Zion could not believe he was in her room while everyone was asleep.

"OMG. Would you chill out, please. We have been on numerous assignments together. Everyone knows we honor the Warrior's Code. The streets are different. That is a place of no rules, but normal every day, we honor the code."

He nodded and physically relaxed. Breeze fell asleep quickly. He watched her sleep for about thirty minutes then drifted off himself. He heard movement and jumped up. She was still asleep, but she was thrashing around and silently crying. He eased over to her and gently touched her arm. "Breeze, it is me, Zion."

She gasped loudly. She took several more breaths. "Zion," she whispered. "Please stay."

"I'm here."

"Will you hold me? Just to keep the nightmares at bay. Please."

He didn't hesitate for a second. He slid in beside her and wrapped her in his arms. The next thing he knew, her alarm was going off, and it was eight in the morning. He awoke to her moving to turn her phone off. He stroked her hair in a soothing gesture.

"Breeze, how often are you having the nightmares?"

"Nightly."

He sighed. "Have you told Jana or your dad?"

"They know. Well, they know I still have them, but they don't know how often." She rolled over to face him. "Zion, we all have our own demons to face and slay. This is mine. I am ok."

"No, Breeze, you're not. Talk to someone, please."

She sighed heavily. "Zion I am a warrior, twice over and a controlling asshole caught me off guard and broke me. What does that say about me and my skills?"

"That you are human. You cannot change what happened. No one blames you."

"I do. I blame me." She touched his face. "Today is Kidd's day. Let's not worry about me. Ok? I need to shower. Do you have any other clothes?"

He nodded and pointed to his bag on the floor.

She eased up and started for the bathroom. "After we have showered and changed, we are going to mess with Kidd big time."

She grabbed her clothes, went in the bathroom, started the shower, and got in. Her thoughts were all over the place. *I just want one night of no nightmares. I hate this. I don't want sleep aides or anti-depressants to dull or numb the pain. Ugh, maybe I do need them temporarily.* She refused to cry and she refused to have a bad day. She focused on Kidd's birthday and got out of the shower. She was ready to go in just a few minutes.

When she walked out, Zion grabbed his bag and took his turn getting cleaned up and dressed. While he was in the shower.

Breeze text Jana.

> **Breeze:** Kidd up yet?
> **Jana:** Not yet. 10 mins will wake.
> **Breeze:** I'm going to mess with him… play along.
> **Jana:** DO NOT KILL HIM. Especially on his birthday.
> **Breeze:** Where is the fun in that?
> **Jana:** Matt and Mickey just arrived.
> **Breeze:** Perfect… Kidd + Mickey.
> **Jana:** I will alert your father and Han to be ready to do CPR.
> **Breeze:**

Zion walked out just as Breeze had ended her conversation with Jana.

"In 10 minutes we are going to walk down laughing and cutting up. We are going to make sure Kidd and Mickey see you coming out of my room. Jana will text me when Kidd is up. She will probably send him up to wake me up. If that is the case, act like you are trying to hide, or let him see you kiss me just as he opens the door… something to really get him going. Do you think you can handle that?"

"Do you even have to ask?"

Jana sent her a text.

Jana: Kidd up, going to the bathroom, then up to wake you up. Mickey has an airhorn they are going to bust in together. Han and your dad are ready to snap pics and start CPR.

Breeze: WONDERFUL

Jana: On way up

Mickey and Kidd went up the steps as quietly as they could. Breeze ran to her bed, motioned for Zion to get in and she climbed in beside him. They covered up to their necks and acted like they were making out when Kidd and Mickey busted in. Mickey dropped the air horn and Kidd yelled "HOLY CRAP YOU ARE SO DEAD... HAN IS HERE." Breeze pretended to jump.

"Get out," Breeze yelled back.

Han came walking up the stairs. "What about me?"

Mickey was sputtering and running back and forth in front of the door, pointing and flapping his arms. He looked like a chicken that had its head cut off and was floundering in the field. Jon was across the hall snapping pics of Kidd and Mickey. Neither one of them saw him. Han walked in Breeze's room. "Zion, what the hell are you doing up here?"

Zion just looked at Breeze and then the window. "Guarding Breeze."

"I don't think that is what Uncle had in mind," Han said and started to advance to the bed, when he spun, grabbed Kidd, and dropped him on the bed.

Breeze jumped up and started tickling him. "Happy Birthday."

"Oh Hell NO...." Kidd said. "He is in her room AGAIN."

"Jana approved," Zion said

"No way. No way. Not for that."

Zion got up and revealed that he was fully dressed. Mickey was still floundering. Jon walked by him and snapped a picture of his expression. Jana walked in, patted him on the back, and then ran to the bed to help Breeze and Han tickle Kidd.

"Mom," he said and pointed to Zion as he gasped for breath. "What, son?"

He jabbed a finger toward Zion. He couldn't speak due to laughing so hard. Mickey walked over and pushed Zion off the bed, flipped Breeze off, and walked out. Breeze and Zion were laughing. Breeze got up and ran out of the room after Mickey. Zion grabbed the airhorns and ran after her. He threw one of the airhorns to Breeze. They ran beside Mickey and set them off. Mickey jumped.

"Breeze, I thought Han and Jon were going to kill you both."

"Nah, they love me," Breeze said.

"Not that much," Mickey exclaimed.

Matt was laughing to the point he was holding his side. The four finally ventured down the stairs. Kidd would look at Zion and swear under his breath.

At one point Zion looked at Kidd. "What was that, Kidd? I couldn't hear you. Can you speak up a little bit louder?"

Uncle arrived just as Kidd flipped Zion off and walked in the kitchen to take his place at the table.

"What was that about?" Uncle asked.

"He's jealous that Zion was in my room, and he wasn't."

Kidd ran back in the room, pointed his finger at Breeze, then at Zion, ummed a couple times, swore, and ran back to the kitchen.

Uncle started laughing. "I am so sorry I missed whatever happened."

Breakfast was wonderful. Kidd and Mickey had finally started to recover about the time Kidd was to open his presents. That was until Zion leaned over and whispered something in Kidd's ear and he gasped. Kidd was speechless. Jon captured everything on camera. This was definitely a birthday worth remembering. After breakfast they all loaded up in Jana's Escalade as well as a couple other vehicles and drove to the Memphis Zoo. Kidd had never been to the zoo before. He had said something to Jana several months ago when they were casually talking about things. She often forgot how his life was before he joined their family. When they pulled into the turn off for the zoo, Kidd squealed with delight.

Jana smiled. "I know this is not action and adventure, but I wanted your birthday special."

"Are you kidding me? This is perfect. Are we here all day?"

"They close at nine."

Kidd was jumping up and down in his seat. He couldn't wait to see all the animals. The monkeys were top on his list. Jon snapped a pic. Kidd truly looked like a little kid at Christmas. Jon touched Jana's hand and smiled. Breeze hugged Kidd. They jumped out of the Escalade as soon as they were parked.

"Hurry up." Kidd yelled as he ran to the admissions line. "Seriously. Hurry up." He waved his hand forward as he was running.

Uncle walked up to Jana and Jon. "He really does make it as fun as Breeze and Jazz."

"Trust me, we know."

Han walked up with Zion. "I never thought the Zoo would be your son's 17th birthday, but I can see it was well worth it," Han said to Jana.

They all joined Kidd and Breeze at the gates, got their tickets, and went in. Kidd was on cloud nine. When they stopped at the food court for lunch, Jana almost had to drag Kidd out of an exhibit.

"Son, we are not leaving, just eating. We will be back." Jana explained.

Kidd shuffled his feet and went to the food court. His thoughts were not on food; it was on all that he had not seen yet. Jana bought him a cup with all the animals on it to go with his lunch. He kept staring at the cup and absentmindedly ate what was on his plate. When his fingers hit an empty container he jumped up.

"Go. We will be there in a minute," Jana said.

Kidd took off. Breeze, Matt, and Mickey were all right there with him. They stayed until the zoo closed. They had stopped at a few of the carts for souvenirs throughout the zoo. Jana bought him a t-shirt and a large Orangutan stuffed animal. Breeze got him a key chain and a postcard. She leaned over and whispered something, and he smiled.

Kidd walked up to Jana and Jon and hugged them both. "Thank you so much. This was amazing. I am so glad that you call me son."

Jana wrapped him in a bear hug. "You are our son. That will never change. We want to make every day special, not just your birthdays."

"You do. More than you will ever know. Thank you again." Kidd said.

The drive home was quiet. Kidd fell asleep almost as soon as they got in the SUV.

Breeze touched Jana's shoulder. "Mom and Dad, you really did make it extra special for him. Thanks. I didn't know he had never been or I would have taken him sooner, but I am glad that he got to go for his birthday. It meant the world to him."

Jana choked back a sob and smiled.

THE FOLLOW UP APPOINTMENT

Jazz called everyday while he was out of the country for his tournaments. Jon and Han actually went to his tournament in Japan. Jon was happy when he arrived home. He was bragging about Jazz, his wins, and he made the comment that it was nice to see that he could behave. Jon was not expecting Breeze's comment but he should have.

"Well, Dad, we will just have to fix that," Breeze said and danced off.

"You are still on medical restrictions or we would go to the gym."

Breeze simply shrugged, which caused Jana to bust out laughing. Jon just stared at his wife and daughter, then shook his head. Breeze was thinking about that day and all of Jazz's tournaments. The ones that she missed out on completely. She had gone to a couple of local tournaments with Jon and Jana to support Jazz. She loved the atmosphere in and around the ring, but it wasn't the same. She was tired of waiting for the next attack from Taylor and, most of all, she was tired of being sidelined.

Breeze was chomping at the bit for her Dad and Jana to hurry home so they could take her back to Memphis for what she hoped would be her last follow up appointment and she could receive clearance to start training again. Her Sensei had recommended a Maui Thai Sensei in Jackson. She had gone last week to meet her and absolutely could not wait to train under her. She knew that she would have to start off slow so she didn't pull or tear something or worse, have a major setback. Breeze heard Jon's truck turning in the drive. She grabbed her purse and ran out.

"Slow your roll. I have to use the bathroom, and we are waiting on Jana."

"You better hurry, or I will hot wire that truck and drive myself," Breeze teased.

Jana pulled in and parked in the garage while Jon was in the bathroom. Jana knew that Breeze was hopeful about today and wanted to start training as soon as possible. Jana was anxious that the doctor might not clear Breeze, and she was afraid that would cause Breeze to spiral back into a deep depression. Breeze had started seeing a therapist a couple weeks ago and it seemed to be helping. The therapist recommended herbs and natural solutions to help Breeze relax as well as massage therapy. Breeze had been honest with the therapist and told her that she didn't want anything that could be habit forming, and she didn't want something long term. The therapist respected Breeze's request with the herbal approach, but also put her on a light dose of Bupropion to take the edge off. She reassured Breeze that it was not habit forming and was one of the easier medications to come off of. When Jana walked into the house, Breeze was tapping her foot.

"What?"

"I can drive myself."

"Whatever."

124

"I ain't playing with you. The dojo is calling my name, and I need to hear the doctor say that I am cleared."

Jana started to speak, and Breeze held up her hand.

"Only positive vibes."

"Where is Jazz?"

"Flying home. He is planning to come here once he lands to finally meet Kidd." Breeze said with serious attitude.

"Oh, man... I need to alert Uncle and Han."

Jon walked out and grabbed his keys. "Why are you alerting Uncle and Han?"

" Breeze is hoping for all clear from the doctor today. Jazz is flying home. Oh, and Jazz is planning to meet Kidd, finally."

"Oh, hell no, I forgot I need Kidd to go with me to Japan for a couple of weeks."

"That is ok. We know where Han lives. We could always see if the three of us could add another painting to Han's collection," Breeze said.

"Sass. Lord have mercy the sass is just rolling today. Maybe we should call Han once the doctor gives the all clear," Jana teased.

"Bring it. You three can be in the gym while me, Jazz, and Kidd take Japan by storm."

The three climbed in the truck and took off for Memphis. Breeze's appointment was at 1:15 p.m. with Dr. Witkowski. Breeze mentally reached out to Jazz. *"You landed yet?"*

"Yep."

"Good. Be ready."

"Always."

"I love you, Jazz. Thank you for everything."

"You ready to drink?"

"No."

125

"You are killing me." He shook his head. *"It would help you heal in ways the doctors can't."*

"I know."

"Let Matt and Mickey know that I will be there tonight. Tell them to invite Kidd over, but don't tell him I am coming. It is time I met him and not just over the phone and at a distance."

"Do not kill him."

"I wouldn't dream of it, darling."

"Jana will kill you if one hair is out of place on his head."

"Nah, she loves me."

Breeze busted out laughing. Jon looked in the rearview mirror and Jana turned around to look at Breeze. "What is Jazz up to?"

"Ya know, planning his meeting with Kidd."

"He better not kill my son, or he will be in the gym with me."

"He knows."

"Jon, you need to deal with that," Jana said with a laugh.

Jazz started cursing in Korean, which caused Breeze to laugh harder. They pulled into the doctor's parking lot and Breeze jumped out of the truck.

Jana looked at Jon. "For her sake, I truly hope she is cleared."

"For our sake, I pray she is cleared," Jon said.

Breeze had already signed in and was filling out her form about her level of pain when Jon and Jana came into the waiting room. When Breeze was called back both Jon and Jana went back as well. Breeze passed the physical with flying colors and was cleared to start training. Dr. Witkowski reminded her that if there was pain or discomfort besides normal sore muscles then she was to stop immediately and come in. Breeze agreed. Jazz was still linked with her and was excited as she was that she could get back in the ring.

"Breeze, your body is not ready for tournaments at the caliber that you were used to doing. That is still going to take time." Dr. Witkowski said.

"Trust me, I know."

"You will not be at that level for several more months."

Breeze nodded her agreement and left with her parents to go back to Jackson. She texted her new sensei a copy of the medical release form and asked when they could start the private lessons. Her sensei responded quickly.

Sensei: Is Sunday at 2 p.m. ok with you?

Breeze: Absolutely.

Sensei: We will start off light.

Breeze: Yes, ma'am.

Breeze told her Dad and Jana the news. She was so happy. Jana and Jon were relieved to see a spark of hope in her eyes. When they pulled into the drive, Jazz was sitting in his car in the driveway. Jazz got out and stood by the driver side door, while they parked. Breeze jumped out of the truck and ran to Jazz. He picked her up and spun her.

"It is about time," Breeze said.

"Sorry I couldn't make the plane go any faster."

Breeze grabbed his hand and pulled him towards his car. "Ready to meet Kidd?"

"Absolutely."

Jana was walking by to go inside when she heard the exchange. She quickly turned to face them. "Do NOT kill Kidd or you will be in the gym with me."

Jazz just laughed, Breeze got in the passenger side and they took off toward Matt's house. Matt and Mickey had gone to the Casey Jones Catfish house and picked up five plates of food on the way to get Kidd. They did not want him to see there was extra food because then he might ask questions. Before they placed the order they ran to town, went to the gas station, and they both noticed this breath taking beautiful young woman that was standing near pump three.

"Holy cow. She must be a tourist because you sure as hell don't forget beauty like that," Matt said.

"You ain't lying. Lordy, I would love to see her at the streets. I am sure Breeze could help her accent in all the right ways," Mickey said.

They both composed themselves and got out of the car. Mickey walked past the woman and had a sense of other worldly. There was more to her than beauty, he could tell. He didn't say anything, but he tapped Matt to let him know. As they were walking into the store two guys were coming out, one was taller than the other and the other one was bulkier, but you could tell they both were fit. Matt's skin tingled. It wasn't bad but he knew they were not like most people. Matt and Mickey watched as they both walked out to pump three.

Mickey was now on alert. Were they here as part of the hit on Breeze? He hadn't got the feel of trouble from them. Surely they were tourists. When they pulled out, Mickey saw their license plate. Now he was really on edge. They were not visitors, they lived here. Mickey was used to the family and their abilities and on rare occasions he might meet one or two people that had abilities, but now there were more than just the family here. He would call Yu or Zion when he got in the car. They got their drinks and gas then headed to go get the food.

When Matt went in to get the food Mickey made the call. "Hello."

"Zion, It's Mickey. Any info on the hit on Breeze and Jazz? Are there any unfamiliars in town?"

"Uncle has spoken with two on Mr. Smith's payroll. No, not that we are aware of."

"Matt and I just got gas and we bumped into three individuals with abilities, but we did not pick up trouble. They had plates for Jackson, so not visitors."

Zion asked for the name of the gas station, the make and model of the car, and the direction that they were headed. Mickey relayed it all. He knew that Uncle would not take any chances and would check things out.

"Have you let Jana know?"

"No. I did not want to set off alarms if they weren't needed. You know Jana is already on edge, which is never a good thing."

"That is one person that I never want to piss off."

"Amen, brother."

"I will let Uncle know."

"Oh… Jazz is meeting Kidd soon."

"Oh Shit.."

Mickey busted out laughing. "Later."

Zion hung up. He shook his head and laughed. He would love to be there for that meeting. It would be interesting for sure. He called Uncle and relayed everything that Mickey had told him. Uncle thanked Zion and hung up. A few minutes later, Uncle called back.

"Go."

"Yes, sir."

Nothing else was said. Zion grabbed his helmet and took off out the door. He went to the gas station and began tracking from there. The plate was easy to track. It was registered to Blade McGroff. Upon a little research, he found that he was a senior in high school. The same school Breeze would be attending. He had a twin brother and a younger sister. The sister was also a senior, even though she was two years younger. A little more digging revealed their dad was a doctor here in Jackson. The mother was deceased. Zion relayed everything to Uncle and then he made his way to Matt's house. He might actually get to see the initial meeting after all. He laughed at that thought.

He called Breeze.

"Hey."

"Hey, Zion. What's up?"

"I will be there soon. We will be working."

"Attire?"

"We are on the bike."

"Just yours?"

"Yep."

"I will be waiting."

"I'm coming in for a few minutes. I need to speak to Matt and Mickey."

"Jazz is here. Is he needed?"

"Nope. Just you and me, babe. It will be over night."

"Lovely. Do I need a small bag?"

"Yes. Essentials and a change of clothes. Don't forget your piece."

"See you soon."

Breeze walked over to Jazz and hugged him. They heard Matt's car pull into the drive and Jazz pulled her over to the couch to sit with him. The car doors opened and closed and there were feet running up the steps. The door busted open and in ran Kidd. He was bouncing with excitement.

"Breeze, Breeze. What did the doctor say?" Kidd was saying as he ran in and abruptly stopped when he saw her on the couch. Jazz stood and stuck out his hand.

"Hey, Kidd, I'm Jazz."

Kidd shook his hand and smiled. He looked at Breeze and grinned. "Tonight she sleeps with me."

Jazz flipped and pinned Kidd to the floor. "Actually tonight she sleeps with Zion."

"No way."

"Way." Breeze said and stepped over to look down at Kidd. "He is on his way."

"That is ok. You are here now, so more time for us."

Jazz's ears turned red and he looked straight at Breeze. "Have you not taught him how to block?"

"No, we were too busy with the streets or just everyday stuff."

"Block? What the hell is he talking about. I train with Jon, not Breeze."

Matt and Mickey were in the kitchen sitting out the food when Zion strolled in.

"He means your thoughts." Zion said with a cocky tone and walked over to Breeze. He pulled her in his arms.

Kidd began swearing which caused Matt and Mickey to come running out. Matt busted out laughing and Mickey just shook his head. Breeze had already told Jazz about Kidd's birthday surprise. Jazz started laughing, stood up, and pulled Breeze out of Zion's arms and wrapped his arm around her. They walked into the kitchen like that and got food. Breeze yelled for Zion and Kidd to move their tail feathers. Kidd grinned, jumped up, and ran into the kitchen. Zion simply walked in, like it was any other day. Breeze split her plate with Zion. It was a lot of food and she could not eat it all. If they had known sooner that he was coming, they would have ordered him a plate.

Kidd looked at Breeze with a goofy grin and Jazz's ears went scarlet.

"KIDD!" Jazz roared.

Kidd jumped. "What?"

Zion laughed and patted Kidd's back. "He is a telepath just like our girl here."

Kidd's mouth dropped open.

"While I am on assignment. You boys are going to race, play nice, and Jazz is going to teach you to block your thoughts from others."

"All I can say is he has one hell of an imagination. Breeze does not own a hot pink and black thong and bra set."

"Not yet, but I can buy her one."

Zion took Breeze's plate and Matt grabbed Kidd's before it hit the floor with him. Breeze flipped Kidd and Jazz stood with his foot on Kidd's chest.

"Not bloody likely." Jazz said and then walked into the living room.

Everyone was laughing including Kidd.

"You can't blame a guy from trying."

Zion sat on the couch and handed Breeze her plate back. They all took their places. There was this unspoken rule that everyone seemed to know and respect, including Kidd, that Jazz would sit with Breeze. Everyone was just talking when Zion asked Breeze if she was ready for school to start.

"Yes."

Kidd groaned.

"I thought you liked school."

"I do but it is my Junior year and there is a lot that I am going to need which means I will have to pay for it. You know my old man isn't going to pay for anything, except liquor and beer."

"Jana is taking care of all of your senior pictures and your class ring."

Kidd shook his head. He didn't want to have to ask Jana to do that.

"It is already done. Jana called and put the deposit down on your pictures. That is why they sent you the card that your appointment is tomorrow afternoon. Aren't you and Jana shopping tomorrow morning?"

"Yeah, but I thought just simple school stuff."

"Jana is excited to go with you. She missed out on mine because of my mom, which is a whole other story, but she is really excited."

"She has given me so much. I hate that she is spending more money on me."

"Why? You are her son. You are family. It makes her happy when you are happy. Just enjoy it."

Jazz had sent Zion a mental image of Kidd in a dress and Zion almost choked on his fish. Kidd looked at him as he was trying to swallow which caused Zion to start gasping and choking more. Jazz simply kept eating and Breeze shot him a look. He was blocked so Breeze did not know what he had said to Zion but she knew he had said something. Zion finally recovered and went back to talking with the group.

"Do you know a Blade McGroff or Rocky McGroff?"

"I know of them. They kind of keep to themselves. I think they train in martial arts, but not sure where. I have heard them talking about tournaments. Blade is kind of popular with the ladies, but again I see them talking to people but not really hanging out that much. I think I have seen them at a couple of football games, here and there. I don't really run in their circle, they are upper class, where I am not. They have a sister named Summer and OMG she is hot. I mean beauty that will melt your retinas. The only person that is hotter than her is Breeze. Not only is Summer beautiful she is a freaking genius. Most of the guys are intimated by her beauty and smarts. I have never had the opportunity to ask her out or anything. She is senior, but is supposed to be a sophomore. Why?"

Breeze threw a cushion at Kidd and he dodged it. Mickey looked at Zion and saw the brief nod. Mickey now had names and knew they were going to school with Breeze. Mickey would get with Matt about surprising Breeze as a welcoming committee for her first day of school. Maybe they could get a feel of the siblings there. Jazz was just taking everything in. It was hard for him to hear about her new school, since it was their senior year and they were now going to be a part, but he never let on. He did not want Breeze to get depressed or sad because of him.

Jazz grabbed a cushion and hit Kidd with it. "I swear I am going to kill him, Breeze."

"Jana." Breeze said and went back to eating.

"It might be worth the gym time." Jazz said.

Zion took his plate in the kitchen and placed his dirty dishes in the dishwasher. Breeze followed him in the kitchen and did the same.

"Do we have time for me to make coffee? I am running on fumes."

"No, but we will be stopping at the coffeeshop in town and

having dessert at the café."

"Well, what are we waiting on? Let's go."

"Yes ma'am."

"Coffee and Cheesecake, seriously, let's go."

Zion laughed. Took her hand and gently turned her to face him. "We are going out as a couple for this assignment. Are you ok with that?"

"Of course. Why wouldn't I be?"

"You are starting a new school here soon. People will know that we were out together. I just didn't want to cause you any unease."

"Zion, I do not care what anyone thinks when it comes to my personal life, especially when it comes to my friends and family. You are both of those things to me."

"Let's roll."

Zion walked into the living room, said his goodbyes, grabbed his jacket and helmet. Breeze did the same and grabbed her small overnight bag. It would go in the saddle bag. Jazz got up and hugged her tight.

"I will see you sometime tomorrow. I train Sunday."

"So do I."

Jazz kissed the top of her head and then swatted her butt hard as she walked out the door.

Kidd gasped when Jazz did that. Jazz turned, looked at Kidd, and cracked his knuckles.

"Let's race." Jazz said.

Matt and Mickey strolled out back toward the garage, like it was any other day. Jazz immediately started tapping Kidd's mind, which frustrated him and made him mad.

"If you don't want me in your head, then block it." Jazz said as he got on a bike.

They worked for hours on images, blocking, listening, and blocking some more. Kidd was a quick learner and he was observant. Kidd actually broke through Jazz's barriers a couple of times, but Jazz slammed his thoughts down quickly. By ten o'clock Kidd was exhausted. Jana called him at ten fifteen.

"Hey, Kidd, I just wanted to remind you that I will pick you up around nine in the morning. Please be ready when I get there."

"Ok, no problem."

"How is everything?"

"Good."

"Is Breeze and Jazz there?"

"Jazz is, but Breeze is on assignment with Zion."

"Ok. I will see you in the morning."

Jana was really calling to see if Jazz had given him a heart attack or not. She was relieved to hear that Kidd sounded normal. A thought struck her and she ran into the living room.

"Kidd, Jazz, and Breeze together."

"Oh Crap. Call Han immediately and tell him under no circumstances does Taka come to the states. We cannot handle the four together. I mean we knew Jazz was going to meet Kidd, but when you say it like that, we are screwed." Jon said.

"Apparently Uncle had the same thought, because he has Breeze and Zion on assignment together now." Jana said.

"I will send that man his favorite whiskey for that one." Jon said.

AUGUST 4 - NEW SCHOOL

Breeze stood facing the mirror, spiking, and styling her sassy auburn hair. She was reflecting on the hell she had been through. Her eighteenth birthday had not been what she expected. She never had any intentions of spending it in the hospital. As she was sitting at the vanity, she decided to try to cover the dark circles that were under her eyes. If any of the guys saw her, they would know that the nightmares were still causing her sleepless nights. She pulled on her knee length boots over her jeans. She admired herself in the mirror one final time and grabbed her book bag.

"I wish Jazz was here, I miss him." Breeze said to herself and her empty room.

Man this sucks... I can't shake the darkness that is encompassing me. Maybe I should talk to the doctor about increasing my anxiety meds. I was cleared last month to start working out and training again, I thought that would help me to feel more like myself. It does and it doesn't, there is just this big gaping hole in my heart and mind. She shook herself and focused on getting all her stuff together so she could leave for school. School was a sense of normal for her and she was looking forward to it.

Breeze looked in the mirror, the scar on her cheek was obvious as well the scar on her neck, but only people who knew her knew they were relatively new scars. She didn't want any questions or comments from anyone at her new school regarding the accident, several people from the streets went to school here, not to mention others lived in Jackson. She hadn't been to the streets much this summer since Taylor was still lurking around. *My concentration is horrible right now. I need to focus. It is not the first time that I have been beaten, though it is the first time anyone has crushed my spirits like this. Damn it, Breeze, get it together.* She sighed and took in her room as if she wouldn't return. One bookshelf was filled with all her favorite books. Her Harry Potter books were front and center even though they were tattered and worn, they were well loved. She had the English version, Japanese version, and Korean version of the series.

She admired her chic handmade desk. It was organized with school supplies on one side and art supplies on the other side. She had old records that had been converted to decorative cork boards hanging all over her room with pictures from Japan, Korea, muscle cars, music groups, Jazz, her family, and her friends. She briefly glanced over her neatly made bed with the red and yellow blanket that her Grandmother Lee had made her then her eyes went to the black and red dragon painting beside her bed. She quickly made her way down the stairs to the kitchen, grabbed the largest insulated cup she could find for her coffee, and then made her way to her car.

Breeze pulled up in the school parking lot in her Yellow 1965 Mustang with her radio blaring the new Iggy Azalea cd. Everyone was staring before she even got out of the car.

"Well Hell, I better get this party started," she said to herself as she was getting her coffee and backpack. She was getting ready to place her ear buds in her ears when she heard a familiar voice yell, "Yo, Breeze. What's up girl?"

She ran across the parking lot to where Matt and Mickey were parked. Matt was driving his black Charger. Mickey was riding shotgun, looking cool and relaxed as always. She smiled to herself, she wished she was blessed with Cherokee cheekbones like they had, however, that would require her to be Cherokee. She ran to Mickey's side of the car and tugged at his long ponytail. He started to jump out when she caught a thought from the backseat. She pushed Mickey back into the car and reached into wave at Kidd. Kidd smiled, but she could see a light bruise on his cheek. *Damn it, his dad had struck him again, Kidd deserves better.*

"What are you doing here? I know you are not coming to school since you both are done."

"We thought we would ease your nerves, you know with a new school, first day jitters and all that jive." Matt said.

"Yeah, you look a little pale," Mickey said laughing.

"I told these guys a new school couldn't scare you. Cause you're the bomb," Kidd said.

"Aren't you supposed to be going into the school with me, since it is your first day of a new school year and all?" Breeze asked Kidd.

"Nah, I'm skippin'," Kidd replied. Breeze shook her head. She hoped that her dad did not find out, because if he did, Kidd would be in the gym more than he already was. Not to mention if Jana found out. Breeze made the sign of the cross and Kidd simply grinned bigger. "She loves me."

"Your funeral if she finds out and no, I am not telling. I am not stupid, especially after our last adventure. The alerts are still up."

139

The three guys got out of the car. They all turned when they heard Jazz's car pulling into the lot. The sound of that engine was like music to their ears; it should be, after all the blood, sweat, and tears that the three of them had put into it. Jazz came rolling up in his red 1965 suped up Mustang. All the guys admired the car from a distance. He parked right next to Breeze's car.

The ladies could care less about the car. They were too busy admiring the drop-dead gorgeous man getting out of the car. Breeze always thought he could be a model, but he enjoyed schemin' and doing Martial Arts with her. She admired his dark eyes; they had an edge to them that could quickly turn you on or make you want to turn and run.

OMG, he is fine. Breeze thought. Jazz's Asian skin glistened in the sun, and Breeze's heart skipped a beat.

What the hell? He is my best friend, and he is the one and only person who knows all my little glitches. We decided a long time ago that we are better off as friends. Ok, so I decided that, but after all the crap that I have just been through, there is no way I am going to do anything to destroy our friendship. Jazz was there every day to sit with me. All Jazz knows is what my mom and Stan had told everyone, and what he had heard the doctors say about my injuries. There had not been any time to discuss all the specifics of my prolonged stay and I'm thankful for that. This burden is mine and mine alone.

She felt a brief sadness and quickly shook it off, to ensure 'her boys' didn't see it. Suddenly, Breeze was lifted in the air and spun around. The pain in her ribs screamed, and she let out a little gasp of air. The bruised ribs were still tender. Her work outs with her new sensei reminded her daily how tender they still were.

"Sorry girl, I forgot." Jazz placed her down gently.

"It's good to see you. Let me guess, here to ease my nerves?" Breeze asked.

"Yeah, how'd you know?" Jazz asked.

She laughed and pointed to Matt's car. Jazz laughed lightly. He wrapped his arm around Breeze, and they walked over to the car. He fist bumped all the guys but kept his other arm around Breeze's waist.

Jazz froze. "Are you all guarded?"

"Yep," They all said at once.

"Do you feel it?" Jazz asked.

"I have felt it since I pulled in the parking lot," Breeze said.

"Can you tell where it is coming from?"

"No, but we can sure find out. Kidd cover your ears and think ONLY about the hottest chic you know. Don't stop thinking about her until I tell you."

Jazz had worked with Kidd on blocking but he had not prepared him for what was about to happen. Breeze was going to open her mind and blast thoughts out. She would shatter Kidd's barriers in mere seconds. That is why they had him covering his ears. Jazz, Matt, and Mickey were prepared for it. They would work on this additional skill later today since Kidd was leaving with them.

"Oh crap, here we go," Matt and Mickey said sarcastically.

Breeze closed her eyes, opened her mind just slightly, reopened her eyes, and screamed as loud as she could inside her head. Three cars over, a guy standing with another guy and a girl grabbed his ears and began holding his head. Breeze mentally quit screaming and closed her mind back off. Matt and Jazz high fived her.

"Bet he won't try to listen in again," Mickey chimed in.

"Doubt it. He now knows I can hear voices and others' thoughts. He will be curious now more than ever," Breeze said and turned to Kidd. "Kidd you can stop drooling now."

"You should have left him alone. Girl, always ruining our fun," Matt said.

Mickey was laughing hysterically and gasping for air at the sight of Kidd's expression. Jazz had a look of murder in his eyes.

Breeze put her hands on her hips and looked at Kidd. "I know you weren't picturing me naked." She said with attitude.

Kidd's face turned scarlet.

"Naked wouldn't have been so bad. All I can say is he has one hell of an imagination," Jazz said with a hint of irritation.

Kidd's face got even redder. "Sorry, Breeze. You said the hottest chic I know and that would be you," Kidd said through a grin.

"Boy if I were you, I would run," Mickey said in between laughs.

Kidd shook his head, even with his hands over his ears and focusing on images and other things, he still felt raddled from what had just happened. He looked over and saw Blade McGroff holding his head. He elbowed Mickey lightly and told him that was Blade that was holding his head. The only reason he even mentioned Blade's name was because it had been brought up the other day. Mickey nodded and looked at the girl near him. "Is that his sister Summer?"

"Yep. Smokin', I told you." Kidd said in a cocky tone.

Mickey looked briefly over Kidd's shoulder and Matt nodded. Their suspicions were confirmed, they had other abilities and Breeze would be here alone today. Zion and other warriors had been keeping tabs on the McGroff siblings and nothing was off. They made no mention of Breeze or even acted like they knew her name. It was determined that they were not sent here to target Breeze. In fact they had lived here for years. They moved here when Summer was two and the twins were four. How none of the family had ever seen or met them before now was a miracle.

Jazz took Breeze by the hand, and he gently touched her wrist. Mentally she heard his voice, and she responded with her mind. *"You Ok?"*

"Yes," Breeze said.

"Have the nightmares ended? Are they coming any less frequent?"

"No and No."

"Please will you let me take on some of the burden?" Jazz asked.

"You can't take any of it away," she sighed.

"You make me crazy."

"Yeah, I know, and that is why you love me."

"We will discuss this more later; you better go before you are late to class."

Jazz slid his hand off her wrist and spoke. "Do you wanna skip?"

"On my first day, would love to, but then you can explain it to my dad," Breeze said with a grin.

"Nah, I don't think Jon would be too happy with that. You better get to class." Jazz gently popped her on the butt and motioned toward the front door.

Kidd choked and swore lightly. He still was adjusting to Jazz touching Breeze all the time. The weird thing was he even did it in front of Jana and Jon, and they didn't kill him.

"I will see you all here at three today." Breeze said.

"School is out at two thirty." Kidd was still in shock over

143

Jazz, but he knew what time school ended, and it was not three.

"No joke. I have permission to use the school gym to train in both Martial Arts and Gymnastics. Before that, I was thinking about a little crumpin' and dancin'. You know I was cleared a month ago. I am at the dojo every other day; however, I need to work on my gymnastics too. What a better way?"

All the guys yelled their agreement and stated that they would be there by three. When Breeze was leaving, she walked past the guy who covered his ears and his two friends or siblings. He was cute in a bad boy kind of way; he had ash brown hair that was neatly cut, a great athletic build and stood about six feet or maybe six feet one. He didn't slouch; his posture was rigidly straight. He gave off the air of cocky, but not stuck up. She decided to make sure her test was accurate. Gently she let her guard down only enough for him to hear exactly what she wanted him to hear.

"Why were you trying to hear my thoughts?"

She heard an unfamiliar voice respond, *"I just want to know more about you."*

"Then just ask. Being inside my head will only give you a headache. Not to mention the only way you will get inside my head is IF I allow you in. Now I need to go to class, see ya. Oh, what is your name?"

"Blade McGroff."

"Nice to meet you."

Summer and Rocky were walking with Blade when Breeze walked by. They heard Blade let out a long sigh.

"What?" Summer asked.

"She has abilities," Blade said just above a whisper.

"What? No way," Summer said.

"She has my ability, plus the ability to completely block out others. I think her friends have similar abilities or something along those lines."

"How is that possible? She is not like us," Rocky stated.

"I felt pain from her when she came near us," Summer said.

"What kind of pain?" Blade asked with concern.

"I sensed trauma. Her ribs are hurting, and her left ankle is hurting as well. Why?" Summer asked casually.

Blade shrugged. He didn't want to discuss her with his siblings. There was something about her that he couldn't explain. He walked to class in a fog thinking about the new girl. He hoped that they would have at least one class together.

"Hey, what's crumpin'?" Rocky asked.

"No clue, but we will see at three today, won't we?" Blade responded.

Breeze had walked in and went straight to the office for her schedule. She remembered briefly Zion asking about Blade and Kidd talking about his sister Summer. The girl outside must have been Blade's sister. Was the guy with them a brother or a friend? It did not matter. She was in no way interested in a relationship right now. Lord have mercy! Jazz would stroke out at that thought. She sighed. She really wished he was here with her. She shook off the loneliness and went back to getting her schedule.

Breeze was a little shocked by the schedule that was handed to her but figured it was because she registered in the summer and possibly all the classes that she would normally be taking were full. She arrived in class just a couple of minutes before the bell rang. In English class, Breeze found out they were going to be reading *The Scarlet Letter*. *"Ahhh, just shoot me now. I have already read this,"* she groaned internally. Breeze felt like she was in absolute hell. She raised her hand and explained to the teacher that she needed to go to the office due to a scheduling mistake. She wasn't about to explain that this class was one of them. She was thrilled when Ms. Hall allowed her to leave. She was ready to run down the hall, but she didn't. It really wouldn't be a good thing to get detention on the first day of school. *If I don't get in AP English, I will scream. There is no way I can sit through The Scarlet Letter again.*

Thankfully, the office staff were nice and apologized for not placing her in the AP classes such as English, Spanish, Korean, and Advanced Art. Apparently her schedule had been accidentally given to another new girl. That student was in the office, too, and she was sobbing. Breeze walked over to the girl and apologized for her accidentally getting her schedule. The girl looked up at Breeze and tried to smile. Breeze stuck her hand out. "I'm Breeze. You are?"

"Whitney."

"Are you a senior?" Breeze asked. Whitney simply nodded. "Great. I will see you around. We can be new together."

"I'm not near as smart as you," Whitney said.

"I am sure you are smart in other areas. Language and culture are my thing. I need to go. Good luck," Breeze said.

Whitney seemed to relax after Breeze spoke to her. Breeze mentally heard Whitney's insecurities and the schedule mishap just sent her over the edge. Breeze walked down the hall relieved that she was going into her AP class. She had received the reading list this summer to begin reading for this class, plus the study guides to work on. Just as she was about to enter her new English class, she noticed Blade, his sister, and the guy that he was with earlier. They were all sitting in the back left side of the class.

Oh, great, this should be fun. She opened the door and walked in. The teacher turned when she heard the door open.

"Hi, Miss Lee, I was expecting you earlier," the teacher said.

"Sorry, I was given the wrong schedule," Breeze explained.

"Please take your seat in front of Miss Alexander."

Breeze thanked the teacher and took her seat. She then looked at the board for the full reading list for the first semester. There was also a note stating that the second semester reading list would be posted before they left for winter break. She was thrilled with the books listed. *Dante's Inferno* was the book listed for this week. *A book a week. This is my kind of class, an actual challenge.*

She had just sat down when she felt a light tap on her shoulder. It was Miss Alexander handing her a note, looking nervous.

"Thanks," Breeze mouthed and turned back around. She opened the folded piece of paper and read it quickly. **Can we talk like earlier? Simply nod or shake your head**. Breeze breathed in. She knew that she could listen to the lesson and talk at the same time. She and Jazz used to do it all the time back home, but she wasn't sure if she should let this person in or not, so she nodded.

"Why are you so guarded, and do your friends have similar abilities?" Blade asked.

"I'm an extreme fighter," Breeze replied simply.

"That is not why you are guarded."

"It's not?" She sighed. *"Ok, I'm guarded to simply to protect myself. As far as my friends, one has similar abilities, but it is not my place to say what they are. All of them know how to guard their minds."*

147

"Miss Lee, where in the levels of hell are rapists found?"

"Level seven, the level for the violent," Breeze said.

"Very good," Ms. Steinbeck said. She was pleased to see that this group of students had actually done their summer reading.

Blade was shocked that Breeze could communicate mentally and still fully function in class. That took real talent. *"Wait, you said you are an extreme fighter. Do you train with your father?"*

"I did until I started training in Muay Thai and kickboxing."

Breeze did not question that Blade knew of her father; most people in Jackson had heard of him, especially if they were in any martial arts.

"Aren't you worried about getting hurt?"

"No. Sore muscles get better and broken bones eventually mend. You seem fit. Do you just work out in the gym or do you study martial arts as well?" Without realizing it she reached up and touched her ribs.

"Do your ribs hurt?" Blade asked. He wasn't trying to avoid her question he was just concerned when she touched her ribs.

"Oh, UMMM, yeah, a little."

"Did you get hurt in a competition?"

"Not exactly," Breeze said.

"Well, what then?"

Breeze hesitated. *"I'd prefer not to discuss it. Besides it's time to go."*

The bell sounded and Breeze gathered her things as quickly as she could. She noticed that Blade was talking to his sister. She looked sad for some reason. Breeze also noticed that they were talking below a whisper. *Oh well...off to Spanish.* Breeze had learned a long time ago to tune out hearing everyone's thoughts. If she had her mind open all day everyday, it would sound like bees humming in her head. It would be absolute noise. She didn't care to hear all the teenage babble and drama. As she was walking she realized that Blade had not answered her question. He did seem really concerned though. She felt stupid for touching her ribs. She was feeling off today. She assumed it was her nerves and the unease of Jazz not being there with her.

The only time she completely listened to others with her mind was when she sensed trouble or when she was on assignment. If she had listened harder to Taylor, maybe she would have picked up on his intentions to try to kill her. She was thinking about what Jazz said about Kidd. She didn't need to be a telepath to know how he felt. She had known for years, but she also let him know that they couldn't be together. She made her way to her next class and found Blade near the door.

How in the world did he beat me here? He was still in class when I left the room. Who is this guy? Is he stalking me? Nah, I just met him. Plus, my instincts aren't screaming. If I trust anything, it's my instincts and Jazz. Since Jazz is out playing with the guys, my gut will do.

Breeze figured that Blade was smart to be in the advanced classes. She asked him about his classes as they walked in together. "Are all your classes AP?" she asked.

"Yeah. Yours?" Blade asked.

Breeze explained her dislike for math and chemistry. She also explained that she had four advanced classes: English, Spanish, Korean, and Advanced Art. After she ran through her schedule Blade started grinning. She thought about pushing him over; he had such an air of cockiness about him that it was irritating, and kind of cute.

" I will see you in advanced art seventh period."

"Can't wait," Breeze said and took a seat in front of Blade. He touched her mind. *"Do you want to continue talking?"*

"Sure, that is fine."

"Why are your ribs hurt?" Blade asked.

"The why is not important. I have four broken ribs and the rest are pretty bruised. I don't have time for the pain, and I will continue to train. Ok?"

"Sorry. Yeah, ok," Blade said. He was a little shocked by her irritation but respected it. Blade noticed a guy walking over to them. It seemed by his thoughts that he knew Breeze.

"Hey, Breeze, what's up girl? Wow, you look fine even when you're not at the streets," Chad said.

"Hey, Chad, I didn't realize you went to school here. It is nice to see a familiar face. Yo, you still crumpin' and dancin'?"

"Absolutely."

"Today at three, front lawn."

"I'll be there. Who else?"

"Jazz, Matt, Mickey, Kidd, and myself."

"Sounds like a party."

"You know it. Bring anyone you know who can keep up. Thirty to forty-five minutes and then I need to train. How does that sound? Let others from the streets know. I haven't seen anyone else yet, so I will let you have the honors of getting the word out." They talked cars and dance moves briefly, then Chad went back to his seat.

"What is crumpin'?" Blade asked once Chad was gone.

"Street dancin' with attitude. Would you and your friends like to watch or join in?"

150

"Sure," Blade said.

"What are your friends' names?"

"My siblings are Summer and Rocky," Blade said.

"Don't you think you should ask them first before you commit them?"

"Nah, it'll be cool."

Spanish class was extremely interactive. Breeze decided they needed to focus on the class; they could talk later. The class went quickly. Once the bell rang, she had four classes that weren't with Blade. Chemistry was well...Chemistry, and Algebra II was a bunch of numbers...*AHHHHH. Thank goodness for lunch.* Breeze grabbed a fruit salad and went to find a quiet place to sit and read. She spotted Chad, Angela, and several others sitting at a table and decided to join them; she could read later. There was a bubbly girl at the table. Her name was Wendy. Breeze thought briefly, but apparently loudly: *'Less talk and a lot more music'* because Blade started laughing. Breeze started hearing Bach in her mind and shut out everything else. *I'm really slippin'.*

Study hall was fifth, so she caught up on her reading in there. Sixth period, Korean class was great; her teacher knew her through Jazz's mom. She entered the class and spoke fluent Korean to Mr. Lu; it was hard for several of the students to keep up, and he would have to repeat the information a few times.

Breeze heard one of the students mumble something about her being a showoff, and she responded in rapid Korean and then wrote it down so the student could keep up. Mr. Lu had to step out of the room so the other student wouldn't see him laughing. If this class only knew how often she spoke this language they might rethink some of their snide comments, but she didn't need their approval and she didn't care about their opinions. *What a great first day*, Breeze thought sarcastically.

Blade was waiting when she entered their Advanced Art class. The teacher, Ms. Appleton, explained that they would have a partner for a major project. They would have three weeks, maybe a little longer, to finish the project and present it. The art would also be used for the Senior Art Show, which would be in April. Fortunately, and unfortunately, Breeze and Blade were paired up. Summer was paired up with Wendy. Breeze really felt sorry for Summer, and she hoped Summer had some earbuds so she could tune Wendy's talking out. Maybe Summer was used to it, or maybe it didn't bother her. It would make Breeze crazy if she had been paired up with her.

Breeze and Blade discussed ideas for about five or ten minutes. Blade loved Breeze's idea of including items from books that they were reading in English. He mentioned a demon from Dante's *Inferno* or something from *Beowulf*. Breeze liked all the ideas; they were all stories that she liked and could really wrap her brain around. She just wanted something that was unique and different. She expressed that desire to Blade. She didn't expect his response.

"Oh, so you want it to be like you?" Blade asked.

She pretended to fluff her spiky hair. "Exactly. Fun and Spunky. Now let's get our blueprint drawn." Her original assessment of him being cocky was shining through.

"You're funny," Blade said.

"Whatever. Let's work." Breeze knew there had to be a fun side to Blade because his sarcasm was as big as his ego. She couldn't wait to see how good of an artist he really was. She laughed a little to herself. *He may be good, but I am better.*

Blade thought he was seeing an interesting side of Breeze. It seemed that art and the discussion of books really brought a spark to her eyes. The spark of adventure as well as the possibility of learning about the past, mythological creatures, and intertwining them through reality seemed to entice Breeze. He was also interested to see how good of an artist she was. He knew she had to be good to get into this class. They both agreed to draw a blueprint and then they would work to pull them together for the project.

Blade grabbed his art supplies from the closet and began sketching out an idea. Since Breeze was new, she had her materials with her in her backpack. Once she got a feel for the class, she would bring in her tackle box with all her art supplies. She got her sketch pad out and began drawing a dragon with a castle in the background. Breeze felt funny, and then the images started flooding her. Oh, she wished Jazz was here. He could ask the right questions and guide her back. She did not need this now. *Shit.*

She reached her mind out. *"Jazz, help me, please."*

"I'm here. What is it?" The images were fast and rushed at first. *"Relax. Focus on your art. Now show me what you saw."* The images became clearer.

- **Car**
- **Taylor**
- **Taylor driving in the city limits near her mom's house**
- **Him stopping at her mom's house**
- **He knows I am not there**
- **He is on the interstate, coming here**

Jazz could feel tension coming from Breeze.

"Breeze, breathe; relax, honey. I will be in the parking lot when the bell rings. I will be there. Stay near people until you see me."

"Yeah, this time, but what about the next time he comes or when the visions start flooding in? I'm scared. I hate being this broken," Breeze said.

Jazz could feel the fear in her mind and in her words. He hated to see her like this. She reminded him of the hits that had been ordered and had been intercepted by Uncle. Jazz continued to talk to Breeze mentally and reassure her that everything was going to be ok. She knew better. Taylor was going to finish what he started. Jazz hated Taylor for everything that he was and stood for; there was no way he was going to let that creep touch her again. If he had to move in with Jon and Jana to protect her then that is what he would do. He reassured her again that he would be there waiting when the second the bell rang. He blew her a kiss mentally and told her to go back to her drawing.

Blade sat there staring at Breeze. He knew something was wrong, but he couldn't tell exactly what it was. He was concerned. He tried to touch her mind, but she was completely blocked to him and she was unwilling to let him in. He waited until she finally sighed a little.

"Breeze, are you ok?" Blade asked.

"Yeah, I'm good," Breeze said.

"You kind of zoned out and got really pale."

"I'm ok. Let me see what you have drawn."

Breeze was amazed by Blade's artistic abilities. The demon that he had drawn was incredibly detailed. He had also drawn a castle in his sketch, however it seemed to be built at strange angles like it was leaning or had a magic mirror effect. It was interesting. Breeze was also impressed at how Blade had finished that much in less than an hour. It was pure genius. Blade was as impressed with Breeze's art as much as she was with his. When he saw the sketch of the dragon it seemed to be alive, it was as if it was breathing. The scales were each evenly spaced; there was so much order to them. Blade didn't get the feeling that was who she was as a person, but what did he know? He had just met her.

"Do you think we can build these?" Breeze asked.

The excitement at the challenge was already building inside of her. She couldn't wait to start on this project. She was thinking about the materials that they had in the workshop, and she thought everything they needed was in there, but she would double check when she got home.

"Sure," Blade said with confidence.

Breeze rubbed her hands together with excitement. "Great, I will see what I can do this evening, and then we can work on it in here daily or you could come over to my house and work on it. My parents won't mind."

Blade was shocked that she would invite him over since she had just met him, but they were partners on a project. It made sense to work on it outside of school to finish it on time.

"Bring in what you can tomorrow. Once we figure out the dimensions, then we can figure out how much time we need and if we will have to work on it outside of class or not."

Blade smiled at her. He was about to say something when the teacher told them to put up their supplies. He looked at the clock in shock. Breeze quickly put her supplies back in her bag. She wrote down her address and phone number and handed it to Blade just as the bell rang. He put it in his pocket.

SET BACK

The bell rang for the end of the day. Blade was disappointed. The class felt like it ended too quickly. He wanted to talk with her more and get to know her. He knew once she left for the day that he wouldn't see her until tomorrow in English class. Breeze interrupted his train of thought.

"Are you ready to see some crumpin'?"

"Yes."

"I need to change. I'll be out soon," Breeze said.

Breeze changed into some cute gray shorts and a halter top under a decorative cropped t-shirt, and then she threw on her tennis shoes. When she walked out, all her boys were sitting on Matt's hood.

"Holy crap, girl," Kidd yelled. Matt elbowed him.

"Mickey, you bring the music?" Breeze asked.

"Sure enough; Girl, you know I'd never let you down," Mickey said.

"Let's hear what you got," Breeze said.

'Imma Be' by the Black Eye Peas started playing; about ten seconds into the song, techno started mixing with the beats and a little bit of reggae. Jazz got up. Breeze ran toward him as he cupped his hands and threw her in the air. Breeze flipped three times and landed. She turned, stepped in his hand, and climbed up to his shoulder and pushed off. They were both in the air tumbling. Chad and Angela started dancing. Kidd was in the grass jumping and spinning.

Chad, Matt, Mickey, Kidd, Jazz, and Breeze all stopped instantly to look at their phones. About fifteen other people dancing did the same thing. Apparently, a text had come through. They all high-fived, smiled big, and went right back to what they were doing. Four more songs played. There were so many people dancin' and crumpin', it was great. Rocky and Summer joined in. Blade stood off to the side and watched. He couldn't take his eyes off Breeze. He saw Breeze and her friends start to slip off, but before they got too far, Chad said, "See you at the streets."

"Absolutely, we will be there," Matt said.

"Yeah, I got something new to show off," Breeze said.

"Uh oh, our girl is holding out on us," Kidd said with a laugh.

"Will you take care of all that?" Breeze asked and pointed to the crowd that was dancing.

Chad nodded and walked off. The five made their way to the gym. Blade continued to watch Breeze and her friends until they were no longer in sight. He decided that he would try some crumpin'; it was actually fun. No one was paying attention if you were good or not, it was all about having fun and feeling the beats.

Jazz, Kidd, Breeze, Matt, and Mickey walked into the gym. Breeze hit the lights.

"What's the plan?" Jazz asked.

"One hour of Muay Thai, no holding back. One hour of gymnastics with you guys spotting." While talking, she took off the t-shirt and tossed it. She was wearing her halter top and was in total work out mode.

"Are you sure that you're ready for that? Your ribs aren't healed and that ankle isn't much better." Jazz was seriously concerned. He couldn't bear to see her hospitalized again.

"Are you here to help or lecture?"

"Fine. You can explain it to your dad when you're back in the hospital," Jazz said.

"Fine."

"Is that a tat?" Kidd squeaked with a huge grin.

Kidd was bouncing with excitement. He was the most fun-loving person you would ever meet even though he came from a crappy home. He reminded Breeze a lot like Shaggy from Scooby-Doo. He was adorably cute. Kidd absolutely loved Breeze in so many ways. He had wished more than once that he had her parents since they were so cool. He had always wanted a tattoo, but he would have to wait until he had a job, could pay for it and was on his own. His grin was infectious.

Breeze grinned. "Yep, my mom got it for me for my sixteenth birthday. I thought you knew. I mean hello, the streets."

"Awesome. I knew you were planning to get one, but when we were at the streets I hadn't noticed," Kidd said.

Mickey clucked his tongue at Kidd in a disgusted manner with a how could you not notice expression. Matt started laughing when Kidd flipped Mickey off. Breeze just rolled her eyes at them both. She turned her attention back to Jazz.

"Jazz, will you help me tape my ribs and my ankle?"

"Yes," Jazz said with a hint of anger and frustration.

"Look, you can help me train, or I'll do it myself. Which do you prefer? Make your decision because I don't have time to wait," Breeze said.

"I'll help. I'm just concerned."

"Don't be."

Jazz, Kidd, and Breeze sparred for the full hour. First it was Jazz and Breeze. Second it was Breeze and Kidd. Third it was Jazz and Kidd. Finally, it was two on one, Breeze being the one.

"Thanks, guys. That was great. Now you guys rest and spot me when I need it."

She rested for about ten minutes and drank some water. Breeze felt alive and more like her old self. She missed training like this. Matt and Mickey helped drag out mats and set up the uneven parallel bars. Mickey started the music once Breeze stepped on the mat. It was the same upbeat stuff they danced to earlier. "Perfect," Breeze said.

Breeze practiced her floor routine twice and then decided to work on her uneven parallel bars routine. Jazz and Kidd were there. Jazz lifted her to the first bar. All was going well until she released from the low bar to the high bar; she missed and hit the mat face first. Her ribs screamed in protest. She was seeing stars. She heard feet running toward her. Breeze held up her hand. "I'm fine, I just need a minute," she said.

"No. You are done," Jazz insisted.

"No, I'm not. You chose to stay. Now, shut it."

"Fine," Jazz growled in frustration.

Breeze finally got up. Jazz walked over to her, touched her waist, and pulled her to him. He ran his arm down hers and gently held her wrist in his hand. Mentally she heard his voice. *Do you need my blood?*

"Not right now. Matt, Mickey, and Kidd would freak. That is just one of many secrets that we can never share with them or have

159

exposed," Breeze said.

"*Later?*" He asked.

"*Maybe,*" she said.

"*Ok. You scare me, you know that?*"

With a cocky grin she said, "*Yeah, I know. Now spot me.*" Jazz moved and the connection was broken. He kissed her forehead and returned to the bleachers with the guys.

Twice Breeze did the routine flawlessly. The third time she was feeling exhaustion but she decided to continue. Low bar to high bar release – perfect. The next release, from high bar to low, she completely missed and landed extremely hard face down. It hurt to breathe; there was blood, and she could smell it. She could hear Jazz faintly. Kidd was running. Everything was foggy and sluggish.

"The ambulance is on the way," Kidd said.

In her mind she was screaming, "*No,*" but nothing was coming from her mouth. She was tired and gave in to the darkness. She heard a familiar voice.

"*Breeze stay with me, I can't see you laid up again,*" Jazz said.

"*I'm here, I'm not going anywhere,*" Breeze said.

"*I called your dad.*"

"*What? Why? I'm fine, just let me regroup.*"

"*No, you are not. You have been out for five minutes. The ambulance is here,*" Jazz said.

"*No. No hospital,*" Breeze insisted.

Their connection was broken by the EMTs working on her. The ride to the hospital was agonizing for her. She couldn't imagine being back in the hospital. Once there she heard her father and Jana enter the room.

"Honey, are you ok?" Jana asked.

"Yes."

"You are pushing too hard," Jon said. He had worry all over his face. Jana's face looked just as anxious as her dad's did.

"No, I'm not. I have a big competition in four months, remember, in Thailand," Breeze said.

"Sorry, Sweetie, you might not be going to Thailand. We will have to see what the doctor says," Jon said.

"What? No. I have worked too hard for this." Breeze said.

"There is always next year or the year after," Jon said. His only concern was his daughter and her well being. He knew the competition meant the world to her, but he would not risk losing her.

"Haven't you always told me to follow my dreams? Now you're telling me no. WTH?"

"Honey, your father isn't telling you not to follow your dreams. We both think your injuries are worse than we originally believed," Jana said with a grim expression.

"AHHHHH. That SOB, I hate him. How could he do this to me? How?" Breeze demanded. She slung her head back in frustration and looked at the ceiling.

A man looking about thirty-five or forty entered the room while Breeze was ranting. He gave Breeze and her parents a weak smile. "Hi. I'm Dr. David McGroff. Breeze, upon looking at your x-rays I will say, you are an incredibly lucky young woman."

"Lucky. How do you figure that?" Breeze asked with a lot of attitude. Lucky did not describe how she felt. Pissed was more like it.

"You are still alive." Dr. McGroff explained.

"Alive but BROKEN, so broken it's not even funny. Just tell me the damage." Her anger and frustration were causing her to be ruder than she would typically be to an adult. She didn't care at the moment. She just wanted to get out of the hospital as quickly as possible.

"Mr. and Mrs. Lee, may I speak with Breeze for a few minutes? Then I will call you back in to explain everything," Dr. McGroff said.

"Sure," Jon and Jana said.

"Thank you." Dr. McGroff waited for Jon and Jana to leave the room. He spoke barely above a whisper. "Breeze, I have reviewed your file from when you were hospitalized after the incident, and you have been through some serious trauma. I know it has only been three months. That is not near enough time for your body to heal completely. Can you please look at me?"

Breeze stopped looking at the ceiling and turned her head to face the doctor. She was trying hard not to cry or scream; she just wanted to go home, and she didn't want to discuss the accident that put her in the hospital in the first place.

"When you said you were broken, you didn't mean just physically, did you?" Tears started streaming down her face, and she gently shook her head no. "Breeze, the incident that placed you in the hospital, it was domestic, correct?" She nodded yes. "Did you know that you have some internal bleeding going on?" Dr. McGroff asked. The fear on her face told him all he needed to know. "Ok. I'm surprised County General did not catch it. Maybe when you fell, it caused an old injury to reopen, but I don't think so. Have your cycles been more painful and heavier than normal since the incident?" Slowly she nodded. The words internal bleeding just kept repeating in her mind. She was scared in a way that she hadn't been before. The tears just kept coming. "That's what I thought. We need to bring your family back in."

Gently she reached up and touched his arm. "Doctor, am I dying?"

Dr. McGroff lightly patted her hand. "No. It is just going to take you awhile before you are un-broken. Does your father know that you were...?"

"No. Please don't tell him. Not even my mother knew. The doctors told me of my loss when she wasn't in the room at County General. I don't need my family thinking bad of me, especially now," she said with a sigh and a sob.

"I think if they knew that it might help you heal faster, but that is for you to tell them that and not me."

"Sir, is your son Blade?"

"Yes."

"Can you please not tell him, Summer, or Rocky? I really don't want them to think badly of me, either. I know I just met them, but it is nice to have friends that don't know of the accident."

"No problem. I don't normally take my work home with me."

"Thank you." Tears were streaming down her face.

"Let's get your family." Dr. McGroff gently placed his hand on her shoulder and gave it a light squeeze. It was a sign of reassurance. Breeze was grateful for a doctor with bedside manners, but she just wanted to be healed and go home. It had already been three grueling months.

"And Jazz, please," Breeze said.

"I will ask your father if that is ok."

Breeze knew her dad would allow Jazz in, ultimately it was her decision since she was eighteen, however she didn't need to push that issue. When they entered the room, Jazz moved to the opposite side of the bed and held her hand. Tears were still streaming down her face. Jazz kissed her cheek lightly.

"Ok. There are numerous injuries that we need to discuss. There are four broken ribs, and all the others are still badly bruised. Her pelvic bone is fractured. Her hip is fractured. Her left ankle has a hairline fracture. Her right wrist is also fractured. Those are all mending so there is no need to re-break them, place pins in them or anything like that. I do want her ribs taped for two weeks. Her ankle and her wrist also need to be taped between two to three weeks; the only time the tape is to be off is when she bathes. Now, we need to discuss a more serious issue," Dr. McGroff explained.

"A more serious issue? What?" Jazz asked. He looked down at Breeze and held her hand tighter.

"There is some internal bleeding that needs to be discussed," Dr. McGroff continued.

The room erupted in frantic discussions. Internal bleeding had not been mentioned previously. Jon looked pale when he was talking to the doctor. Everything Breeze had been through was flooding back to him. His thoughts were becoming cloudy. Jana lightly touched Jon's arm.

"Mr. Lee, County General did the absolute best they could do. Yes, they probably missed it. To be honest they were trying to save her life, and they did that. Since a good portion of the injuries have healed and a lot of the swelling has gone down, it is now easier to see this injury. There is a slight tear between her ovary and fallopian tube on the right side. It can be repaired through an outpatient procedure called a laparoscopy. We would use a laser to fix the affected area. I would really prefer not to wait; however, she would need to be out of school for seven days. Even though it is an outpatient procedure, we would have to tilt her body and place a gas in her to expand her abdomen so we could see all the organs. The gas does cause discomfort after the procedure. This is the reason for the seven-day restriction, and if we do it today, she could go back to school next Wednesday. Her follow up appointment would be next Tuesday. I will call the school first thing tomorrow morning and have home bound arranged for the week so she won't miss any days or any class work. I will step out so you can discuss it."

"There is no need. We will do the procedure today," Jon said.

"Dad, don't I get a say?" Breeze asked through her tears and sobs.

"Honey, you can't let this go on. You need the procedure," Jon insisted.

"Dr. McGroff, will this affect me in the future when I decide that I want to have children?" Breeze asked.

"I don't think so, but only time will tell."

New tears started. Jazz touched her wrist and touched her mind. *"Breeze have the procedure. I will help you heal,"* Jazz *begged her.*

"You don't understand. I hate that SOB; he has taken so much from me. I hate him."

"I know. I hate him, too," Jazz said.

"I need to ask the doctor one more thing."

"Doctor, will I be able to compete in four months in Thailand? I just received clearance a month ago to begin training again. When will I be able to train again after this procedure?"

Dr. McGroff looked at Breeze. He could see the hope in her eyes. He knew that mentally what he was about to tell her would probably cause her a huge set back, and he hated it, but professionally, he had no choice.

"Breeze, I am sorry, I don't see you competing in Thailand in four months. You are on medical restriction for six to eight weeks. I am sorry."

Breeze slung her head back in a frustrated gesture. "Let's do the stupid procedure." She started sobbing uncontrollably. "I HATE HIM. I HATE HIM," Breeze yelled.

Jazz whispered in her ear. "I love you, and I will help you heal."

"Jazz, can you step out with her parents so we can prep her for surgery?" Once the family was out of the room Dr. McGroff began administering her IV. He spoke to her while he got her ready for surgery. "It looks like he really cares about you."

"He's my best friend."

"I see love in his eyes."

"He's my best friend, so of course he loves me. I don't deserve him," Breeze said.

"Sure, you do. This was not your fault," Dr. McGroff explained.

"I should have fought harder."

"You fought and you survived. You ready?" he asked.

"No, but let's go. Wait. Can I see Jazz quickly?"

"You had better hurry before the medicine kicks in." Dr. McGroff left the room and motioned for Jazz to come back.

Jazz quickly followed the doctor. He could feel Breeze's frustration and anxiety regarding the surgery. It made him anxious as well. Jazz entered the room. "Touch my wrist," she told him softly. She touched his mind. *"Go to the streets tonight, please. Win for me. Bring back a pink slip or two."*

"No way, I'm staying with you," Jazz said.

166

"Please. Take Kidd; he is really good. Besides, I have a week at home, so you get all my attention since you don't start school for another week, plus you can help me with my art. I really could use a new bike and maybe a new car. Get the guys and go for me," Breeze said.

"Ok, for you. I don't like it, but ok. I will win you a pink slip or two. If you need me, just call out with your mind."

Breeze paused for a moment. She knew what she wanted, but she felt that she didn't deserve it. Jazz was so good. She bit her lower lip with uncertainty. Jazz stroked her wrist to ease her anxiety. She sighed slightly and then spoke. *"Hey. Tomorrow when we are alone, can you help me heal?"*

"I thought you'd never ask." Jazz was relieved that she had finally asked. *"Good night. I see the fog moving in."*

"Hey. One more thing, work with Kidd on guarding when I cast out."

"Already taken care of. Oh, he is observant," Jazz said.

"What?" she asked.

"Later."

"Promise?" she asked as the darkness moved in.

She didn't like the darkness; too many things came to her there. Jazz kissed her forehead and gently laid her arm on the bed and stepped out of the room. When he walked into the lobby he saw Jana sitting with Kidd. Jana was reassuring Kidd that Breeze would be going home after the procedure was complete; she would not have to stay in the hospital overnight. Kidd was rattled. Jazz understood fully. Jazz motioned to the guys, spoke briefly to Jana and Jon. The four got ready to leave when the guy from her school walked in and spoke to them. Jazz was having second thoughts about going, but he told Breeze he would. *Damn it. She makes me crazy.*

As the darkness closed in around Breeze, she could see a battle going on. *"Tell my sister I love her, please, tell her,"* a young soldier said.

Breeze decided it was time to stop ignoring the visions and time to start listening. She would even begin helping if she could; it didn't matter what her mother thought. She wasn't crazy, she was a Seer and a Telepath, and she was going to embrace those gifts and all of her other little glitches. *"What is your sister's name? What is your name?"*

"You mean you will tell her?"

"I will," Breeze said.

"Her name is Mary Adler. I am SFC Charles D. Smith. Tell her that I love her and tell her to look in the back of her old closet at Mama's for the jewelry box. There is something special inside it. We are from Charleston, SC. Thank you, Ma'am." The vision faded.

Note to self: I need a notebook to keep a journal for information like this. Also ask the doctor about racing. Remember to stay guarded; don't need any ease droppers listening in. HEE-HEE. I feel funny.

"Breeze can you hear me? I need you to open your eyes. The surgery is over. You are in the recovery room. Please open your eyes for me." Dr. McGroff was talking to her while checking her pulse. She slowly started coming around.

"Hey, there; how do you feel?" a friendly nurse asked.

"Like I have been hit by a big train," Breeze said.

"You are so full of personality, aren't you?" Blade asked.

Breeze jumped slightly. She almost thought she was dreaming, but she was fairly sure that she was awake.

"What the hell?" she asked in shock.

Breeze turned her head to try to see Blade. She heard him

168

laugh and tilted her head up so she could look back toward the door. He was standing there leaning against the doorframe with his arms crossed. She groaned.

"Nice to see you, too. I was still at the school helping Chad when the ambulance arrived. Matt and Kidd said you were unconscious and bleeding. When I got here everyone was in the waiting room. Your dad said you were in surgery having a procedure done. Jazz told me to tell you that he would fulfill both for you. Then your friends left. I asked your dad if I could see you when you came to, and he said it was ok. Chad was here earlier, too. He said to tell you, 'Bummer about tonight; maybe in a few days.'

"Ahhh, they're my boys," Breeze said with a croaky voice.

"Breeze, you will be in recovery for about forty-five more minutes. Are you ok with Blade being in here with you?" Dr. McGroff asked. Breeze nodded. Dr. McGroff turned to face his son. "Blade, you know the rules with recovery," Dr. McGroff said.

"Yes, sir," Blade said. He walked over from the door, got a chair, slid it over near the bed, and sat down.

The doctor and the two nurses left the room. Blade started laughing. Breeze's emotions were all over the place. She didn't know if it was the drugs in her system or truly her own feelings. She was confused as to why Blade would feel the need to come to the hospital to check on her. She had just met him for heaven's sake. Breeze's thoughts were interrupted by Blade talking to her.

"You know you are so funny."

"What are you talking about?" she asked as she was trying to shake the fog from the meds.

"You even have an attitude when you are unconscious. You

169

would say, 'I'm guarded, come back another day.' One time your friend Jazz popped into the message and you two were rapping, 'We're guarded. We're guarded. Come back another day or don't come back at all.' See Attitude."

"That is too funny. That was something we did probably four years ago. At least it was effective," Breeze said.

Blade slid his chair closer to Breeze's bedside. He gently touched her arm, but he accidentally touched her wrist. There was something like a jolt of electricity that ran through his body, and he saw bright scattered images.

- Blood
- Cars
- A knife
- Breeze screaming and begging.
- More blood
- Then he felt a tear through his chest, neck, and cheek.

Breeze moved her arm and Blade sat in shock. "What the hell?" he asked.

"Sorry."

"Don't I get something more than sorry? What was all that?"

"Memories, nightmares, and I wasn't completely guarded when you touched my wrist. It is a glitch, so to say."

"A glitch? Those images were so bright. Was that all your blood from your incident?"

Breeze did not want to be having this discussion. She was hoping that she could change the subject and not focus on what Blade had just seen. "Why do you and your dad call it an incident and not an accident?"

"The guy who hurt you didn't accidentally do this did he?

170

It is more of an incident than an accident."

"What do you know?" she asked with irritation.

Blade was not backing down. She needed to discuss those images. "Summer could sense pain in you. In English you held your ribs, and when I asked you about it, you were vague. Normally that means a person is protecting someone or something. I know if it was related to martial arts, you would have said so. Now, were those images from the incident?" Blade demanded.

"Most of them, yes. Some were not."

He could feel his anger building. He didn't know Breeze, but he hated any man who would place his hands on a woman. Blade pressed forward. "I felt a cut across my chest, neck, and my cheek. Did he cut you?"

"Yes."

"Is that what the scar on your face and neck are from?"

"Yes. I had plastic surgery for the cut on my chest; however, my face was too swollen at the time and the one on my neck is too close to an artery. Can we change the station, please?"

"One more question."

"What?" she said through gritted teeth.

"Where is he now?"

"He is on his way here," Breeze said with absolute conviction.

"What?" There was tension in Blade's voice when he asked the question.

Breeze felt the tension in his voice, but she couldn't understand why. He didn't know her. "Well, he was a few hours ago, anyway."

Blade couldn't believe that all her friends had left if they knew this piece of information. Everything that Blade had seen of her friends said that they would jump in front of a train for her. Did she not tell them, and if not, why? He was confused and angry. He was having an internal struggle. The complexity of the whole situation perplexed him. One thing was for certain - she had more abilities than just mind reading.

"Did he call you?" Blade asked.

"No."

"How?"

"Another glitch," she insisted.

"You saw it?"

"Yes. Are you always so nosy and persistent? ENOUGH." Breeze's frustration was apparent in her tone, but Blade also felt the tension in the air.

"Ok," Blade said and held his hands up in surrender.

Breeze laid back on her pillow and took in as deep a breath as she could without screaming in pain. *Why did he have to see those things? Why does he care where Taylor is? I just want to sleep without any nightmares or visions. Just one night would be nice. Maybe once I see Jazz. I want Taylor to go away and leave me alone. As long as he is texting, calling, and stalking me, the longer I will be broken.* A tear slid down her cheek. She flicked it away.

"You ok?" Blade asked.

"Yeah."

"I'm sorry I upset you."

"No biggie. More upset with myself than anything," she said.

Blade was determined to not let the evening end on such a sour note. "How many... ummm... glitches do you have?"

"Too many," Breeze started laughing. "Ouch, Owwww,

Ouch. That hurts worse than breathing."

Blade couldn't believe that she was hurting this bad after he had seen her dance earlier in the day. "How come when you were crumpin' and dancing you weren't screaming in pain?"

"I blocked it and ignored it mostly," she said.

"Hey, what are we going to do about our art project?" Blade asked.

Breeze grinned her famous Cheshire cat grin. "No worries. I've got it covered," Breeze said.

"If you think you are doing it alone, then you have lost your mind," Blade said.

"You mean more than normal?"

"I've known you a day. What exactly is your normal?"

Breeze was laughing and gasping in pain. She felt Jazz's mental nudge and saw a big smile on his face. *"What's up?"* Breeze asked.

"Kidd just won against Ice on bikes. Matt just won a pink slip. Oh yeah I've won two slips and you a nice pretty red bike, already souped and juiced," Jazz said.

"You ROCK."

"Is that guy still there?"

"Yes. His name is Blade. Relax."

"Yeah," Jazz said, a little annoyed.

"Don't go getting pissy. Hey, can you be at the house tomorrow at eight in the morning? Jana is supposed to work, and I think she feels she needs to stay home with me because of me having this procedure. I'd rather stay home with you."

"Yeah, I'll be there with your pink slip in hand and my blood in my veins. Ha-ha."

"Ouch. Crap. Don't make me laugh," Breeze said.

"You'd better not have me over, because you will be laughing

173

until you pee yourself."

"You are so stupid...ouch." She took a breath. *"See you tomorrow."*

"Why don't I come over tonight? I could sleep until six, slip out and be back by eight."

"Yeah, right. What if you get caught? No way."

"Please. Where's your sense of adventure?"

"Hey. I could ask my dad. It wouldn't be the first time you stayed.

"Not since our last trip."

She smiled. *"Hey, he knows nothing can happen."*

"Ok. Ask, but if he says no, I'm coming through the window. Deal?"

"Deal. I'll text you."

"Ok. See you soon." (Their connection ended)

Blade sat there watching Breeze. Her eyes were open, and her facial expressions were changing, but she wasn't talking. He took in every facial expression with great care for understanding. He realized that something was going on. Her expressions were that of someone having a serious dream or an intent conversation. He was worried that she was seeing something else about Taylor.

"Breeze, why are you so quiet?" Blade asked.

"Oh, umm, just thinking."

"I said your forty-five minutes are almost up, and you will be going home soon."

"Great. Hey, do you have any other glitches?"

"Nope. No other glitches," he said with a smile. *Other secrets, hell, yeah but no other glitches.* Blade thought the last part to himself and that part of his thoughts was completely blocked off.

Breeze's family came into the room with the doctor. Blade slid the chair back and stood when they entered. Dr. McGroff explained her discharge orders. Home bound services would begin tomorrow. Blade volunteered to get all her assignments from the teachers and get her books. He said he would drop them off tomorrow right after school. Breeze waited until Blade had left the room and she was waiting on the nurse with the wheelchair to ask her dad about Jazz.

"Hey Dad, I know you and Jana both have to work tomorrow, and I don't want you to worry about me. How would you feel about Jazz staying at the house tonight and with me tomorrow?" Jon gave her a questioning look, but before he could answer, Jana spoke softly.

"He does watch over her," Jana said.

"You are correct, he does make sure she is safe and if anything was to happen, I know he would call us straight away." Jon sighed. "I guess." He was having thoughts of their last adventure, not about something happening between them. Hell, if they took off again, they may not find them for a year, if ever.

"Thanks, Dad, I will text him and let him know." She grabbed her cell.

Breeze: Cool. Come when can.

Jazz: On way now

Breeze : K. Bring clothes and stuff

Jazz: And stuff?

Breeze: Pink slip and keys

Jazz: Ohhh. That.

Breeze: What about bike?

Jazz: Matt's garage

Breeze: Cool.

Breeze sat her phone down. Jon stepped out, and Jana helped her get dressed. She was sore and thankful that Jana helped her. The nurse entered with the wheelchair and rolled her to Jana's Escalade. Jazz arrived about twenty minutes after Breeze and her parents arrived home. He was surprised to see her in the living room and it was set up for her to sleep there instead of in her bedroom.

She saw his questioning look and laughed. "Ouch. In here is better than my room because of the stairs, at least for a couple of days."

Jazz was shocked to see how pale she was. He did not like that, but he would take care of that tomorrow. "Dang, girl, did they take all of your blood? You are awfully pale."

"Just tired," Breeze said.

"Nightmares again?"

"Yes, and then some. Speaking of which, I need a spiral notebook. I've decided to listen and help if I can."

Jazz shook his head. He had been trying for years to get her just to accept who she was and see what all the spirits wanted. He was shocked in a way, but this was Breeze; anything was possible. "Dang, I leave you for a few hours and you have some type of revelation or something."

"Oh. Speaking of revelations, Blade got a jolt."

Jazz stood straight and looked at Breeze. "What happened?"

Breeze explained the situation. "His first question, besides what the hell, was, 'was all that your blood?'"

"What all did you tell him?"

"Not much. He knows I am a telepath; we have talked with our minds in class. I simply told him it was one of my glitches. He asked where Taylor was now, and I told him on the way here. When he realized I hadn't spoken to him, he asked if I saw it. We changed the subject after that."

Jazz was shocked that Breeze would even say that much to a stranger or someone that she had just met that day, especially about the visions. That was something that she kept guarded from most people. She had never even told Matt and Mickey that she had visions. They simply accepted that she knew things. "He didn't get freaked out?"

"No actually, the opposite. He was more curious or interested than anything else."

"I don't like it," Jazz said and walked over to the couch. He sat on the floor in front of her and stroked her arm.

"I know. Shhh. My gut says it's ok."

"Your gut. Oh, hell, then I really don't like it."

"You know I am going to go crazy for six to eight weeks. I guess I will be at Matt's a lot. I wonder how many cars we can build."

"Oh, dear, we better call Matt and tell him to add on."

"Ouch, would you stop making me laugh. I'm really tired. The meds are kicking my butt. Your sleeping bag and pillow are on the floor. You ok with that, or do you want my room?"

"This is good. I will see you in the morning."

Jazz was sound asleep when he heard Breeze scream at the top of her lungs. Jon and Jana came running into the room. Breeze was thrashing, kicking, and screaming. "No, damn it, I won't let you. Get the hell away. I'm done, it's over, get out." Another blood curdling scream and tears were streaming down her face. Jazz and Breeze's parents were frozen. Breeze screamed again and she grabbed her throat. "No. No."

Jazz ran to her side. Gently he touched her hand, and the other arm touched her wrist. A violent jolt ran through him. He saw Taylor choking her and pounding her head; she was bleeding horribly. There was blood everywhere. Her tears even looked like they were bleeding. Jazz focused on calming his breathing and started talking softly to Breeze.

"Breeze, sweetheart, I'm here. He will <u>NEVER</u> hurt you again. Come back to me. It is only a nightmare, nothing more. Please, Breeze, for me."

The thrashing and kicking were becoming less, and the screaming had stopped. She was drenched in sweat. She had never shared any of those images with him, not even in the hospital. She was guarded the whole time. This procedure must have really shaken her. Jon and Jana walked over to the couch and started gently talking to her. The thrashing and kicking finally stopped after about ten minutes of them talking to her.

"Does she do that often?" Jazz asked with tears gently rolling down his cheeks.

"We have heard thrashing around every now and then, but never screaming," Jon said.

"She didn't scream like that even at the hospital. I really think the procedure today just brought everything flooding back," Jazz said while he was stroking Breeze's hair and holding her hand.

"Please don't go," Breeze whispered.

"I'm not going anywhere." Jazz didn't care that her parents were in the room; he slipped the covers back, gently lifted her head and back, and slid behind her. He wrapped his arms around her and whispered in her ear, "I'm here and I'm not going anywhere. Sleep, I have you."

Jon looked pale and in shock. Jana took Jon's hand. "She is safe now. Let's go back to bed."

"I can't believe that SOB hurt her so badly. Jana, I swear if I ever see him again, I will make him pay."

"I don't think you are the only one who would like to get their hands on him." Jana shifted her gaze to Jazz. He was still silently crying, but he was holding and soothing Breeze. Breeze had no idea how much he truly hurt when he saw her like that.

I wonder why Breeze won't give Jazz a chance. Is she afraid of destroying her friendship with him? Does she not realize that their friendship could make the relationship even greater? I will talk with her after Jazz goes home from break. She deserves someone who accepts her for who she is. Jana quickly cleared her thoughts and led Jon back to their room.

When Jazz knew that Jana and Jon were back to sleep, he leaned down and gently kissed Breeze's cheek. She mumbled sleepily, "What's up Jazz?"

"I swear to you that he will never hurt you again."

"You are an hour away once you go back home, so that is not something you can guarantee. Even if you were here, you couldn't guarantee it. I have a feeling that he will try sooner rather than later, simply because I am weak now."

"We will fix that as soon as everyone leaves tomorrow. I should have insisted when you left the hospital the last time."

"You did insist."

"Obviously not hard enough."

Jazz stroked her back and continued to speak soothing words to her. He was speaking Korean, soft lulling words. She got goosebumps and blushed slightly. Thankfully it was dark and he couldn't see her blushing. *"Breeze, I'll be here all night, holding you. Sleep, I mean truly sleep, shut out all the nightmares and visions, I have you. Tomorrow we will work on your speedy recovery."* Breeze snuggled into Jazz's arms and quickly fell asleep.

COMFORT

For the absolute first time in God knows how long, she slept like a rock. When she woke up, it was eight thirty in the morning. Jazz was still asleep; she could hear his breathing in her ear. She didn't want to get up, but she really needed to. Jazz moved slightly like he was stirring. His mouth was on her ear nibbling, and he started laughing.

"Everyone left about an hour ago. I have had to pee like a Russian racehorse for about that long but didn't want to wake you, but now MOVE."

"Oh, what if I tickle you?" Breeze teased.

"I will piss all over you and your couch."

Breeze was laughing while she let Jazz get up. Once Jazz got back, he helped her up and helped her walk to the bathroom door.

"Can you grab me some baggy clothes? Like a T and some simple, loose gray shorts?"

"Who are you getting sexy for?" Jazz asked.

"Aren't you going to help me heal? I thought I could at least try to look better than roadkill for you." Breeze said.

"Girl, if you only knew. Hey, do you own any baggy clothes?"

"Yes, I own baggy clothes. Skimpy is for the streets." She

gave him a sly smile and closed the bathroom door.

Jazz went to her room to get her stuff. He sat on her bed for a moment and sighed. She had been through so much; it truly was a wonder that she survived. *I will get her to talk, even if it kills me.* Jazz simply cracked the bathroom door and laid her clothes on the counter, closed the door, and waited. When she came out, she had her hair in its normal wild-yet-styled look. Besides moving a little slowly, she looked wonderful. "Turtle," Jazz teased.

"Shut the hell up."

"Make me."

"I may be slow, but I can still kick your ass." Breeze tried hard to look serious when she said it.

"In your dreams, sweetheart."

"I'm hungry. You cooking?" Breeze asked.

"Yeah, right. I can cook you up a big bowl of cereal and a cup of whoop-ass stew," Jazz laughed.

"Cereal sounds great, but I was thinking of Jazz a' la carte," Breeze teased.

"It's good to see your sense of humor back."

"Yeah, that's me: Good Ole Smart Ass," Breeze joked back.

"Let's eat."

"You eat. I'll nibble."

"What is up with you? You act like a Kat on the prowl," Jazz laughed while he poured his bowl of cereal.

"Not a Kat on the prowl… I'm a Breeze on the prowl."

"You know I could take that the wrong way," Jazz said with a smirk.

"Take it how you will. Now pass the Capt'n Crunch." The two ate their cereal. Once they finished, they went into the living room. "Jazz, are you sure you are ok with helping me

182

heal?"

"Breeze, come on, you know I don't mind. Hell, you could ask when you don't need to heal. You know I love the rush we both get."

"I love it, too. That is why I hate to ask. It feels too good."

"You should ask more often," Jazz insisted.

"I'm asking now," Breeze said softly.

Jazz gently scooped her up in his arms and carried her upstairs to her room.

"You know I'm going to have to bite you where no one will see the marks."

He nodded. They spoke briefly about the location of her biting him. Once the location was decided, desire flooded him. It had been so long since she had drunk from him. Every nerve in his body was awake and screaming for Breeze.

"You've never bit me on my upper thigh before."

"I know, which should make the rush even greater," Breeze said.

Every time she drank, he had thoughts of making her his mate. *Lordy, lordy what he wouldn't give.* They both knew she couldn't kill him from drinking, nor could he kill her. If a full vamp bit either of them, they weren't sure what would happen.

She drank until she was dizzy. When she finished drinking, they were hot, sweaty, and breathless. Jazz pulled her in his arms and held her.

"Wow," Breeze sighed with satisfaction. It had been too long since she drank because she was feeling the full affects.

"You know that is going to leave a mark, a real pretty bruise."

"Complaining?" Breeze asked.

"Never."

183

Breeze was giddy. Jazz laughed, it was like Breeze was intoxicated, and in a way, she was, but in a legal sense.

"You know if you go to the doctor on Monday with not even a scratch let alone a fracture, the good ole doc might think something."

"Whatever. Don't care," Breeze said with attitude.

"Silly girl, what am I going to do with you?" They laid there talking and cutting up.

"Hey, you know your teacher will be here at one."

"Crap. I forgot all about school. Ok, you eat while I gather my art stuff. You know I really do want you to drink from me before you leave. It always seems to make our connection stronger."

"After that, if our connection was any stronger, you would feel it if I farted." Jazz was laughing hysterically. Breeze rolled her eyes.

They both stopped instantly when they heard the doorbell ringing. They both looked at her alarm clock; it was only eleven in the morning. Fear shot through Breeze. Jazz jumped up, dressed, and ran down the steps. Breeze saw his posture and knew he was ready to fight. Breeze was on the steps when he reached the foyer and slung open the door. Jazz's posture changed.

"Breeze, it's your boy." Jazz turned and walked past her with a sly look on his face.

"My boy, what?" She saw him as she got to the foyer. "Blade, what are you doing here?"

"Bringing your books, remember?"

"Yeah, but I thought you were coming after school."

" now is lunch. I worked it out to miss PE, and Ms. Appleton thought it would be great if we worked on our project. The home bound teacher will vouch for me, that is, if you invite me in," Blade said.

Breeze heard Jazz laughing in the kitchen.

"Yeah, come on in," Breeze said. *"What?"* she mentally snapped to Jazz.

"If he had arrived ten minutes earlier, he might have received an ear full." He started laughing again. She gave him a huge mental eye roll.

"Ummm, am I interrupting something?" Blade asked.

Jazz was laughing so hard that Breeze got the giggles. "No, nothing. I'll get the art stuff." She motioned Blade to follow her. She was still giggling when she yelled, "Jazz." He started laughing harder.

"Are you sure I don't need to leave?" Blade asked.

"I'm sure," Breeze insisted.

"Yeah, you can join the party," Jazz yelled and he went back to his hysterical fit.

"You look great, by the way," Blade said.

"Uhhh, thanks. Did you bump your head or something?"

"No. Your color is good, and you are moving more than I expected."

Jazz yelled from the kitchen, "She should." He lost it and started laughing again to the point that he started hiccupping. "I'm (hiccup) going to (hiccup) get a (hiccup) shower."

"Good," Breeze said with a hint of irritation.

"You know you really aren't supposed to have sex until like six weeks after the procedure," Blade said bluntly.

Breeze's mouth dropped open. "What? No. Absolutely not. Are you always this bold?"

Breeze could feel the heat in her face. Jazz touched her mind (All she could see was a huge grin) *Shut it,* she yelled back at him mentally. She could hear him laughing again.

She looked Blade in the eyes. "Blade, let me get one thing straight with you right now." She took a deep breath and let it out so she wouldn't yell. "My sex life is no one's business but mine, and just because a guy and a girl are close, that doesn't automatically mean that they are sexually active. Jazz is my best friend, like it or lump it. Period, end of discussion." Breeze turned and slowly walked into the kitchen.

Blade could follow or leave. She didn't care. She grabbed her pain pills and took one.

Blade walked up behind her. "Breeze, I'm sorry. You're right. I shouldn't have assumed anything. I really am sorry that I upset you."

"Fine. Jazz and I have a special, intimate connection, just not that kind of intimate."

Jazz touched her mind. *"We could always make it that way."*

"Please, you are not helping, especially with you showing me images of you drying off," Breeze said.

"If you like, you could help me. I'm sure 'he' won't mind." Breeze mentally glared at him. *"Hee-hee. You know I sensed a little jealousy when I opened the door,"* Jazz said.

"Yeah, right. He has known me for like a day and a half."

"Our connection took less than that. Remember?"

"I remember, but that is so different."

"Really?"

"Yes, really. What, you want me to run to him and confess my undying love?" Breeze felt Jazz tense. *"What?"* she asked.

"He's here." Jazz growled out the words.

"What? No."

Breeze looked at Blade. He had his fists doubled, back straight, and looked tense. Panic ran through her. "What is it,

186

Blade?" Breeze almost yelled.

"I sense him here," Blade snapped.

"What? Who? Jazz?" Breeze asked.

Jazz slammed open the bathroom door; he was fully dressed, and his shoulders were back. She knew that look. It was the one she saw so many times on the streets or in the ring.

"No." Blade snapped. "The one who hurt you."

How in the hell did he know that? He hadn't heard her and Jazz's conversation. They were guarded. He does have other abilities; he must, because he has never met Taylor. Breeze heard the engine rev outside; her hair stood on end and not in a good way. Was she healed enough to fight? She would never let him hurt Jazz, never. The engine died. Blade stood rock still. Jazz looked similar in form; Breeze could hear her heart pounding. Everything felt like it was in slow motion. Breeze took in a deep breath and moved between Blade and Jazz. She opened the door just as Taylor was raising his hand to knock.

"What the hell do you want, Taylor?"

"Hey, Breeze. What? You have bodyguards now? Can I come in?"

Blade answered before Breeze could. "You are not welcome here."

"Yeah, you need to step before you end up worse than she did upon your last unwelcomed visit," Jazz snapped.

Fury spread across Taylor's face. He couldn't believe that these two guys would even speak to him when he was speaking to Breeze. *Jazz would never learn. Breeze is mine, not Jazz's, she is MINE. I can't even believe they are looking at me let alone talking to me. I knew her dad and Jana were gone. I waited as long as I could before I rang the bell. I should have known that Jazz would be here. I should have went after Jazz as well as*

Breeze, then maybe I would be rid of him at least. Jazz, Blade, and Breeze all heard his thoughts. Taylor had no idea that any of them had special abilities. He did not believe in those kind of things.

"I wasn't talking to either of you maggots, I was talking to Breeze," Taylor said with a sense of control, though his face did not show that same control.

"Breeze, what about it? Can he come in?" Jazz asked with his cocky grin and a wink.

"Yeah, Breeze, can we play?" Blade asked with the same air of cockiness.

Breeze realized that Jazz and Blade were talking mentally with each other. They had a plan for some serious pain for Taylor, but she feared something bad would happen to them. She straightened herself up, squared her shoulders, and said, "No, Taylor, you may not come in, now or ever. Don't ever come back here, to my mom's house, or to any of my friends' homes. What we had is over."

"We will never be over," Taylor snapped. Before Breeze could say anything else, she was jerked back behind Jazz and Blade. They were shoulder to shoulder.

"Breeze said it's over. That means it's over. Now leave," Jazz snapped.

"You're a whore, you know that? Your little boyfriends won't always be around. I can promise you that."

"We both may not be here, but one of us will always be, and you will never lay your hands on her again. I can assure you of that," Blade growled his words at Taylor.

"Bitch, I don't know why I love you so much. You always treat me like crap," Taylor said.

Jazz snapped. He grabbed Taylor by the shirt and pulled

him closer. Jazz landed his first punch squarely in Taylor's nose. Blood went everywhere. Blade growled and began throwing punches. Breeze ran to the phone. "Dad, Taylor is here. Jazz and Blade are fighting him."

Jon was home in less than five minutes. His truck was still rolling when his door was slung open and he threw it into park. Taylor was still fighting Jazz and Blade when Jon walked up.

"Jazz and Blade step back," Jon said. No questions asked, they did as they were told. Jon stepped forward. "Taylor, you are twenty years old and on my property. You have hurt my daughter in more ways than one. It is now time I taught you some manners."

With that Jon was in the air doing a spinning roundhouse kick directly in Taylor's chest. A couple of sidekicks landed on Taylor's ribs, punches were added to the ribs to make him really hurt and finally a knee to his stomach. Jon stood up and bowed.

"Now get in your car and drive back to wherever you came from."

Taylor was holding his ribs as he slowly picked himself up. He turned to leave and looked over his shoulder.

"This isn't over between us, Breeze. You hear me. This isn't over by a long shot. "

Jon stiffened. Blade and Jazz were by his side. Breeze stepped out.

"Oh, it is over. Long over. Now go." Breeze yelled the words and pointed toward Taylor's car.

They all stood there until Taylor had raced out of sight. Breeze turned to Jazz and saw that he was bleeding from his mouth and nose. His knuckles were also cut. She looked at

Blade. He didn't even look like he had a hair out of place. She looked at her dad; she knew he wouldn't even be winded. She had seen him at too many competitions. He was composed.

Jazz is an awesome street and arena fighter; why is Jazz bloody and Blade doesn't even have a scratch? I know Taylor connected with him. Oh well, glitches, mere glitches.

"Thank you," Breeze said to all of them.

Jon turned to Blade and Jazz. "Thank you for protecting her."

"No problem," Blade said.

"My pleasure," Jazz said.

Both Jazz and Blade gave a cocky grin and winked at Breeze.

"Uhhh, men," she said.

"Are you guys ok if I go back to work? Blade why are you here?" Jon asked.

"He brought me my books, and we were getting ready to work on our art project when Taylor showed up," Breeze said in a carefree way.

Jon just nodded. "OK. Call me if you need me. I will see you this afternoon. Jazz, are you crashing here again tonight?"

"Yes, sir, if you don't mind."

"Good. I will see you later," Jon said.

Breeze looked at Blade while Jon was talking. She saw a flash of jealousy touch Blade's eyes when Jon asked if Jazz was staying the night, and then it was gone.

"Blade, I'm sure Jana wouldn't mind if there was one extra for dinner," Jon said.

"Thank you. I'd be honored," Blade said.

Jazz walked over to Breeze, placed his arm around her, and placed his hand on her waist. He bent to her ear and whispered, "I think I will drink before I leave. I want our connection to be as strong as possible. I will visit on weekends when I can, and I will see you at the streets."

Breeze grinned. "I thought you'd see it my way." She winked and bumped him with her hip.

He laughed. "I have more than one thing to keep an eye on." Together they looked up and saw Blade staring at them.

Breeze laughed and whispered, "You are so bad. I could just hold out on you."

"Nah, because when I drink, you will get to drink from me as well."

Her eyes lit up. "You mean it?"

"Absolutely."

"You know I love the rush. The only thing that could possibly be a bigger rush might be sex and a drink at the same time. Can you imagine THAT rush?" Jazz asked with a grin.

A chill ran through her. She could only imagine how great that would be. She blushed and he started laughing. Her thoughts briefly wondered to actually giving Jazz a chance at them being together as a couple, but quickly shook the thought. He was her absolute best friend and she would never ruin that. She knew what it was like to be lonely and she would not go back to a time when Jazz was not in her life.

"Hey, behave while I'm gone," Jon yelled to them.

"We will," Jazz and Breeze yelled back and started laughing.

"Yes, sir," Blade said. He still couldn't wrap his thoughts around Jazz and Breeze. What was up with them? Breeze said they have a connection - a special connection, but nothing sexual.

Jazz had reiterated that when Taylor showed up. Jazz truly hated Taylor, not just because of the abuse, but also because he was Breeze's first. Of course, Jazz didn't know that he had opened that part of his mind to Blade. Jazz had become completely blocked when he grabbed Taylor by the shirt. Blade had just a brief glimpse at Jazz's thoughts, but it was enough. They loved each other; that was obvious to everyone. Her friends and her parents saw it and accepted it without question. Hell, Kidd even saw it and accepted it, but it didn't stop him from advancing on her. It was like there were these underlying rules or something. Maybe it had to do with the streets, but he really doubted it. Blade shook his head slightly, to clear his head. He wasn't even sure what the streets were.

Good grief, I've known her a day and a half, and I already wish it was me touching her that way. What the hell is wrong with me? One thing is for sure, Jazz and I, not to mention the others, will have to work together to protect her. Taylor's thoughts were of pure hatred, and he wanted Breeze dead in a bad kind of way.

"Hey, Blade, are you coming or are you going to stand there all day?" Jazz yelled from the front step.

Crap. Jazz still has his hand on her waist, and she is standing in the doorway. God she's beautiful. "Yeah, I'm coming."

NEW FRIENDS

"Breeze, again I'm starving. Can we order some pizza or something?" Jazz asked.

"Bro, you read my mind," Breeze said. All three started laughing. "Blade and I will set up at the kitchen table with all the art supplies. You call and order the pizza. Blade, what do you like on your pizza?"

Blade smiled shyly, "Pineapple and ham."

"Awesome. That's our favorite; two large pineapple-and-ham pizzas, cheese sticks, and a two-liter coke. Don't forget extra garlic butter."

Jazz laughed, "Girl, you hungr-r-ry?"

"Nah, I know how much you eat. Now go order the food before I start drooling on my art supplies," Breeze laughed.

Blade felt relaxed, something he hadn't felt in years, or a lifetime for that matter. The art project was coming together nicely. They decided on the three-headed dog "Fluffy" from *Harry Potter and the Sorcerer's Stone*, and a demon from *Dante's Inferno*. Breeze designed the demon; it was a dragon with snakes coming out of one of its eyes with a big ugly horn on its head. They also decided that they would build a unique castle, the dragon and the three-headed dog would stand in front of the draw bridge. They had been working about thirty minutes when Jazz walked in.

"You know taking characters from books and creating them is cool," Breeze said.

"You are such a geek," Jazz laughed. He walked over, slid behind her in the chair and placed his hands around her waist.

"What are you doing?" She asked.

"Admiring your work," Jazz said.

"When will the pizza be here? I'm hungry," Breeze said.

He whispered in her ear, "I'll feed you." He bent over and kissed her gently on her cheek and slid out from behind her in the chair. "The pizza is here, my lady." He bowed to her in a silly knight gesture.

"Talk about a geek," Breeze said and Blade started laughing.

"Yeah, but you love me," Jazz insisted.

"Always. Now get out of my way. Haven't you heard ladies first?" Breeze teased.

"Find me a lady, and she can go first."

"Kiss my BIG TOE," Breeze jokingly yelled back.

Blade just watched as the two laughed and threw jabs at each other. He wondered if they acted like this around her parents. Well, he would see this evening. Her dad did ask Jazz if he was staying tonight. *Wow. I wonder if I will ever get their relationship. Her dad completely trusts Jazz with her, even though it is so obvious that there is something there.*

"Are you ok? Hello. Earth to Blade. Dude, you better eat before Jazz eats it all. What are you thinking about?"

I guess it's best to be honest. "I was trying to figure you two out. One minute you are like an old married couple, the next you are 'one of the guys', and then the next you're like secret lovers. I just don't get it. You're not together, but you are," Blade said.

194

"Don't try to figure it out. We are what we are," Breeze said.

"Yeah, what she said," Jazz mumbled through a mouth full of pizza.

"We instantly connected when we met five years ago. We have been like this ever since. We are like this in front of everyone including our parents. When Jazz has a girlfriend, if she can't handle me hanging out with Jazz or him hanging out with me, he simply dumps her. Same thing when I have a boyfriend, if he doesn't like it, then goodbye, boyfriend. Jazz is a part of my life. I am a part of his life. There is nothing else to figure out." Breeze took a sip of her coke and then continued. "We discovered the streets together and have been going ever since. Matt, Mickey, and Kidd don't question it, and neither should you. The more you are around us, the more "normal" it will feel. Seriously, we are what we are."

Jazz leaned over the counter and kissed her forehead. "I couldn't have said it better myself."

"Did Taylor have an issue with your friendship?" Blade asked.

Jazz and Breeze both nodded. Jazz spoke first. His hatred for Taylor was as obvious as his love for Breeze. "Taylor had an issue with everything."

"I had to train a lot, and he was out of town a lot, so Jazz and I took advantage of that time. Taylor's biggest issue was and is me. He hates everything about me. He wanted complete control over me and everything in my life. When he couldn't have those things, he would go into mad rages. There were times he would get so mad that he'd leave for a couple of days," Breeze said.

"Why did you put up with it?" Blade asked.

Jazz walked around to her, placed his arm around Breeze's

waist, and kissed her gently.

"I'm ok. Stop worrying," Breeze said and patted Jazz's hand. "I stayed for several reasons. When I first met him, he was sweet and kind. That changed after about two months after we started dating. He said something, and I made a sarcastic comment. The next thing I knew was that I had a fat lip and a bloody nose. I immediately grabbed my purse and left. I went straight to Jazz's house. We left and went to the docks. The next day I received a dozen roses at school as an apology. For the next couple months, things were good between us until one night, Matt called, and Taylor snapped. He called me every name in the book. I was on my guard, and he wasn't able to hit me. He stormed out, and I didn't see him for two weeks. Ever since then, it has been a complete love - hate relationship. Second, I thought he would change. Third, I loved him."

Jazz looked tense the whole time Breeze was talking. She could sense it, because as soon as she finished, she placed her arm around his waist and turned him to face her. "Loved, past tense, Jazz. I won't ever take him back again. He knows that, and that is why he hates me so much right now. One thing about the evening of the "incident" that you don't know is that I told him when he was cutting me, that even if we were both in our graves, I would never take him back. He was already in a rage, and he came to kill me, so I figured being honest wouldn't change his mind. I wasn't willing to lie and say I loved him just to make him stop. If I was going to die, I was going to do it honestly. Please stop worrying." She kissed Jazz lightly and ran her hands over each of his cheeks.

"Hey, you know I'm still here, not to mention your home bound teacher just arrived," Blade said.

"I told you we are what we are, and we don't hide it from anyone, including you. Now you two play nice and eat while I let my teacher in and do some schooling." Breeze chuckled a little. "Jazz, will you call Matt and ask him to bring the bike over? I really want to see my prize."

"Hey, speaking of prize, wasn't there something new you were going to show us last night?" Jazz asked.

She turned, reached for the key hook, and threw Jazz a set of keys. "In the garage, third on the left, check it out, and take Blade with you. No drooling on the merchandise."

The home bound teacher stayed for two hours. She did thirty minutes on English, Spanish, Chemistry, and Algebra II. Before she left, she checked to see the art project and confirmed that Blade was there. Jazz couldn't wait for the teacher to leave. As soon as she was out the door, he ran to Breeze.

"Nice ride. Who helped you? Can we take it for a spin? Can I drive?" Jazz asked.

"Thanks. Dad. And, yes, we can take it for a spin. I'm driving, but I might pull over and let you drive."

"You rock. Let's go."

"Ok. Blade, you coming?"

"Absolutely."

She felt Blade gently nudge her mind. *"Yes?"*

"You build cars, too?"

"Yep, and race them. Problem?"

"No. You just keep surprising me."

"I am me."

Jazz chimed in. *"She is Breeze. Gotta love her."*

"What else?

"Besides cars?"

197

"Yes"

"Bikes," they both said with a big grin and bumped hips.

"Am I missing something?" Blade asked.

"We will show you sometime." Their connection ended

Jazz was grinning like a kid on Christmas morning. They went out to the garage and fired up the Camaro.

"Wow. Listen to that engine purr," Jazz said with a tenderness to his voice.

"You are such a brat. Here, you can drive to Matt's," Breeze said while she slid from behind the wheel.

"Move over, babe. You don't have to tell me twice," Jazz said.

"I'm driving back," Breeze said with confidence.

"We will see." Jazz said.

Breeze sat between Jazz and Blade. Matt was worse than Jazz over the car. He showed off his prize.

"Speaking of prizes, where is mine?" Breeze asked.

Jazz pointed over beside the garage. He was still admiring the car.

"Can I drive it?" Matt asked.

"Drive what?" Breeze asked. Her focus was not on the car, but the bike that Jazz had won for her.

"The car. HELLO."

"Yeah, take it for a spin, grab Mickey, and don't scratch it," Breeze said. She was admiring her bike while Jazz was walking away from the car and walking over to her. He knew she would love it; he thought that it would be a perfect fit, but he wouldn't know for sure until she tested it out.

"Breeze, get on it," Jazz said once he was at the garage.

"I'm not sure I can. The procedure, remember?" Breeze said with a slight nod in Blade's direction.

"Blade, what do you think?" Jazz asked.

"Probably not. My dad is pretty strict when it comes to appropriate recovery and the restrictions that go with it."

"Jazz, you get on it and fire it up. I want to hear it," Breeze said.

"Sweet. Two treats…correction… three treats in one day," Jazz said with a grin.

Breeze blushed. "Brat."

Jazz started the bike. It roared.

"I would love to be on that right now. To feel it. UMMMM," Breeze said with desire.

"Girl, I'm glad it turns you on.," Jazz teased

"More than you know." She touched Jazz's mind. *"Drink later?"*

"Me or you?" he asked.

"Me, you, both," Breeze said.

"Seriously? What about your parents?"

"Fine. Tomorrow?"

"First thing in the morning?"

"You know it."

Jazz and Breeze grinned. Blade sensed that the two were talking, but they weren't inviting him in the conversation so he figured they would block him if he tried. Jazz had a mischievous grin on his face. Blade wasn't sure what that could mean, but he was sure that it didn't involve him.

"Ready to go?" Breeze asked.

"Wow, Matt has a lot of cars."

"Most he sells, but the best we keep. He is one hell of a mechanic, but not as good as Breeze," Jazz said.

"Is there anything you can't do?" Blade asked.

"YES," they both said.

"I suck at Scrabble and word puzzles. Now let's go. We need to help Jana with supper and work more on that project."

"Yes, ma'am," Blade said with sarcasm and saluted her.

"Oh, hell," Breeze said.

"Oh, no, he didn't," Jazz said through a laugh and snapped his fingers.

"Around me two days and already cockin' an attitude." Breeze laughed. "Hey, you did let your dad know you were eating with us, right?"

"Yes, while your teacher was there," Blade said.

"'Tude. We will work on it."

They all started laughing. Breeze placed her arms around both Jazz and Blade's waists. She bumped both their hips and walked to the car. "Now you get to see some real driving," Breeze said.

"Hold onto your lunch, dude. You're in for the ride of your life," Jazz said.

"I have a feeling just being friends with Breeze is one wild ride," Blade said.

Matt and Mickey were standing by the car. All three guys said, "You ain't lying, but it sure is worth it."

Breeze's expression caused all four guys to go into hysterics. "Y'all suck," she said.

"Nope," Jazz said.

"Definitely not," Matt laughed.

"No way," Mickey said and shook his head.

Blade was laughing. He knew what the guys were thinking. Breeze caught a glimpse of the thoughts. All she could do was roll her eyes and place the key in the ignition. She had not meant the comment in a sexual manner, but the three had interpreted it that way, and their thoughts were quite clear. She fired up the car and threw it into drive. They arrived home before Jana or her dad, so they started cleaning up. Jazz knew where everything went just like he lived there. Blade started preparing a salad to go with dinner. Breeze straightened up the living room and washed dishes.

"Breeze, how do you guys afford those cars? You don't steal, do you?" Blade asked with a hint of concern.

Breeze laughed. "We build all our cars from the ground up or we win them at the streets. When we don't race for slips, we race for cash. We get parts from all kinds of places: junk yards, classified ads, Craig's List, eBay, etc. Matt is an awesome mechanic. Not only does he help me and Jazz with our cars, but he also builds for others. Often when we win a car, we will either sell it or strip it and customize it for ourselves, but normally we sell them.

"It is easier to customize when we start fresh. My dad and I built my first car when I was thirteen years old. We sold it, and with the money we bought parts for two more cars. By the time I was sixteen, I had built fifteen cars, thirteen of which were sold. At the streets I not only race cars, but I also race bikes, compete in motocross, compete in dance offs, and compete in fights. It is all about the money and who you beat at the streets. I have only lost fifteen races at the streets; thirteen in a car and two on bikes, not to mention Jazz, Matt, and Kidd are racing, too. That's a whole lot of cars and bikes. Mickey races in bikes and motocross."

"How many people race in the streets?" Blade asked.

"Thousands," Breeze said.

"The fights are separate?"

"Yes and no. Each event is separate, but if there is a race, you can guarantee there is a fight somewhere. The streets are like me and Jazz; they are what they are. Once you are in, you are in. There is always someone better than you and they are just waiting to prove it. You always have to be on your guard."

"Trust no one except your inner circle and sometimes not even them," Jazz said. He and Breeze smiled at each other.

"Could I go with you to the streets?" Blade asked.

"Depends," said Breeze.

"Depends on what?"

"How do you feel about skipping school every now and then?"

"No problem."

"It also depends on if we think we can trust you," Jazz said.

"You just said trust no one," Blade said

"Wow, quick learner," Breeze said with attitude.

"There has to be some level of trust in the people you run with. There is always someone out there trying to steal secrets. We don't just meet people and place them in our circle. We have been friends for a long time. Breeze grew up with Matt and Mickey. When her mom married Stan and moved to Memphis, the three never lost touch. She would see them almost every weekend when she was here visiting. Breeze had been in Memphis a year before I moved there, and we became instant friends. We became closer friends than Breeze, Matt, and Mickey. Breeze met Kidd about two years ago, and she introduced him to Matt and Mickey. He was hanging out with her for six weeks before he went to the streets with them. I just met him a month ago, but I trust him because Breeze has such faith and trust in him. I don't like some of his thoughts about Breeze, but that is not an issue of trust."

Jazz winked at Breeze and she rolled her eyes at him. He

walked around, stood behind her, placed his hands around her waist, and kissed her neck lightly.

"Hey, guys," Jana said as she came into the kitchen.

"Hey," Jazz and Breeze said as one.

"Hello, Mrs. Lee," Blade said.

Jazz and Breeze laughed.

"Hello, Blade. Really, please call me Jana, and if you are a friend of Breeze's, you are welcome anytime."

"Thank you, Jana."

Blade noticed that Jana was gorgeous. Her long black hair was silky with a natural blue sheen and auburn highlights. She had her hair pulled back where it was braided at the top of her head, to the base of her skull and then it was flowing down her back. Her Asian skin was flawless. He also noticed that Breeze and Jazz didn't move because she was home. In fact, Jazz kissed Breeze again on the neck, he kissed her on the mouth and kept his hands on her waist. Blade felt a burning in his stomach; he realized he was jealous. *There is no reason to be jealous. I am not with her. I would like to be, but I'm not.*

"Blade and Breeze, how's the art project coming?" Jana asked.

"Good. You wanna see?" Breeze asked.

"Sure."

Jana leaned close to Breeze and whispered. "He is cute. I think he is a little jealous of you and Jazz." Breeze shrugged. "This is cool so far. Can I see the blueprint?"

"There are two blueprints, and we are combining both designs," Breeze said. Blade grabbed the sketchpads and handed them to Jana.

"Blade. Wow. You are an amazing artist. Breeze, have you thought about him doing some art for the cars?"

"I hadn't thought about it, but I'm sure it would have come to me, eventually."

Jazz was laughing and Blade was grinning. Blade looked like he had just been caught with his hand in the cookie jar.

"Jana, I don't know about you, but I get the feeling they were talking about us."

"Ummm…not about both of you; just about you, Breeze," Blade said.

"Oh, well, do tell." Breeze had her hands on her hips.

"HELL, NO. Guys can have secrets too, you know," Jazz said.

"We will see about that." Breeze decided to play dirty.

She opened her mind just enough so both guys could see the images that she wanted them to see, and she let the fun begin. She showed them herself undressing and being in a revealing bikini, walking around Jazz's red mustang, and then lying on the hood. She visualized Kidd placing oil on her body and then leaning over to kiss him. Then she closed her mind.

Jazz yelled, "HEY."

Blade's face flushed.

"That was so wrong, especially after Kidd yesterday morning," Jazz said.

"Yeah. Wrong - so wrong," Blade stammered.

"Girls can have secrets, too," Breeze teased.

"Breeze, were you playing?" Jana asked.

"YEP," she said with a big grin.

"Blade, I think we are going to have to work together in more ways than one. Not only are we going to keep an eye on Taylor, but now we are going to have to keep our eye on the men she chooses."

Jon walked in and laughed. "Who are you watching besides

Taylor?"

"Kidd," Jazz and Blade both said. Breeze laughed.

"I don't think you have to worry too much about that one," Jon laughed.

"If you only knew," Jazz said sarcastically.

Jon looked at Breeze. She signed the word crazy and pointed to the guys. Everyone started laughing. Jazz walked over to her. "I'm crazy about you." He kissed her.

"Yeah. Yeah. Whatever." She hugged his waist.

FEAR

They had dinner, cleaned up, and then Jon and Jazz went into the living room and turned on a UFC fight. Jana went upstairs briefly and came back down to watch the fight with the guys. Jana and Jon couldn't keep their hands off each other. Their love just shined. Blade followed Breeze's lead.

"Blade, would you please relax, just be yourself. We can work on the project, sit in here and talk, or go in there and watch the fight; your choice."

"I'd really like to talk."

"Ok." They sat at the counter facing each other. "What is on your mind?"

Blade thanked Breeze for a wonderful day. He wanted to know so much about her; he wanted to know everything. He didn't know why. He had just met her, but it was beginning to feel like he had known her for a lifetime. It was weird. He took a breath. "A lot; Taylor, Jazz, you, and the streets."

"Ok, go on."

"I saw Taylor's thoughts. He totally hates you, and he wants you dead. I don't get it. You seem to be a great person."

"It's a control thing. He can't control me, and it makes him crazy. I am too independent, and he can't stand that. His idea of love is control. My idea of love is complete acceptance."

Blade nodded. "Why don't you and Jazz date since you have such a great connection? I see you two together, and I see love."

"We decided a long time ago that we valued each other too much to date."

"I feel so comfortable around you." He took a deep breath and continued. " I do feel a little funny when I see you and Jazz kissing, but I will get over it." Blade's expression was priceless. He could not believe he had just blurted that out.

"Ha ha. I will say it again; Jazz and I are what we are. I'm glad you feel comfortable around me. I feel it with you as well." Breeze encouraged Blade to continue.

"The streets. Are they safe? Don't you worry about getting hurt fighting? After all you've been through, is that something you still want to do?" Blade asked.

"The streets are often referred to as the underground. It's as safe as anything else. I love fighting. It is a part of me. I will do it if I physically can. What has happened to me had nothing to do with the streets. It had to do with a self-absorbed, control freak. Since I recently turned eighteen, I will still do the streets, but I will also be competing in the UFC and the MMA arenas, once all the medical restrictions are cleared." She sighed deeply.

She lost Thailand and entering the UFC and MMA may be delayed as well. Her plans were always to compete in Thailand, then after graduation join the UFC and MMA arenas full time. Blade sighed. He was worried that she would get hurt. During the conversation with Blade, Breeze could tell that he was truly worried about her wellbeing. She just figured it was because he truly wasn't a part of that world. She had grown up in that world and loved it.

"That's part of it. Accept me for who I am because that's the only way to be a part of my inner circle. Can you do that?"

"Yes."

Breeze expressed how tired she was and recommended that they go in the living room to watch a fight. She got up and took her next pain pill. She knew she had to take them as recommended to stay ahead of the pain.

"My dad would have a fit if he knew all you've done today. You are supposed to be resting and healing," Blade said.

Breeze's mouth dropped open and looked at him. "I am," she said with indignation in her tone,

Blade laughed. "I better go. I'll see you tomorrow to work some more on the project."

"See ya." She walked him through the living room to the door. Jazz got up and joined them at the door. "Thanks for today with Taylor. Will you be by tomorrow?" Jazz asked.

"Yes. You're welcome. She is so worth it," Blade said.

"You got that right," Jazz agreed.

"Hello. I'm right here."

Blade turned without thinking and kissed Breeze on the forehead. She didn't pull way and Jazz didn't go crazy, which he assumed was a good thing.

"See you tomorrow, Blade." She smiled at him.

He turned and walked off. He heard Jazz say, "Oh great, now I have got to worry about two people trying to be with you, him and Kidd. We will make our connection super strong."

"Promises, promises," Breeze said.

"Oh, I promise starting first thing tomorrow," Jazz said.

"Starting… Oh, I like the sound of that," Breeze said. She did a silly little dance and turned to go back inside. Jazz wrapped his arm around her waist and went into the house with her.

Blade had no clue what they were talking about, but it really didn't bother him. Their relationship was growing on him, or at least he hoped it was. Breeze went back to the kitchen to look at their project and the blueprints. Jana came in and stood beside her.

"What?" Jana asked.

"Something is missing. I just don't know what," Breeze said and shrugged. "We have weeks to work on it, but I would like to figure it out now instead of week two."

"You'll figure it out. Will Blade be back tomorrow?"

"Yeah"

"He likes you," Jana said.

"I know, but I'm not ready for anything more than friends. I am so broken."

Jana was concerned with how Breeze was using the term broken. Breeze was healing physically; however, her spirits still seemed to be far from normal. Jazz always picked up Breeze's spirits, but even he seemed to be struggling to help her get back to normal. Zion had helped some, and the last several challenges seemed to have helped, but she kept slipping back. The thought crossed her mind to call Han and ask him to send Taka home, but she quickly dismissed that thought. She could not handle those three together at the moment. Hell, she would need all the Korean and Japanese warriors here if that happened. They would find another way to get Breeze back to herself.

Jana motioned for Breeze to sit. She gladly accepted. Maybe Jana could help her figure out what her project was missing. Probably not since Jana typically let her figure those things out for herself. In Jana's opinion, it was more gratifying that way, and it was one hundred percent truly your art. Breeze agreed, but she really would like some assistance with this project. Breeze looked at each part of the project. It had a long way to go before it would be complete, but there was still something missing. She glanced at the blueprints again. It wasn't Blade's section that was bothering her, it was hers, but what could it possibly need at this point? Breeze was deep in thought when Jana lowered her voice so none of their conversation could be overheard.

"Breeze, I know you love Jazz. Why don't you give him a chance? He loves you. He trusts you completely, he is always good to you, and he would never hurt you or let anyone else hurt you."

"I know all that. I'm scared I would screw up our friendship or hold him back, and I couldn't live with myself if I did either. I love him too much."

"You'd rather him find someone else?"

"No, of course not."

"Just seriously consider giving him a chance. I think your friendship would strengthen that relationship."

Breeze nodded to Jana. They sat there and talked for about twenty minutes. Jana was someone you could tell anything to and know that it would be in the highest confidence. Jana talked to Breeze about Jazz, Blade, and Kidd, even though she knew that Kidd was not her type. He was a brother to Breeze.

Breeze laughed. "Jazz didn't like Kidd's crush."

"Typical."

"I know, right? That is one of the reasons that I love him," Breeze said sarcastically.

"Let's go watch the fights. You look a little pale."

"Jana, I hate to ask this, but can Jazz sleep with me tonight? I slept so good last night, something I haven't done in forever.

Nothing will happen, I promise."

"Oh honey, I know that nothing would happen and not just because of the procedure. He respects you too much, and he respects us too much for anything to happen in our living room. He really is a gentleman most times."

"Will you make sure that it is alright with Dad?" Breeze asked shyly.

Jana didn't say anything, she simply winked. Breeze hugged her. She knew it was all good. Breeze walked in the living room. Jazz was in the chair with the ottoman, and her dad was on the couch. Jana joined Jon on the couch, and Breeze decided to sit in the chair with Jazz. She sat in front of him. He scooted up so he could place his arms around her. She remembered watching a fight, but not much more than that. She awoke with a jerk. Jazz whispered in her ear, "I'm here."

"Something is wrong."

"Where?"

"Mom's," Breeze said.

"Should we call her?"

"Not yet. You know she thinks I'm crazy if I ever say I saw something." Breeze took a breath and gasped. "Jazz, oh God."

"What?" Jazz asked.

Jana and Jon came over to the chair. They reassured her that they would believe whatever she told them. Jana spoke softly, and Jon took her hand. They knew how her mother treated the visions and wished that they could change how Mary handled it. Breeze began speaking rapidly.

"I see the house, and there is someone in the shadows. Mom and Stan are just getting ready for bed. Stan locked the doors, set the alarm, and turned off the lights. Mom is upstairs in her room. The person in the shadows is watching the house closely. He has flicked a cigarette, he is walking toward the house, and he has something in his hands. It looks like hedge clippers and a teddy bear. He has cut the phone lines. He is walking to mom's car, he is bending down near the car, and I hear hissing. He is now standing, he is lifting the handle on the driver's side door, it is unlocked, and he is placing the bear in the seat. He is reaching for something in his back pocket. It is a piece of paper and a knife like a hunting knife. He is stabbing the paper into the bear and stabbing it to the seat. The note is too dark to read. He is closing the car door. He is bending again; he is checking the tires. They are flat. He is grinning. He is lighting another cigarette and walking back to the shadows. He is laughing."

Breeze looked at Jana and her dad. She was so thankful that they believed her. Her dad was reaching for his cell. Breeze couldn't believe that her dad was even considering calling her mother. She knew he would try to tell her mom the truth; if she accepted the truth or not, would be another story. Jana gave Breeze a reassuring smile and took her hand for comfort. Breeze knew that if her mom would just accept what she said as the truth then their relationship would be a lot better.

"Breeze, you are who you are, and that is what makes you special. This may make her believe," Jana said.

Jon walked into the room. They all could hear the screaming on the other end. Stan had gone out to the car and the tires were flat. He used his shirt to open the door and saw the bear with the note and that was what caused the screaming. Stan was now on the phone.

"Tell me what it says."

"It says… 'The bitch will die and there is nothing you can do.'"

212

"Stan, listen to me. Call 911 on your cell and don't touch anything. He was smoking in the bushes. Make sure the police search the whole area of your property. Tell them you heard a noise, you thought you heard a car door, you got up, came down to check, and you saw someone run through the bushes. Got it?"

Stan gave his agreement. Jon reassured Stan that Breeze was safe. Once they hung up, Jon told Jazz to call Kidd, Matt, and Mickey. He told Breeze to call Blade. Jon had people to call. Taylor was not getting to his daughter again. Jana followed Jon out of the room. She also had a call to make.

Breeze didn't know Blade's phone number; she mentally reached out to him. Thankfully, he heard her call. *"Call me ASAP."*

Breeze's phone buzzed

"What's up?" Blade asked.

Breeze explained everything that had just happened. He assured her that he was on his way. "What about your dad?" Breeze asked.

"As long as your parents are home, then my dad is fine with me being there. Why'd you call me?" Blade asked

"My dad told me to. Jazz is calling Matt, Mickey, and Kidd," Breeze explained.

"Cool. Sleep over at Breeze's house."

"Funny. Can Rocky fight?"

"Yeah, and so can Summer," Blade said.

"If you want, bring them."

Jon walked in. "Is that Blade?"

"Yes."

"Do I need to speak to his father for him to stay here?" Jon asked

Breeze shook her head. She pointed to her dad and gave thumbs up. Jon gave a slight nod. He was beyond angry that Taylor would threaten his daughter again.

"Blade, see you soon and thanks." Breeze said.

"I'm glad we can help. Plus, I get to spend time with you."

"I question your sanity to want to walk into this craziness, but, whatever. See ya soon." She ended the call.

Everyone arrived about fifteen minutes after the calls. Kidd looked rough. He walked over to Breeze and hugged her tight. "No more hospitals, please. I can't take it."

Breeze hugged him tight then ruffled his hair and stepped back. "I will try to honor that request."

"Good." He nodded and walked over to a bean bag and took his seat.

Jon was in complete warrior mode. He stepped into the living room with Jana at his side. They both were standing straight, ready to take on the world.

"Thanks for coming. Here's the deal; Taylor's bad news. He tried to kill Breeze once, and he is threatening to do it again. He got his ass kicked today, and he is still running his mouth and sneaking around. The restraining order is about as good as the paper it's on. I have made some calls." Jon took a deep breath to keep his composure. "Matt and Jazz, I want calls made to people who know this guy and his family. I want to know his every move. Jazz, please let Uncle know the latest development and see if the amount is the same or if it has been raised. Mickey, do you know where he lives and works?" Mickey nodded. "Good. Work your magic. Kidd and Blade, Breeze does not leave your sight at school. I guess that includes you two as well." He pointed to Summer and Rocky. "He will **not** touch my daughter again." Jon said.

214

Matt and Mickey grabbed their phones and began making calls. Mickey walked in grinning. Blade was honored that Jon would trust him to protect Breeze. Kidd was grinning like a fool. Jon shook his head. Summer and Rocky nodded. Jazz and Matt were both on the phone and gave a thumbs up.

"Kidd, Blade, Summer, and Rocky, since you have school tomorrow, we will get you blankets and pillows so you can crash."

"Dad, Summer can sleep in my room. Rocky can crash on the floor there or here. Blade and Rocky can crash on the floor in here or take the spare bedrooms. Kidd can crash in his room."

Matt and Mickey spoke softly to Jana and Jon before they made their exit for the evening. They would be close by in case they were needed. Jana quickly made a call to Japan before she showed everyone where the blankets, sleeping bags, and pillows were located. Jana showed everyone where they could sleep. Jon shook his head and Jana grinned. She loved a full house, but this was beyond full. Jon and Jana said goodnight to everyone. Jana made sure the doors and windows were locked. She would not risk Taylor slipping in or trying to slip in.

Kidd came bouncing back into the living room with a blanket and pillow. "I'm sleeping with Breeze," he said with a smile.

"The hell you are," Jazz yelled. He hopped on the couch and pulled Breeze in his arms.

"Man, you are always ruining my fun. Fine, I'll sleep on the floor right here so I can smell her and have wet dreams," Kidd teased.

Breeze hit him with a cushion. Blade, Summer, and Rocky

were standing there with their sleeping bags and pillows.

"What's up? You'd prefer the floor compared to a nice bed?" Breeze asked.

"We thought we'd protect you better in here," Summer said with a smile.

"Protect me, from what?" Breeze asked.

They all pointed at Kidd.

"Busted," Jazz yelled.

Breeze thanked everyone. She was grateful for all her friends.

"Hey, since Jazz is sleeping with you, do I get Summer?" Kidd said with a sly grin. Everyone threw their pillows at Kidd. He threw his arms up in the air and was trying to deflect some of the pillows. "I give."

Breeze looked at Summer. She was blushing.

"Kidd, you couldn't handle Summer. I think she could take you here or at the streets," Jazz laughed.

Breeze knew that tone. She looked at him and kissed him. She touched his mind. *"Do you want to extend the invitation or me?"*

"I will, but I got my eye on your boy."

"Still first thing in morning?" she asked.

"Oh yeah, as soon as they are all gone. Your parents will go, right?"

"Yeah, you are here. Feeling greedy?"

"Yes, I am," Jazz said.

"I love you."

"I better get this over with before I change my mind."

Their connection ended.

"Hey, Blade, you've earned it and so have your siblings. This Friday night, 6:00 p.m., meet us here."

Rocky and Summer looked at Blade for answers. Kidd's mouth dropped open. "No way," he said.

"Way."

"Thanks, man. We will be here. Do we need to bring anything?" Blade asked.

"Yourselves. Everything else will be taken care of. Kidd, close your mouth and call Matt. Tell him three additional, my approval," Jazz said with a grin.

Kidd ran from the room to make the call. "Stop messing with him before I kick your ass," Breeze said.

"Medical restrictions, remember? You can't," Jazz insisted.

They began poking at each other and throwing jabs at each other. Blade was staring at them.

"Matt said cool." Kidd said as he bounced back in the room..

Breeze looked over her shoulder at Jazz, gave him a nod, and turned to Kidd. "Kidd, move over. Jazz is hogging the covers," she said with a huge grin.

Kidd grinned and clapped his hands with excitement.

"Hell, no, I'm not sharing you tonight. Sorry, bro. She is staying right here with me," Jazz said.

Rocky started laughing.

"What?" asked everyone in the room.

"All of y'all. Kidd is a horny toad, you two are hilarious, and, Blade, your expression is priceless. Summer, your expression is not any better than Blade's. You are all funny as hell," Rocky said. They all grabbed their pillows and hit him. Everyone took their places in the living room and started to go to sleep. Jazz held Breeze. He was asleep quickly.

Blade touched her mind. *"Hmm,"* Breeze asked in a sleepy tone.

"Can you show me what you saw? I think it will help me piece

all this together," he asked.

"Not tonight, I'm too tired. But tomorrow I will. I promise."

"Ok. Thank you for calling me. This is nice. Rocky and Summer are happy to be here as well. It's nice to be included."

"You need to fill them in about the streets," Breeze said.

"Hey, we are going to the races, right?"

"Yes, of course." She yawned. *" Can I see your hand?"* He looked at his hand and mentally showed it to her. *"I mean on the couch, not in my mind...Dweeb."*

"Dweeb? Isn't that like a word from the 70's?" Blade asked.

"KMA." Breeze said and mentally shook her head. Blade placed his hand on the couch. She touched his hand, brought it to her mouth, gently kissed it, and laid it back down. *"Thank you again. Good night."*

THE STREETS

The next three days were uneventful. Blade came over every day at eleven thirty in the morning. They would eat lunch, then Jazz would leave to go to Matt's garage until about five thirty in the evenings, and then he'd return to help with dinner. Friday rolled around and there was electricity in the air. Kidd was there right after school. Matt and Mickey arrived at five that evening. Blade, Rocky, and Summer were there by five thirty. Jazz and Breeze walked out of the kitchen with duffel bags draped over their shoulders. Breeze grabbed a set of keys from the key holder and headed for the garage. Jazz grabbed his keys.

"Blade, Summer, and Rocky choose who you are riding with and let's go."

Rocky chose to ride with Jazz, and Summer chose Matt's car. Kidd was excited that she was riding in the back with him. Blade chose to ride with Breeze, surprise, surprise. The three cars left and headed for the streets.

"What was that all about?" Breeze asked.

"For some reason Rocky really likes Jazz; he likes his attitude. I can tell you our dad is thrilled about that. For some unknown reason Summer likes Kidd and, I wouldn't pass up an opportunity to be alone with you."

Since Wednesday morning Jazz and Breeze had connected even more than normal, so when her heartbeat picked up, he touched her mind.

"What's up?" Jazz asked.

"Nothing," Breeze insisted.

"Liar."

"Love ya."

"Do I need to ride with you and have Rocky drive my car?"

"Yeah, right. You don't let anyone drive your car."

"I could make an exception," Jazz said.

"All is good. Now pay attention to your driving." She mentally flashed him a smile. "Oh, by the way, I asked Chad to invite Angela," Breeze said.

"What?"

"I thought you'd like that."

"How'd you know?"

"Come on. I know you better than anyone. She's your type and she's cool with our friendship. Still want tomorrow and Sunday?" Breeze asked with a grin.

Jazz grinned mentally.

Breeze and Jazz talked for a couple more minutes, then she ended the connection. Blade was watching Breeze when she got silent. He realized that she must be talking to someone, and the only logical person would be Jazz. "Hey, are you talking to Jazz?" he asked.

"Yep."

"Tell him it's my turn, and I'm not sharing. Never mind, I will tell him." There was silence for a few minutes. Then he started laughing.

"What?" Breeze asked.

"Oh, nothing."

Breeze knew there was no point to push the issue. He wouldn't tell her. It was between Blade and Jazz. She could only imagine what Jazz had said to Blade. That thought made her smile. Blade sighed and looked at her. "Hey, Breeze, how long until we get there?"

"You sound like a kid. Are we there yet?" she laughed. "Ten minutes and we will start rolling in."

Breeze sensed Blade's anxiety. She remembered what it was like the first time that she went to the streets. She patted his leg and told him to relax because he was with her. His eyes widened with excitement when they pulled in. He hadn't seen anything yet. All three cars pulled over. Jazz and Matt got out. They headed to a tent. Chad, his girlfriend, and Angela came walking over to Breeze's car.

"Breeze, thank you for inviting me. This is cool. Where's Jazz? Is that Blade McGroff? Girl, he is fine. Are you two dating?" Angela asked.

Breeze laughed. She couldn't remember ever seeing Angela this talkative. "You're welcome. He is over at the registration tent. Yes, it is Blade. No, I'm not ready yet." Breeze took a breath. "Angela, I brought us some clothes. Are you ready to change and get your sexy on?"

"Absolutely," she said.

When Angela and Breeze started walking to the restrooms, everyone else got out of the cars. Breeze motioned to Summer so she would join them.

"Where are you going?" Blade asked.

"To get our sexy on," Breeze said.

Blade gave her a questioning look as the three ladies walked off. *Oh, dear lord, I hope Breeze did not mean they were going to dress like the other ladies here. I am already having thoughts about Breeze that I shouldn't be having. And, Oh hell no, my sister is NOT dressing like the women here. I will be fighting a whole lot of men off and probably Kidd, too.* He swore under his breath.

Once in the restrooms, Breeze broke out the clothes; hers were a pair of black leather short shorts, a black leather halter top that strapped around the neck. It was open in the back and came right below the bra line. She had black mid-thigh boots that had a red dragon running up the outside of each boot.

Angela's clothes were a white leather mini skirt with short black stretch shorts that went underneath the skirt, a black and white leather halter that was like Breeze's, and white mid-thigh boots which had a black and red dragon on them. Breeze's tat was obvious in her outfit, and she made it look awesome. Breeze brought Summer a halter top that was red and white plus red boots with a white dragon on them. She wasn't sure if Summer would be comfortable in a short skirt or shorts, so she told her to wear some sexy jeans. Summer listened, and the jeans she wore hugged her ass exactly right. Breeze walked out first with Angela right behind her, then Summer. All the guys were sitting on the hoods of the cars. Kidd, Matt, Mickey, and Jazz all got up at the same time.

"Oh, my," Blade said.

"You ain't lying," said Jazz.

"The girls are smokin' hot," Kidd said. Matt elbowed him, but grinned. Mickey whistled.

Blade got off Breeze's car and started walking toward her. He reached his hand out and she took it. Jazz did the same to Angela, and she also accepted his hand. Blade was on Breeze's right, Jazz was on her left, and Angela on Jazz's left. The four led their group in. Kidd bounced with excitement. He looked at Summer and grinned. She gave him a shy smile in return.

"Time to race. Guys, let's roll," Breeze said.

Jazz, Breeze, and Matt got their cars and lined up. Breeze was first. She won hands down. Next was Matt. He won a slip and cash. Jazz won cash. Now they waited for their next race. Blade came up behind her, and he touched the right side of her hip.

"Are you racing for slips?"

"Why? Do you see a car that you like?"

"What?" Blade asked. Breeze repeated what she said and winked at Blade. "I like them all."

" I can't win them all; there's not enough hours in the day."

Blade shook his head. Breeze was a different person here. It was like she was free of all worries and troubles. She seemed to have more sass and attitude here, and that was saying a lot. "I like the yellow one," he finally said.

"Done," she said and walked toward her car.

Jazz was right behind her. "Are you racin' for your boy now?"

"Are you racin' for your girl now?"

They bumped hips and walked off. Matt was allowing Kidd to race his car. Kidd won by a car length. Rocky was so excited about all the races he could barely stand still. Breeze tapped Jazz, Kidd, Mickey, and Matt's minds.

"Tomorrow I want to see what Rocky, Summer, and Blade have. I think Rocky would do well in a car, Summer a bike, and Blade, well, we will see. Kidd, let's get you a car that truly fits you. I was thinking that orange one with yellow faded at the top. You can use my car for slips. You're up next so go and make sure you win. I really like that car." Kidd ended his connection so he could focus on racing.

"I know the perfect car for Rocky," Jazz said.

Mickey chimed in, *"Summer has spunk, and I think she's afraid to show it. Let's put her on a bike that lets her personality show."*

"Are you thinking Kidd's?" Breeze asked.

"Yeah, and I don't think he will mind." Mickey smiled.

"We will leave Blade's to you, Breeze," said Matt.

"Jazz, what is your feel on Angela?" Breeze asked.

"She doesn't want to race; she likes watching."

"You sure?"

"Positive."

"Ok. Now let's race."

Kidd came running over with a pink slip in hand. They ended the connection. "We'll get it to the garage and tweak it. Then you can start racing it," said Matt.

Kidd was grinning. "Thanks, Breeze."

"No problem. My turn." Breeze won Blade the yellow Camaro. "Matt, I want him to test drive this one tomorrow. Once I see him in it, we'll decide if tweaking it will be enough or not." She turned and looked at Kidd. "Can Summer test your bike tomorrow?"

"Can she ride?" Kidd asked with hesitation.

"Dunno. Let's ask," Breeze said.

Summer and Rocky were in a zone watching the races. Breeze walked over and tapped their shoulders. "Summer, can you ride bikes?"

Summer, Blade, and Rocky looked at each other and grinned. "I've been riding dirt bikes and motorcycles since I was ten years old," Summer said.

"Do you have a street bike?"

"Yeah, but it wouldn't win any races if that's what you are asking."

"No. I just wanted to know if you can ride. Blade, can you get the bike to Matt's house tomorrow? Can either of you ride?" Breeze asked.

Rocky preferred to ride street bikes and drive cars. Blade was fine with dirt bikes, street bikes, and cars. He did mention that even though he could ride bikes that Summer really was the best. Breeze looked at the guys and gave a thumbs up. Zion and Yu walked by, and she bowed slightly. They returned the gesture. Jazz and the others did the same. Zion smiled and walked off.

"Good thing we weren't on an adventure," Jazz said to Breeze.

"Why? It wouldn't be the first time they have had to track. Would you like me to issue the challenge now and see if the newbies can keep up?

Jazz busted out laughing. Zion whipped around and so did Mickey. Zion walked back over to Breeze, stroked her face, and touched her mind. *"I am not working tonight, and I really don't feel like tracking that beautiful ass of yours all over creation tonight. Can you behave just for one night?"*

"Jazz did you hear that I have a beautiful ass."

"Duh, tell me something I didn't know."

"We were thinking of seeing if the newbies could keep up. Would you like to play?" She stroked Zion's face. "You would be with me."

Zion looked at Jazz, Kidd, and then Mickey. He threw his head back and busted out laughing. Mickey and Kidd took off running for Breeze. Zion grabbed her and threw her over his shoulder and took off. Jazz was holding his side from laughing so hard. Blade looked at Jazz, Kidd, and Mickey for an explanation. Mickey was cussing. Kidd was speechless and Jazz was laughing.

"Who issued the damn challenge?" Mickey finally spoke.

"Challenge? What challenge? Who was that?" Blade asked confused.

"One of the best trackers, and he is now with one of the best schemers. Bro, why were you left behind?" Mickey asked and shook his head. He turned just as Angela walked over to Jazz.

Breeze came walking back with a whole lot of sass. "Mickey, darling. Thank you for that wonderful compliment. Oh, no worries. I am quite sure that I see a challenge in your future." She sashayed off to stand by Blade, Summer, and Rocky. She picked up the conversation right where they had left off.

"Matt's up right now, then Jazz, and we will explain everything in the cars. Remember, trust no one because there are too many ears here. Oh, Blade, here ya go." Breeze tossed him his keys and handed him the pink slip.

"Thanks."

Jazz and Angela walked off toward the location that Jazz would be racing in.

"Don't worry; you don't have to drive it home. We have a truck where we load our new rides. We'll load it once Matt and Jazz race. That is, unless you want to drive it home."

"And miss being alone with you? No way," Blade said. He kissed her hand. A chill ran through her from her head to her toes. She giggled.

"Knock it off. That felt funny," said Jazz.

"Then tune it out because I like it," Breeze snapped back.

"Oh, hell; Well, two can play at that."

Breeze felt a weird sensation on her mouth. She realized Jazz must have been kissing Angela. *"Ok. We need to work on this connection. You don't want to feel who I kiss or whatever, and I sure don't want to feel who you are kissing or whatever. I love our connection, but seriously, there are just some things I don't want to feel."*

"Or whatever? Is there something I need to know?" *Jazz asked.*

"No."

"You're not going to sleep with him, are you?"

"Jazz, I've known him a week. You know me better than that."
Jazz felt her tense and the flashes started.

"Breeze, breathe, hold onto Blade. I will tap him. You'll be ok. I will be there as soon as I win. I would come now, but I'm being cued to start my engine." He quickly tapped Blade. "Blade, take her to her car alone. She is having a vision. I will be there in five."

"What do I do?"

"Nothing besides what I said."

Blade did just that. Breeze grabbed Blade's wrists and extremely fast images were flashing in his mind. He was seeing their surroundings; Taylor was there with three of his buddies, and they were watching him and Breeze.

"Shit," Blade swore out loud and then tapped the others. *"Jazz, Kidd, Matt, and Mickey HE IS HERE."*

"Get to Breeze's car," *Jazz said.*

Kidd was holding Summer's hand and running along with Matt, Mickey, and Rocky. Jazz wasn't far behind with Angela in tow.

Jazz tapped Blade. *"I told you not to do anything."*

"I didn't, she grabbed my wrist."

"Where is he?"

Blade turned to his left, and Jazz immediately saw him. Jazz turned to Kidd. "Call Jon now. Matt, get the extras loaded, we have to get her out of here," Jazz said with authority.

"On it," Matt said.

"Mickey help Matt," Jazz said.

"No problem," Mickey said.

"Breeze, get in your car." Jazz was extremely angry and worried at the same time.

"No way. I'm not running," Breeze said.

"You're not. You're leading him out of here so we can get him in a more private location for his royal ass whipping. Blade I need you to go with her. Angela, you are with me unless you want to leave with Chad."

"I'm with you. Is that the guy that hurt Breeze?" Ang asked.

Jazz explained that Taylor doesn't race, but he knows Breeze does, so he came to finish what he started. "Rocky you are with me. Kidd, you and Summer with Matt. Get to the car now. Matt should be there. We will split up and meet at Jon's gym. Is that correct, Kidd?" Kidd nodded. He was shocked that Taylor would show up here. "We will drive calmly out of here. Once we hit the gates, we gun it. We will be followed and that's the point," Jazz explained. "I will alert Zion and Yu."

"Jazz be careful, please," Breeze said with concern. Jazz walked over and kissed her. Taylor saw this and fury was clearly displayed on his face. All her friends saw the fury.

"He's pissed," said Kidd.

"Good, he's sure to follow," said Blade.

"I wonder if you kissed her if it would make his fury worse. I'm up for some serious ground and pound," Rocky said.

"Do you mind?" Blade asked Breeze. She shook her head and he then looked at Jazz. He shook his head and turned to Angela. Blade wanted their first kiss to be special and he wasn't going to let the public scene or her ex-boyfriend ruin that. He turned to her, gently touched her face, lightly pulled her to him, and placed his lips to hers. Everything else went away. She was the only thing that mattered. She pulled him closer and kissed him passionately. He felt her tongue against his; everything about her was soft and sweet. It was perfect.

Blade heard Rocky say, "Hmmm. I think it worked."

Blade and Breeze turned. Taylor looked like he was about to spit nails.

"Jazz, if this doesn't go the way we hope, then we will call Uncle. I'm not playing his games anymore. He will NOT hurt me, my family, or my friends," Breeze said.

Jazz didn't look happy, but he didn't argue. "Are you sure?" He asked her and she gave a nod. "You know Uncle will want to know everything," he said as he gently touched her cheek.

"Part of the hold is all of the secrets," she said and touched his hand. "I am done with his hold on and over me." She got in her car, started the car, Jazz stepped back, went to his car, got in, and Breeze led the cars out. She was followed by Jazz, Matt, and finally the truck with all the cars brought up the rear. The truck wasn't part of the trap; it went out, got on the interstate, and headed back to the garage. When they turned out, they went three separate ways. Taylor and a buddy followed Breeze. His other two buddies followed Jazz. They hadn't been on the road long when Taylor rammed Breeze. Jazz was linked to Breeze the minute they got in their cars. They both heard the shots ring through the air. Blade growled and he clenched his fist.

"Are you ok? Did the shot hit you?" Breeze asked.

"No. I'm not ok. I want his blood."

She made a mental note to never make Blade mad. Another shot was fired, and it hit her back glass. She was ticked. She really liked this car, and Taylor was now ruining it. She flipped the console open and turned on the nitro.

"Ever been in a car with nitro?"

"No," Blade said.

"Hold on." She punched the switch, and they were gone. She heard another shot and decided she had had enough. She threw the wheel to the right, spun the car around, and was headed straight toward Taylor's car.

"Breeze, what the hell are you doing?" Blade asked with concern.

"I want to see how much balls he really has. I want him to know I'm **NOT** scared anymore."

"There are better ways."

They were getting closer to a head-on collision when Taylor spun out and hit the ditch. She turned the wheel hard left and was headed back the original way. She was laughing, Jazz was cussing her mentally, and Blade was looking confused and upset at the same time.

"Have you lost your mind? You could have killed yourself. Not to mention I think Jazz is going to kill you. I think he about crapped on himself when you pulled that stunt."

"I'm perfectly fine and, no, I wouldn't have killed myself or you; I was going to break right. It was either that or have Taylor continue to shoot at us. Look at my car; the next one could have been one of us. Jazz will be ok once we are back at the gym."

They both looked over their shoulders at the sound of a car flying up behind them. "Ready for round two?" Breeze asked. Blade looked like he was ready to kill. "The gym is not far up ahead. Blade, how am I supposed to get out of the car?"

"None of us expected a gun."

"I did. I know how badly he wants me dead. I just didn't think he'd be stupid enough to use one. Call my dad and warn him that Taylor is armed. I'm going to call Matt."

"Jazz, get Angela and Summer to my dad's house for their safety."

"No time. They knew what they were in for when they got in the cars," Jazz said. "Oh, by the way, when this is over, we will discuss that little stunt of yours."

"I love you."

"I'm still pissed."

Breeze tried to flatter Jazz to ease his anxiety. It was not working. Breeze and Blade arrived at the gym second. Matt, Mickey, Kidd, and Summer were already there. Summer was holding a shotgun.

"Blade?" Breeze asked with a confused tone.

"I think that's how you get out of the car."

"I won't ask."

"Better that way," Blade replied.

She looked at Summer. All shyness seemed to be gone, and she looked like she could take on the world. Jazz was flying around the corner to the right on a side street. Blade and Breeze were walking toward Mickey when they heard a car flying up from the left. Taylor didn't see Summer because his focus was on Breeze, until he spotted Jazz. He stuck his left hand out the window with the gun in hand. There was a loud sound and Taylor started swerving all over the road. He dropped his gun in the street. Summer had shot out his tire. Jazz pulled into the grass. Jazz, Rocky, and Angela got out and moved over to where the other four were located. Taylor's buddies were pulling up. Summer shot out one of their tires as well.

Breeze shot Blade a confused look. "They won't be driving out of here, I guess," he said with a shrug.

"Wow. Ok," Breeze said.

"Never a dull moment around you, girl," Kidd laughed.

Taylor was running across the road. "I told you; you are a whore. Bitch, I'm going to kill you."

Before anything else could be said, a whole lot of things happened; four UFC fighters stepped out from the side of the gym, Jon stepped down the steps and Blade, Rocky, Jazz, Matt, and Kidd were moving across the grass. Summer got in front of Breeze and Angela.

Jon spoke in a calm manner, but Breeze could see his anger. "Taylor, why are you here?"

"I'm here for that bitch."

"If you are talking about my daughter, I can assure you, it's not going to happen."

Blade was the first to move toward Taylor; he was so fast. Rocky was right at his side.

"Breeze is not a whore or a bitch. You need to have some respect for her and all women," Blade said through gritted teeth.

"Kiss my ass," Taylor yelled at Blade.

Taylor's friends were at his side, though they didn't seem too sure of their odds. Blade was on Taylor before anyone could do anything. Rocky took the largest of Taylor's friends. Matt took one and Jazz took the other. Blade busted Taylor up good. He made sure to break four ribs and bruise all the others. He broke his wrist and hurt his leg badly, not to mention that he broke his nose, his jaw, and blacked both of his eyes. Taylor tried to defend himself, but he was too slow. Jon walked over and slowly touched Blade's arm. Blade stopped.

Rocky, Jazz, and Matt were standing beside the UFC fighters, and the guys that they had been fighting were on the ground. The fighters said their goodbyes and left. They were only there to run interference if needed. Kidd and Mickey came walking out of the gym in shorts and T-shirts. Jazz, Matt, Rocky, and Blade were walking toward the gym.

Jon was on the phone. "Yes ma'am, I'd like to report a disturbance at my business property. Four guys were threatening my daughter and her friends. The man is her ex-boyfriend, Taylor Smith. Yes, ma'am, there is a restraining order against him. No, ma'am, the boys were working out when Breeze and her friends pulled up. The guys heard shots fired. They ran out and saw Breeze's back glass shot out and two carloads of guys following her. They confronted the guys. Taylor pulled a gun, and it is in the road from when his tire blew out and he hit the other car. Taylor and his friends got out and started fighting the guys from the gym. all four, Taylor and his friends, are on the ground. You might want to send an ambulance or two. The police have arrived, thank you."

Jon hung up and greeted the officers. They documented Jon's story, took pictures of Breeze's back glass, pictures of the gun in the street and dusted the gun for prints. The ambulances arrived and transported Taylor and his friends to the hospital. Two police cars followed the ambulances. As soon as the men were discharged, they would be arrested. Several officers went in the gym to get everyone's statements. That's when Breeze noticed Blade, Jazz, Matt, and Rocky in shorts and t-shirts looking a little sweaty.

Breeze just sat in shock while the others talked. She heard Angela say they were coming back from the movies to meet the guys here when they heard cars coming up from behind them fast. They heard a shot and then another one. The second one hit the window. We were screaming and Breeze kept saying that he'd come to finish what he had started and was crying. She heard Summer across the gym telling the same thing, but she also had pulled out a movie stub as proof. She heard Jazz say that he and Blade had been sparring when they heard gun shots.

"Where were you, Mr. Lee?" one of the officers asked.

"I was here with the guys, overseeing the workouts and sparring. I had gone to the back to get cleaning supplies when I heard the shots. I ran out and saw these four fighting with Breeze's ex-boyfriend and his friends. That's when I saw Breeze's car. I ran over to make sure the girls were ok, and I called 911."

"Thank you, Mr. Lee. Miss Lee, I'm sorry your ex got this close to you. He will be in jail for a couple of months, so don't worry."

She nodded.

"Good night, officers." Jon walked them out.

The room was quiet until Jon returned. Breeze was worried that Taylor and his friends would tell a completely different story. Jon reassured her that it didn't matter, since none of the guys would even be able to remember their own names. They were completely wasted. All the guys went and changed into normal clothes. Breeze remembered Ang and Summer's statements.

"Summer, how did you get a movie stub?"

"From your dad."

"Jana and I were at the movies. It had just ended when Kidd called," Jon said.

Breeze leaned forward and placed her face in her hands. She began sobbing. Blade and Jazz walked up to her; they both placed their arms around her.

"Breeze he won't touch you, I promise," said Jazz.

"I promise you that as well," Blade said.

"You guys shouldn't make promises you can't keep. In a month or two he will be out of jail, and he will wait until I'm alone. He will come after me again."

"We will be there," they both said.

"We all will be," Matt said, and all her friends agreed.

"Are you all crashing at my house?" Breeze asked.

Kidd yelled, "Hell, yeah."

Matt and Mickey said their good-byes. "See you tomorrow at ten in the morning. Don't come any earlier. I need my beauty sleep, not to mention Tisha is coming over," Matt said.

"Yeah, and she's bringing Lisa with her, so definitely not before ten in the morning." Mickey winked and walked out.

Jon made sure that he didn't need to call Blade's dad or Ang's mom. They all assured Jon that there was no need to call their parents. Ang told Jon that her mother expected her to stay the weekend with Breeze. Jon nodded and looked at Breeze. She gave Jon a weary smile.

Blade placed his arm around Breeze and whispered in her ear, "Now, you might be a bad influence on her." Breeze was laughing so hard she was crying.

Jazz tapped her mind, *"Crap. How will we drink now?"*

"Very carefully, Greedy," Breeze said with a teasing smile.

"Hey, kiss Angela. She really likes you and she kind of got thrown into this mess. Just not now. Some place with a little privacy."

"You owe Blade one in private, too," Jazz said shyly.

Breeze and Jazz continued to talk mentally for a few more minutes. Jon was planning to meet everyone at the house after he locked up the dojo.

Blade took her hand. "Are you ready to go?"

She nodded. "You?"

"Always ready to be with you," Blade said.

"And you question my mental state? You should be worried about your own." She kissed his hand gently.

Jazz walked up, "Oh, yeah, we need to talk about that stunt."

"Nope, it's over. It's done. Nothing to say, plus I bought us a little more time. If you will excuse me." She pulled Blade to her car. She was still laughing when she started the car. Blade touched her hand. She looked at him and smiled. "Thank you."

"You're welcome. May I kiss you again?" Blade asked.

She nodded. She explained that she would like a little privacy. He agreed. Breeze decided to take back streets to her house. They pulled over a couple of blocks before her house. This time she took his face in her hands, and he placed her face in his hands. They sat there holding each other's face for what felt like forever, which was probably like thirty seconds. He leaned over and passionately kissed her. He scooted closer to her. She really enjoyed his touch. She had butterflies when he kissed her. He moved back slightly. "We better go, everyone's waiting. By the way, that's how I imagined our first kiss."

"Now that I'm out of breath, we are going to roll up in the house. One more kiss before we go."

He pulled her to him and kissed her a little bit harder, but even more passionately. She had her hand around his neck and was pulling him more into the kiss. He gently released her grip and laughed. "Girl, I want nothing more than to keep kissing you, but they will wonder where we are," Blade said.

"Well, crap," Breeze said in a playful and frustrated tone. They pulled up just as Jazz and Angela pulled in. She realized she wasn't the only one making out. She tapped his mind.

"Have fun?"

"I had to do something when I felt you making out. Yeah, we had fun. You?"

"Absolutely."

"Ok, you don't have to gloat," Jazz said with a grin and attitude.

"We will work on that part of the connection."

"Yeah, I can see myself sitting in class and then start drooling and looking all gooey eyed," Jazz said.

"OHHH, I'll buy tixs. Better yet, I'll sell them."

"Har har har."

Their connection ended.

"I'm hungry," Breeze said.

"Me, too," Jazz said. The four walked in together.

"I ordered pizzas. I thought you'd be hungry. There are movies on the counter. Good night. We are going to bed," Jana said. She walked over and hugged Breeze. "I love you. I am glad you are ok."

"Thanks, Jana. Dad, thank you, too. I really appreciate it. I love you both."

"No problem, baby. I'd do anything to protect you."

"You're welcome. The pizzas should be here in five minutes. They are already paid for," Jana said.

"You rock." Kidd yelled.

Everyone called our their thanks. Jazz and Angela were on the couch. Kidd, Rocky, and Summer were sitting on big bean bag chairs. Blade was in the chair with the ottoman. Breeze walked over to Jazz, kissed him on the forehead, and walked over to Blade.

"May I sit with you?"

"Sure. He started to move over when Breeze sat in front of

him. He leaned over and kissed her neck.

"Oh, I need to change. Angela, do you want some comfortable clothes?"

"Yes, Please."

"Summer?" She got up and followed Breeze upstairs.

"Blade, will you get the pizzas when they arrive? I would ask Jazz, but he'll eat them all."

"He better not. I'm starving." Angela giggled.

"Sure," Blade said.

Breeze was walking up the stairs when she stopped and turned to look at Jazz. "You still have that friend in Mono-Valleo?"

"Yeah."

"I need to pay him a visit."

Jazz nodded. "When?"

"Sunday ok?" Breeze asked.

"Sure. I'll call."

"Thanks."

Blade tapped her mind. *"Who's in MonoValleo?"*

"Someone who can help me train without training because they were broken once, too."

Blade gave a slight nod.

TAYLOR AND HIS FRIENDS

Taylor refused to answer anything in the ambulance except his personal information. The police arrived at the hospital just as Taylor and his friends were unloaded from the ambulances. They were all given drug tests and blood alcohol levels were checked. Taylor's blood alcohol level was almost three times the legal limit. He was read his rights and cuffed to the bed. He was beyond angry and started yelling and cussing at the officers. His friends were in rooms across the hall and they were being read their rights as well. They were not yelling and cussing.

Taylor called his attorney once he was in a room and asked that his father be notified. If he was in Memphis, his father would have ensured that he was released as soon as he was patched up, but since he was in Jackson, he wasn't sure how soon his dad could get him released. Taylor was patched up, and he passed out. The next morning when he woke, he forgot where he was and that he was handcuffed to the bed until he tried to move. His head was pounding. He had one hell of a hang over and wished they would give him some vodka and orange juice, but he was pretty sure that wasn't on the menu.

Taylor's attorney and father arrived at eight in the morning.

The officer that was posted outside the door alerted his supervisor that Mr. Smith's attorney had arrived. Fifteen minutes later another officer arrived and explained the charges to Taylor and his attorney.

Taylor's father interrupted him. "There has been a huge misunderstanding."

Before Mr. Smith could say anything else the officer spoke over him. "No sir, there has not been a misunderstanding. Your son and his friends were harassing Miss Lee and her friends. You son shot at her and her car. The gun that was found on the scene has come back with Taylor's prints all over it. Please do not try to downplay domestic violence to me. I know what your son is capable of, and he will be going before the judge Monday morning. Until that time he is under arrest. Now, Mr. Smith, you may leave the room, or I can have you escorted out; it is your choice."

Mr. Smith started to speak, but the attorney shook his head. Mr. Smith walked out as smugly as he walked in, but he was mad. He was mad at his son for being stupid enough to have witnesses, he was mad that this was going to cost him dearly to get his son out of jail, and, most of all, he was mad that the hits had not been executed. He got in his car and called the first associate that was hired to follow through with Breeze and Jazz. To his shock, it went to voicemail. He tried again and then called his second point of contact for the contract, and it went to voicemail as well. They never rejected his call. He called them both back and left a terse message on both voicemails. They both had been on his payroll for a long time; in fact, when Taylor's mother decided she was leaving, his first acquaintance had helped him remove the possibility of having to pay alimony. Taylor did not know anything of that and never would. No woman ever left Mr. Smith unless he decided it was time for her to go.

"I can't believe how stupid Taylor has been when it comes to Breeze Lee. There are plenty of women out there that would not give Taylor the attitude that Breeze did. If there was a way for me to take care of her and Jazz myself, I would. I taught Taylor no witnesses and always take care of personal issues behind closed doors." Mr. Smith said to himself and the empty car. He punched the seat in his frustration.

He sat there thinking about how much this was going to cost him both financially and in his time to clean up this mess and to make Breeze disappear. He wondered if he knew any judges in Jackson. He couldn't think of any off the top of his head. He would reach out to one of his business partners in Memphis to see if they could call in some favors. Once Taylor was home, he would give him a week or two to heal and recover, then he was sending him either out of the state or out of the country. He would work recruiting for him. Mr. Smith smiled. That bum leg might come in handy. Taylor could use it to attract women to feel pity for him. He was thinking about the preferences of his Asian and European associates. Yes, Taylor would be a valuable asset in recruiting for those preferences. Taylor was a ladies' man for sure.

Once the attorney had left Taylor at the hospital, he called Mr. Smith to fill him in on everything. The judge that Taylor was supposed to go in front of was not someone that was easily bought, and it was likely that Taylor would be in jail for a month or two at least, but he would try his best to get bond set and would try to delay trial as long as possible. Mr. Smith groaned. He tried his associates regarding the contracts again, but both went straight to voicemail. Mr. Smith reached out to a couple of business associates in Memphis. Fifteen minutes later, the first business partner called back. He confirmed what his attorney had said. The second business partner called a couple minutes later. Not only did he confirm that the judge could not be bought, but he also confirmed that the judge had zero tolerance for domestic violence, especially since his only daughter and grandson had been killed by his daughter's husband. Taylor would be lucky if he just received a couple of months.

Mr. Smith was in such a foul mood when he arrived home that no one wanted to be around him. He was on the phone for two hours trying to track down his associates regarding the contracts. No one had seen them for a couple of weeks. Mr. Smith could not believe it. He was beginning to think they took his money and ran. That thought infuriated him even more. At that moment an email came through that made his blood turn cold. They hadn't run at all; they had been relieved of their duties permanently. The pictures made his stomach turn. He deleted the pictures and email quickly. He did not need anything leading a connection back to him. He sat down hard in his desk chair and poured himself a tumbler full of whiskey. He drained the first glass and poured himself another. He drank the second slowly. Who are these people? Who the hell is Breeze Lee and Jazz Dubre? Mr. Smith did not come out of his office until it was time for dinner. He was staggering drunk when he went down to the dining room. He was served and everyone slunk back to the shadows to avoid Mr. Smith's gaze and mood.

During his meal, he raised his glass and said, "To my son, the biggest idiot in the world." Then he lowered his glass to his mouth and threw the contents back. He stumbled from the room and went to the library. He woke up the next morning when sunlight was pouring in the window. Someone had given him a blanket and a pillow during the night, but he didn't know who. It didn't matter. Monday could not come soon enough.

THE MORNING AFTER

A police officer called at seven in the morning to inform Breeze and Jon that Taylor had been arrested for breaking the restraining order, public intoxication, reckless driving, stalking, attempted murder, DUI, and discharging a firearm in public. Since he didn't touch her this time, the attempted murder charge probably wouldn't hold, so he would be released in a couple of months, but he would not see the judge until Monday morning, so the officer did not know if bail would be set or not. He would have some serious fines for the DUI and firearm charges, not to mention he would lose his license for at least a year. Jon hung up. He sat at the table with Breeze. "Honey, I wish they could keep him longer."

"I know, so do I, but it is what it is. His family is so loaded; he basically walked when he landed me in the hospital for three weeks. His dad did tell him that he wouldn't bail him out again. We could only hope, but I doubt it. His dad abused his mom for twenty years until she had enough and ran. Taylor's mad at his mom, not his father."

"I will never understand why a man feels the need to hit a woman," Jon said.

"Control, Dad, complete control," Breeze said.

"Still, there is NO excuse for it."

"I know."

Jon began talking to Breeze about Blade and her interest in him. Then he switched to her evening attire. When she hesitated, he held up his hand. Breeze hugged him.

"Oh, Dad, I love you."

"I love you, too, I just worry now more than ever with you on medical restrictions again," Jon said.

Breeze agreed with her dad that the timing was kind of lousy.

"I'm glad you have such loyal friends."

"Me too," she said and laid out her plans for the day. They were all going to Matt's house to work on her back glass and get a few parts for a car that she was planning to build.

"Jana and I are going to the mountains for today and tomorrow. Will you be ok alone?"

"Alone? I'm never alone."

"Yeah, I noticed." They both smiled. "You know your friends are welcome, though you might have to hang Kidd from the ceiling to keep him from Summer."

"I think she can handle herself," Breeze said.

"I think so, too," he laughed. " Have fun, behave, and try not to get in any trouble while we are gone."

Breeze sat and talked with her dad a little while before he got up to go pack their bags. Breeze enjoyed sitting with him, talking, and having a cup of coffee. They could talk cars and martial arts, whereas with her mother, you didn't mention either without her blood pressure rising to stroke level. Everyone else was still asleep as they should have been since they didn't go to sleep until four in the morning. The one person awake was Jazz, and he came walking into the kitchen. He looked rough. Breeze greeted Jazz with a smile and light kiss on the lips. She gave him the run down on what the officer said, her dad's plans, and hers.

Jazz tapped her mind. *"What did you have in mind for MonoValleo?"*

"Tribal band."

"Where?"

"Left ankle."

"How will you hide it?"

"Tape, of course."

"Ok. It's your head."

"No, it's my ankle." She sighed heavily. *"It's only been five days of restrictions, and I'm going crazy."*

"Hey, you are still doing toning and strengthening, right?"

"Not right now because of the procedure. I'm waiting for the ok from the doc on Monday."

"We both know that you're completely healed from that, and probably most of the others as well."

"We know that, but they don't. How would I explain all those fractures completely healed or almost completely healed when only days ago they were still there?"

"Good point," Jazz said.

"Don't worry. I do plan to continue to train, but it's kind of complicated now. I will NEVER be this broken again."

"You are not broken, Breeze. You've just had a setback."

"I'm broken more than you know," she said.

"Will you show me? Please?"

"No. It will not be your burden. I love you too much," Breeze said.

He walked around and faced her with his hands on her hips. *"I love you too much to let you hold the burden alone."*

"I know."

Jana quietly walked in, smiled at them both. She kissed Breeze on her forehead. "We'll see you tomorrow afternoon."

Jon entered the kitchen after Jana. He had their luggage. Breeze hugged them both and told them to have fun. Jon told Jazz to protect Breeze and to call if he needed them. After Jon and Jana left, Jazz went back to their conversation. This time he slid his hand to her wrist. *"Please."*

"I can't."

"I will never leave you. You know that, right?"

"I know," she sighed.

She decided to show him everything when Blade walked in.

"I'm not interrupting, am I?"

"Yes," Jazz said with great irritation.

"No," Breeze said with a sense of calm.

"Breeze, I know you were going to show me. I could feel it," Jazz insisted.

"Later. I promise."

"Tomorrow?"

"Yes, after we see your friend. We will go on to the mountain and find some place private, drink, and I will show you everything. We will drink again after that. Just remember I didn't want you to share this burden."

"Thank you."

"Save it until you have seen everything," Breeze said and ended the connection.

"No, Blade, you are not interrupting. Do you want to go out back and sit by the pool?"

"Sure." He knew they had been talking; he just wished he knew what about. He also wasn't sure he'd ever get used to

Jazz having such a strong connection with her or seeing him with his hands on her. He would have to because he liked being a part of her life. It felt right. He also got the sense that Breeze and Jazz shared a greater secret or two that the others weren't involved in.

Rocky really liked Jazz, which was odd because, normally, Rocky didn't like anyone who wasn't family. When Blade asked him why, he just shrugged. Rocky honestly seemed ok with all her friends, but he really liked Jazz. They went out and sat on the swing that was off to the side of the pool. Breeze just wanted some alone time with Blade. She was beginning to like him. She needed to clear the air first, though.

"Blade, you know I'm still healing emotionally, mentally, and physically from my last relationship, right?" Breeze asked.

"I know."

"Please be patient with me," Breeze said.

"I will."

"Can you accept that Jazz and I are what we are?"

"I'm trying," Blade said.

Breeze explained that she liked him, but she needed a little more time before she agreed to date him. Blade was ok with that. He felt strangely close to her, and he would give her the time she needed. He hoped it wasn't a long time from now, but he had already agreed to be patient, and he would honor that. They sat there talking for a little over an hour when Summer and Rocky walked out. They were pale.

"Hey, man, we need to go. We need to change, load up my bike and be back by ten so we can go to Matt's garage, not to mention I'm starving," Summer said. Rocky just grinned.

"I'll be right there. I'll meet you at the car. Now go away," Blade said. He waited for the door to close before he spoke.

"Do you think you can stay out of trouble for a couple of hours while I'm gone?" he asked.

"I'll think about it." Breeze winked at him. "The question is, can you stay out of trouble while you are away?" Breeze asked.

"I don't know. You are rubbing off on me." They laughed. He gently kissed her lips and then her forehead. "I'll see you at ten."

"I better go cook for those beasts before Jazz chews off his arm or someone else's. See you then," she said. They walked to the front door together, Breeze said her goodbyes and kissed Blade lightly.

Jazz grabbed her the second the others were gone. *"You have a promise to fulfill. Since Kidd and Ang are still asleep, this is the perfect time."*

"Three times in one day?"

"Absolutely," Jazz said.

"Outside; now, so they don't hear us."

They quietly ran out the back door. They ran to the back of the pool house. Jazz bit her, hard and fast. It took every ounce of her will power not to rip Jazz's clothes off. He could sense it, and it made him bite her harder. It was getting harder and harder to keep this secret. They were out back for about twenty minutes before they went in and started cooking breakfast. Breeze cooked, and Jazz ran to get a shower. Kidd and Ang both woke up quickly when they smelled the bacon cooking.

Blade, Summer, and Rocky returned at nine forty. They all had a lot more color to them. They all loaded up and headed to Matt's about ten thirty in the morning. Matt and Mickey had all the bikes out waiting on them. Kidd helped Summer unload her bike, and then he fired his bike up and took off. He was still working the kinks out of it.

"Let's see what you got," Matt said.

Summer jumped on. She was good, but she was right: her bike wasn't ready for the streets. Breeze and Matt would work with her on getting it fit for her and the streets. She would be an awesome racer. Breeze threw Summer the keys to her new street racer, the one Jazz had just won for her.

"Jazz, show her the basics, and let's race." She flashed him a grin and turned to Mickey. "Mickey, let's get some of the dirt bikes and do some motocross."

Breeze was excited as she headed straight for the line of bikes. Blade placed his arm around her. "Do you think you should?"

"Why not?"

"The procedure. My dad hasn't cleared you yet."

"Crap." Breeze shot a look to Jazz. He shrugged. "Rocky and Blade, grab a dirt bike and follow Mickey." Breeze was beginning to realize that Blade was as serious on medical restrictions as his dad was. She would have to work on that. She tapped Zion. *"Where are you and Yu?"*

"Working."

"Ok. We are at Matt's; I was thinking you could show the newbies a thing or two on dirt bikes. I am on medical restrictions."

"Since when has that stopped you?"

"Since the newbies are the doc's kids."

"Priceless. Let me know how that works out for you."

"Should I issue it now?"

"I wouldn't. Jana and Jon are on high alert. You know Han is flying in, right?"

"What? Why?"

"Taylor."

"Sounds like the perfect time. Gotta go. See ya."

In the back of Matt's garage, there are five acres set up for motocross and tricks. Rocky's mouth fell open. "What the hell?"

"Motocross track and extreme tracks. Mickey will do a run on each. If you have never done tricks on a bike, now is **not** the time."

"We haven't," Blade spoke for all three of them.

"Ok, just watch. It's all yours, man." Breeze motioned for Mickey to start.

Mickey did the tricks first. When Mickey was finished, Blade looked at Breeze. "Do you do that?"

"I'm much more extreme."

"Seriously?"

"Seriously. Let me show you. Just don't tell your dad."

"Promise not to break anything?"

"Promise." Breeze crossed her heart and gave Blade a shy smile. He gave a slight nod. Breeze waved Mickey down to let him know that she was taking the track next. She took the bike that Blade was holding and Mickey's helmet.

"I mean it. DO NOT BREAK ANYTHING." Blade yelled.

He started to sweat. He was seriously having second thoughts about agreeing to let her do this. Mickey started laughing. She took off. The thrill and the rush made her feel alive. Her last trick was a back flip. Before she knew it, she was at the end of the track. Breeze was grinning when she walked back to Mickey. She threw him the helmet. Mickey picked her up and spun her around.

Blade was completely speechless. He knew the streets made her seem free, but he never dreamed of her doing something like this. They would talk later. Her safety was a priority. Breeze could tell Blade was in shock, and she didn't care. She walked over and kissed him lightly.

"Nothing is broken or torn, just like I promised. Rocky, you ok?"

"Yeah, I think my stomach is still on one of the jumps you did. You should have seen Blade's face. He was freaking out."

"Good thing I didn't; it would have ruined my concentration," Breeze said with complete sass.

After they ran the motocross track a few times, they went back to the garage. "Blade, Summer, and Rocky, we are going to see what you got in a car. All are loaded with nitro, same with the bikes that we race except for the dirt bikes because it's not allowed," Breeze said.

"Matt, do we have the cars from last night?" Matt nodded. "Great. What about the ones from last week or two weeks ago?" she asked.

"We have yours and Jazz's from last week. We have the orange and the purple from two weeks ago."

"Ok, let's get the yellow one from last night for Blade, and the purple and the orange for Rocky and Summer. I want to try out mine from last week. Hey, bro, since we are here, can we fix the Mustang today?"

"We may have to go to the junkyard," Matt said.

"I need to go, anyway."

"Wow. Is she always this bossy?" asked Rocky.

"Only when racing; she knows her stuff, so you do what she says," Jazz said.

Jazz raced Rocky first in the orange car. It wasn't working for him, so he tried the purple. Neither one worked for him. Jazz waved to Matt. There was a roar and the garage door opened. Jazz's black Challenger rolled out.

"Holy crap," yelled Rocky.

Breeze ran over to Jazz. "What are you doing?" she asked, a little confused and concerned.

"I told you I knew the perfect car for him. He's sure to win."

"Are you sure? You love that car."

"We will build another one, I'm sure," Jazz said.

Breeze shook her head and walked out to count them off. Jazz was right, the Challenger was perfect. Breeze raced Summer in the car Jazz won for her; it was almost perfect, and she decided to keep it. Summer was a match to the purple 1977 Corvette. Of course, they would tweak it. Next, Blade raced Kidd. It was close. Both cars seemed to be made for each of them.

"I think that's got it," Jazz said.

"No, there's one more race," Breeze replied.

"Really? Who?"

"You and me."

"What? Mustang to Mustang?" Jazz asked.

"Charger to Charger."

"What?" Jazz asked shocked.

"I'm glad I can still surprise you. Matt, can you bring out the Chargers?" Breeze requested.

"Sure thing," Matt agreed.

He ran behind the house, and was gone a couple of minutes before they heard the engines roar to life. Mickey came around the corner first, driving the car from her garage, and then Matt came from behind his house in a red and black Charger. Jazz's mouth fell open. "Are you serious?"

"Yep."

"OMG. Let's go."

Jazz and Breeze took their places at the starting line. Blade noticed Kidd and Matt betting on who would win. They revved their engines; Angela took the position to count them off. Her arms went up and dropped. Breeze and Jazz were neck and neck. Jazz pulled ahead, Breeze got beside him again, gave him a wink, gunned it, and hit the nitro. She won by half a car length.

Kidd threw his arms up and paid Matt. Breeze walked over with sass saying, "Was he betting against me?"

"Yeah," Mickey said and nodded.

"Sucker," Breeze announced.

They stayed at Matt's until about seven that evening, then they headed back to Breeze's house. "You know you all are welcome to stay tonight. Jazz and I will leave about ten tomorrow morning."

Kidd plopped on the couch. "You know I am staying."

"I have to get home. My mom expects me by nine," Angela said.

"I'll drive you," Jazz said.

Breeze shot Jazz a look and shook her head. Breeze made it clear that she would be driving Ang home so her mother wouldn't suspect anything. Jazz gave a grumble but agreed. He really liked her and wanted to see her again. Breeze motioned for Jazz and Ang to go out back to say their goodbyes. Jazz didn't hesitate. He grabbed Ang and gently pulled her out the back door. Ang blushed a little but took Jazz's hand and went willingly with him. Breeze turned her attention to Blade, Summer, and Rocky.

"What about you guys?

"We're staying, or at least I am," Blade said with a grin.

"Yeah, the party is better here," Rocky laughed.

"I'm staying. I kind of like it here," Summer winked at Kidd. Kidd's mouth dropped open.

Rocky shook his head, "I need a date." Blade was laughing so hard he fell off the ottoman. Breeze sat with Blade for about an hour. She patted Blade's leg, stood, and turned her attention to Rocky.

"Rocky, you can beat Jazz at extreme snowboarding on the PS3. He really needs to be beat. He is getting on my nerves. Blade, are you riding with me and Angela?" Blade nodded and started walking toward Breeze. She held up her hand for him to stop, then ran to the back door and yelled for Jazz and Ang. Blade took a seat back in the chair while he waited for her. "Don't make me come out there," Breeze said.

"Whatever," Jazz said from the swing area in the yard.

Blade was still laughing when Breeze came back into the living room.

"I'm glad you are staying. How does your dad feel about you guys being here all weekend?"

"He doesn't mind. He is glad we are out and not staying home. He thinks we don't socialize enough," Blade said.

"Pretty soon he'll be complaining you're out too much and I'm a bad influence on you."

"Nah."

Angela and Jazz came in looking a little breathless. Breeze started laughing. "Let's go, Juliet."

Breeze drove. Ang rode in the backseat so her mom would know that Blade was with Breeze and not her. Ang's cheeks were still a little pink. Breeze was glad that Jazz liked Ang. She was cool, a bit shy, but Jazz would take care of the shyness.

Sunday morning everyone left by nine thirty in the morning. Breeze assured everyone that she would let them know when she was back, and everyone could come back over. Kidd was going to Matt's house.

After everyone left, Jazz scooped Breeze up and carried her upstairs. "I leave tonight because I have school tomorrow. I want our connection as close as possible."

A sadness touched Breeze's eyes.

"I would move here if I could, you know it," Jazz said.

"I know."

He sat her on her bed and gently lifted her chin up so she met his eyes. "Blade is here."

"It's not the same, and you know that."

Jazz nodded. He flicked his finger under her chin. "My other thigh has your name on it."

"You first," Breeze said with confidence. Jazz did not hesitate. He was gentle this time when he bit her, but she became really excited. She was not gentle; in fact, she was so keyed up she ripped the side of his pants down the seam. Jazz sat up. "You owe me some new pants."

"Complaining?" Breeze asked.

"Hell, no."

BLADE AND HIS SIBLINGS

The week had been crazy since Blade and his siblings had met Breeze and her friends. They had no idea that the streets even existed before now. When they arrived home Sunday morning, Blade immediately showered and went to work out. He might not be a warrior but he still knew and practiced martial arts. He had a private Sensei in Jiu Jitsu ever since he and Rocky were four years old. Summer preferred trapping, but she still worked out with Blade and Rocky at least two or three times a week.

Blade loved to work out with weapons, and Rocky was always willing to go against him. They all loved archery as well. The long bow was Blade's favorite. Rocky liked the crossbow, and Summer loved the compound bow. Their house had a pool, a small pool house, and a fenced in backyard. Behind all of that sat twenty acres with a building that had been converted to a gym/ work out area. Beside the building and over three acres of land, there were various targets set up with land markers for distance so they could practice their archery. To the right of that was an area set up for target practice for guns. They were all diverse in their skills and talents.

Their home and the shooting range had been Summer's

sanctuary for many years. They had friends; however, they preferred the company of each other. It was easier to keep family secrets when you stayed close to the family. Plus, Summer didn't really fit in with any of the kids at school. Her IQ was through the roof, not to mention how beautiful she was. Most women were jealous or insecure around her, and most guys couldn't even find their voice around her. Around Breeze, they all could be themselves, and no one judged them. Blade seemed more competitive than normal since Breeze entered his life.

Blade and Rocky were out in the gym sparring.

"Wow, what has fired you up today? Was it Jazz, Kidd, or both?" Rocky asked as he was rolling to get up from the mat yet again. Blade simply shrugged.

"Have you told Breeze that you are in a tournament in a few weekends?"

"No."

They began drying off since they were drenched in sweat. "Why not?"

"I don't know, I just haven't. I just feel like it would be salt to a wound. Especially with her on medical restrictions."

"Jazz still competes, and she seems fine with it." Rocky shook out his hair. "Summer has a trapping competition that weekend, and we are in a martial arts tournament. Will Jazz be here this weekend?"

"I don't think so. I think he has a tournament, but I could be wrong. You know how the conversations go around them: sometimes I do well to even know what we are talking about or when we are supposed to be somewhere."

Rocky stood straighter and looked at Blade with a smile. "Maybe it will be the same tournament that we are in... I would really like to go against him in the ring."

Blade threw his towel at Rocky. Blade walked over to the bar mounted on the wall and started doing pull ups.

"I am going to practice shooting," Rocky said.

Blade nodded and asked him to turn on the music before he went out. Metallica started pouring out of the speakers. Blade worked out for about thirty more minutes, then he went in to take another shower. Breeze was all that he could think about. He wondered about MonoValleo again. He had a feeling it was more than what she had said but had no idea what it could be. Blade thought about what Mickey had said about the guy who had thrown Breeze over his shoulder. *What the hell was a tracker?* He shook his head. He understood the term, but tracker of what?

Blade wondered how he had not picked up on thoughts from people at school about the streets. He realized he had picked up thoughts of cars, motorcycles, and fights but, he had thought it was normal teenage stuff just their wants and desires, so he tuned it out. Plus they weren't people that he hung out with, and most weren't even in his classes. He was washing his hair when he remembered a passing conversation in the hall between two guys. *OMG. One of the guys had said the name Breeze.* Blade thought back, trying to remember what was said. *It was a fight in New York. She had been hurt bad but rolled the last second and barely won. When was that? December or January. CRAP ... flashes of other conversations of both guys and girls came to him...*

- *Breeze kicked ass this weekend*

- *I can't believe Breeze got beat this weekend*

- *Did you see Breeze on the track,? She rocks, Mickey seems to live on the track to be able to beat her.*

- Breeze and Jazz should just hook up. It would make things easier.

- Have you seen Zion with her? He is fine. If she doesn't date him, I would love a chance with him.

- I wish I could understand what Breeze and her friends say, but I guess I would have to learn Korean, Japanese, or whatever it is that they speak.

- Can you believe Kidd beat Breeze on bikes... HOLY COW.

Blade was shocked that he had heard not only her name a lot at school, but he had also heard her friends' names as well. It was almost every Monday now that he thought about it. He finished his shower in a daze. Those were actual conversations that he had heard and not thoughts of others. Blade decided he was going to Memphis; he had some research to do. Rocky walked in just as Blade walked out of his room.

"I will be back before four or five."

"Ok. I am going to clean the gun. After that I might go Matt's house. I will be back before you get home," Rocky said.

Blade nodded and walked downstairs to go out the back door. Summer was coming in and stopped him. "Ang called and invited me over. I am going to go over there and then go to Breeze's around five or five thirty."

"Rocky is planning to go to Matt's, and I was planning to go to Memphis. Do you want me to drive you, and then I could pick you up and us all go to Breeze's house together so we don't have three cars over there?"

"Yeah, that sounds good. I need a quick shower."

"Tell Rocky, please, when you go up."

She nodded and ran up the stairs.

Blade sat down to play a game on his phone and got lost

in his thoughts again. He was thinking about Breeze, her friends and their devotion to each other, their loyalty. They were truly family, whether they were blood or not. Blade was amazed that everybody just seemed to accept her and Jazz. Their relationship was growing on him, but man, it was hard seeing Jazz put his hands on Breeze. Angela didn't seem to mind Breeze and Jazz's relationship or them touching each other, which was interesting. Angela didn't seem like the kind of person that Breeze would hang out with, but then again, neither did Kidd, and they were pretty close. Angela seemed to know a lot about Breeze and had nothing but respect for her. She also knew the others, but how? She wasn't a part of the streets until recently. What was it about Breeze that he was so interested in? Why was he drawn to her?

He thought about the upcoming tournament. He wouldn't mind going against Jazz. It would be nice to see what he was up against. When they had fought Taylor, he wasn't watching his style or technique; he was focused on Taylor and causing him as much pain as possible.

His thoughts drifted back to the trackers and why they needed them. Did Breeze take off a lot? When she was at the streets, they were everywhere anyway. She left for a minute, then returned. It wasn't like she left the country or anything like that. His head was beginning to hurt from the complexity of Breeze, her friends, and the streets. He worried that she would get hurt when she entered the ring again. Yeah, it was a risk for all of them, but Breeze had been through a lot because of Taylor and the domestic violence that she endured. *Holy crap... I sound like an Old Fart. She is a mixed martial artist, she will fight. She will win some and lose some. There will be blood. There always is.*

Blade grabbed some lunch while he waited on Summer and Rocky. He made them a plate as well. Summer came bouncing down the stairs. It normally took her an hour to get ready but here she was, showered, dressed, with her hair and make-up done in twenty minutes flat.

"Ummm, since when can you get ready in less than an hour?"

"Since now… because I have places to go and people to see."

"We need to talk about your clothes at the streets."

"What about them?"

"You need more clothes on than what you had on at the streets."

"No way. I have to fit in, and I liked how I felt in them. No one was judging me or being all self-conscious around me. It was great. I like those clothes and I will wear them again. Besides, Angela and I really rock those outfits."

Blade held up his hand to get her to stop talking. Her mind was in overdrive, and he did not like what he was mentally hearing.

"Lunch is ready. Let's eat, and then we will leave."

As they ate, Blade asked Summer about Angela. They seemed to become instant friends, which was abnormal for Summer.

"She's quiet, but there's a fun side to her that I noticed while we were talking at lunch. She doesn't judge me. Hell, none of Breeze's friends do, and that is a good feeling. I like fitting in."

"It's nice to be hanging out with other people and not just staying to ourselves isn't it?" Rocky said.

Summer agreed. "We should have done this a long time ago."

"We tried that a couple of times and it didn't end well." She drank some soda then continued. "I mean, between you getting ticked off at every man that had a thought about me and Rocky standing up in the lunchroom and knocking one guy out and then breaking another guy's nose because of a comment they had said to me or about me. Not to mention all the drama with the girls and their insecurities…"

"Yeah, Kathleen for example."

Blade groaned at the memory of the cheerleader that he had tried to date and was so self-conscious that anytime she was around Summer, she would break out in hives. At one point she demanded that Blade sit with her and her friends and their table and not with Rocky or Summer. When he refused, she went into a temper tantrum for all to see. Blade told her it was over and walked away. Blade shook his head at the memory and was thankful for meeting Breeze and her friends.

Summer finished her lunch, took her plate in the kitchen, and walked back out with some serious attitude.

"Take me to Ang's, take me to Ang's," she said as she threw her arms out in front of herself and acted like she was flying out the door. Rocky and Blade looked at each other in shock and amusement. They quickly followed her.

"I can't wait until Dad hears you talk like that."

"No worries, Dad likes Breeze and Jazz. Well, he is not sure about Jazz, but he seems to really like Breeze. Breeze's attitude can rub off on me all it wants," Summer said.

Blade just shook his head.

Blade dropped his siblings off and decided that he might have some friends in Memphis and Dyersburg that might know Taylor. He decided to call them instead of driving there. If they weren't comfortable talking over the phone, then he would drive to Memphis. Right now he was willing just to call. That conversation needed to be in private. Blade called several friends and was surprised that all of them knew of Taylor, and all of them warned him to stay away from him. He was bad news and so was his father.

"You know he beat down a girl here in Memphis several months ago. Stabbed her, beat her, and left her for dead in her own home. She was one of the best mixed martial artists around, and he beat her down. If her stepdad had not returned home when he did, she probably would have bled to death. It was bad. You also have to understand that his dad might be in a lot of shady business. There are rumors that Mr. Smith has connections with the mob, is a gun runner, and he has his hand in a sex trafficking ring. It is also rumored that Taylor helps out in some of the activities. Neither have been arrested, because they always have alibis, but the ones that cover for them are on Mr. Smith's payroll or they are individuals that run in similar circles. It is also rumored that Mr. Smith may have helped Taylor's mom disappear for good."

Blade's friend Chris was happy to tell Blade everything he knew as long as Blade agreed never to hang around with Taylor. Blade ended the call and sat there for several minutes. He had learned a lot in a short amount of time. Now he needed to figure out how they could use that information to protect Breeze. He decided that he would fill everyone in when they got home tonight.

SECRETS REVELED

Breeze told Jazz that they needed to get ready to go; they did not need to be late. They arrived in MonoValleo by eleven in the morning. She knew exactly what she wanted. It took Jazz's friend an hour from start to finish. She left the tape off and switched shoes.

"Let's eat, and I know the perfect place for privacy so you can tell me everything," Jazz said.

He took her hand and gently stroked it. Breeze tensed. She had promised to tell Jazz and knew that she couldn't back down, but she really didn't want him to hate her or think badly of her. He pulled her close and stroked her hair. He kissed her forehead. He was trying to reassure her, but it wasn't working.

"It can't be that bad."

She just looked at him with doubting eyes. She didn't want to hurt their friendship.

"Honey, I will not leave you no matter what."

"Even if I'm a horrible person?" Breeze pulled her hand away and looked down.

"You are not horrible."

"Let's eat, and then we will see."

They went to Burger King. Afterwards they went up the

mountain to an old dirt road that led back to a trail. They parked and walked up the trail to a cave. They sat off to the side of the cave on a flat area and leaned against a boulder.

"Take my wrist before I change my mind."

He gently touched her wrist, and he heard her familiar voice. *"Ok, Jazz, I'm going to show you a month prior to the incident with Taylor, and then I will show you everything from that day. If it becomes too much, please tell me."* He agreed. *"Ok, you ready?"* Breeze asked with a sigh.

"Yes," he said.

The images were sharp and clear:

- *Breeze was in the bathroom sitting on the floor holding a pregnancy test, crying.*
- *She was at the doctor's office at the health department. "Miss Lee, you are pregnant. Now we need to get you on your vitamins and get your next appointment scheduled."*

"How far along am I?"

"Approximately five weeks," Dr. Suzanne said.

- *She was calling Taylor.*
- *They met, she told him, and he went off. He punched her hard in the chest and then slapped her. "You crazy bitch. Trying to trap me. You whore, it's probably not even mine, and it's probably that asshole Jazz's." He punched her in the face. She got in her car. "We are done. I won't have my child raised like you were." She gunned it and left him standing there.*
- *Her phone had twenty-five voice mails and fifteen texts, all from Taylor. She refused to answer them; she simply deleted them.*

- She went home, packed all his stuff up, including the box for the ring. She slid the ring back in the box, closed the ring box and put the lid on the box.
- She texted Taylor a location to meet.
- She waited in the public lot, she saw him pull in, and before he could get out of his car, she rolled down the window, and dropped the box on the ground. She pulled out of the lot with him standing there staring at the box.
- A month later she returned from her appointment at the health department. No one was home yet. She went in and she immediately knew something was off, but she ignored it. The air felt disrupted. She assumed it was because Stan or Mary had recently left, but it felt different. She went into the kitchen, fixed herself a snack, then she headed upstairs. She threw her backpack on her bedroom floor and headed for the bathroom. She froze when she heard a noise in her room. She turned and he was facing her. There was pure hatred written on his face. She turned to run. Taylor grabbed her, threw her against the wall, and he punched her.

She was trying to regain her composure; she was fighting back, but he slung her again this time toward the stairs. She was going to run. He grabbed her by the throat and pounded her head into the wall; he threw her face first down the stairs. She screamed. She landed hard and she was bleeding. She was crawling to get up; she would fight for her life and her baby's life. She screamed. "No, damn it, I won't let you. Get the hell away. I'm done, it's over, get out. Even if we were both in our graves, I would never take you back, WE ARE DONE."

"Oh, we're done alright," he said, laughing, and he punched her with all his might in her stomach. She screamed. He pulled *out a knife and stabbed her. She was bleeding everywhere. She was holding her stomach and crying. She blocked the next punch, which broke her hand. He punched her, he stabbed her in her face, and he stabbed her in the left side of her chest, cut down to her right side in a diagonal movement. He continued to stab and slice, she lost count of how many times the knife came down.*

She was down. She was cramping. She was holding her stomach and crying. "Not my baby. Not my baby." He kicked her hard in the stomach.

"Yeah, bitch, and now you." He kicked her in her ribs breaking four and bruising the rest. He stood up and walked out the front door. Once he was gone, she dragged herself into the living room, knocked the phone over, and dialed 911. "911 what's your emergency?"

"Help me. My ex-boyfriend just stabbed me. Help me. Help me." Then silence.

- *Stan arrived home, saw all the blood in the foyer, saw Breeze's feet and screamed. He picked up the phone. "Please hurry. My daughter is lying in blood."*

The images ended. Jazz was crying. Breeze took his hands from her wrists. She started to get up, and he stopped her. He grabbed her in a tight hug.

"I'm so sorry. I had no idea you were pregnant. Why would you think you were horrible? Did your mom or dad know? I'm so sorry. I wish you had told me. I love you so much. I would have been there, right by your side the whole time. You should not have carried this burden alone." He held her and placed his lips to her hair.

"I thought you'd hate me. No, my parents didn't know and

268

don't know. The procedure I just had was caused when I had the miscarriage. Jazz, what if I can't have kids because of all of this? I'm a horrible person because I couldn't protect my precious child."

She was sobbing. Her secret had finally been shared, and she couldn't stop crying. He held her and cried with her. He cried for her, her pain, and the child she had lost. Jazz reassured Breeze that there was nothing that she could have done and that no matter who he was with, he would always be there for her. She leaned her head against his chest and listened to his heartbeat.

"I have an idea. Will you come with me?" Jazz asked.

She nodded, stood, and took Jazz's hands to help him up. They walked over to the side of the mountain. They could see everything from up there. The landscape below was so green and full of life. Jazz placed his hand in hers and kissed the top of her hand. He gently released her hand and turned her to face him.

He looked in her eyes and spoke. "What were you going to name the baby?"

"Justice."

"For either, boy or girl?" Jazz asked.

She nodded. Jazz turned them to overlook the mountain again. He wanted this to be special and help her heal. She needed some type of closure.

"I love it. Take my hand and repeat after me. Justice Lee, I love you. I'm sorry; I fought as hard as I could. Please know you will forever be in our hearts."

Breeze repeated the words, and she felt a huge burden lifted from her. She finally had told someone her secret, and she got to say goodbye to her baby. Breeze hugged Jazz with absolute love. He kissed the top of her head. He wasn't done with honoring Justice. They would buy necklaces with Justice on them. Breeze loved the idea. A tear had started to roll down her cheek again. Jazz gently kissed it away.

"We will wear it always. It will be our secret," he said.

"One of many," Breeze said with a smile and choked back a sob.

He pulled her to him and held her close for a couple of minutes. He was thinking about everything. If he had known, he would have married her in a heartbeat and raised Justice as his own. He understood her terms of 'so broken' now. How did Jana not know it? Maybe it was because she lived in Memphis. Breeze broke his train of thought.

"I want a coffee milkshake from Arby's," she said.

"You mean Jamocha?" Jazz asked with a grin.

He knew how much she loved coffee. Breeze lightly poked Jazz's ribs in a playful manner. He picked her up and kissed her. She climbed on Jazz's back. He carried her piggyback down to the car. They went to a little jewelry store in the mall, and Jazz found two silver dragon charms with a simple silver chain. He had both dragons engraved with Justice. He placed Breeze's necklace on her and kissed her ear.

"I love you, Breeze, and we will always remember Justice together. I love Justice as well."

"Thank you, Jazz. Now may I place your necklace on you?" He nodded. "Jazz, you are my best friend, and I love you more than you know. Thank you for carrying some of the burden. Thank you for loving me and Justice. This is so we can remember Justice together forever." She placed the necklace on him and kissed him. "Let's go home."

Once back in the car, Breeze rewrapped her ankle and put

her other shoes on. On the way home, both of their phones buzzed.

They looked at the message, it was Matt.

Matt: A little warning next time would be nice.

Jazz: What?

Matt: Han is here.

Jazz: Oh. Zion told me yesterday that Han was coming, I forgot.

Matt: You forgot Han was coming... seriously.

Jazz: Why is he there and not at Dad's house?

Matt: He wanted to surprise us and see if we were behaving

Jazz: And?

Matt: Thankfully yes.

Jazz: Thumbs up. Home in 30 to 45 minutes.

Jazz looked at Breeze and rubbed his hands together.

"Damn, I have to go back home tonight. It would have been perfect to break in the newbies and them see Han tracking us." Jazz said.

Han was waiting for them when they arrived. He greeted them at the door. "Young Ones."

They bowed and walked in. Breeze helped Jazz pack, kissed him good-bye, and waited for Blade to arrive. Some people might think that she and Jazz were cheating on Blade and Ang, but it wasn't like that. If either of them had a problem with it, they would be happy to talk with them, but they weren't changing for anyone.

"You'll be here this weekend, right?" she asked him.

"Absolutely." *Now more than ever he wished he lived here. She needed him.*

"Thank you again for the necklace; I love it." She smiled at the thought of the streets. "Are we racing or fighting this weekend?"

"You are on medical restriction, remember, so racing it is." Jazz ran his finger down her nose in a playful way.

"You can still fight, and I will cheer you on."

"Yeah, right. Since when do you sit out of a fight?"

"Oh. Ummm, good point," she said.

Blade had just pulled up. Jazz smiled at her. "I'm always going to be here. If you need me, call."

"I will."

He tapped her mind. *"Seriously, Breeze, I'm not going anywhere."*

"I know. I'm not either. I'm back, and I will NEVER be that broken again. It was a hard place to be."

"By the way, your boy is growing on me."

She laughed at Jazz and winked at him. She was standing on the porch step as Jazz was walking toward his car. Blade was walking up to the porch and passed Jazz to get to Breeze. They nodded to each other. Rocky and Summer were walking up behind Blade. Rocky and Jazz bumped fists. Blade made it to the porch quickly, though it felt like it took a hundred years. He wanted to run to Breeze and kiss her, but he held back. Blade touched Breeze's hand.

"Hey, sweetheart."

"Hey," she said.

"See you soon," Jazz yelled just as he got to his car.

"Yep. See you Friday." She blew him a kiss and touched her necklace. He did the same.

"Am I missing something?" Blade asked

She shook her head, opened the door, and motioned for Summer and Rocky to go on in. Blade shook his head lightly. He wasn't sure he would ever understand the Breeze and Jazz connection. Blade rolled his eyes at her and smiled. She was holding his hand and led him to the kitchen. He about jumped out of his skin when he saw Han in the kitchen. This caused Han to bust out laughing.

"Blade, this is my Uncle Han."

Blade stretched out his hand. "Nice to meet you."

Han shook his hand in return. "Did Jana not tell you all I was coming?"

"No."

"Imagine that." He was laughing when he walked into the living room.

Breeze heard Rocky yell, "Holy shit, you scared me."

"Sorry."

Rocky quickly walked into the kitchen. He pointed to the living room and looked at Breeze.

"My Uncle Han."

"He is huge. What did you do?"

Breeze laughed. "Nothing, but I can if you want."

Rocky held his hands up in surrender. "No, I am good. Thanks." He turned and went back into the living room. Breeze could hear Han, Rocky, and Summer talking.

Breeze turned to Blade. "I want to finish our project. There are a few things that I want to add."

The project was complete. It was a unique castle with a demi-dragon on top of the castle, holding an egg in the talons of her right claw, watching, and guarding her home. In front of the moat were the two demons guarding the castle. There was a draw bridge with spikes on it, and there was a head on each spike. It was a warning to all that dared to invade their home.

Blade was amazed with all the added details. It really added to the piece. It was unique for sure. "What should the title be?"

"For Justice." Breeze said with great confidence.

"I like it."

Breeze made sure that Summer and Rocky weren't bored to tears. Han was playing against Rocky on a racing game. Summer was cheering Han on. Breeze just shook her head and walked back into the kitchen. Blade couldn't keep his eyes off of her. There was something different about her, not just the necklace. She had an air about her like she did at the streets. She sat in the kitchen chair playing with Blade's hand. Blade kissed her lightly. She was a million miles away. He had a feeling that she was thinking about her day with Jazz. He felt the jealousy building again and pushed it away. He wouldn't screw this relationship up.

He was right she was thinking about her day. She finally felt a sense of peace and a little bit of her old self back. She was absent mindlessly stroking Blade's hand. She was beginning to have feelings for him. She felt like it was too soon for that, but too late now. They sat in the kitchen and talked for a while.

"Hey, I noticed your planner has X's. Why?" Blade asked.

"It is a count down on my restriction days. If you go back six weeks and eight weeks there is a big smiley on both."

"What if it takes longer?"

"I will go absolutely crazy. It wouldn't be a pretty sight."

"Friday are we going to the streets?"

"Yes. This time we are taking the cars, bikes, and the dirt bikes. We will race in what we feel comfortable."

"Are the three of us racing?"

"I did say we."

"Cool. Now maybe Rocky will shut up," Blade said while shaking his head.

"Doubt it. He's got the racing bug. It doesn't go away; it just gets worse," Breeze said with a huge grin.

Blade gaped at her. He wasn't sure he could handle much more from Rocky. Every chance they were alone and away from their father, he was talking cars, the streets, and racing. He was even making plans with Jazz and Matt to build a car or two. Once he found out that he was racing, it would be all he wrote.

SCHEMIN'

The week after the procedure was finally up. Breeze went to the doctor; he cleared her to go back to school and said she had healed beautifully. At school Rocky, Blade, and Summer joined the table with Chad, Angela, and Breeze. Angela whispered to Breeze about clothes for Friday. "No worries. I got you and Summer taken care of."

"Cool. Jazz will be there, right?" Angela asked. Breeze grinned and nodded. "Good."

Friday rolled around quickly. Jazz raced in everything, as did Breeze and Matt. Rocky focused on cars, though he did race on bikes a couple of times. Summer raced bikes and motocross. Blade focused on cars and bikes. Kidd did the same as Blade. Mickey only did motocross and extreme motocross. Kidd raced for slips on bikes and won two. Jazz mainly raced for cash, with the exception of slips for a bike; he didn't like the guy's attitude, so he adjusted it for him. Blade raced for cash. Rocky raced for slips; he won in both cars and bikes. Summer raced for cash; she smoked the competition, and she could have won several slips. Mickey walked away with a pocket full of money. Matt won a car and cash. All in all, it was a good night.

Breeze was becoming bored and decided it was time to play.

It was time for a test to see if her new friends could keep up or not. Breeze made sure that some final challenges for the night were issued. Sasha challenged Blade. Brian challenged Rocky. MaKayla challenged Summer. All of Breeze's friends went to watch the various challenges. Breeze used this as her opportunity to embrace her schemin' skills.

In the second race, Mickey turned around. He did not see Breeze, but he did see Jazz. He swore lightly. He strode over to Jazz and touched his shoulder. "Jazz, where is Breeze?"

"Shit! I should have known. I can't wait to see how Blade handles her schemin' and that she has left for the evening." Jazz said.

Matt walked over with a piece of parchment in his hand. He just smiled.

Kidd turned. "Crap. Who is calling the trackers? Better yet, who is telling Blade?"

Blade came over with a pink slip and cash in his hand. "Who is telling me what?"

Mickey blew out a breath and then spoke. "Remember when you asked who that guy was not long ago, and I told you one of the best trackers talking to one of the best schemers." Blade nodded. "You might want to call that tracker, because the schemer has left the building."

Blade was confused at first. He thought Breeze was watching all the challenges, and then it hit him.

"OMG. Did she set up all of those challenges?" Blade asked.

Everyone looked at their shoes, whistled, or did something to avoid answering the question.

Mickey patted Blade on the back. "Welcome to Breeze's world. You will have to keep up or be left behind. We all have been left behind a lot. That tracker I mentioned earlier has only found her once or twice when she was completely at her best. He has found her several times lately, but at most he has found her five to seven times over the last several years. Good luck, she could be in Mexico by now."

Blade lost his mind. He was ticked. How was he to watch over her and protect her if she was going to take off? He had no idea how to even begin tracking. Matt handed him the parchment. It was in Breeze's handwriting.

"Where did you get this?"

"One of the bouncers gave it to me. He said Breeze gave him a $100 bill, asked him to wait five minutes and then give it to me."

Blade opened the folded piece of paper and read it out loud for everyone to hear.

> *Friends, Romans, and Countrymen.... I digress. I hope you all enjoyed your challenges, but there is now another challenge on your plate. To all my new friends, welcome to the Breeze Challenge. You have exactly three hours from the time you read this note to find me. If you don't find me, then I win. If you find me, well count yourself lucky, because you win. You may use any resource at your ready except for calling Jana, Han, Uncle, or Dad. Good luck to you all. Ang, this challenge includes you as well, though I'm sure you will use Jazz as your aide. The clock starts NOW.*

"Mickey, I need the tracker's number," Blade said.

Summer and Rocky were laughing. Blade needed a little adventure in his life, and now he had it. Blade called Zion and

Yu. They met all of Breeze's friends about a mile down the road. They were there within ten minutes of the call. Blade handed Zion the note.

"Who all touched this?"

"Breeze, the bouncer, Matt, and myself."

Zion took a deep breath and focused his energy on Breeze's signature. He handed the paper back to Blade. "I will call with updates. The clock is now at two hours and forty-eight minutes." Zion turned the car and took off. Jazz just laughed. He took Ang's hand and led her to his car.

"Wait, are you going to help me?" Ang asked.

"Yes." He smiled. "If the trackers went that way, then we are going the opposite way. Matt and Mickey will help the others. Kidd has not had this kind of challenge yet either, which surprises me."

Blade, Mickey, and Rocky worked together. Matt, Kidd, and Summer worked together. Every time they thought they had her, they quickly realized it was a decoy. The trackers checked in every twenty minutes. At the three-hour mark, everyone met back at Matt's, including the trackers. Breeze pulled in five minutes later. She was driving a car that wasn't hers.

She got out of her car and blew on her nails. "Oh, so close." She smiled and sashayed over to Zion and Yu. "Nice tracking; better luck next time."

Yu just laughed. Zion shook his head but chuckled. They left.

Blade came over to her in a fury. "What the hell, Breeze! I can't protect you if I don't know where you are."

Breeze simply slid her hand over his cheek and smiled. "If you don't know where I am and the trackers can't find me, then no one else can either." She slid her hand off his face as she walked over to Kidd. "Little Brother, you have skills, but remember I am the Master." Breeze looked at Jazz and winked.

Blade was in disbelief. He could not believe that everyone was not upset. This was not going to be the norm. He would always know where she was so he could keep her safe. He just had to figure out how to master that. Blade joined her in the house. Her excitement was contagious to everyone except him. He was in a foul mood. Breeze simply kissed his lips and wished him better luck next time. His foul mood was not going to dampen her win.

Breeze whispered that she would like to go outside with him for a few minutes. He agreed and went out with her. She took his hand. "Do you still want us to be an item?"

"What?"

"I am asking if my scheming is going to be the deciding factor if you want to date me or not."

"Of course, I want to date you. I am not pushing the issue."

"I know." She walked over to Matt's truck and let the tailgate down. She hopped up on it and sat down. Blade sat beside her. "Here is the deal. When I get bored, I issue challenges or I scheme and/or both. It is as much a part of me as Jazz is. I am who I am; can you accept that?"

He blew out a breath of frustration. "I have been frantic with worry. I kept thinking what if Taylor found you, and we didn't know."

"As I said earlier, if the trackers can't find me, then neither can Taylor." Breeze looked at him. "Can you accept me for me? Yes or No?"

"Yes."

"Do you want to be a couple?"

Blade leaned over and kissed her with complete passion. The kiss ended.

"Hell, yeah, I want to date you."

"Good."

Even though he agreed to accept her for who she was, he was going to learn everything he could about tracking. Mickey tried to reassure Blade that being left behind by Breeze was normal, but Blade was trying to figure out how to ensure that did not become his normal. He would sit on her if he had to so he would know where she was. There was no way that Taylor was getting to her on his watch.

Breeze was planning and thinking about another scavenger hunt, a few challenges. *OH YES.* She mentally imagined rubbing her hands together and thought of the challenges that were supposed to happen before the incident had occurred. She wondered how Blade would handle losing his clothes during a challenge. Breeze busted out laughing and jumped off the truck.

"What?" Blade asked, seriously confused.

"Nothing. Absolutely nothing." She ran in the house and flashed Jazz a smile. He looked at her for a second and caught her brief line of thinking and busted out laughing, too. Mickey looked at them both, then looked at Blade as he stood there. Mickey thought of all of the challenges then realized what kind of challenge Breeze was thinking. He tilted his head up to the ceiling so he wouldn't bust out laughing.

"So, Blade…how do you feel about running around town naked?" Breeze asked.

Kidd spewed his drink everywhere. There was the sound of a car pulling up. Zion and Yu knocked then walked in.

Zion walked straight to Breeze, put his arms on her shoulders, and looked her right in the eyes. "Can you behave for like five minutes?"

"I am behaving now."

Zion gave her a skeptical look. He removed his hands and walked over to the couch. He sat beside Kidd. "You know your sister could work the nerves of a saint, right?"

"I know. That is one of the reasons that I love her."

"Has Kidd played that kind of challenge?" Zion asked.

"Not yet." Breeze said. "But then again, neither have you."

"What type?"

"Hello, the find your clothes kind," Mickey said and rolled his eyes. "Lord have mercy. No one pays attention around here."

Blade looked at Breeze with concern. Surely they were joking. Breeze looked at Blade and shook her head no. His mouth dropped open. There was no way that was happening. Breeze shrugged and walked into the kitchen. She yelled something in Japanese and Matt responded. Blade heard banging around and realized Breeze was making a snack. His stomach growled at the thought of food. Everyone went into the kitchen. They had sandwiches, chips, pickles, and sweet tea. They were starving.

"Yo, Yu, why are you guys back?" Jazz asked.

"Uncle sent us."

"Well... welcome to the party." Jazz said and walked over to Breeze.

She nodded to the unspoken question. She was on cloud nine. At least Blade wasn't mad at the world right now.

She turned to Kidd. "Don't forget on fall break we are going with Jana to go Christmas shopping."

"Fall break, seriously?" Blade asked

"Ugh, yeah. That probably still won't be enough time for Jana to shop," Breeze said.

Kidd nodded his agreement through a mouth full of food. "Everyone, while you are here, write down three things that you would like for Christmas. Jana typically gets one thing off the list and then gets tons of other stuff not on the list. Halloween and Christmas are her favorite holidays, just so you know."

Blade, Rocky, and Summer didn't write down anything at first, but Kidd insisted that they put something on the paper.

"If you don't, it will hurt Jana's feelings," Kidd said seriously.

Blade read over the list of the others. The items varied from inexpensive to astronomical. "Mickey, does that seriously say a strip club?" Blade asked.

"Don't worry, he won't get it. He has listed it for years." Jazz smiled big. "Last year..." He started to speak and got tickled. Mickey pushed past him, went into the spare bedroom, and brought out a record player.

Kidd busted out laughing. "OMG, he kept it."

"Hell, yeah, I kept it."

Blade, Summer, and Rocky all stared at the record player. The original top had been removed, and a taller lid had been added. There was a metal rod running down the center. There was a Ken doll wrapped around the pole with money laying around on the bottom of the player. Mickey plugged it in and a mini disco ball started flashing & spinning, the record started spinning and Ken was spinning on the pole.

Rocky roared with laughter. "That is priceless."

Mickey unplugged his treasure and carried it back to the spare bedroom. Zion was still laughing. Yu just looked at

Zion and shook his head. Breeze texted Uncle and asked him for his three items. Breeze quickly wrote down his items. "Uncle said for you both to write down three things so Jana is happy." They were both shocked by this but obliged.

"Perfect. I am sending Jana a text. We will probably have to draw names in the next week or so."

Breeze was about to push send when she realized she had not got Dr. McGroff's list. She quickly asked Blade to call his dad and explain why she needed his list. There was a lot of discussion between Blade and his dad. Finally, Dr. McGroff listed three things and Blade added them to the list. Breeze took the picture and sent it to Jana.

Jana: Thank you. Now, you, Jazz, and Kidd will be going with me to Gatlinburg the first Saturday of Fall Break.

Breeze: I will let Jazz and Kidd know. How long will we be in the mountains?

Jana: Several days.

Breeze: Ok.

Breeze relayed the message to Kidd and Jazz. They both nodded their agreement. Everyone made their way back to Breeze's house except for Matt, Mickey, Zion, and Yu. Blade was now thinking about the holidays and what he could get Breeze. Rocky was still talking about the record player. He mentioned it when he walked in. Jana smiled.

"You ain't seen nothing yet," Jana said.

This Christmas was going to be so much fun. Blade was glad that they were included. They always had nice Christmases; however, since his mom died, it hadn't been the same. From everything that Blade had observed about Jana, Jon, and Breeze so far, was that family meant everything to them. That thought made Blade smile.

CHRISTMAS AT THE LEE HOUSE

When Jana had asked everyone to give Breeze a list of three items for Christmas, Kidd made sure to list two things, then he put a star by number three and asked Breeze if he could write his third item down and place it in an envelope just for Jana to see. Breeze agreed and texted Jana to let her know. Breeze handed Jana the envelope the minute she walked in the door.

They were all hanging out and laughing. Blade, Rocky, and Summer left around nine that night. Their Dad wanted to spend time with them because he had to work emergency room rotation for the next two weeks. Matt texted Breeze and told her that they needed to work Uncle had called. Matt pulled up five minutes later. Breeze ran up to her room, changed clothes and ran back out to Matt's car. Jana had waited until she was alone to read the note from Kidd. As soon as Breeze left to go with Matt, Jana sat down on the couch with a cup of coffee and opened the envelope. She took out the folded piece of paper. She quickly sat down her cup. Her hand was shaking, and tears filled her eyes. She clutched the piece of paper to her chest and smiled.

Jana,

Thank you so much for showing me what a family really is and for showing me love. You are amazing. Even though you did not give birth to me, you are still my mom. You have showed me love and acceptance. You have encouraged me and helped me to believe in myself. The other two items on the wish list are not important; my one true wish is to call you mom from here on out if that is ok with you. I love you.

Kidd

Jana cried tears of joy. She was thrilled. After a couple of minutes she called Kidd.

"Of course you can call me mom from this day forward. Thank you so much for the best gift ever. I love you, Son."

"Thanks, Mom."

They hung up, and Kidd thought about something special to get Jana. He knew they were drawing names, but he was still getting Jana something. He sat down and began drawing. He was just doing free thought drawing, and when he looked at the picture, he was shocked to see a beautiful ring. He decided that in the morning, he was going to a local jewelry store. Kidd woke up early and knew that it was too early to go to town, but he planned to be the first person in the store. He found Jana a beautiful mother's ring. He got his and Breeze's birthstones in it. Inside the band he had it inscribed with To The Best Mom Ever. Love, Kidd & Breeze

As soon as he had the ring wrapped and he was back in his car, he called Breeze. Now he was nervous. He should have talked to her first before he bought it. He was worried that he would offend her. Breeze answered and sounded out of breath. He quickly told her about the ring. She was thrilled.

"Kidd, that's wonderful. Thank you so much for putting my name on it with yours. Jana will absolutely love it."

They talked briefly. While he was at the jewelry store, he bought Summer a beautiful brooch with a dragonfly on it. He thought about what Blade would get Breeze for Christmas. He wondered if it would be a ring, an engagement ring possibly. He wasn't sure that Breeze was ready for that. Kidd liked Blade, but that was still his sister, and he wasn't sure that he liked how possessive Blade was of Breeze, even though he knew it was nothing mean or hateful. He hated what Taylor had done to her. He saw sadness touch her eyes more often than he liked. He had hoped when she and Blade had started dating that the sadness would fade, but it hadn't yet.

He needed to talk to Jon now that he had talked to Jana. He had to find Jon something. He would wait on that until he went shopping with Jana in the mountains. Jana and Breeze could help him figure it out. He called Breeze back.

"I'm bored."

"Ohhh…. Now that you mention it, so am I." Breeze paused for a second. "Meet me in fifteen minutes at IHOP."

"Purrfect," Kidd said.

Kidd arrived right on time and they were quickly seated. They knew what they wanted and ordered as soon as the waitress came over to their table. They ate and talked.

Breeze sent Jana a text to make sure that no red flags went up.

Breeze: *Shopping with Kidd*
Jana: Ok
Breeze: *We will be home by 11 p.m.*
Jana: Sounds good…BEHAVE.
Breeze: *Duh – Christmas shopping*

Breeze showed Kidd the texts and grinned.

"What shall we do?" Kidd asked.

"I did say we were shopping; I just didn't say where we would be shopping."

Kidd bounced in his seat. He had a feeling it would be New York or Atlanta, but he would just wait and see. Breeze had planned with Mike for the trip of the day when Kidd had called and said he was bored. After they ate, Kidd followed Breeze to the private airstrip. Breeze grabbed her duffle bag and purse out of her car. Mike greeted Kidd by his actual name. Kidd looked at Breeze for an explanation.

"No need for a different identity. We are shopping."

Kidd grinned and danced onto the plane.

"Wheels up in ten," Mike announced.

"Thank you," Breeze said.

"Your flight will be an hour and forty-five minutes," Mike said, and he made his way to the cockpit.

Breeze nodded slightly as acknowledgement. They both pulled out a book and began reading when the plane took off.

Thirty minutes before they landed, Breeze opened her duffle bag and handed Kidd a warmer coat, some fur lined gloves, hat, and some warm boots. Kidd kicked off his Vans and put on the boots.

"These are nice." Kidd flexed his foot and turned it to look at them. They fit like a glove.

"I know, and they are yours. I love mine."

Breeze was wearing her boots. They were dark brown in color. Kidd's were black. They both had on light sweaters with a jacket. Obviously, wherever they were going, the jackets would not be warm enough. When they landed, Kidd recognized the landscape.

288

"Yay!" Kidd said and ran off the plane.

A black SUV with a driver was waiting when Kidd exited the plane. He waited as Breeze walked off like she didn't have a care in the world. Kidd looked at her with confusion. He thought one of their rides would be there.

"There is no way that I am going to waste time by trying to find parking this time of the year. This makes things easier on many levels."

"You are so wise. I should call you Obi-wan."

"That title is already taken. I could be Yoda," Breeze said.

"No way. We could change Han's name to Yoda and you could take Obi-wan."

"Nah," Breeze said and flipped her hand out. She walked to the SUV and got in. Kidd ran to the other side and jumped in. If he didn't hurry she might leave him standing there. He was not missing New York for anything.

Kidd noticed the duffle bag when he got in and pointed.

"You know, a little of this and a little of that," Breeze said with an air of cockiness.

Panic set in. Kidd had a feeling that she would be fighting. He had none of the stuff he would need to treat her if she was injured. Breeze patted his shoulder.

"Relax. Shopping first, and after that, I have us covered."

"I hate when you do that."

She shrugged. The driver dropped them off in front of Central Park. They walked over to Rockefeller Center. Kidd took a picture of Breeze with a large soldier nutcracker statue. Breeze snapped a pic near a large Christmas display that was being put up. They paid for skates and took to the ice. They skated for about an hour. After they skated, they went up to the 70th floor to the Observation Deck. They went back down to the lower level. Kidd ran over to the Radio City Music Hall. He purchased two tickets for Dec. 27th to see the Rockettes.

Kidd asked Breeze if she would take a panoramic picture of him in front of the Prometheus and all the international flags. She gladly took the picture. She knew how much he loved New York. They took several pictures for other families there, and in return, one father took a picture of Breeze and Kidd in front of several of the flags.

"We should print three copies of that," Breeze said.

"Me, you, and ?" Kidd asked.

"Oh yeah… five then." She grinned. "Jana, Han, and Uncle, plus our copies."

"Or…" He thought for a second and then gave a thumbs up. "Why don't we come back two weeks before Christmas and take one in front of the Rockefeller Christmas Tree."

Breeze grinned. "Little Bro, I like how you think."

"I learned from you."

"Yes, yes you did."

They shopped for a couple of hours. Kidd bought Jana a couple of Broadway tickets to an upcoming play. The ring was his personal gift to her. The Broadway play tickets and the Rockettes tickets were her gifts for drawing her name. He also bought her a pair of boots at Saks Fifth Avenue. He would put the tickets in separate envelopes inside the box. The picture that they planned to take in front of the tree would be taped inside the top of the lid.

Breeze bought Uncle some of his favorite cigars. She couldn't buy his favorite drink here, but Jazz was helping her with that. If Kidd thought it was cold here, she wondered what he would think about the temps in Russia. Jazz had left

Memphis yesterday after school and flew to Russia and was staying a couple of days, then flying home, but no one needed to know that. His parents were out of town on a business trip for his dad. He would be back home in time for school on Tuesday. Monday was a teacher in-service day.

Breeze bought Grams her favorite tea and a beautiful teapot. Kidd got Grams a silk scarf with Japanese Cherry Blossoms on it. After lunch at Lenny's, Breeze motioned to Kidd that they needed to go. Kidd's anxiety kicked up when he saw a flyer for a tournament. She shook her head. They did not have time for that. It was a two-day tournament. Just as they got in the SUV, Kidd received a password for an underground fight.

He looked at Breeze. His heart was pounding. She took his hand.

"Kidd, I need this. Always looking over my shoulder is stressing me out. Not to mention all the hovering everyone is doing is making me insane. It is better than when Taylor landed in me in the hospital, but the hovering is still there to a certain degree. The two months when Taylor was in jail recently was great. Everyone relaxed a little bit, not fully, but some."

Kidd relaxed. "I get it." He let go of her hand and hugged her. "I'm in your corner all the way."

Breeze smiled. They made their way to a dojo that was an hour away from Central Park. Breeze got out of the SUV with confidence. Kidd loved to see the confidence of the fighter shining through. She was in a zone. This was only her third fight since the incident. Kidd was excited to see her in the ring. His anxiety had subsided, and now excitement flooded him. Breeze entered the dojo to chants and whispers. She had every intention of squashing the murmurs, here and now.

Her first opponent was cocky. Breeze thought about every fight that she had ever seen this opponent in. Breeze went to the locker room, changed, and when she walked out, she handed Kidd her duffle back and the first aid materials that he might need. She waited for her name to be called to enter the ring against Deja. Breeze entered the ring with determination to get some of her respect in the circuit back. Her opponent's cockiness just really ticked her off. She made it her mission to bring her down several notches. Forty-five seconds in, Deja punched Breeze straight in the eye, Breeze spun, swept Deja's legs out from under her and was on her. Breeze repaid the eye punch with several face punches and head blows. Deja tapped out in two minutes and ten seconds.

Breeze took her mouthpiece out and spoke directly to Deja. "Confidence and cockiness are NOT the same thing. You are a hell of a fighter, but your cockiness takes away from that."

Deja growled and advanced on Breeze. Breeze was ready. One punch from Breeze and Deja was waking up on the mat, Knock Out. Breeze exited the ring and waited for her next match. She won her second match, but her third match she lost. Kidd thought Breeze would be mad even though she fought hard; he was surprised when she just shrugged.

"I can't win them all. No one can. Win some. Lose some. Today was about getting some respect back, and I did that."

They watched a few more fights which took a couple hours, then they left for home. Once they were on the plane, Kidd asked her about her eye and how were they going to cover it.

"Shoe sale."

Kidd roared with laughter. He hugged her tight. "God, I love you."

292

They were home by ten thirty that night. There were no questions about her eye or knuckles. I mean come on, she is a warrior twice over and a fighter. It was when she wasn't sporting cut knuckles or bruises that they worried. Blade, on the other hand, was a whole other issue. They had no plans this weekend because he and Rocky were out of town for a tournament. Hopefully by Monday her eye would not be that bad.

Jazz had been sparring Rocky often, and he had told Breeze that he was really good. Rocky had told Jazz that all three of them had taken private lessons for years. Blade and Rocky still did, but Summer focused on trapping. She still sparred them often to stay in shape and because she liked to take her brothers down at every chance she got. Blade knew that Breeze was and is a fighter when he started seeing her, so Breeze never understood why he reacted the way he did when she had a black eye or was sporting bruises from trainings or a fight. The following Monday when they returned to school, Blade about lost his mind when he saw her eye.

She held up her hand and simply said, "Shoe sale, now if you will excuse me."

Kidd heard the exchange and started laughing. Friday was the last day of school for two weeks due to Fall Break. Blade knew that Jazz, Breeze, and Kidd were going with Jana to Gatlinburg to go shopping. He planned to talk to Matt about what he should get Breeze for Christmas. He really loved her, but he didn't think that an engagement ring would be a good idea, not right now, anyway. He knew they would be gone for several days. He texted Matt that he needed to talk to him once Breeze left for Gatlinburg. Matt agreed. They all saw how much Blade loved Breeze. She loved him, but she still had her guards up when it came to completely trusting someone with her heart again.

Blade, Kidd, Angela, Summer, Rocky, and Breeze all received a text at the same time. They all thought it was about the streets, but then they saw it was from Jana. She was sending everyone the complete list of names drawn, just in case anyone wanted to knock out their shopping well before the Black Friday sales. Breeze made the mistake of going to Black Friday sales one year. She and Jana were at the Mall waiting at four in the morning, and by eleven in the morning, Breeze was in such a bad mood that Jana threatened to buy her a pacifier to shut her up. Breeze vowed that she would be done with her shopping well before that craziness or she would just order online.

The Christmas Exchange List for the Lee Household:

1. Jazz picked Kidd
2. Jana picked Zion
3. Jon picked Angela
4. Kidd picked Jana
5. Breeze picked Uncle
6. Matt picked Yu
7. Mickey picked Debra (Ang's mom)
8. Han picked Rocky
9. Jim picked David
10. Kim picked Cindy
11. Grams picked Breeze

12. David picked Jon
13. Blade picked Jim
14. Rocky picked Grams
15. Summer picked Henry
16. Uncle picked Jazz
17. Zion picked Kim
18. Yu picked Han
19. Angela picked Mickey
20. Debra picked Summer
21. Cindy picked Matt
22. Henry picked Blade

Angela ran over to Breeze and Kidd. "I need your help. How in the world do I top the record player? Whoever made that was freaking brilliant."

"You have his list of his likes, dislikes, interests, and favorites, right??"

"Yeah… have you seen his list?"

"Women, money, and more women and money. That's pretty much his list."

Breeze laughed. "Ok, so get him a girly calendar. He loves music. Anything that he can spin and create great beats with, and you could always dress up in a naughty Mrs. Claus outfit and take a picture of you in that outfit and make him your own calendar."

Angela's mouth dropped open. She could not believe the last one had even come out of Breeze's mouth, but then again, she wasn't sure why she was surprised. Kidd, Rocky, and Blade were laughing at Angela's expression. Summer could not look at her because she knew she would start laughing.

Kidd began bouncing up and down. "Oh, oh, I know. You

three plus Sasha could make him a calendar! You could be naughty elves."

Kidd took off running at the end of his comment and slid into his next class before any of the three ladies could strangle him. Rocky walked into class and just shook his head, but he was grinning. Kidd was thankful he already had his presents for Jana. He could not wait to go to Gatlinburg.

The week passed quickly, and Jana was waiting when they got home. "Where is Jazz? Does he not know we need to go?"

"You do know he goes to school in Memphis, or did you forget that minor detail? He will be here soon. I thought we were leaving in the morning."

"Change of plans. We are going tonight. I extended our reservation at the cabin by another night and day."

Kidd gaped at Jana. Breeze busted out laughing and patted his back. He had never been Christmas shopping with Jana before. He had no idea how much she really liked to shop. The big get together was on Christmas Eve for the gift exchange, but Christmas day, Kim, Jim, Han, and Grams always came over; they would have breakfast and open stockings. Of course, Kidd had been to Christmas at the house before, but the shopping experience was something that was going to be new for him.

"Remember, children, one bag for clothes, nothing more. The Escalade will need the room." Jana said.

"Yes, Mom," Breeze yelled from the top of the stairs.

Kidd was still speechless. They were now going to be gone five nights and four days. What in the world would they be getting? He quickly went to his room and made sure he had everything. He brought his bag out and sat it by the door. Breeze sent Jazz a text and told him to hurry up, that Jana was ready now. Breeze brought her bag down and sat it by Kidd's. Jazz made the drive from Memphis in record time. He was not going to feel the wrath of Jana for making them late. As soon as Jana heard Jazz's car, she yelled for Breeze and Kidd to grab their stuff. Kidd looked at Breeze and mouthed HELP. Breeze got the giggles, grabbed her bag, and ran for the garage. Breeze and Jazz jumped in the back and left the front seat for Kidd. Jana walked out with her bag, purse, and had a huge smile on her face.

Kidd looked at Jana. "So, Mom, what's on the agenda."

"Shopping, shopping, and more shopping."

"Are we doing anything else?"

"What else is there?"

"Uhhh… FOOD."

"Oh, I guess I will stop and get you a hamburger, if I must."

Breeze and Jazz started laughing. Kidd turned and looked at them.

"Little Bro, just sit back and enjoy the ride."

They checked into the cabin at eleven that night. Over the next several days Jana made sure that they went all over Gatlinburg. Jana was about unique gifts and supporting local artists. It wasn't bad; Kidd enjoyed spending time with the three of them. By the third day Kidd thought his legs were going to fall off from walking so much.

When they returned home and carried everything into the spare bedroom, Kidd was like the walking dead. He fell face first on his bed and did not wake up until ten the next morning. Jon laughed when Kidd shuffled out for breakfast. Kidd was relieved that all of his shopping was complete, and he could just sit back and relax. He was ready for school to be back in session, that was something that Kidd never thought he would think or say. Their next break would be for Thanksgiving, and that was always a big kick off to the Christmas holiday in the Lee house.

The day after Thanksgiving, it was custom to put up all the trees in the house and start decorating for Christmas. Every bedroom had a small three-foot or four-foot tree, and each person decorated their own tree in their room with the theme of their choice. Kidd's was decorated with shotgun shells and fishing lures. The topper was turkey tail feathers from Kidd's first turkey.

Jazz decorated the spare bedroom tree with cars and motorcycles. The top of the tree was the General Lee car from the Dukes of Hazard. Breeze's tree in her room was decorated with origami objects, Korean flags, Japanese flags, Japanese Cherry blossoms, paper teapots, and the top was a Korean hand-blown glass doll. The big tree in the living room was the family tree with ornaments that had been collected over the years. Every year, a new ornament was added by members of the family. There was another big tree in the foyer upstairs. The one upstairs had beautiful origami swans and origami Japanese women on it. The top of the tree was topped with a huge origami star. The stair banister was decorated with red ribbons and candy canes. It took a full day to get the house decorated. No one minded. Everyone came over, drank homemade apple cider, ate cheeseball, oyster crackers with ranch seasoning, and fruit trays. Everyone started decorating the stairs, mantle, and kitchen, then they moved to the living room to decorate that tree. Jana had Santas from around the world set up through the living room. The front foyer smelled of cinnamon, cranberries, and oranges. It was welcoming. Time flew between Thanksgiving and the Winter Break.

Finally, Christmas Eve arrived, and Jana was doing her traditional Pineapple Duck for dinner with fried rice, yoki-mondo, and a Japanese noodle dish. Everyone arrived at five. Even though everyone had drawn names, they still each got Jana, Uncle, and Grams something each. Zion laughed when Breeze danced past Uncle.

"Young One," Han said.

"Yes Obi-wan," Breeze said and batted her eyes at him.

Uncle and Han exchanged looks.

"Breeze, remind me, whose name do you have?" Yu asked.

"Uncle."

"Oh yes, I remember now. Jazz, who do you have?" Yu asked.

"Kidd."

"Hmmm."

"Ya know, it's been a coon's age since…" Breeze started to say.

"DINNER," Jana yelled before Breeze could finish her statement.

The dining room table would have put Martha Stewart to shame because it was breath taking even though it was decorated with simple accents and touches. Kidd walked in the kitchen and hugged Jana tightly. "Thank you, Mom. It's beautiful as always, and the duck smells divine."

"You're welcome. I love you."

"I love you, too."

After dinner everyone went into the living room and spread out to start the gift exchange. They went around the room, and each person presented their present to the person that they had drawn. Kidd was first to pass out his gift. Jana opened her boots, and when she opened them and found the envelopes with the two sets of tickets, she gasped. She hadn't noticed the lid of the box yet, but Han and Uncle did. They both stood and were looking at the lid when Jana turned and looked at them.

"What are you doing?"

Han just held up the lid so Jana could see it. She looked at Kidd and Breeze. "Children."

They both jumped up and did a happy dance and quickly sat back down. Uncle just shook his head. None of them had picked up on anything, especially not a trip to New York. Uncle had a feeling that he would be just as surprised with his gift, especially since Breeze had his name. She did not disappoint him. The gift of the evening was Angela's gift to Mickey. She had taken the record player idea and had put a Barbie doll in it and had it dressed up like Mrs. Claus. Then there were three other Barbies that were dressed like elves from the Lord of the Rings. Each Barbie had a candy cane to support them, and Christmas lights twinkled on. As music started playing, there were four poles strategically placed, and the candy cane had a magnet on it so when it started turning it would pull the cane and dolls to the poles, and they would swing around the poles. Mickey laughed and clapped and continued to play with it. Jana threatened to take it away if he didn't pay attention while others opened their gifts. Angela had also given him a blues cd and a calendar of supermodels. He was on cloud nine.

Grams was brought to tears from Breeze and Kidd's gifts. Kidd presented Jana with her ring last. Grams was not the only one crying; Jana was so proud of the gift and her children. Her heart felt like it would explode. After the gifts were exchanged, Christmas music was put on, and they broke out card games. They played games until around eleven, then everyone went to their own places so they could spend the day with their families. Grams, Han, Jim, and Kim stayed at Jana's house. Breeze gave Grams her room, Kidd gave Jim and Kim his room, and Han took the spare bedroom. Breeze and Kidd slept in the living room. Everyone knew that Christmas was Jana's favorite holiday because it was all about family. Kidd loved this family.

TIME MARCHES ON

Several months had passed since that challenge and race, and Breeze had not issued any major challenges. Blade had assumed it was because of fall break, shopping with Jana, Christmas. Now they were preparing for exams, and spring break was not that far away. Little did Blade know those items would not stop Breeze from a challenge or two. Zion and Yu stopped by often; they knew that Breeze had cabin fever, which was never a good thing. She was a warm weather kind of girl, and her taking off for the tropics was a real possibility, if the opportunity arose. Zion had pulled Han to the side on Christmas Eve and told him the sadness was touching Breeze's eyes again. Han had seen it, too. Breeze was trying hard not to let it show. Zion was scared to death that she was going to slip back into a state of depression.

Breeze had started entering as many competitions as she could after Christmas. It was nice to be in the ring. Her dad and Jana were at those competitions. Jazz knew that she was missing the intensity of the streets and the fights there. Jazz called Breeze in early February and surprised her with the news that Taka was coming to town. Breeze danced around her room. Breeze and Jazz were entering a tournament together, and Taka would be here for that. Breeze was thrilled to see her old friend. Breeze hoped Taka had not told Han that he was coming to Tennessee, or she had a feeling that he would have an assignment come up before he flew out. Blade and Rocky were going to be at one of Summer's trapping competitions the weekend of the tournament. Two days before Taka flew out, he had to fly to China because his dad had to have emergency heart surgery to put a stent in and he was unable to come. Breeze was ok; she missed him, but it was probably for the best. If Jana, Han, and Uncle found out that Taka was in town with Breeze and Jazz, they would probably sit on them.

Breeze was in her third fight of the tournament when she threw a kick and felt a pop in her ankle. There was a burning sensation up the back of her leg. She dropped onto the mat; she lost that fight by tap out. She was rushed to the hospital; thankfully, there was an orthopedic surgeon on call. He did an MRI and determined that the Achilles tendon was severely strained but not torn. She would have to be in a boot for six weeks, and then it was to be re-examined. At that time, if everything was good, she would have to wear a brace to support that ankle any time she was in a sporting event.

Jazz took second in the tournament. Jazz knew that Breeze was bummed.

"Old times, we could go see Han," Jazz said.

Breeze was laughing so hard that her side hurt. She had tears rolling down her cheeks and she was gasping for air. Jazz helped her into his car and drove her home. Matt and Mickey were waiting when they pulled into the garage. They did not know that Breeze was in a boot. When she hobbled out they gasped. Jazz looked at Breeze; she just nodded.

"We thought now would be a good time to go see Han in

Japan… you know for old times' sake."

Jazz walked into the kitchen, and Breeze clumped behind him. Matt and Mickey were laughing and couldn't stop. Jana's phone rang, and she handed it to Breeze.

"Hello?"

"Young One," Han said.

Breeze laughed and hung up. She pointed to Jazz. "You're up next."

Breeze had barely finished her sentence when Jazz's phone rang, he looked at the screen, and saw it was Han.

"Yo."

"Yo? Really?" Han said in disbelief

"Yep."

"Don't even think about it, Young One."

"What?"

"You know what."

"Gotta go. Love ya, bye-bye," Jazz said and ended the call.

He began dancing into the living room with Breeze clumping behind him. Blade arrived about thirty minutes later and was shocked to see her in a boot, but in good spirits. She told him about the tournament and the new round of restrictions. The room seemed to be popping with energy, and Blade had no idea why. Mickey and Matt could not look at Breeze or Jazz without laughing. They all heard motorcycles pull up. There was a knock, Zion entered and bowed.

"Breeze and Jazz, Uncle said to tell you that he is in Korea with brethren, and Han called."

Breeze stood up and saluted Zion with a whole lot of attitude.

Zion laughed. "I will relay that."

"You do that," Breeze said.

Jazz ran around, and Breeze jumped on his back. "Old Times," Jazz yelled and ran out the back door.

Zion shook his head, bowed, and left. *Now this was more like the old Breeze,* he thought. Zion wasn't sure how Blade would handle that. He had seen a brief glimpse of the old Breeze, but Blade had not experienced it full on. Zion wasn't sure Blade or his blood pressure would survive.

Zion looked across the street before he got back on his bike and spotted Taylor in a black Escalade. *SHIT.* Zion mentally called out to Jana, Jon, Breeze, and Uncle to relay the information. When Jon and Jana walked out the front door Taylor took off. Everyone went on high alert again. Breeze was tired of this song and dance. She had six to eight weeks, then she had some plans to take care of.

She texted Mickey

Breeze: *The Friday before spring break let's make noise in circuit. Keep it QUIET for now, but it's my name... Only RING circuit receive texts when time, nothing early.*

Mickey: *Location?*

Breeze: *Multiple – you pick. Four and counting.*

Mickey: *Really?*

Breeze: *Yeah*

Mickey: *Jazz?*

Breeze: *Of course, but closer to time. Block so Blade doesn't get a sense.*

Mickey: *Yep. Yep. Got it.*

LONG OVERDUE

Breeze was finally out of the boot, but she did have to wear a brace for all tournaments and competitions. Her ankle was weak, and if she didn't want a torn Achilles, she would follow that rule to the letter. She was not about being sidelined again any time soon. It sucked that she still had some restrictions until she completed physical therapy. Spring was in the air, and Breeze was getting antsy. Everyone could feel it. The trackers were on high alert. Blade was even expecting something. He was on edge, and he hated it.

Blade and Breeze were coming home from a date when Mickey called. They could hear the song "Bad Girls" by M.I.A. playing in the background.

"Hey, Breeze, I have made you a peace pipe," Mickey said.

"One? Oh, how disappointing," she teased.

"Actually, four; do you want them all?"

"I'd love them. Hey, tell Matt to call me."

They hung up and about thirty seconds later Matt called. "Mickey said to call."

"Are you with him?" Breeze asked.

"No. Call waiting."

"Yeah. Set it."

"What about...?" Matt started to ask, however Breeze cut

him off.

"What about it?"

"Done."

They hung up, and her phone vibrated a few seconds later. She looked at her phone, sat it down and smiled. Blade looked at her. He had a feeling she was planning something, like schemin'. She told him nothing was going on, but he doubted her. He knew something was going on because he could feel excitement in the air. It still made him crazy that all the others seemed to know so much when he knew so little. Ever since the last challenge that was issued, he made it his mission to always know what was going on, but he felt like he was failing miserably. The call came from Mickey and then Matt, not Jazz. Jazz was almost always involved. He had to remind himself of the time frame that they had been dating, and to have patience. The next day at school, Breeze seemed distracted.

"Hey, Blade, do you want to go to the movies tonight? It would be just me and you," she asked.

He quickly agreed. He commented on her attention span. She brushed it off and simply blamed it on the medical restrictions. She explained to him that two more weeks of being sidelined might actually put her in the looney bin. He laughed until he saw her expression. She was guarded, so Blade couldn't pick up a hint of anything else. Blade had to go to the other end of the building, so they parted ways at her locker. Breeze's locker was close to Ang's, so she walked over and whispered low to Angela so no one else could hear. She explained her plans to Ang and asked her to nod if she agreed. She nodded. Breeze said thanks and walked off to class.

School ended for the day. Blade walked Breeze to her car.

"I'll pick you up at seven, ok?" Blade asked.

"That sounds wonderful."

She kissed Blade and left to go home. She had things to take care of before her date that night. She ran into the house, packed her duffle bag, made sure she had tape, nasal spray, and gloves. She needed enough clothes for possibly four days. She grabbed her small purse and placed her i.d., keys, sunglasses, and wallet in it. Matt had her tickets. Jazz would meet up with Matt and Kidd. She reached her mind out to the four guys. As she was talking to the guys, she placed her duffle bag in her car.

"Pick me up at 10:30 tonight. Everyone needs to stay completely guarded. Blade has been extremely curious since Mickey called last night. I will distract him this evening with a movie. Once the five of us are on the road I will call him later and ask him to pick me up at Ang's in the morning. I will block all background noise and show him me and Ang hanging out. We will be long gone by the time he arrives in the morning to pick me up for school, and Ang will give him the message I have left."

"Breeze, Blade can read Ang's mind, remember," Jazz said with *concern.*

"Relax. By the time Blade knows I'm sleeping over we will already be gone. I will tap his mind and give him images. I will feel him when he tries to tap me, so I will talk to him or let him think he's seeing my dreams." Breeze ended her connection with the guys and focused on getting ready for her date.

She put on a cute short blue jean skirt and a sexy t-shirt with a pair of long socks and boots that came up mid-calf. She put her mind solely on the date. She would have a great time tonight. Blade arrived five minutes early. He was wearing loose fitting jeans with a nice short sleeve polo shirt. Blade was talking to Jon when Breeze walked down the stairs. He smiled wide. He was thinking about how much he would like to take her back up to her room. Blade reminded himself where he was at and whose house it was. He complimented Breeze on her appearance and finished his conversation with Jon. Jon told them to have fun, and they left.

They went to Arby's before they headed to the movies. Blade couldn't take his eyes off of Breeze. She was gorgeous. They got back to her house around ten fifteen that evening. She kissed Blade passionately and told him good night. She watched him drive down the street. She waved one final time before he turned the corner to go down the block. She ran in, asked her dad if she could stay at Angela's for the night, and mentioned that this weekend they were going to Memphis to see Jazz. Jon nodded his approval. Breeze ran out, grabbed her bag from the backseat, and Kidd fired up her car. He drove her down the street and let her out where she got in with Matt. Jazz was in the backseat with Mickey. They pulled up to Angela's. She came out and Breeze handed her the sealed envelope for Blade.

"Blade will come here in the morning to pick me up. Simply give this to him and don't say anything to my father."

"What's up?" Angela asked.

"Nothing."

Jazz leaned out the window and took her hand. "Ang, trust us please. There are some things we need to take care of."

"Ok. No problem," Angela said.

"I will see you next weekend. It will be you, me, and the movies, ok?" he asked and then kissed her hand. Ang blushed and giggled. She couldn't wait to be alone with Jazz. She really liked him. She couldn't believe that with all the women at the streets he would rather spend time with her. Jazz loved to see her blush. He kissed her hand lightly again and gently pulled her down toward the car. He got close to her ear and whispered, "I promise to make it a wonderful night." He kissed her neck. Angela was scarlet.

"Thanks, Angela. I will see you at school Monday," Breeze said.

"Welcome," Angela mumbled back. She was still trying to recover from Jazz's lingering kiss on her neck. Ang watched the cars pull off and the truck with the other rides go by before she went back into the house. Breeze waited until they were on the plane before she tapped Blade. She made sure to guard all background information so he wouldn't know her true location.

"Blade."

He sat up. *"Yes?"*

"Hey, sweetheart. I wanted to ask you if you could pick me up for school tomorrow."

"Sure. Is there something wrong with your car?" he asked, concerned.

"No. I just want to ride for a change. Pick me up at seven in the morning at Angela's, ok?"

"Angela's?"

"Yeah, I'm staying the night."

"Ok, I'll be there."

"Thank you. Good night, handsome."

She showed him an image of her and Angela sitting on the bed looking at photo albums. She yawned, pulled back the covers, and climbed in. Angela was placing the photo albums on her desk. She showed Blade that they were talking boys.

"Would you ever go all the way with Blade?" Ang asked.

310

Blade was paying close attention now. He couldn't wait to hear Breeze's answer. He had desired her since the first day he met her. Breeze blushed at the question.

"Maybe, someday, but not like tomorrow or anything. What about you?"

"Would I go all the way with Blade?" Ang asked in shock.

"No. He's mine. Remember? I was referring to you and Jazz."

Angela blushed and giggled. "Maybe, one day, but I'm still a virgin."

Breeze ended the connection with Blade.

"Laying it on a little thick, weren't you?" Jazz asked. He grinned and lightly kissed her.

"Nope. He doesn't want to hear Angela's dreams, especially about you. He knows I'm guarded even when I sleep."

SECRETS

Blade arrived at Angela's at exactly seven in the morning.

"Hey, Ang, is Breeze ready?"

She shook her head and handed Blade the envelope. He opened the envelope and read the note inside.

> *Blade,*
> *Please DON'T be mad, but I will not be at school today, and I won't be home this weekend. Restrictions or not, I have some business to take care of. I will see you on Monday.*
> *With love,*
> *Breeze*

Blade looked at Angela. "When did she give this to you, and where did she go?"

"She brought it by last night, and all she told me was to give this to you and not to mention anything to her dad. Matt, Breeze, Jazz, and Mickey drove off."

"What? She wasn't driving her car?"

"No. Kidd was following in her car, and there was a guy driving the truck with all the street bikes on it."

"She never said where they were going?" Blade asked. His

anger was coming to the surface.

"No. I heard Matt yell to Kidd something about the garage and all the tickets were taken care of."

"Get in."

"OK."

"What was Breeze wearing?"

"Shorts, a cute T-shirt, and flip flops. Hey, did she get a new tat?"

"No. Not that I know of. Why?" Blade asked, but he was really trying to hold onto his anger.

"No reason. I thought her ankle looked tattooed, but it was probably just a cool anklet."

"Which ankle?"

"The left, you know, the one that has been in a boot and brace. OHHH, sorry."

Blade was getting madder the longer they talked. He calmed himself. "Did she have anything with her?" Blade finally asked.

"Her duffle bag."

"What time did she stop by last night?"

"Ten thirty."

Blade growled. How could he have missed the guys or the truck? He had been with her until ten fifteen last night. He was beyond mad. He was tired of all the secrets. They were supposed to be a couple, and he only knew what she wanted him to know. Ang was feeling a little uncomfortable with Blade's irritation at Breeze.

"Sorry. That's all I know. Wait, she did say something about the beach."

He felt like all the air had been knocked out of him, and he heard Breeze's voice in his mind. *Don't try looking for me.*

You won't succeed. I will check in every six hours to let you know I'm fine. IF anything happens to me, all guards will be let down and you will know our location immediately. IF I'm hurt, Jazz will be the one to contact you. Every six hours one of us will be in contact to let you and your family know how we are. I am safe. No worries, my love. I will also let you know when we return. Go to school, and don't be pissy all weekend. There is nothing you could have done to stop me. Do not mention any of this to my Dad or the trackers. I have to take care of some business."

Their connection ended, and he was thinking to himself; *We will just see about that. The first time it was a challenge, but this is something more than that. Three hours compared to possible days, no way. Pissy? Pissy. She has no idea how truly pissed and worried I am. If she was racing, she would have told me, which means the bikes were either a decoy, or she was planning to race as well as going to the streets to fight, though I doubt it. The bikes were a decoy. I know it.* He pulled into the school parking lot and sat there for a second. "Please wait." He touched Ang's wrist. He was trying not to yell at her.

He read the note again.

. . . restrictions or not, I have some business to take care of. . .

"SHE IS GOING TO FIGHT IN THE STREETS," he screamed. Angela jumped.

"No way, she has been careful not to train or do anything to hurt her ankle." Ang shook her head.

She knew Jazz wouldn't let Breeze fight because he had told her about how hard it was to see Breeze in the hospital for three weeks. She knew the guys would keep Breeze safe.

How could Blade be so sure that they were fighting?

"Yeah, I know. However, her note indicates she's ignoring her restrictions. Read it yourself."

Angela read the note in shock. She shrugged and smiled.

"We better get to class, there is nothing we can do. You know, to get to the streets is guarded and coded. We have only been a part of the racing. We know nothing of the fighting or dancing. I know it's all probably connected, but we don't have an 'in' to that part of the underground."

Blade put his password in his phone and called Rocky. "You and Summer meet me in the courtyard. Call dad and tell him we may be taking a weekend road trip." He hung up and looked at her.

"That's it, Angela. See if you can find Chad. If he is here, ask him to see me."

Ang quickly got out of the car. She was shocked by Blade's reaction. This was Breeze. She couldn't remember a time when Breeze wasn't working on cars, fighting, or competing. Blade seemed so possessive of her it was like she was his wife or something. She laughed a little and quickly found Chad. She relayed the message to him for Blade. Chad approached Blade about five minutes later. Blade was pacing when he walked up.

"What's up, bro? Where's Breeze?"

Blade stopped and looked at Chad. "Have you received anything about the streets this weekend? Anything, race, fight, competition, or etc.?"

"Yeah, bro, there's a race in Ohio. Motor cross in GA. Dance off in FL. Nothing big, normal weekend stuff."

"There is something you are not telling me. What is it?" Blade took a couple steps toward Chad. Chad cringed. He had an odd feeling without Breeze being there. It was an uncomfortable feeling that made his skin tingle.

"Breeze will be pissed. I can't."

"You can and you will." At that moment fear ran through Chad, and the tingling sensation became unbearable.

"There is some major shit happening this weekend in the fighting arena. There are four major fights lined up in four major cities across the US this weekend. Which means there will be competitions, step offs, and racing as well. They will be spread out in surrounding cities to ensure nothing gets busted up. Everything was thrown together quickly and sent out instantly with the expectation that the location may change with a five-hour window notification before the 'event' happens. The first alert was sent out Wednesday night at eight fifteen. Dude, you look like you've seen a ghost. What's up? Again, where is Breeze? OH CRAP, NEVERMIND. Oh, she is going to kill me."

The realization hit Chad hard that Breeze was fighting this weekend, and she had not told Blade. He felt horrible for outing her secret. Blade's heart sank. He was remembering Wednesday evening when they were in her car, and she had spoken to Mickey and Matt. He had sensed an air of excitement.

"Chad, thanks. No worries, Breeze will be mad at me, not you. Do you know the cities and states?"

"No. Remember the location will be announced five hours before the event. No one knows; we are just waiting. I do know the first location. It was announced two hours ago."

"Why a five-hour window? Where's the first location?"

"The window is so the location can be changed, and the competitors can still make the flights and be there in time to warm up and get ready. Not to mention to let fans get there in time to see the event. There is not enough time to alert outside forces. When you arrive, there are clues to the actual location. The first location is Baton Rouge."

Chad's phone vibrated. His face went pale and he handed the phone to Blade.

Circuit: Cities just went from four to seven for the weekend.

"Does that mean there are now seven fights and not four?" Blade asked.

Chad nodded in agreement. His phone buzzed again.

Circuit: Window now three and a half hours, not five hours

Blade looked at his watch. "That means her first fight is in an hour and a half. How do so many people travel with such a short window?"

"Tickets are purchased the night of the first alert with the rule being purchase for the farthest place from your home, multiplied by the number of nights of the event. Once the location is announced, you log in, change the destination, and you are good to go."

"Chad, do you have tickets?"

He nodded again.

"Here's my number. Send me the next alert you get."

Chad's phone buzzed again.

> *Breeze:* Don't tell him anymore. I'll send you fake alerts to send to him. Smile and tell him first fight still a go.

Chad looked at Blade. He knew that Blade knew. He could see it on Blade's face.

"She knows I know," Blade said.

"Yes, and it's weird how you both know."

"We have a special connection."

"More like FREAKY. Look, bro, Breeze is one of the best underground street fighters. When her ex beat her, a lot of crap was started about her losing her edge. Four cities is something she has done before, seven is not. She is out to prove that she has not lost her edge. If you interfere, she may choose the streets over you. If you go, go to support her, NOT to stand in her way. Those restrictions have been harder on her than you know. The restrictions are a constant reminder of the SOB that broke her and how easily she was beaten."

Blade listened to everything that Chad had to say. He had not known her prior to the incident. He sighed.

"Please send me the real alerts. She doesn't know we are still talking," Blade said. "I promise I will support her." He turned and quickly hurried to his car.

Chad had a feeling he should do as Blade said, but he really didn't want Breeze's wrath. Blade seemed like he really cared, so he decided he would send him the alerts. When Blade, Summer, and Rocky arrived home, their dad was standing at the door.

"If you go, remember these are street fights. It means there will be lots of fresh blood. If you don't feel like you can control yourself, then stay home. Blade I understand your desire to go; remember, she chose to go. I'm not sure if she is doing this to prove to others that she can or simply to prove to herself that she is not weak. Either way, she is determined. I will be going with you to tend to her injuries. I'm sure there will be many. Summer, go get us each two bottles so we can drink before we go."

Blade's phone vibrated. It was Chad; first fight starts in thirty. Blade's stomach tightened. *He doesn't have to be so excited, but knowing Jazz and Breeze, their excitement was probably ten times worse than Chad's.* That thought did not help his nerves. He took the bottles that were handed to him, and he drank. He knew he could control his thirst, especially when it came to Breeze.

"What's up with you, Rocky? You look all keyed up," Blade said with a little frustration.

"Just excited," Rocky said.

"Excited about what?" he asked.

"You know, the streets, the fights, all of it." Blade just shook his head. "Jazz was planning to take me to his next fight," Rocky grinned.

Blade swore lightly under his breath. Rocky grinned even bigger. They packed quickly. Blade's stomach was in some serious knots. All he could think about was Breeze. He wanted to be with her, he wanted to know all her secrets, but mostly he wanted her to love him above all others. He knew the fight was probably underway because he had some serious anxiety going on. *I wish I was there.* His phone buzzed again.

First fight - Breeze won TKO 2 minutes first round. Next location announced, Miami, FL.

"Crap. She just fought and won, and she is fighting again in three and half hours." He yelled to everyone and no one.

Rocky came around the corner; "What was her time?"

"Two Minutes, first round TKO."

"Cool," Rocky said, bouncing on his toes. "Where are we

going?"

"Miami, FL."

"Beaches, girls, and fights... who could ask for more?" Rocky was grinning like he had just won the lottery.

Summer said one of Breeze's favorite lines. "Uhhhh Men." They all laughed.

They left in a hurry to get to the airport. The airport was packed. Thank goodness Summer purchased the tickets online or they would never have made it on time. Blade spotted Chad, and he came over.

"Dude, you must have flown to get here. I was here waiting when the text came through," Chad said.

Blade looked around, and he couldn't believe how many people were there. Chad let Blade know that another flight to Miami had to be added because of all the people going there. Blade looked at Rocky; he was useless. His excitement was unnerving to Blade. Blade shook his head and sat down.

Chad's phone buzzed. "No way," he said.

"What?"

"Another fight has been added for tonight... back-to-back."

"She is going to kill herself."

"Nah, she's the best," Chad said with a big grin. He was excited to see Breeze fight, and it showed.

Blade was concerned, and he voiced that concern to Chad. He was worried that she hadn't been training or working out; she couldn't. She had several restrictions back-to-back, and when she finally entered a tournament, she ended up in a boot with another round of restrictions. Chad laughed a little. He explained that the Breeze he knew wouldn't stop training simply because she was told to. He also reassured Blade that if Breeze fought and was not in appropriate condition, then her father would kill her. She knew better.

"Have you been with her every minute?" Chad wanted Blade to really understand.

"Well, no. She normally goes home for a couple of hours. I go over around dinner time and stay until nine at night."

"Plenty of time to train or workout," Chad said with confidence.

Blade felt like Chad even knew her better than he did. "Tell me what you know." There was a hint of irritation but more longing to his voice than he had wanted there to be.

"That's it, bro. Breeze won't let anything, or anyone, hold her back. She is a fighter through and through, mentally, physically, emotionally, and spiritually. When I say fighter, I don't mean just in Martial Arts. I mean if she believes in something, she 'fights' for it." Chad respected Breeze. Blade could see it in the way he talked about her.

When the plane landed, they grabbed their bags and got off the plane. They had everything in their carry-on bags so no need for baggage claims.

"Are you following me or you going on your own?" Chad asked with an air of cockiness.

"With you," Blade said.

He was too worried about Breeze to be on a scavenger hunt in Miami, Florida. Hell, he might lose Rocky and waste time looking for him. Chad interrupted his thoughts.

"That is a wise decision."

It took them forty-five minutes to find the location. They were in the back of the arena. Blade was on edge. Rocky and Chad were bouncing with excitement. Blade didn't try to tap Jazz or Breeze. He wanted her mind completely on the fight. As much as he hated it, he wanted her to win.

"She is supposed to make her first contact in a couple hours, so we wait," Blade told his family.

"We're still watching, right?" Rocky asked, sounding a little unsure and worried.

"Yes, we are staying, but we are going to be unseen until after her first contact," Blade said.

Breeze came out. "Wow she looks fine," Chad said and blushed. "Sorry, man, I know she's your girl and all, but OMG."

Blade smiled, but kept his mouth shut. Breeze's opponent came out. She was probably ten pounds heavier, four inches taller, and had a good two inches on reach compared to Breeze.

"Chad, how many rounds?"

"Three rounds. Three minutes per round."

Blade held his breath, and the bell rang. The opponent "Vixen" threw the first punch and connected with Breeze's nose. Vixen connected again. Her third punch was blocked. Breeze did a sidekick and connected, followed with a sweep kick, taking Vixen down. Breeze was on her. She had Vixen pinned by holding her leg at a funny angle. Vixen tapped out in just forty-five seconds in the first round.

Next fight would be in ten minutes. Blade stood stunned at her speed and her skill. Watching her, she looked completely healed, but there was no way that was possible. He noticed she had both ankles taped, both wrists and hands taped as well. He saw Jazz and Matt doctoring her. They were extremely gentle; he saw them both touch her wrists and they both nodded. Kidd came over beside her with water and some nasal spray. She tilted her head back, Jazz re-aligned her nose, and she didn't even scream or anything. Jazz did something

322

odd though; he rubbed his wrist under her nose, and she took a deep breath in. He touched her wrist, and she gently touched his. They both laughed and nodded.

"What the hell is between those two?" Blade said through gritted teeth.

Chad jumped. "Dude, you were so silent I thought you had left. You mean Jazz and Breeze? They've been like that ever since I can remember, but they never hook up. It's just them; no boundaries and complete acceptance."

"Has the next text come through yet?" Blade asked, still gritting his teeth.

"Nah, we'll probably sleep a few before the next one."

The fight started. This one was a better match to Breeze's skills. Breeze got pinned and just when everyone thought she would tap out, she rolled and flipped China. First round was over. The bell rang to start the second round. Breeze came out hard and fast. She had China pinned against the fence. The ref broke it up before China could tap out. Two minutes and twenty seconds into the second round, Breeze pinned China again and held her throat until she passed out. Breeze won by KO. Breeze touched Matt; he nodded. She looked pretty rough. One of her eyes was swelling shut, and her lip was busted. Matt and Kidd led her out. They went down the back into the alley where doors were off to the side.

"Let's get a couple rooms so we can rest. We don't know when the next fight will be. The fights only get harder from here on out."

"Harder?" Blade stopped walking and gaped at Chad.

"You know, opponents tougher?" Chad was shaking his head. He couldn't believe how little Blade knew about the Underground, and he was dating the hottest chick in the circuit.

"I don't know if I can take this." Blade looked like he was going to throw up or pass out.

"If she can, you can." Chad's phone vibrated. "No way."

"Please tell me they didn't add another fight."

"No, but the next one is in twenty minutes."

"What? Is she insane? Her body just took one hell of a beating." Blade was frustrated, confused, and angry all rolled up in one. His face was turning red, and he had his hands in a fist.

"Do you remember me telling you that Breeze has done four fights in four cities in a weekend before, but not seven? Well, she hasn't done four fights in a night. If she wins tonight, she earns her respect back and then some."

Phone vibrated again. Special feature + main event.

"What does that mean?" Blade was anxious.

"It means someone fights before her. She will fight second."

Rocky was bouncing with excitement. He figured it would either be Jazz or Kidd to fight before Breeze. Either way, he didn't care. Kidd had been working with Jon for several years from what they all had told him. Jon was as tough on Kidd as he was on Breeze. Jazz was amazing. Breeze was as amazing as all the guys had said she was. Blade was shaking with fury and anxiety. Dr. McGroff was concerned about all of Breeze's injuries. Summer was just taking everything in. She was especially taking in Kidd. He looked so adorable.

"Here comes Jazz. Obviously he is before her. Mickey has come out with him. Oh, boy, Ice is his opponent." Chad was sounding excited and shocked at the same time.

"I've heard that name before," Blade said.

"If you've been to the streets, you've heard his name. He is

324

into everything. Jazz won a car from him a few weeks back."

Blade was talking to Chad about the possible outcome of this fight. Chad simply shrugged. He honestly didn't know who would win; they were both good fighters. Rocky was so excited that Blade wanted to strangle him. "What is your deal?" Blade asked with absolute irritation.

"I've sparred with Jazz. He really is an amazing fighter," Rocky said.

"I thought he was here to help Breeze."

"They help each other. Speaking of which, here she comes," Chad said.

Blade saw her; she had changed clothes and had cleaned up. Her injuries didn't look half as bad as he thought they would. Jazz and Ice pounded on each other, blow for blow. The bell dinged. Breeze took care of Jazz's nose, the cuts on his face, and the gash under his eye. She touched his wrist, and he touched hers. She kissed him and then whispered something. The bell rang, and he was back in the ring. Jazz and Ice were a total match.

Jazz did something odd: he winked at Ice. Ice dropped the punch he was getting ready to throw, and Jazz took full advantage of it. Jazz tore into Ice. Ice stumbled back a couple of times. Jazz got him in a neck hold on the mat. Ice didn't tap out; instead he passed out. The ref pulled Jazz off Ice and worked with him. When Ice came to he swore loudly. He had never lost by KO before.

Breeze was going to be against Lady Ice. Chad was jumping up and down with excitement.

"What?" Blade asked rather reluctantly.

"Lady Ice wants Breeze's head. She's Ice's Old Lady, and she is just as ruthless as he is. Breeze beat her before, down in Austin."

Chad's phone vibrated.

Circuit: Main event rules changed, following men's rule of time by request of the champ.

"Ok, maybe you're right; she's trying to kill herself, or she's insane. Read for yourself." Chad handed Blade the phone.

"If she survives all eight fights, I might kill her myself," Blade said. Chad laughed, but he noticed how pale Blade was.

"Three rounds, five minutes each, no holds barred match," yelled the announcer.

Lady Ice landed the first few punches. Her fourth punch was to Breeze's ribs. Instead of Breeze grabbing her ribs in pain, she took a deep breath and did a roundhouse to Lady Ice's face. Lady Ice hit the mat. Everyone waited for her to get up, but she didn't. She was out. Breeze won by KO in fifty-two seconds in the first round.

"Awesome!" Rocky was bouncing on his toes.

"Yeah, awesome; only two more days of this," Blade said with sarcasm and rolled his eyes.

Rocky bounced harder on his toes. Blade grabbed him by the front of his shirt. Rocky simply grinned. That irritated Blade even more. Breeze, Jazz, Matt, Mickey, and Kidd had already left the arena. She should be contacting him soon, and while they waited, they checked in to a hotel. Chad roomed with the guys, and Summer had her own room.

Blade felt Breeze touch his mind. *"Hey you, I'm fine. Letting you know that I've won four for four."*

"Four for four?" Blade was trying to sound like he didn't have a clue what she was talking about. He was biting his lip.

"I've won all four fights so far."

"Four fights. How many fights are there?"

"Enough. No worries."

"No worries. I'm sick with worry. Where are you?"

"I'm fine. Jazz is fine. We're all fine. I'm checking in like I said I would. Now stop worrying. I'll be home Sunday."

With that, the connection ended. He decided that he and his family would stay out of sight until after the last fight or until she was really hurt, whichever came first. At twelve thirty in the morning, Chad's phone vibrated. He woke everyone up. "We gotta go. Dallas. The text just came through."

"Are you kidding? She's fighting at four in the morning?" Blade asked.

"Yep."

They woke Summer. Summer was not someone that you wanted to mess with in the mornings. She needed a full eight hours of sleep, or she was a complete bear to be around.

"Breeze better stop this schedule because I need my rest. I may beat her ass myself," Summer said angrily.

"Now, now," Rocky said, talking in baby talk. She growled and he jumped back. "Oh, you are such a kitten," he sneered.

They barely made the flight. When they landed, they ran to the next fight location. Everyone's phone vibrated at once.

Circuit: Main event x 2. Standard rules. First fight: Breeze vs. Venom; second fight: Breeze vs. Jade.

Chad swore, shook his head, and handed Blade his phone.

"She is going to kill me," Blade said.

"Not easily done," Summer laughed. She was holding her coffee and looking extremely tired.

The first fight went rather quickly. Breeze got Venom in a guillotine chokehold and won by KO in one minute fifteen seconds, first round. The second fight was rough for Blade to watch. Breeze was bleeding badly. She had her knee kicked and was not able to put a lot of weight on it. She had a horrible gash on her head, and her nose was broken. Her opponent was just about as badly banged up. The mat was covered in blood. It was the third round, and they were two minutes in. They were blow for blow. The score was basically tied. Blade knew Breeze was throwing more kicks than her opponent. There was a loud pop, and Jade dropped. The ref ran over. He called the fight at two minutes thirty-seven seconds in the third round, TKO by submission. Jade wasn't getting up, and then Blade saw why: Jade's leg was snapped.

People up front were getting sick. Medics were called in, and she left in an ambulance. Breeze stepped out of the ring. Blade had to see her, he had to talk to her and know that she was able to continue. He quietly told his dad to get Summer something to quench her thirst. Rocky was fine because he was loving the fights. Blade asked Rocky to go with him. He didn't know what he would find once he got to Breeze. He needed some moral support. Blade told his father that they would drink once they got back to the hotel, or they would find a donor bank if they needed to. His father reluctantly nodded.

"Chad, go get some sleep. You are looking a little dead on your feet."

"You ain't lying. I wonder where we will be next. HM-MMM, she never disappoints."

THE REALIZATION

Rocky and Blade followed Breeze and the guys to where they were staying. Blade didn't try to tap her or Jazz's minds; he wanted to see her in person. Matt, Mickey, and Kidd went in one room. Jazz and Breeze went in another. He heard Jazz saying she really needed a stiff drink, and they both laughed.

Breeze yelled to Matt, "You guys get some sleep; we have a serious match or two soon."

"You know you kick ass, but you're seriously a pain in mine." Matt yelled back to her.

Breeze grinned at Matt and blew him a kiss. Matt shook his head and reminded them to keep the noise down.

Jazz leaned out of the room. "Jealous."

"I'll send Kidd over to babysit," Matt yelled back.

"Quit hatin'," Jazz laughed.

Breeze waved good night to everyone. She was giddy from her wins. It felt good to be back in the game. Jazz took her by the arm, gently led her into the room, and closed the door. Breeze was talking when Blade heard Jazz tell her to hush and drink. It was completely silent. Rocky was standing at the door ready to knock when Blade stopped him. He placed his finger to his lips. He heard Breeze talking to Jazz.

"Thanks for everything. I can't drink to completely heal; it would be a little strange for all the people who've been to all the fights, but you can drink and satisfy us both." He heard Breeze laugh, she gasped, and nothing.

Rocky looked at Blade. He was clenching his fists. He nodded, and Rocky popped the door open, but he did it where the others couldn't hear it. He couldn't believe what he was seeing. Jazz was holding Breeze in his arms with blood on his lips from the inside of her bicep. She froze at the sight of them. Rocky closed the door, and Blade stood frozen.

Jazz spoke. "Blade, we are not like you; we are half breeds."

"What? How? Are you saying? No way." She was speechless.

"We are day walkers," Rocky said.

"How long have you known?" Blade asked.

Jazz thought for a moment before he answered Blade. "I have known since the first time we fought Taylor."

Blade was in complete disbelief. None of his family had any idea about Breeze or Jazz. How could they be like them? Blade was furious. He was tired of all the secrets. At least this secret he understood. He knew the cost of others knowing something like this.

"I didn't know," Breeze said and walked over to Blade.

He wasn't sure he could touch Breeze without her truly feeling his hurt. He felt angry that Jazz shared in this secret with Breeze. He was also mad that Jazz knew his secret.

"Technically, I'm only half. Same as Jazz," She was trying to comfort Blade.

"Is this one of the secrets ONLY the two of you share?" Blade asked. Breeze nodded.

"Blade, he is helping me heal. We don't drink for thirst. We drink to heal or for pleasure. We don't drink from others."

330

"I get your connection now, but I'd rather you drank from me," he said through gritted teeth. His anger wasn't fading.

"This is only part of our connection. Our connection was strong before we found out we were both half breeds," Jazz said. "Breeze, Rocky and I are going to step out. We'll be back."

She nodded, never breaking her gaze from Blade. How could she not have seen it? She touched his arm and demanded that he look at her. He was still trying to get his temper under control. He snapped his head up and growled. She growled back.

"You were so broken when I first met you. Why didn't he heal you then?"

"I wouldn't let him," she said.

"What?"

"Taylor broke me in so many ways, and I had to heal on my own. These fights are part of that healing. Do you understand?" she asked. He merely nodded. "I don't think you do," Breeze said as she touched his arm with gentleness. She touched his wrist, he felt the jolt, and she showed him everything that Taylor had done, how Jazz sat with her and talked to her when she just wanted to die; the mountain, the message they sent out over the mountain; the importance of the necklace that she only removed during fights. She showed him her pain, hurt, and desires.

Rocky and Jazz had come back in. Jazz walked in and touched Blade's other wrist. He showed Blade how he felt when he received the call that Breeze might not make it. He showed him how she looked. He could think of nothing else but getting back to the hospital to make sure she was safe. He showed Blade the night of the procedure and the morning after, the hate he felt for Taylor, and how he planned to get even. He showed him that the necklace meant as much to him as it did to Breeze.

Breeze and Jazz tapped Blade's mind at the same time.

"You have now seen another secret or two that only we share. We are what we are. Are you ok with that?"

"Yes," Blade insisted.

"Good. Would you like to share in this connection one hundred percent of the time?" Breeze asked. He nodded.

"Will you always make sure Breeze is safe?" Jazz asked.

"Yes, with my life," Blade said.

"Will you always stand by Jazz like he is your brother?" she asked.

"Yes."

"Will you stand by me no matter how extreme I get?" she asked with a smile.

"This weekend has about killed me, but, yes, I will."

"Promise to keep the secrets we just showed you? We are the only three who know those things," she said shyly.

"Of course."

"Your family is included in that promise," she said.

"I promise."

"Will you help me take care of Taylor?" Jazz asked.

"Already in the works."

"Can you ask Rocky to go to the guys' room? We want to finalize this bond without any witnesses." Breeze said as she touched Blade's arm in a reassuring manner. Blade nodded. *"I'll let Kidd know. He rarely sleeps,"* Breeze said.

Jazz took Rocky over to the guys' room.

"Blade, do you know how rare this is that Jazz and I let anyone this close?"

"Yes."

Breeze shook her head. There was no way that he understood. "Blade, this means that not only do we trust you, but that we accept you fully. We trust Matt, Mickey, and Kidd, but they are not a part of this secret." Blade wrapped his arm around Breeze and pulled her close. Jazz came back into the room laughing and shaking his head.

"Kidd is so stupid," Jazz was saying in between laughs. "Rocky crashed."

"Why did you say Kidd is stupid?" Breeze asked with her hands on her hips.

"As soon as I told him Blade and Rocky were here, he wanted to know where Summer was and started drooling."

Breeze laughed. She knew that Kidd really liked Summer. She would work on that later. She took a breath and steadied herself. Breeze turned to Blade, took his hand, and led him to the bed. Jazz held her other hand. Jazz and Breeze touched each of Blade's wrists.

"Blade, we are going to solidify this bond. You both are going to drink from me at the same time." They both felt Blade tense. *"You won't hurt me, Blade, and neither will Jazz. You must drink from me. I'm the one with all the glitches, remember."*

Jazz laughed. *"Glitches, yeah, I'd say. Seriously, she will be okay."*

"Do you trust us?" she asked.

"Yes."

"Do you want to be connected with us?"

"More than anything."

They removed their hands from his wrists. Breeze sat in the center of the bed. "Blade, I offer myself and my blood to you. Do you accept?"

"Yes." She held out her right arm to Blade.

"Jazz, I offer myself and my blood to you. Do you accept?"

"Yes." She held out her left arm to Jazz.

"Then please drink." Breeze said to them both.

They both lifted her arms and turned them over. They placed their mouths to the inside of her biceps and bit her. She gasped. Blade heard her moan, and he drank, as did Jazz. Both Blade and Jazz stopped at the same time. This was Blade's first drink from a living, breathing human. Breeze and Jazz could feel all the emotions flood Blade. They could also hear his thoughts freely as he could hear theirs.

"You may tell your family that we are half breeds, but that is as far as it can go," Breeze insisted.

"Don't worry, they won't say anything. The same goes for you two." They nodded their agreement.

She touched Jazz's wrist. *"Do you mind if I drink from him?"*

He shook his head. "Do you want me to leave?" Jazz asked.

She shrugged.

"I'll call Kidd," he said.

"You don't have to go." Breeze said.

"I love you too much not to leave. You deserve a little privacy. It's your first drink from him. Not to mention, I think he wants to be alone with you."

"Are you really ok with this?"

"Breeze, have I ever lied to you?"

"No." She grinned, "Well, what are you waiting for?"

"GREEDY." Jazz said and winked at her.

"You know it."

Jazz left the room and went to the guy's room. Blade was sitting on the side of the bed. He was unsure as to what he should do. He knew what he wanted, but he didn't think she was ready for that. Breeze scooted over to Blade and pulled his arms around her. She nuzzled her nose into his neck. She could feel his heart beating. She loved how it sped up every time she kissed his neck and chest. He loved having her in his arms. He knew they had only been together about eight months, but he was having feelings about her that he had not experienced before. He got the feeling that she wanted to ask him something. He gently lifted her chin so he could look into her eyes. "What is it?"

"UMMMM, can I drink from you?" Breeze turned her head a little and shyly looked away from him.

He stroked her hair and pulled her even closer to him. "Breeze you can drink from me any time." He spoke softly and reassuringly to her.

"I've only drank from Jazz, I'm nervous," she said.

He could feel her desires and knew how badly she wanted to drink from him. He looked her in the eyes and said, "Breeze, please drink."

She was shaking from nerves and exhaustion. She decided she would drink from him in the same place on his body as he drank from her. She slowly moved to his right inner bicep. She sank her teeth in him. He stroked her hair, wrapped his hand through it, and gently pulled. He leaned his body into her. A low deep moan poured out of him. She finished drinking. He pulled her to him and kissed her passionately. "Breeze, can I have one more drink from you. I promise you may drink again to ensure your strength."

Breeze nodded and guided his hand down to her inner thigh. He kissed his way down to her thigh, grabbed her, and bit. Desire, holy shit, she wanted him badly, but she was not ready for that. She touched his mind.

"Can I bite you NOW?"

"Yes," he moaned as he said it.

She didn't hesitate for a second. She bit him and was slammed with his desires. That was not helping her control her own desires.

"Will you hold me all night?" She asked as they finished drinking. Blade pulled her tightly in his arms and reassured her that he wasn't going anywhere. "Will you be ring side in a few hours?" Breeze asked him hesitantly, unsure if he would stay for the fights or not.

"I wouldn't miss it," he said.

At one in the afternoon, they woke up and were starving. She tapped Jazz.

"You awake, bum?"

"Yeah, but Matt isn't up yet."

"Don't wake him; he needs his beauty rest."

"Kidd asleep?"

"Yes, thank goodness. We are cutting his caffeine intake. I thought Rocky was going to kill him. He kept waking Rocky up and asking him about Summer. Rocky finally told him that he would talk to her for him, but he had to lay down and shut up."

"That work?"

"Yep, because I whispered in his ear and told him that he could dream about her. He was out so fast. The boy was smiling in his sleep and he's still smiling."

"Dog."

"Don't be a hater."

"Whatever. You hungry?"

"Hell, yeah."

"I'm going to order lunch for everyone and pick it up from the local diner."

"Make sure your boy goes with you. I don't need you jumped or anything."

She ended the connection and grabbed her cell phone so she could call the order in. She saw her reflection in the mirror when she passed by to go to the bathroom. "Wow. Roadkill," she groaned.

"You are beautiful."

"Whatever."

"Breeze?" She turned and looked at him. His tone seemed more serious than a second ago. "I love you and I don't mean like Jazz loves you."

Butterflies were in every part of her body. Plus, she had goosebumps. "It's only been eight months, but I know what you mean."

Breeze showered first and got ready while Blade showered. He was amazed that she was fully dressed, and her hair was done when he came out. "WOW."

"What?" She asked confused.

"It takes Summer forever to get ready."

"She's never schemed on a dime and got the heck out of dodge. I will work on it with her."

Blade grabbed Breeze and kissed her. When he broke the kiss, he looked her directly in the eyes and said, "I don't think so."

Breeze was still laughing when they left to go get all the food.

REVELATION

They all ate lunch. Matt was finally feeling alive. Breeze's phone vibrated, she looked at Blade. She told him to call his family and have them meet them. Blade confirmed Breeze's suspensions about them having assistance from an insider. She assumed it was Chad and she was right. Blade called his dad, told him the plan, and whispered so Chad wouldn't hear on the other end.

"Pack some bottles for Rocky, because he's really pale."

"What about you?" Dr. McGroff asked.

"Bring me one, but really I'm fine. I'll explain later," Blade said.

Jazz, Matt, Mickey, Rocky, and Kidd all looked like kids on Christmas. They had their bags in hand and were waiting for Dr. McGroff, Summer, and Chad. As soon as Chad was close enough, he high-fived Breeze and Jazz. He couldn't stop talking about all the action.

"Just wait for today's action." Breeze said and winked at Chad.

"Come on give me something," Chad begged.

"Can't," Breeze teased.

"Please."

Jazz grabbed Breeze around the waist, stuck his head over

338

her shoulder, laughed, and said, "She can't and won't. Surprise and anticipation will make it even better. Let's just say it'll be more than you ever hoped for."

"Man, that's messed up," Chad said.

All her friends laughed. "We know."

They boarded the plane. Thirty minutes later Chad's phone went off. Chicago, IL.

2 bonus features + 2 main events.

Two minutes later it buzzed again.

Second main event, three rounds five minutes each.

"Girl," Chad said with a huge grin.

"Yeah, just wait until you see it. I truly hope you're not disappointed." She winked and wagged her eyebrow at him.

Blade was sitting beside her, holding her hand. "Does this mean I can hang out at you place all the time, put my hands on you, and kiss you whenever I like?" He asked with a hopeful grin.

"Yeah, right. With Jazz, we are what we are. With you and me, we are dating. My dad would kick your ass from here to Taiwan and everywhere in between."

Jazz and Kidd were laughing uncontrollably. "I'll sell tickets," Rocky said.

"See, the bug only gets worse." Breeze lightly punched Blade's shoulder.

"Great. I think your bad influence has rubbed off on Rocky," he teased back. They landed. "You're a little nervous. What's up?" He asked.

"Prefight jitters." She shrugged a little. "I need you to go with your family and Chad while we get warmed up and ready. You're going to be ringside for these fights, which is quite different than the viewpoint you had before. Can you handle it?"

He nodded. She leaned over and kissed his lips gently. "See you soon," she whispered against his lips.

Jazz and the guys walked up. Blade had already walked off with his family. "Breeze, you look a little green. What's up?" Jazz asked.

"Prefight jitters."

Jazz didn't believe her. She was normally keyed up with excited energy before a fight not nervous. He didn't like it. "I can't believe you won't tell me who the second contender is. I've only seen you this freaked from one other fight."

She smiled. "You won't be disappointed."

"You're completely guarded, knock it off, Breeze. I don't like it."

He knew that when Breeze blocked him out it wasn't good. The last time was when she was hiding Justice from him. It made him anxious and on edge.

"You won't like it either way. You will see," she said.

"Breeze, what do you mean 'I won't like it'?"

He was concerned and that comment put him on edge even more. This wasn't Breeze. She always told him what was on her mind or who she would be up against. It really upset him.

"We need to warm up and stretch."

Chad's phone buzzed:

2 bonus features first: Rocky vs. Ice, second: Jazz vs. Jake the Snake

2nd main event contender a surprise

Chad showed Blade

"Why is the second a surprise?" Blade asked. He had a bad feeling. He heard Breeze and Jazz's discussion. Jazz didn't seem to like it either. "Wait, let me see that again. Rocky's

340

fighting, what the hell?"

Blade tapped Jazz. *"Jazz, are you sure he's ready?"*

"He wouldn't be in the ring if I wasn't."

"What's up with Breeze? I'm having a bad feeling about the second fight."

"Yeah, me, too; It's not good, she is never this keyed before a fight or competition with nerves. She's not talking, and she's completely guarded."

Blade sighed, he promised to support her and not get in her way, but something was wrong. *"I'll be ringside if you need me."* He ended the connection because the bell sounded for Rocky's match to begin.

Rocky beat Ice in the first round. He won in two minutes and forty-five seconds by TKO by way of submission. Jazz won in the third round in four minutes and ten seconds with a KO. Breeze's first fight went better than anyone suspected it would. KO, first round in forty-five seconds with the second kick.

Chad received a text:

Next fight thirty minutes.

Breeze and Jazz went back to stretch out some more. Breeze refused to tell Jazz who the next contender was going to be. He was furious. He was tempted to call the fight, but when he looked at Breeze, he saw how anxious she really was. He softened a little, but not much. He was still frustrated.

"I will tell you three minutes before we go out and not a minute before."

Jazz began pacing, he couldn't let her walk out and not be prepared. He would never forgive himself if she got hurt. Jon would kill them both. She was getting into her fight zone.

She spoke softly, "Think of all the people who have beaten

me.   Go through that list and pull their strengths and weaknesses."

"How far back?"

"Two years," she said.

"There are nine."

She shook her head. "No, there were ten."

"Ten?"

"Who beat me the worst?"

"That SOB doesn't count," Jazz yelled.

"Yes, everything counts."

"Breeze." He sighed. "You make me crazy." He resumed his pacing. He went through the list. He couldn't shake the thought of her wanting to include Taylor as part of the list. What was she thinking? He was ready to call Jon and see if he could talk some sense in her, but he quickly dismissed that idea.

"Just promise me, you won't let me be that broken again," Breeze said in a choked voice.

"You won't be. I promise." She gave him a weary smile and hugged him. Jazz didn't like where this conversation had gone.

He tapped Blade. *"That bad feeling just got a hundred percent worse. She won't tell me who until three minutes out, and she made me promise her that she won't be that broken again. I don't like it."*

"We got other issues. Taylor's boys are here."

"Keep an eye on them. Let Rocky know as well. I will keep an eye on her."

"No problem. Just keep her safe."

"Easier said than done, but I will." The connection ended.

342

"Breeze five minutes." Matt yelled.

"Thanks." Jazz walked over to her, she buried her head in his chest, and he stroked her hair. She took a deep breath all jitters were gone. She was focused and determined. She waited until the three-minute mark. She raised her head and took a deep breath

"Ok. Don't be mad. The second fight is against Taylor Smith," she said.

Jazz exploded with anger. It was official, Breeze had lost her mind. He would sit on her if he had to. This fight was not going to happen. He refused to see Breeze busted, broken or worse, dead. He refused.

Breeze took his hand. "Do you trust me?"

"Yes, I trust you. However, this fight is not happening."

She explained how this was for complete closure, her final healing for herself and for Justice. He wanted to scream. All he could think about were the memories of her in the hospital with tubes everywhere. Breeze took his hands again and kissed him lightly. Jazz surrendered. He would stand in her corner. It was for her and Justice. If she started to lose, he and Blade would make sure that Taylor paid. She would not be broken again, that was for sure.

Jazz tapped Blade. *"Taylor, it is Taylor, second fight.*

"No. I won't let her," Blade insisted.

"No choice," Jazz said.

"It was just announced," Blade told Jazz. "I'm on my way to the corner."

Jazz ended the connection with Blade and turned his focus back to Breeze. He had to talk some sense in her. "Breeze, I love you. Please allow me and Blade to handle him."

"This is my fight. You promised not to let me be that broken again. There is not a day that goes by that I don't think about what I lost. This is my final healing. You and Blade will get your chance. Tonight, will just piss him off even more. Will you stand in my corner and support me?"

"Yes," He said through gritted teeth.

There was electricity in the air that everyone could feel. She walked out and went to her corner. Blade came over. "I'm in your corner today."

"No interference," Breeze said.

"No. I'm here to support you."

"I love you, Breeze. Promise me you will win," Jazz said.

"I promise. I love you, too," she said.

"Breeze, have you lost your mind?" asked Mickey.

"You know I've heard that somewhere before. Mickey, Taylor hates my type of music and it's already been approved for music during the fight: Champs choice. Can you hook me up with something with a lot of bass and funk? About twenty minutes worth." Mickey jumped off the ring and ran to the announcer's booth. He handed them a CD.

"My heart has stopped, Breeze. Please be ok," Kidd said. He was worried sick. There was no way he could see Breeze laid up again.

"My garage is full. If you are on restriction again, we are going to have to build another garage," Matt said.

"Kidd, I'll be fine. Matt are you hoping?"

"No, just worried," Matt replied with a waver in his voice.

"I love you all. Now let's kick some ass."

Breeze spotted Blade's family and Chad. They looked as tense as "her boys." She stepped to the center of the ring and touched gloves with Taylor.

"I will be clear. This will be a CLEAN FIGHT. Bow to each other and to me. Ready." The MC said loud and clear. The music started playing. Breeze was psyched. The bell rang. Taylor threw the first punch and missed. Breeze connected with his jaw with a right hook. Then she connected on the left side of his head and he was bleeding just above his left eye. He was pissed.

He swung hitting her on the left side of her ribs. She saw Blade shift and Jazz touched his wrist to stop him. Breeze did a sidekick to Taylor's right ribs and a sweep kick to his left leg. His left eye was bleeding so bad that the ref had to call time so he could get it looked at.

Jazz touched her mind. *"Breeze kick his ass. He is taking too much pleasure in hurting you."* She gave a slight nod.

The bell rang and the connection was broken. Taylor was still bleeding, but not as bad. He swept her leg, and she went down. Taylor didn't hesitate. He was on the mat ready for some ground and pound. She rolled, he hit the mat with his right hand, and it popped. She rolled again when she saw his foot coming down, she swept his leg, and he fell. She was on top of him before he could get up. She locked her knees around his waist where he couldn't buck her or roll.

She started pounding on Taylor. He was blocking as much as he could. She was doing body punches wherever she could. She tapped his ribs a couple times he was trying to roll. He threw a punch straight to her face breaking her nose. She kept throwing punches; she caught him on the side of his head, just above his right eye, and he started bleeding from there as well. The bell rang ending the first round. The ref pulled her off him. Taylor sucker punched her.

The ref turned to Taylor. "That's your one warning, and

345

the next time you won't lose points. I will declare her the winner." Taylor cussed. "Corner now or I will call it." The announcer said it for all to hear.

Breeze was in her corner. Jazz set her nose and took care of the cuts. She drank from her blue bottle. She felt a jolt of energy. Jazz touched her mind.

"Not too much. We don't need you healing before everyone's eyes."

"I don't think I will. I didn't heal from Blade's blood, at least not externally. Your blood heals me and gives me energy. His blood gives me strength and energy. Together I think I am just energized and stronger."

"Yeah. Well, let's not experiment with that theory too much here ok." Their connection ended.

"How y'all holding up?" She asked.

"Girl…

..My nerves…

…Are shot." Mickey, Matt, and Kidd said together.

Blade shrugged. "To be honest, like a train ran me over."

"Yeah, that about explains it," Jazz said.

"Good. Suck it up. Two more rounds and then home."

"Breeze, we are going to talk about your extremes when this is over," Blade laughed.

"No doubt," Jazz said.

"Matt you sell tickets, I'll call the media, and Mickey you call the morgue." They all looked at Kidd and laughed. "Seriously," Kidd yelled.

She connected with Jazz and Blade. *"Just because we are bonded, that doesn't mean you are going to tag team me."*

She stepped out of her corner ready for whatever Taylor threw her way. He was pissed and it showed. He threw several

346

punches back-to-back, but Breeze had her guard up.

"Get away from the fence before he pins you." Jazz yelled.

She listened. She started throwing punches back making Taylor get his guard up. She jump-kicked backing him into the fence, she was still punching, and she put a knee in his stomach. He pushed her back and started throwing body shots. She kicked his chin and started pounding again. He tried to do a foot stomp. She did a knee to his stomach again, he punched her in the ribs, and pushed her back again. He wanted her backed into the cage badly. He threw a punch and kept his thumb out, jabbing her in the eye. The ref saw it, asked Breeze if she could continue. She nodded. The ref called time and sent her to her corner to be evaluated.

The ref yelled, "Illegal contact, jab to the eye, penalty. I warned you, Mr. Smith, clean or I call it." The ref was getting ready to call a TKO, but Jazz ran out on Breeze's behalf.

"Her eye is fine. She wants to continue."

"Fine."

Taylor laughed. Jazz ran back to the corner to psych Breeze up. "Breeze you got one minute in this round. Save the ground and pound for the next one. Right now, sweep the left leg and go for the knee. Make him hurt and reopen some injuries. He needs to hurt and bleed." He leaned over, kissed her, and whispered, "For Justice."

Breeze came out of her corner fired up. She punched Taylor in his mouth, and he started bleeding. She did a fake sweep for the right leg and connected with the left as planned. She threw a punch just above the left knee. He hit the mat; she was throwing punches. She threw a right punch and connected with the side of his head. He was rattled. He couldn't get up and his eye was bleeding again. The ref came over to look at his eye. "Can you continue?"

"Get the hell out of my way." Taylor pushed the ref away. Taylor was finally up, and the bell rang. Breeze knew he was coming, so she kept her guard up. The ref was yelling at Taylor, but he was still coming. She looked at the timekeeper and yelled, "Ring the bell." The bell rang for the third round with no break. She did a spinning hook kick and connected with Taylor's head. He went down. She went after him, got his left knee in a knee bar, and pulled hard to let him know that she would cause injury. He tapped out.

The fight was over. Third round TKO by submission in one minute and twenty-three seconds. Taylor didn't get up. Blade and Jazz both came over to Breeze and helped her to her corner. The arena erupted in screams and cheers for Breeze. Breeze heard the music that was playing and laughed. It was Vanilla Ice's song, Ice, Ice baby. "Mickey, that song is perfect. It makes me think of the original Ninja Turtles and them dancing to this song."

The guys rushed her and hugged her. The announcer walked over to Breeze and announced her the winner. Breeze was excited that the fights were over and ready to go home and just relax.

"Speaking of home, your dad is pissed," Matt said.

"What? How does he know?" Breeze asked.

"Don't look at us. It's our asses, too," Jazz said.

"Hello. Your dad is in the UFC and some of those guys were there in Dallas this morning. Not to mention the whole Martial Arts world is all about this weekend. Eight fights in two days. That's INSANE." Matt said.

"Great. Medical restrictions are the least of my worries. Matt, I'm crashing at your pad until Sunday evening so I can sleep and at least race a little before I go home."

They all laughed. Blade picked her up and kissed her.

"Dude, get a room." Rocky yelled.

Blade ensured Breeze that they would all go with her to talk with her Dad. Mickey and Matt looked at Blade like he had a second head. Kidd was swearing and telling Blade that he had lost his mind. Jazz began laughing and agreed to go as well. Matt and Mickey slowly recovered from the shock of Blade's statement. They nodded. It wasn't the first time they had to face Jon for doing something stupid with Breeze and they were sure that it wouldn't be the last. They all groaned. Jon would have them in the gym for a year over this stunt. Kidd swore again but agreed that he would stand by Breeze no matter what. Breeze protested the most. She just wanted to rest before she had to enter the gym again. Rocky and Summer were ready to stand in her corner as well, even if it was against Jon. She proved that she was worth fighting for and with. She seemed to have Blade's heart which meant she was family.

Dr. McGroff came around the corner with Chad. "Breeze I just spoke with your father. He called asking about your medical restrictions. I told him they had been removed last week, but you are to do weekly follow-ups for a month. He said he was relieved, but he still had matters to deal with."

"Uhhh, maybe crashing at your pad is not a good idea. So, I guess we are going straight home."

"Another ground and pound?" asked Rocky.

"Selling tickets as we speak," Kidd said. Breeze pushed him over.

They boarded the plane and headed home. When they landed, Jon and Jana were waiting at the airport. Matt and

Mickey agreed that she wouldn't be going to Matt's house tonight and she probably wouldn't be visiting for a long time. Kidd patted Breeze's back lightly. Breeze walked forward. Blade was on one side with his arm around her waist. Jazz was on the other side with his arm around her shoulders.

"Hey, Dad, I won."

"I've heard. Are you insane? Four fights in one weekend."

"Actually Dad, it was four fights in one night, eight in two days. Taylor was my last fight, and I won that one by TKO by way of submission. I won all eight. Who needs Thailand?"

Jon's mouth was open, and shock was written all over his face. He whirled around and faced Jazz. He started asking Jazz if he was insane and how could he let her fight Taylor. Jazz stood tall and met all of Jon's questions. He wanted Jon to understand that this was Breeze they were talking about.

"Let her? You know when she sets her mind to something there is NO changing it. She didn't tell us until three minutes prior to the fight. Blade and I both tried to stop her, but she was determined to prove he would never break her again."

"Breeze, you scared me. I have been sick with worry since four this morning when I got the call that you were in Dallas. If you do something like this again, I may kill you myself."

"Hell, we'll help," Jazz said.

"Definitely," Blade said.

"Ok, let me look at your injuries," Jon said.

Breeze protested that she was fine and that Dr. McGroff had checked her out. Jon wasn't hearing it. He gently guided Breeze back to Dr. McGroff.

"We will check your injuries. Then we all go to the house so I can hear all about it."

"See I told you party at Breeze's," Rocky yelled.

"Wait, I thought you were pissed?"

"Oh, I am, but I'm also thrilled that your home in one piece, and that you taught that SOB a lesson. I'm proud of you for standing up for yourself. However, don't think that you are not in trouble, because you are in serious trouble, but that can start Monday." Jon hugged her and kissed her on the head.

Jazz bumped her hip. Blade kissed her. Breeze went with her dad and Dr. McGroff so they could look at her injuries. She finally felt like her old self. She was ready to throw down another challenge to Jazz. Blade wouldn't even know that she was gone. Jazz looked at her and shook his head with a smile. She winked. She finally had the all clear from her father and Dr. McGroff and she ran over to be with her friends.

"Hey, guys, let's go home and crash for the rest of the weekend before I'm grounded for life."

"That's my girl," Kidd yelled.

"Chad, you are welcome, too. Jazz you better call Angela and tell her she can crash at my place."

"Ahhh, man, I was so into the fights that I forgot to look for a girl," Rocky sighed.

"We'll hook you up man, no worries," Mickey said with a huge grin.

"Dr. McGroff, you're welcome to come over as well. We will cook out and the adults will have a few beers."

"I'd like that, thank you."

Jana walked over to Breeze and hugged her. "We were worried, but you look more like yourself. I'm proud of you. You are lucky to have such great friends. You and Blade look closer." Breeze hugged Jana. It was finally time that she talked to Jana, woman to woman. Jana was happy to have her home and agreed to talk to Jon for her. She simply smiled. Jana hugged her again and motioned for her to go back over to Blade.

Her phone buzzed. Text message from Taylor.

Taylor: Don't leave town. I will take care of you.

She showed Jazz and Blade. She texted him back.

Breeze: We'll be waiting and you will never break me again.

She turned her phone off, placed her arms around Jazz and Blade's waists, and they walked to the cars.

"Looks like you boys may get your wish sooner than later."

"I'm not going anywhere," Blade said.

"Neither am I," Jazz agreed.

"Thanks." Breeze wrapped her arms tighter around the guys' waists and kissed them each on the cheek. "Game on."

About the Author

Sharon Barnes is a Native American author who lives in rural TN with her husband, children, grandchildren, and fur babies. She holds a Bachelors of Science Degree from Austin Peay State University and two national certifications for Interpreting for the Deaf and Hard of Hearing. She has received several awards for her poetry. Shanghai Sunset was a top ten finalist in the Actions/Adventure category of the 2023 Claymore Award.

Sharon is an avid reader and loves to do research about other countries. She has a passion for other cultures, languages, fairy tales, folklore, myths, and legends. It amazes her how many countries and cultures have dragons in their legends. The supernatural world has always fascinated her and it is often incorporated in her stories. Rarely will you see Sharon without a cup of coffee, no matter the time; if she is awake, then coffee is close by.

You can connect with me on:

🌐 https://sharonabarnes.com

🐦 https://x.com/Barnes_S76

Also by Sharon Barnes

Grab your coffee or tea, settle in, and let's explore these enchanted stories together! Keep an eye out for new releases and exciting updates—adventure awaits!

Midnight the Witching Hour

Midnight The Witching Hour is a modern-day Romeo and Juliet with a flare of magic. Liz Krimshaw has been on the run for a long time. Thankfully after her parents were murdered, a man by the name of Lucas arrived to help her and her baby brother. She quickly learns that Lucas is her protector. Liz knows her heritage and family history. She has been working in the local archive which has assisted her in gathering the evidence she needs to bring Katherine Blackthorne down. Liz is ready to right the wrongs of the past in a very big way. Revenge is sweet, especially when your opponent underestimates your skills and talents as a witch.

The Dragons Lair

THE DRAGON'S LAIR

Lizza is on a mission to get a new book when she bumps into a man, The tattoo on his left arm is the most unique tattoo she has ever seen, then as he moves to go around her, she can see the clear design of the tattoo it is a Dragon. Her father's last words on the dreaded day of his death, 'Trust the Dragons. Follow the Dragons,' echoes in her head every time she sees the biker club. The crest on the back of their jacket is The Dragon's Lair with a black dragon. Honestly, did her dad mean for her to run to a club of bikers? Surely not.

www.ingramcontent.com/pod-product-compliance
Lightning Source LLC
Chambersburg PA
CBHW050537260626
47157CB00002B/332